COME CLOSER

Closing his eyes, he imagined what it would be like to hold Emily in his arms and feel her delicious nearness. Tristan felt himself being pulled to her, a siren's song promising sweet intimacies he had only heard of but had never experienced.

It was too easy. Unable to resist any longer, he let his thoughts travel closer, until his mind was on the verge of touching hers.

The idea of slipping into her mind both intrigued and frightened him. He should have known better. It should have frightened him enough to make him turn away. It would have, but another, stronger emotion took hold. Loneliness pushed him over the edge of abandon.

IF YOU
COULD READ
MY MIND

Pamela Labud

ZEBRA BOOKS
Kensington Publishing Corp.
www.kensingtonbooks.com

ZEBRA BOOKS are published by
Kensington Publishing Corp.
850 Third Avenue
New York, NY 10022

All Kensington titles, imprints, and distributed lines are available
at special quantity discounts for bulk purchases for sales promo-
tion, premiums, fund-raising, educational, or institutional use.

Special book excerpts or customized printings can also be created to fit specific needs. For details, write or phone the office
of the Kensington Special Sales Manager: Attn. Special Sales
Department. Kensington Publishing Corp., 850 Third Avenue,
New York, NY 10022. Phone: 1-800-221-2647.

Zebra and the Z logo Reg. U.S. Pat. & TM Off.

ISBN: 0-8217-7868-4

First Printing: April 2006
10 9 8 7 6 5 4 3 2 1

Printed in the United States of America

Once again,
for Bill, Jamie, and Caitlin,
who sustain me every day,
and also for Hailie,
who persistently made sure I didn't forget
to include her on the dedication page.

Acknowledgments

First and foremost, I'd like to thank Hilary Sares, editor extraordinaire, for being so smart, patient, funny and wise, and for giving me the chance to see my books in print. Also, thank you to my agent, Paige Wheeler, and her staff for sharing their expertise and wisdom. Lots of thanks also to the Romance Unleashed authors, who are undoubtedly the best of the best! And finally, I'd like to send my heartfelt appreciation to the wonderful ladies of the Central Florida Romance Writers, the most awesome RWA chapter I know. I truly am a better person and writer for having known you.

Prologue

November, 1795

It was well past noon when the murderer returned to his uncle's country estate. Covered with mud, Lord Griffin Whitehall, second son of the earl of Kendall, trudged along the road until he reached the entrance to the grand old house. Ignoring the questioning glances from the house staff, he made his way to his uncle's parlor.

"Well? Did you find them?"

Baron George Cantor of Darrowby stood hovering in the doorway. Old and brittle, he looked more like a stick figure covered in dry leather than the robust man in the portrait that adorned the main hall of the mansion.

"I found her. About a mile down the river. She'd thrown herself and the boy into the water."

"Where is she now?" Cantor leaned close.

"She's dead."

"Did you kill her?"

Griffin hardened his expression. It was enough to make the other man look away, his hand nervously rubbing his chin.

"Never mind. What of the boy? Is he still alive?"

Griffin grunted. "I never saw him. I searched the area

most of the morning and didn't even find so much as a muddy trail."

"Too bad. With that boy's magnificent mind, he could have been of use to us. If only we could have saved him. He'd be reading the minds of our enemies, learning of valuable secrets . . ." He glanced into his nephew's hard expression.

"He's an abomination. If he tells what he knows . . ."

"Pah!" Cantor waved his hand. "You have nothing to be concerned about. A child that age can't possibly get too far in this weather. With the wind picking up, the temperature has barely been above freezing all week. He'll die of exposure before the day is out."

Griffin paused a moment, studying his uncle's face, looking for any chance that he was lying. Would he have given the demon child shelter? He doubted it. George Cantor was a man who was only concerned with his own well-being. If he couldn't profit from the child, he'd have no interest in saving him.

"I must go. My regiment leaves in the morning. I'll resume my search when I return. I warn you, old man, if you help the little fiend and I learn of it, I'll make certain you perish along with him."

With that, Griffin turned on his heels, the vision of his uncle's fear assuring him that the old man wouldn't dare cross him. He knew well Griffin always kept his promises.

Cantor watched in silence as his nephew rode to the end of the estate. He waited a full half hour before summoning his servant.

"Bennett! Get my cloak and have the groomsman saddle my horse. I'll go after the lad myself."

Two hours later he found the boy, cold and wet, staggering along the road west of the estate. Though he'd journeyed a far piece, the child still had not gone outside of Cantor's reach.

Seeing the old man spurred the boy to break into a run, though it was a poor effort at best. Tripping on some loose stones, he fell face first onto the road and though he desperately tried to crawl out of Cantor's reach, he hadn't been fast enough.

"Come now, Tristan. I've a warm bed and some hot food for you. You'll catch your death out here."

"Leave me alone! I won't go back!"

"If it's your father you're worried about, you can put your mind at ease," Cantor said as he halted his mount a few paces ahead of the child, blocking his escape. "He's gone off with the army. He won't ever be back to trouble you."

He watched as the child's fear of his father's return warred with the lure of a warm bed and sustenance.

"I can't go back there," he said, with less conviction than before.

"Just for a few days. You may leave any time you wish."

The boy looked haggard and had clearly aged beyond his years that night. "He killed her. He killed my mother."

"Come. Your mother wouldn't want you starving in the cold. If you like, you can stay long enough to put some hot food in your belly and get a good night's rest. I won't stand in your way if you wish to leave after that."

Although Tristan was frightened and suspicious, Cantor knew the boy couldn't read his mind too clearly. He was a man used to keeping secrets and he never let his thoughts go astray.

Besides which, Tristan was near to collapse from sheer exhaustion and hunger. Cantor knew he'd give in, because if he didn't he'd not survive in the wilderness.

As if to persuade the child further, the wind picked up and a cold, rain-soaked gale began to beat upon them.

"All right," he said, inching forward. "I'll go, but I'm only staying one night."

The food had tasted like heaven and Tristan had nearly slept around the clock when he woke to new thoughts in his head.

"Here now, take this missive to Lord Danbury. Tell him I have a way to get the information he seeks about the goods stolen from his warehouse last week. If he's willing to pay the price, that is."

What was the old man going on about? Quickly pulling on the clothes the maid had set out for him the night before, Tristan left his room—now so painfully empty with his mother gone—and went out into the hall. Going down the stairs, he could hear his great-uncle's discussion below.

"George, what do you know about Danbury's business?" Lady Cantor asked.

"Nothing, yet. But now that I have Griffin's bastard to myself, I'll be able to learn all manner of interesting things."

"I've always said you were the clever one in the family."

"As soon as I've managed to get a few more pounds in the coffers, I have plans for the whelp. It's a shame about the mother, though. I could have used her to keep the boy in line."

Reeling as a wall of pain slammed against him, Tristan saw the other man's thoughts. Murders he'd planned—a knife through the ribs of one man, poison in the wine of another. One by one the hidden thoughts came forth, all the pain and blood and death.

Tristan nearly fainted from the shock of it.

The flesh-and-blood man before him was nothing but the shell of a snake or a dark, vile dragon with fiery breath and the heart of a monster beating inside him.

"You're a murderer!" Tristan blurted out. "I saw it, the blood on your hands . . ."

The smile on Cantor's face froze into a hideous mask. When he spoke, a forced tone of tolerance laced his voice.

"You've no idea what you're talking about." Cantor slowly rose to his feet, advancing on Tristan as he moved.

"You planned to use my mother to cheat and steal from your business associates, and when she wouldn't, you sent for my father. You told him all those lies about us! You made him kill my mother!"

When the blow came, it was hard and unrelenting. Tristan whirled, his slight, eight-year-old body crumpling to the ground like an autumn leaf tossed about in a storm.

"You keep your lying mouth shut, do you hear? Your mother was a fool to refuse me. All these years I've kept her secret. She owed me. Now, you're the payment, boy. You will do as I demand or I'll flay the hide from your back. You'd do well to remember that."

Grabbing Tristan's shirtfront, Cantor jerked him violently upward until the boy's feet barely touched the ground. Cantor then drew back his hand for a second strike.

"Let me go!" Tristan struggled, but before he could even muster a good fight, Lady Cantor rushed into the fray, grabbing her husband's arm and holding it back with all of her strength.

"George, what are you doing?" she screeched in a loud, high-pitched voice. "You can't hurt the child like that. What will people think?"

"They'll think he's a lying, sniveling ruffian, that's what. It's no concern of yours, Lavinia."

"What will you do?"

"I'll take him to the country and lock him in the root cellar for a while. Perhaps a little seclusion and starvation will teach him to respect his betters. The boy needs to learn discipline."

"He's so small and thin already. What if you kill him?"

"I've no intention of really harming him. I'm meeting with the solicitor at the end of the month, before we travel to Kent to meet with Bradley. If my half-brother were to die, there's a chance I'd inherit. I'll need the brat alive until then. Best to know what's in Bradley's mind, eh?"

"I won't help you! I won't!" Tristan struggled in Cantor's grasp.

"Oh, you'll change your mind, young man. You'll change your mind, right enough."

Cantor's true intentions burst into Tristan's mind. He saw the man smiling, his clothing stained with red powder, his thin, bony hands stirring a pot of steaming liquid, and then pouring it into a cup. Seated around a small table, the old man smiled over his own brew and gazed into the final terrified expression on the face of a corpse.

Murder. Cantor was planning to kill his relative.

Taking advantage while Cantor was off his guard, Tristan savagely kicked his tormentor on the shinbone. With the strength of an eight-year-old boy scared out of his wits, he delivered a decisive blow.

The old man howled and the woman beside him howled. Tristan took advantage of their surprise and bounded for the door. Just as he made the front hall, a tall, dark figure loomed over him.

"I see you've managed to find your way home, boy."

Tristan looked up into the face of his mother's murderer and screamed.

Chapter One

July, 1812

"*It won't make any difference, you know. You're wasting your time trying to save them.*"

Tristan Deveraux ignored the taunting of his weary psyche. A surgeon's apprentice, he did his best to focus his attention on the task before him and not on the constant whispering of his exhausted imaginings.

Outside the infirmary tent, the battle raged on, soldiers from both sides of the conflict engaged in the heat of battle. Even at this distance, amid the roar of cannon fire, he could hear the screams of men and horses dying. He could smell the smoke as the early July wind dispersed it across the open field of death, and he could hear the cries of agony as casualties fell on the bloodied field.

It was a fine line he walked between the battle outside and the turmoil that always stirred within his own mind.

Pulling back the gore-soaked dressing, Tristan gently probed the injury. The cut from the bayonet didn't seem that deep, but the soldier had lain in the mud for a full two days before being brought to the infirmary tent. Now, the swelling and putridity were preventing Tristan from seeing the extent of the damage.

He had two options. If he took the leg and the damage was only superficial, it could cost the soldier his livelihood.

If he left the wound and waited, the man might die. It was not an easy decision to make.

Glancing up, he was surprised to see the soldier was still awake.

"Don't you fret about me, sir, I'll be dancing at yer wedding, see if I don't," he ground out between clenched teeth. Covered in the filth from the battle and smelling of smoke and death, he waited patiently for Tristan's decision.

A brave lad of only eighteen, Fowler had been among the first men to fall at the attack on Salamanca. The reports were that he'd held his post long after older, more seasoned soldiers had fled.

Most men bearing such a devastating injury would have been howling with the pain and fighting to escape the horrendous surgery. Clayton Fowler had remained as quiet as a church mouse since he'd been brought to the infirmary tent an hour earlier.

"No one really blamed you for what happened. You were just a boy, after all."

Tristan gritted his teeth, again disregarding his mind's malicious goading. It didn't help that the sound of his consciousness was housed in the tone of the one man in the world he'd hated the most, his great-uncle George Cantor.

"You're a failure. You were born one and you shall die one. No need to carry on this charade . . ."

The surgeon would have to go deeper to learn the extent of the injury. He had to help this man, no matter what.

"Can ye save it?" Fowler asked in a quiet voice. "I don't want to lose it if I don't have to."

"I have to finish the examination before I can tell you if the leg's viable."

Fowler nodded, laying his head back. He took several deep breaths before speaking. "Do what ye must."

The man beneath his touch relaxed and Tristan felt Fowler's trust cover him like a thick, heavy quilt.

"Give it up, man. You'll only fail anyway. Best to let it go now, eh?"

Tristan shook his head. He would not let his muse have its way.

There was only one thing that he could do. Taking a deep breath, he closed his eyes. It was easier that way. He must tighten his focus on his patient only, use all of his strength to block every other thought, every other image. It was the only way to learn the truth, as much as he hated to do it.

Tristan had an incredible gift. With only the power of his mind, he was able to read the thoughts of others.

It was not something that he enjoyed doing. In fact, experiencing the thoughts of another was worse than unsettling. If a person was in pain, Tristan felt each torturous spasm, if the person was angry it was Tristan who suffered the sharp cuts of the mind's fury. Strong emotions, such as the fear or grief of another could overwhelm him almost into a state of total catatonia.

Surviving the riotous thoughts of another was possible only if one knew how to deflect the flood of such violent emotions. Tristan knew that doing otherwise could mean disaster. He would be like the poor soldier who stood too close to an explosive—when the substance ignited there would be no escaping it.

Furthermore, if experiencing the thoughts and emotions of one person could be debilitating, experiencing the minds of hundreds of people around him each day was worse than madness.

It was like being caught inside a hive of furious whirring activity, innumerable claws of emotion constantly grabbing at him, relentlessly shredding his mental flesh with every touch. Each second of the assault, he would hover closer and closer to the edge of oblivion.

"You can't do it. It will kill you this time for sure."

"No," Tristan said out loud, refusing to let his fears better him. He would do as he must and that was the end of it.

With a trembling hand, he lightly touched Fowler's forehead. Feverish and damp to his touch, barely a second passed before the other man's reality slammed into him.

The pain was unbearable. Bones twisted and broken, blood rushing to an injury that wouldn't be mended without intervention. Torn flesh sending scorching agony to the center of the man lying on the table.

"Damn." Tristan labored to tie off an unwieldy blood vessel. The man before him was now hemorrhaging profusely and wouldn't last long unless Tristan could stop the bleeding.

"No one really blamed you for what happened, boy. You were but a child. A foolish, angry youth, but a child just the same."

"No!" Tristan cursed again as the slippery tissue twisted between his fingers.

When he cut through another layer of tender muscle, the man jerked violently, his hands clutching white-knuckled onto the wood table.

Breathing as hard as Fowler, Tristan did his best to guide his hand deep into the incision.

It was worse than he'd thought. The bone was completely severed above the joint and yellow-green pus oozed out of the incision. There would be no saving the limb.

Disappointment flooded Tristan's mind.

"I tried to warn you. You couldn't change things then and you can't do it now. Give it up before it's too late."

Pulling back, Tristan chose another scalpel and completed the amputation, removing all of the infected tissue as he did so. It was a skill he had learned early in his days on the battlefield so there was no need to give it much thought.

"Go ahead and yell, private. Don't hold back on my account."

Not so much as a grunt escaped Fowler as Tristan then manipulated the tender flesh of the leg wound.

Again and again Tristan had seen it. Brave men from both sides of the conflict enduring excruciating pain and allowing the surgeons to do as they must. Opium was at a minimum and since Fowler was but a lowly private, not even a portion of rum was available to ease his suffering.

Tristan did his best to keep the soldier's discomfort to a minimum, directing Fowler's thoughts to a distant memory when he'd been wooing a young lady on a sunny summer afternoon.

"Easy does it, man. A few more stitches and we'll have it."

By the time Tristan had finished stitching and wrapping the stump, Fowler had thankfully lapsed into unconsciousness. Tristan was glad he had succumbed, although it might be a sign of the man's dwindling health. The next eight or so hours would be his most critical, but at least for the moment, he had a chance.

"It doesn't matter how many of them you save, Tristan. You'll never make up for the one life you took."

Now separated from his patient's mind, Tristan staggered back. Exhausted, he wasn't sure how long he'd be able to keep up the pace. There were so many soldiers, and he felt himself diminishing with every day.

"You need to lie down, boy. You're a fool if you think you can keep this up."

For all he didn't want to believe the voice in his head, Tristan knew it was the truth. Months had passed since he'd joined the army, and he'd worked his hardest to keep up the pace, but he wasn't sure how long he could continue. The more exhausted he became, the harder it was to fight the terrible scheming whisperings that never completely left him.

Just as Tristan was about to abandon it all, a hearty voice called from the tent's opening.

"Hurry up, Tris, there's five more wounded coming down the hill. Mr. Barton will have our hides if we've not cleared out this tent before supper," Harry Blevins shouted over the din of cannon fire and moaning men that surrounded them.

Reginald James Barton was the surgeon who had taken Tristan under his wing upon his joining the army. Though the hours were long, and oftentimes he labored alone, Tristan was grateful for the chance to keep busy. Barton was rarely present to observe his students' efforts. With several young men under his tutelage, he hardly lifted a scalpel himself these days, happy to spend his time entertaining the officers and generally avoiding the messy business of caring for the wounded.

Tristan didn't mind the drudgery of his work. Concentrating on the casualties provided a welcome relief from the constant pummeling of other minds upon his own. During the heat of battle was the worst of it. Such times, when men's passions ran high, the cacophony of emotion and bloodlust nearly overwhelmed him. Too often he feared he might shatter like glass from the constant activity of so many minds intruding into his own.

As Harry approached, Tristan couldn't help but catch the barest of the other man's thoughts. It wasn't intentional, but with proximity, the mental ramblings of his counterparts rang clearer.

Harry was eyeing a fallen French soldier lying prone on the cot beside Fowler's.

"Dirty buggers," Harry's mind rumbled. *"A pox on them all."*

"They're men just like us, Harry," Tristan said as the patient before him finally lapsed into blessed unconsciousness.

The orderly grunted beside him.

"Reading my mind, are you?" A suspicious expression crossed Harry's face.

"Just observing the way you look at the enemy soldiers."

Tristan finished dressing Fowler's wound and then wiped his hands on his apron. At least this patient would know some peace for awhile.

Tristan glanced up to see Harry studying him.

"There, now. You've got that look on your puss again. What're you thinking?"

Tristan chuckled. "Just of how much I enjoy your company." He sighed as he leaned over Fowler once again and gently touched the pulse point at the base of the man's throat.

"How is the lad?" Harry asked.

"His heart is beating a bit faster than I'd like, but 'tis well enough. There's no knowing how much blood he left on the field." He sighed again. "I'm afraid there's not much more we can do."

Harry shook his head. "'Tis a sorry thing, is it not?" Harry nodded at the unconscious patient. "Better off dead, says I."

Tristan sighed. "That's not for us to decide, Harry. We do what we can to mend them and let God sort out the rest."

When the two had finished, Tristan went to change his apron and rinse the blood from his hands. He paused when a strange voice broke into his thoughts.

"Where is he? Are you sure he's the one?" The sound drifted closer. *"This is the most preposterous thing I've ever heard."*

Tristan was not so much surprised at the stray ramblings, but rather the gender of the speaker. It was a woman's presence that had intruded into his mind, but not just any woman.

Cautious, he walked to the tent's opening and peered out. He saw only the usual late evening activity of soldiers preparing for their suppers and a small respite from the fighting. No female was visible at first, but as sure as his soul she was there.

The texture of her mind was different from the other women that followed the army. Most of them soldiers' wives or prostitutes, their tones were distinctive. They were women of the lower classes, wives with little education— their thoughts centered on family life, their children, and husbands—or the working women who made their living off of the desperation and loneliness that was part of the unattached enlisted man's life.

This female was different. A perfect manner of speech, her words were clear and crisp, and not the lower class slang he was accustomed to hearing.

More than that, her thoughts felt like velvet, soft and warm. How such a thing was possible, Tristan wasn't certain. He wanted very much to hear more of her. Inhaling, he thought he might even have smelled her scent of lavender, even though she was still a good distance away.

That was when he saw her. She and the general were walking down the line of the enlisted men's tents, heading toward the infirmary. As they neared, he saw that she had beautiful dark brown hair and a complexion as pale and glowing as moonlight.

Though she wasn't close enough for him to see the finer details of her appearance, Tristan closed his eyes and nudged his mind in her direction. Her skin would be soft, he was certain. He could feel her gaze as she sought him out. Her eyes were the color of violets at midnight.

When he opened his eyes again, he found her staring right at him. A connection formed between them and he felt her tremble at his presence. It gave him a feeling of sudden desire and his body tightened accordingly.

Tristan imagined himself standing behind her, leaning forward and nuzzling her throat ever so slightly. In response, she would tilt her head sideways, and he would caress the length of her neck with the very softest of kisses.

Tristan nearly lost himself in her being, until the bayonet-sharp thoughts of another cut into his mind.

"He's the one, all right. I've been watching him for weeks," a man answered.

Tristan startled, surprised to learn that he was the object of their conversation. Worse yet, he realized he knew that tone well. Uneasiness rose within him like the sea at high tide. It was the voice of his commander, General Robert Henley.

"Hee, boy, they're on to you now!"

"Be quiet, you lout!" Tristan scolded himself, and two nearby soldiers eyed him curiously. He gave them a lop-sided grin and they quickly looked away.

Sighing, Tristan continued his study of the two who'd come searching for him. Something rang odd about this meeting, and Tristan didn't think it boded well for any of them.

Since joining the army, Tristan had gone to great lengths to keep himself invisible. To anyone around him, he was an average surgeon's apprentice. He'd told his counterparts that he'd been orphaned at an early age, which was essentially the truth, and that he'd always had a curiosity about the healing arts.

That he had suddenly become the object of some-one's attention made him instantly nervous, a turn of events that Tristan was sure could only mean trouble.

He'd almost been successful, too, except for one incident that had singled him out from his peers.

It had been among his first days in Spain. There'd been an explosion in the field. When he'd been riding past with his regiment, he'd heard the silent cries of three men trapped at the bottom of the rubble. Alerting his superiors, Tristan and about twenty other soldiers began digging and were able to extract the men from their about-to-be grave. He'd been given a medal. Of course there had been an investigation and when asked how he knew of the men's location, he'd told them he'd heard them calling out.

Tristan knew it had been a poor lie at best. With the deafening sound of cannon fire, men calling out across the battlefield, and even the screams of soldiers and horses as they fell, it would have been impossible to hear with one's ears. Still, the war effort being consumed by other far more important matters, the officers decided it was better to focus their attention on the fighting and not the curious abilities of one so low in the ranks.

All except for General Henley, that was. A twenty-year field veteran, he had made it his business to know his troops well. Many times Tristan had seen the general watching him, his mind strangely silent, his eyes ever scrutinizing. It made Tristan nervous to be at the center of anyone's attention. He knew it was far worse to be in Henley's crosshairs.

Tristan had long ago learned how dangerous it could be for him if anyone knew of his talent.

He quickly decided the best way to keep himself beneath his commander's attention was to stay knee-deep in injured men.

Not long after, he learned that the pain and need of others was a benefit to him.

Tending to the soldiers was how he managed to keep an ordered life. With the enormity of his work there'd been no time to dwell on anything more pressing than the needs of his next patient.

Now, he was facing a new difficulty. The soldiers were fast approaching.

"Are you sure it will work, General? I mean, what if he refuses?"

Tristan could feel the sharp edge of fear that crept into the lady's thoughts.

"He's the one, all right. I've been watching him for weeks. He'll do as he's ordered. He's a soldier, after all. And a damn fine surgeon, too," Henley mused.

Tristan was surprised by his commander's opinion. Just what did he have to base his confidence on, after all?

What didn't surprise him were the young woman's thoughts that followed.

"Foolish man. This is too important to trust my uncle's life on a whim."

Indeed, based on his own understanding thus far, Tristan would have to agree, but he didn't have long to ponder it, or her, for that matter.

Tristan suddenly became aware of two soldiers approaching the infirmary tent. Even before their arrival, the surgeon could feel a myriad of emotions assailing them. Battle weary, they were angry that they'd been summoned from their dinners to make an arrest.

Tristan sighed. He'd already put off two such orders from General Henley demanding he relinquish his post to another and attend to "unspecified duties." Tristan would have none of it. He wasn't about to become the general's errand boy.

"Tristan Deveraux?" the first man asked, passing off his question as a mere formality. Tristan sensed he knew full well whom he was addressing.

"Yes?" He quickly wiped his hands on his apron and took a small amount of satisfaction at the way the two men paled at seeing the amount of blood that covered him and his assistant who, thankfully, remained silent beside him.

"You're to come with us, immediately."

Tristan gave them a shrug. "I still have patients to care for."

"A cutter by the name of Hampstead is arriving in an hour. He'll take up your post."

The second one gave a guttural laugh. "We have orders to bring you immediately."

Feeling the soldier's anger at him like a blast of heat from cannon fire, Tristan thought it best not to argue. "Very well, gentlemen, lead on." He nodded for them to proceed.

The two men flanked him, the one on the right grabbed his shoulder and gave him a rough push forward. Tristan knew something was not quite right about the situation, but the sense he felt from the two of them was nothing more than agitation at having to carry out their duties when both would rather have been eating their dinner.

Without further comment, they escorted him to an area south of the camp through the midst of the soldiers preparing to bed down for the night. They took him directly to a tent that was used for detaining prisoners.

"In you go, sir." The first officer motioned to the open door.

"Am I under arrest?" Even as he said the words, he felt the two men rankle beside him.

"You are what you are. It's not up to us to argue with orders. In you go." The first soldier grunted.

Tristan sighed. After working the last twelve hours straight through, he suddenly realized he barely had the strength to remain standing. Shrugging, he went inside and tried not to let his anxieties build.

When the tent flap fell closed, the thick musty fabric shut out the last remnants of moonlight and fresh air. Although he tried to ignore it, Tristan couldn't help but feel the sense of dread that wrapped around him like a shroud.

Chapter Two

Emily Durbin had always done her very best not to show fear. When she was a child, an older cousin had persuaded her to cross a rope bridge across a small stream that ran the length of her family's property. Halfway across, one of the ropes gave way. She went plummeting to her fate, a mere six feet to the cool water's surface. Yet her scream was said to be heard for six counties and her embarrassment at landing on her bottom in the waist-deep brook knew no bounds.

Although she now was twelve years older, a woman grown and thrice nearly married, it still galled her to show her one true weakness—fear.

In her current situation, Emily admitted she was more than just afraid. She was terrified. When the first threat against her uncle came, she'd been visiting with her cousin Constance at her family's country estate. His carriage had been run off of the road and had nearly toppled into a deep ravine. The attackers had never been caught.

In the days that followed, Emily had insisted on being kept abreast of whatever plans the authorities had come up with to protect her benefactor. Since then, two more attempts had been made. Now, she was determined to take matters in hand and see to it that the proper person was chosen to protect him.

Aldus Branleigh, the viscount of Mabry, was a very important man. Sixty-two years old, her uncle had been working closely with the military to improve weaponry design. It was said that his ideas could revolutionize the armaments, and thereby work toward ending the conflict altogether. The first two attempts on his life had been poorly managed. But it had been the third that had frightened Emily the worst.

On that occasion Lord Branleigh had been taking dinner at his supper club when one of the dishes he'd been served upset his stomach. They had later learned he'd been poisoned. Since then, Emily had kept a constant vigil at her uncle's side—as had the military.

Emily sighed. Even though they were practically surrounded by the entire British army, she didn't feel safe. When General Henley had first approached her with his plan for protecting the viscount, she vehemently refused.

"I don't see how this can possibly work. You say this fellow, this surgeon, has an uncanny sense about him?" she'd asked the general, standing in the midst of the busy encampment peering at the man who walked into the infirmary tent.

"That I do, ma'am. It's the truth. I've seen evidence of it with my own eyes. It's as if he can read minds."

Emily chewed her lip. "I don't see how that's possible."

"Neither do I, Miss Durbin. Deveraux once said that he heard trapped men calling out in the midst of cannon fire. During battle he seeks out the most seriously injured soldiers and manages to get them to the surgical tents quicker. My cook informed me that he could even tell them what food supplies would be available even before the supply officer arrived in camp."

Emily had been appalled. "You're attempting to save my uncle's life with the help of some trickster?" Emily had quickly taken in a deep breath. It was unthinkable to show how terribly upset this affair had made her.

"I'm using what's available to keep Lord Branleigh alive. You know as well as I that his lordship will not long be kept from his business. Already he's snapping at my staff as though they are a pack of small hounds barking at his heels."

Emily had scoffed, though she'd known his statement wasn't far from the truth. So, when he'd taken her to the surgery and she saw just whom he'd intended to entrust their lives to, her anger flared to a new height.

"Surely you don't mean that one!"

"Indeed I do," came Henley's level answer.

The man that Henley indicated was tall and of medium build, he had light brown hair, a square, handsome face, and warm brown eyes. He looked quite nice, actually.

The sight of him sent a sudden rush of heat right through her. When he glanced in her direction, he wore an expression of pure sensuality. His steady gaze darkened and suddenly she had the sense that he was watching her. Her skin tingled and she caught her breath. It was as though someone had just touched her. In fact, she was certain a feather-light kiss had been placed on the very spot at the base of her neck, just beneath her right ear.

Glancing around quickly, she saw no one nearby. It was a most odd sensation, she thought, but not an unpleasant one.

Shaking herself, Emily returned her attention to Mr. Deveraux. A tall, lithe form, lean and muscular, he certainly was well made. His form so perfect, he could have been carved from marble. His face was especially handsome. Medium brown hair of moderate length, worn pulled back at the nape of his neck, framed his face. His high forehead, defined cheekbones, and strong jaw gave him quite a serious expression.

Emily noticed one other feature about Deveraux that

intrigued her. He had the most beautiful hands she'd ever seen. Long fingers, strong and lean, she could imagine how he used them to manipulate broken bones or weave fine sutures into injured flesh. But more than that, she instinctively thought how wonderful his hands might feel in a caress. A light brush across her cheek or a lingering touch on her shoulder or back. Yes, he had the most interesting hands. No artist could have created such a fine structure as the surgeon's hands.

A most fascinating man, he certainly didn't look as if he could thwart a killer. She didn't doubt for a moment other things that Tristan Deveraux might be expert at.

Emily's mouth went dry just considering the possibilities. The general cleared his throat beside her.

"You'll have to trust me, Miss Durbin. If there is anyone alive who can find the culprit behind these attempts on your uncle's life, it is Tristan Deveraux."

The long night stretched out endlessly. Tristan shifted his position, but the narrow cot in the stockade gave him no comfort. It was going to be another long, restless night.

"I tried to warn you, boy. 'Stay away from those louts,' I said. Come back home where you belong. I told you that you weren't good enough to live among them. They know it, too. It's only a matter of time before they cast you out. Then, you'll have to come back to me."

Tristan turned over and pulled the thin wool blanket over his head. He didn't bother to argue with the nagging thoughts inside him any more. It was no use even trying. His demons always returned to haunt him.

Tristan had long known that it was his own guilt that whispered in the back of his mind. He had a past he could never escape from, and even when he was exhausted beyond the point of thinking, the voices still returned. The best he could hope for was to turn his mind to other things.

Eventually, usually sometime before dawn, he would manage a few hours of sleep. For all the good it did him. In the morning, the accusing voice returned, all the stronger for the night's respite.

When he did manage to sleep, he only dreamed of one thing . . .

"Gypsy witch! Where's the creature?" the beast demanded.

"He's safe from you," she yelled back at him.

"You had no right to hide it from me all these years. That thing, that demon, is an abomination. He should never have lived past his first breath."

"You're wrong. Tristan is your son."

"He is not my get! My child lies cold in the ground. I swear to you. I will find that demon and when I do, I'll put him in the grave beside you."

"Please, Griffin! Listen to me! Our son was dying of a terrible sickness. He wouldn't feed. Day by day, hour by hour, his body wasted away. I tried everything. I couldn't stand it. None of the physicians knew what to do. So, I took him to my family and they did the only thing they could. They took him to the magic stones and left him for the fairies."

"You sacrificed my child to your unholy gods! I would rather see my child dead a thousand times than to let that horrid creature breathe in his place."

"The fairies didn't kill our babe. He has a chance with them. A chance for a life."

"You lie! My child is dead. Now you will pay for his life with your own!"

Tristan heard his mother's anguished cry of pain.

"Mama!" Tristan felt the beast man's hand tighten around her throat. In the last seconds of her life she let her thoughts slip through the night.

"Stay safe, my son."

"Please don't go!" he begged. "Don't leave me!"

"I love you . . ."

Like a whisper lost in a windstorm, his mother's voice

was gone. A chasm of nothingness fell between them. Her mind forever silent.

Tristan fell to the ground, a mass of pain and anguish. The beast had killed his mother. The boy had felt the man's thick hands tighten around his mother's throat, shattering her neck and windpipe as though he had held nothing more than a fistful of brittle twigs.

The pain of his mother's loss overwhelmed him. With the very last of his strength he screamed, "I will find you, you bastard!"

Tristan sobbed, angered all the more by knowing that his mother's killer could not hear him. "I will find you when I'm old enough and strong enough. I will make you pay!"

Suddenly the wind stopped blowing and an unearthly chill settled over Tristan. Pain, sharp and stabbing, cut into his brain like a thousand knives piercing his skin. He gasped when a roaring voice broke into his thoughts.

"You killed her as surely as you breathe. It was you who made her sick."

"No!" Though he wanted to deny it, Tristan knew the truth of the beast's words. He had felt his mother's sanity slipping away from him for weeks. He'd not wanted to believe he'd been the cause of it, but the day when he'd first touched her mind with his own, letting her know of his special gift, she had changed somehow. Day by day, more and more her thoughts became consumed with wild imaginings. Fairy princes and magical beasts began to intrude into her thoughts and there was little that Tristan could do to hold her to reality.

The beast called out to him, across the void of pain and loneliness.

"You killed her. I will find you, demon spawn. I promise you, I will not rest until you've breathed your last."

Tristan awoke with a start. Shaking his head to clear it, he did his best to put away the old memory. The past was gone and though he might have to relive it in his dreams, the pain and fear of that other time could never lay its hand on him again.

If only he could convince himself that was the truth. The only way he could find any solace these days was when he would imagine finding a place somewhere, a place apart, alone. A place where there would be no voices to taunt him, no thoughts from others constantly bombarding his own. Peace. It was as ephemeral as a dream, and too far out of Tristan's reach.

That was why he preferred the company of the wounded soldiers. He worked endlessly among them to quell the pain that lived in his own heart until their pain became too overwhelming and he had to retreat. It was at those times he longed for isolation.

Unfortunately, it was a fool's dream. He needed the presence of others as much as he needed air to breathe. He'd learned that lesson as a young child after his mother had died. If he hadn't been found by his uncle, Tristan knew he would surely have died.

It turned out, the only thing worse than the constant bombardment of a thousand minds was the agonizing pit of solitude. Though the thoughts of others battered him constantly, without their substance he found himself virtually sinking into despair.

"You're pathetic, you know. You can't live with them and you can't live without them. You're like a parasite, draining your life from theirs."

It made no sense. A part of him couldn't help but be ashamed. Drawn by the suffering of the wounded, he'd found a strange sort of solace there. True, while he used their minds to find the cause of their injuries and do what he could to help them heal, in doing so he felt liberated from his own isolation. It was a poor replacement for simple human connection, but it was all he had.

There was, of course, the rare occasion when there was someone whom Tristan could not read so readily. General Henley was one such man. He carefully guarded his innermost thoughts, which might indicate that he was even more dangerous to the mind reader than everyone else.

Tristan supposed he could have pushed harder, probed deeper, but he thought that Henley might suspect, and heaven knew Tristan was in enough of a boil as it was.

The woman who'd been with him was another matter entirely. Aside from the utter delight of her physical presence, she had intrigued Tristan with her manner. Highly born, sure enough, and yet her thoughts were neither pretentious nor trite. Her mind was orderly and honest, and in the chaos and deceit that Tristan faced each day, he found it most refreshing.

Still, the risk of becoming too close to another was too high, and he forcibly pushed thoughts of her from his mind.

Lying back on the cot, he sent his mind out. There was something eerie about a battlefield at night. The racket of the day's attack was now silenced to an occasional volley of fire. A question asked, a question answered.

Tristan couldn't help but feel the thrum of so many hearts beating, some faster than others, some irregular, and even others who were all but failing. Out of them all, the strange woman's beat a special rhythm.

"Don't set your sights on that one. She's too far above the likes of you."

Closing his eyes, he imagined what it would be like to hold her in his arms and feel her delicious nearness. Her body would vibrate against his chest—a constant, steady throb of her heart would set his own pulse racing. If he tried, he could feel her breaths blowing out in small puffs of air, inviting him, caressing him. Tristan felt himself being pulled to her, a siren's song promising sweet intimacies he had only heard of but had never experienced.

It was too easy to be pulled along by her sweet presence.

Unable to resist any longer, he let his thoughts travel closer, until his mind was on the verge of touching hers.

The idea of slipping into her mind both intrigued and frightened him. He should have known better. This path could only lead to his destruction. It should have frightened him enough to make him turn away. It would have, but another, stronger emotion took hold. Loneliness pushed him over the edge of abandon.

Emily stirred in her sleep. She was wrapped up in a dream. Mr. Deveraux had just arrived at their country home, bedecked in a full evening suit, sporting a smile, and holding his arms out to her. Laughing, she accepted his offer and the two set off toward a waiting carriage.

"You know, I doubted you at first; I never would have believed it possible."

"What is that, my dear?" she asked.

"That you could ever love me."

Then he kissed her.

Except, it wasn't just a kiss. It was a melding of two bodies, man and woman. Heat stirring between them—warm, soft body against strong, lean muscle and bone. A woman's rounded curves and a man's square, flat planes. Flesh against flesh. Heat becoming fire. Desire becoming an all-consuming need.

His hands seared titillating paths down her shoulders and back, his wide chest pressed against her and his entire body throbbed with a need that Emily neither denied nor understood. It was simply wanting.

It was him.

It was her.

It was the energy of a lightning strike and the calm waters of a still pond. It was knowing that they were meant for each other.

For the briefest of seconds they paused. She opened her eyes, though she needn't have done so. He wore an expression of wonder and lust, of admiration, and love. A wide, slow grin grew on his face. It spoke of secrets shared, of choices made.

He leaned forward until his breath caressed her cheek.

"You are mine."

"Yes." She barely breathed.

Emily Durbin, proper young female that she was, abandoned it all for the touch of a man. But not just any man, she realized.

Him.

The thought of such intimacy with a stranger awakened Emily like a bucket of ice poured on her head.

"The very nerve!" she said, drawing a breath. She settled back wondering what would ever possess her to allow such bawdy dreams to enter her mind.

"It's no use," she whispered into the darkness. Scooting out from beneath her quilt, she foraged around the tent for her slippers and gown. Meaning only to get out of the enclosure for a bit of fresh air, she slid from the tent opening, tiptoed past her uncle's tent, and into the fresh, sharp, early morning mist.

Nodding to the two soldiers who kept guard, she tiptoed to the water barrels. Quietly lifting the lid, she ladled up a fresh cupful and sipped the sulfur-tinged liquid. Despite the bitter taste, it was refreshing.

It wasn't until she'd finished her drink that a strange feeling came over her. She sensed that she was being watched. Glancing up furtively, she quickly scanned her too quiet surroundings.

That was when she saw him. At the edge of camp sat a single tent with two soldiers standing guard at the entrance. On the side facing her, one small flap had been pulled back, and she could see a man, the one from the surgery, gazing at her unabashedly.

"Oh!" For a moment she stood transfixed. She'd seen that expression before.

A lazy smile crossed his face. He was wearing the very same grin he'd worn in her dream. This time, however, he remained silent. His possession of her was clear in the knowing way he nodded to her.

"Mine."

Emily wanted to deny him. She wanted to run away and hide from his relentless stare. She suspected it would make little difference. There simply was no place to secret herself away from him. It both frightened her and drew her to him. Settling her reserve, Emily did as she had always done—met his challenge face on. She sent him a simmering gaze of her own.

"Yours. If you dare."

Chapter Three

The journey into the mysterious woman's mind had not been a difficult one. As though destined to follow the path into her dreams, he was instantly beside her, looking upon the vision of her slumber as though he'd had every right to be there. He thought of turning away, of doing as he should and leaving her to her rest. While he watched, she stirred in her sleep. That small movement had drawn him closer still. She was a mystery he had to unravel. A siren calling out to him and answer her he must. Like a marble statue, he could not turn away.

Tristan didn't know why the female unsettled him so, dressed in her fine skirts and wearing such an arrogant expression.

Now, he'd found her sleeping mind blissfully blank and deep in the snug comfort of her dreams. Her visions were those of her home, her family, herself as a child cradled in the arms of loving parents. She dreamt of cousins, aunts, and uncles, all gathered at some celebration. While he was drawn to it, Tristan couldn't help the slow burn of anger that simmered in his own heart. These were things that had been denied to him, and the ache inside him never completely went away.

He should have left her to her slumber. Or perhaps

made her dream of an itch just between her shoulders in that spot that one could never reach.

Just as one mischievous thought struck him, another came crashing in to take its place. Realizing that she was an unmarried woman, he thought to give her instead something even more startling. Somehow, he sensed that a good unsettling was just what she needed.

Concentrating very hard, he sent her a suggestive thought, a wisp of a dream: The two of them, gathered in a warm embrace, each smiling openly, two lovers on the verge of discovering each other.

Suddenly he found himself staring straight into her soul. She was soft and warm in his embrace. He could feel in her gentle nature, a goodness and passion that he'd never known in another person. She smiled up at him and for a few seconds she drew him to her, closer and closer until he was on the edge of revealing himself to her.

When those large, violet eyes stared up at him, Tristan realized that there was more within her than he'd ever imagined. In an instant, hot desire rushed through him, a wanting consumed him with a need unlike any he'd ever known.

A primal thought burst into his mind, explosive and complete. Suddenly he was filled with her. Her honey-and-musk scent invaded his senses, her soft skin heated and flushed against his own. Her small, round mouth beckoned forth, daring him to taste her lush, womanly flavor.

Without reason he pulled her into his arms, enfolding her, possessing her, taking her into himself. Her skin felt like soft, crushed flower petals, her form pliant and yet strong. He knew she could take any measure of what he gave and still remain her constant, giving self. He suddenly understood that he could never consume her completely. But damn his soul if he didn't want to try.

Suddenly his hands began to roam over her skin—her dress, now gone, his clothing melting away from his body as he pulled her closer still. He felt every inch of her, every breath, every hair, every tear. He nearly lost himself, but at the last second she pulled back. In the space of a breath, she knew.

She was his. He was hers. The strength of that bond was nearly unbearable and yet he surrendered to her as he had to no one before. In his quest to take her, she had possessed him instead.

"I love you," she said. Though his ears had heard her, the words changed when he opened his heart to her. What frightened him more than anything was that he knew instinctively she didn't just love him. She owned him.

The shock of that realization stabbed him like a hot blade. Jumping up from the cot, Tristan grabbed for the tent's wooden frame to steady himself. He shouldn't have invaded the woman's thoughts. Wasn't he in enough trouble already?

In the distant recesses of his mind, he heard only the sound of laughter.

"You're a fool, Tristan. A low, disgusting fool."

Unsettled, he walked to the small opening at the back of the tent. Peering through it, he tried to calm his riotous thoughts. In the moonlight, he could just make out the camp outside. Wanting fresh air and some connection to the world around his small prison, Tristan inched forward to breathe in the cool, early morning air.

That was when he felt her presence near.

Tristan's mouth went dry. Squinting into the dimness, he saw her. His heart quickened in his chest and his breath drew short. A flood of desire rushed through him. Emily Durbin raised an eyebrow. She knew he was watching her.

A slender silhouette in the shadows, she didn't remove her gaze from him immediately, as he thought she might have. Fighting the effect of her presence, he inhaled deeply and once again the scented aroma of her perfume that lingered in the night air. It was damp and feather soft. God help him, he wanted to inhale every last bit of it.

If her presence had unsettled him, he suddenly realized that his had had a similar effect on her. Tristan felt the rush of her emotion as surprise and embarrassment warred within her. That and, he noted smugly, no small amount of aggravation at her realization that she had been discovered watching him. Tristan couldn't hold back his grin.

To his delight, she didn't turn away annoyed or indignant. Instead, she carefully replaced the lid on the water barrel and tightened her already snug wrap. She lifted her chin and began walking toward him.

After a few steps, she paused. Before she uttered her first word, Tristan already knew what she was thinking.

"I've no idea what's going on. You're correct about that," he told her before she had a chance to speak.

Surprise colored her thoughts, her face flushing with irritation.

"How do you do it?" she asked, stepping even closer, though still keeping a respectable distance between them.

"Read your mind? Perhaps I'm just very clever."

"I doubt it," she said, crossing her arms.

"Do you? Then, you have me figured. I'm not clever and I don't read minds."

"Whatever you're doing, it's not amusing. You must stop it at once."

Tristan decided he instantly liked this woman's mettle very much. Her defiant, violet eyes darkened. He found he enjoyed the arrogant way she tilted her chin a tiny bit upward, not to mention the way her mouth bowed up the slightest bit. It made him think how pliant her lips might become if he truly kissed her. . . .

"What's the matter with you?" she asked, an uncertain wrinkle marring her perfect brow. Tristan decided that he liked that, too. Even when he was awake, the woman completely occupied all of his senses.

"I'm thinking about how distracting you are."

"Distracting? You are the oddest man I have ever met."

"Wish you could see more of me?" he'd said as the thought crossed her mind.

"I don't know what you're talking about. Any physical attributes you might have are most certainly overshadowed by your impertinent, arrogant nature."

Tristan laughed. "You don't really think that."

"How do you know what I . . . ? Oh!" The lady stamped down her foot and spun around, sending her soft robes whirling. Her hasty retreat gave Tristan a chance to watch the quick movements of her nicely rounded bottom as she stomped back toward her tent.

A beautiful sight, indeed. White hot, a shot of desire rushed through him. More than anything, he wanted to pursue the captivating woman. As she entered the tent and disappeared from his sight, Tristan felt like a condemned man who's just been denied a king's pardon. But condemned to what, he wondered?

"Infuriating man!"

Exasperated, Emily stormed into her tent, threw open her chest and began to rifle through her dresses. She knew it was too early to begin the day, but nervous energy roiled inside her.

"Has ol' Boney's forces overrun us?"

Emily looked up to see her uncle entering her tent. A force to be reckoned with, Aldus Branleigh was of medium height and build, his white hair always running rampant and his expression one of unconfined exuberance. This morning was no different. He focused his bright gaze upon her.

"Oh, heavens, Uncle. I'm sorry I woke you."

"Think nothing of it. If something has you this vexed, then I should know about it."

She shook her head and relaxed her grip on her handful of morning dresses. "I had a most disturbing dream and I couldn't get back to sleep. I've just come back from getting a drink of water."

"Dearest, did one of the men bother you?"

Emily swallowed. The fellow in the guarded tent did bother her. Quite a bit, actually. Her palms were damp, her chest was tight, and her knees felt like water. In fact, Emily wasn't sure what frightened her worse—that even in sleep, thoughts of him consumed her, or that while awake, he'd sent her usually ordered mind into a full-out riot.

Glancing at her uncle's worried expression, Emily battled to control her emotions. If he knew the extent of her upset there'd be no living with him. Taking a calming breath, she labored to steady herself.

"No, nothing like that. I'm just upset because of all that's going on. Your choosing to be in the midst of the fighting, for one. The attempts on your life, for another. We should go home immediately and hire the best men to protect you until the danger has passed."

"And abandon my work? I'm sorry, Emily, but I simply cannot. There are plans to be made. I have new designs that must be attempted before I continue with the next step of the process. There are other things I must attend to as well." He paused looking away from her briefly.

"But, the danger to you . . ."

"Is nothing if we can save one soldier's life, my dear. We must be vigilant. I do agree with General Henley on one account. This is not a place for a proper young lady. Unfortunately, when we return home and I continue to work, the danger will be doubly fierce."

Emily turned away, pausing a moment to steady her voice. "I don't suppose there's any talking you out of this insanity."

"I'm afraid not. For now, however, it's good that we are

up. I've awakened with a few ideas that I'd like to run past Pemberton before breakfast."

Pemberton. Emily shuddered at the thought of the nervous, damp little man. Nervous for reasons she had no idea, and damp because the poor thing sweated profusely.

Besides his lacking any pleasing physical attributes, the most disturbing thing about Jessup Pemberton was that he leered at Emily almost continually. His mismatched eyes, one blue and one brown, watched her every moment she was in his presence. Her uncle assured her that his assistant's admiration was, while annoying at the utmost, quite harmless. When Emily had arrived to live in the Branleigh summerhouse, the scientist had plainly told Pemberton that his attentions were not welcome where his niece was concerned. He explained that if and when Emily decided to marry, it would be her choice, not one forced by him. According to her uncle, the man had taken the news well enough.

For Emily, the matter was far from settled. Although Pemberton never spoke to her, she always felt uncomfortable in his presence, certain that if allowed the chance, he would do more than just stare at her.

"How much longer will we be here?"

The older man's expression softened. "I apologize, Emily. I knew you would rather be visiting with your friends in Brighton before I uprooted us on this adventure."

"It isn't that at all. I've little care for parties when your life is in such danger. It's just that I feel we would be better protected at home."

"I know that, and I'm hoping to have the last of my design ideas before General Henley by the day's end."

"When that's complete, we can leave?"

"Indeed we can. The general has found us a special protector, a gentleman with a most unusual talent, I'm told."

"I've spoken with the general and I'm certain the guardian he's chosen is not suitable for the task."

Her uncle held up his hand. "Surely, Henley knows what he's doing. The lad sounds quite intriguing and we don't want to miss an opportunity for extra protection."

Emily bit her lip. To say any more would betray her early meeting with the unconscionable surgeon.

Her uncle took her hands in his and gave them a gentle squeeze. "I can see how you are bothered by all this. Don't worry. We'll sort it out. You'll see."

More than anything, she hoped he was right. Unfortunately the heavy stone of dread forming in her stomach told her otherwise.

Jessup Pemberton was not a happy man. He, too, was up at that early hour, fully dressed, and waiting on a messenger. Anxious, he peered through the folds of the canvas to watch the early stirring of the military camp. His position in the center of such violent men made him nervous. He didn't like that he'd been dragged from his comfortable London townhouse and into the center of such dangerous circumstances. Worse yet, he alone knew the purpose of this journey, as well as what fate awaited his employer. The table had been set and there was no changing it now.

Not that he particularly wanted to. He'd spent too much of his life working in the shadows of great men, and to his mind, Aldus was indeed among them. Although none of his previous employers had gained one ounce of his respect, this one did. Not because of his immense accomplishments, though his advances in rifle design were among the best, but for his relation to someone that Jessup desired more than life itself—his lovely niece, Emily.

Miss Emily Durbin was a dream that walked and most unlike other young women of her social standing. Not too tall, she had delightfully rounded curves that were made for a man's touch. But her attractiveness didn't stop there.

It was her quick mind and strong will that drew Jessup's attention. He saw her as a challenge. Once she'd consented to marry him, and Jessup was sure she would once he convinced her the sense of it, he would take great pains to further her education. He would see to it that she wouldn't become just a loving wife, but also a faithful, obedient woman. She would bend to his will, and he gleefully spent his idle moments imagining just how he would make her. She would be the biggest challenge of his life, and he was more than ready to best her.

Emily Durbin was a woman with too much freedom. Jessup knew at the first that he'd have to keep her closely guarded in a remote location. She'd be allowed no windows to entice her and no companions to cloud her thinking. It would be easy to transform her once he had her in the right circumstances. It would take discipline and great strength of will on his part, but he had no doubts he could accomplish the task. None at all.

All he had to do was complete his mission and then be rid of her troublesome uncle. Small obstacles when one considered the delights that awaited him.

"Mr. Pemberton," a man's voice called quietly from the other side of his tent's opening.

"Yes?"

"I've word from London."

Jessup smiled. The future was about to begin. He quickly put thoughts of Emily behind him. He needed to concentrate on the task at hand.

Pushing aside the tent's canvas covering, he motioned his visitor inside. "Hurry. We haven't much time."

"We have enough for this." The man handed a folded parchment to him.

Carefully opening the delivery, Jessup quickly scanned the contents. A small, smug smile slid across his face. Indeed, there would be time, after all.

* * *

"She's mine!"

The declaration struck like a blow against Tristan's psyche. It was a hissing sound, snakelike in the way it slithered into his consciousness.

"She's mine and I'll have her, no matter what!"

The thinker's intentions were dark and dangerous, and arrogant determination resonated like death itself in Tristan's thoughts. Startling emotions, an almost lethal mixture of desire and lust assailed him. Only one other mind had felt like that, and though this latest thinker paled in comparison to his father's tone, Tristan recognized the same depraved evil that consumed him.

More startling than that, the object of the thinker's attention was none other than Tristan's mysterious early morning visitor. It seemed the lady had a dangerous admirer.

Meaning to send his thoughts out and learn more, Tristan's concentration was interrupted when General Henley briskly entered the stockade.

Without looking in Tristan's direction, he motioned the guards to join him. "Escort Mr. Deveraux to the officer's tent and get him cleaned up."

"Sir?" Tristan stood to attention.

"Mr. Deveraux. Perhaps now you shall be more prompt about answering my summons." He nodded once to the guards and promptly left the tent.

Tristan wanted desperately to know what this was about, but as always, Henley's mind remained silent, just out of his reach.

"You're really in the stew now, boy," his inner voice cackled.

Twenty minutes later Tristan had bathed and was outfitted in a clean uniform shirt and trousers. Shaved, hair

combed and his boots shining, he was deemed presentable and escorted to the general's tent.

"Just like a lamb to the slaughter, eh, boy?"

Henley sat sipping his tea at the head of the table.
Before him was set an ample assortment of food—
poached eggs, thickly sliced ham, and rolls of fresh
baked bread. With the long hours in the surgery the day
before and his night in the stockade, Tristan realized he
couldn't remember when he'd last eaten.

"At ease, Mr. Deveraux. Join me for some refreshment.
We've a great deal to discuss."

Despite the offer and his own hunger, Tristan didn't
accept the invitation. Seeing his hesitation, the general sat
back and crossed his arms, evidently willing to wait him
out.

*"He's found you out for sure! Now, you're in deep. There'll be
no escaping your fate, mark my words."*

Tristan swallowed the fear that rose in him. Perhaps
this was the disaster he'd been waiting for.

He decided to put the matter out once and for all.

"You're wondering if I'll accept your terms," Tristan
began slowly. "You've an assignment for me that's a bit
outside my regular duties. My night in the stockade was
only to get my attention."

The general's sharp features broke into a fierce grin. "Exactly. You are a wonder, Mr. Deveraux, a wonder indeed."

"So you seem to think. I'm really not all that special."

"Nonsense. I'm sure you have sufficient reasons for
wanting to stay beneath the stir."

"If I did, I can assure you they would not be ones that
I'd be inclined to share."

"I don't want to know your secrets, Mr. Deveraux. I
don't need to know them. What I do need is your assistance in an important matter. Lives are at stake and you
may be the only one who can prevent disaster."

Tristan could discern that Henley truly believed his
words, which made the prospect all the more frightening.

"Whatever special talents you believe I have, I assure you, you are mistaken. I fear I will fall woefully short of your expectations."

Tristan had thought he worded his denial rather well, but his alarm was raised when Henley only smiled.

"On the contrary, I disagree. I believe you have a gift, sir, a most unusual one that sets you apart from the rest of us. I believe you can read minds."

Tristan sat back, a nervous chuckle escaping him. "I can also foretell the future and cheat at cards. You've found me out."

It was the general's turn to laugh. "I know it sounds ludicrous. Unbelievable, really. But I'd stake my life on it. I've been watching you, Deveraux. I've seen the way you seem to know what's going to happen, the way you react when you're around the men, especially those who are hurt or afraid. Perhaps it's nothing more than phenomenal intuition. Whatever you wish to call the beast, I know of its existence and I intend to use it."

"What do you want?"

"I want you to prevent a murder."

Chapter Four

Emily pulled back from the army commander's tent. A chill went through her at the mention of her uncle's peril. The guard beside the tent eyed her carefully. Giving him a soft smile, she nodded. "I don't wish to be rude. I'll wait until the end of their business."

That seemed to settle the matter. The soldier looked away while Emily leaned against the support pole.

"General," Deveraux answered, "I'm not sure what you expect from me. Even if I had such a talent, I'm no soldier, what could I possibly do to protect the man?"

The general cleared his throat. "Despite what you may think, Deveraux, a soldier's strongest asset is not his weapon, or even his skill at wielding it. It's his knowledge. Any true fighting man knows that knowledge is power. You have the ability to know what others are thinking. That is far more deadly than a blade or a pistol."

Emily watched the trickster's silhouette lean back. "Even if I could help you, which I can't, why should I?"

"You'd be serving your country, for one," the general said in a level tone.

"By patching up his majesty's fighting forces, I serve it now. Isn't that sufficient?"

"I'm sure the crown appreciates your assistance; however, there is more involved. The man in jeopardy is a weapons designer. A civilian whose ideas may well revolutionize our armaments. More power, less bloodshed, less work for men like you."

"You are asking me to help a man whose sole purpose is to create new and efficient ways to kill. I think not."

Emily cringed. How dare he! Her uncle's efforts were meant to aid in ending wars, not in fighting them.

"Perhaps more time in the stockade might give you a chance to consider things better."

"That's the way of it? If I don't do as you order, you'll lock me up?"

The general leaned forward. "I can imprison any man I think might be a threat to my command. I can even have him executed. What's to say that you're not using that incredible talent of yours to spy and to send missives to the enemies?"

Emily heard the other sneer. "Very clever, general. I spend eighteen hours a day, knee deep in blood and death in order to thwart the king's forces."

"I'm not sure what your motives are."

If she leaned to the side, Emily could just make out the general's face through a crack in the tent flap. He didn't look as though he was suspicious of his guest at all.

"Fine. Then arrest me. I could use the sleep."

For a moment the two sat locked in each other's gaze, as though they were trapped in glass. Both were men of strong will, neither one willing to budge in the slightest.

Emily suddenly gained an insight into the surgeon's intention. Tristan Deveraux was a man of conviction, but clearly he was also a man of compassion. She could see the struggle within him. He wanted to save them all, to ease each soldier's pain, to stop the seemingly unending death and destruction.

Seconds passed as she held her breath, but neither one moved.

Emily could stand no more. This wasn't getting them

anywhere. Not really knowing why she trusted the surgeon at all, or even if his talents were what General Henley believed them to be, she decided that this strange man might indeed help protect her uncle. She couldn't understand how, but that morning outside the stockade she'd felt a strange connection to him.

Clearing her throat, she charged inside the tent.

"Excuse me, general, I don't mean to interrupt but I think perhaps I might be able to persuade your officer the importance of helping my uncle."

Both men scrambled to stand in her presence.

For a brief moment the military leader shot her a surprised expression, but then turned his attention back to the surgeon.

"Of course, Miss Durbin. Please join us. Let me introduce you to Mr. Deveraux. He is the gentleman I was telling you about."

Emily nodded and took her first full measure of the serious young man.

"Ah, the mysterious lady," Tristan Deveraux bowed formally, keeping his chin tilted upward so that his gaze never left Emily's. His penetrating gaze sent a shiver through to her core. Emily nodded, doing her best to keep a sudden onrush of emotion under control.

"The two of you have met?" The general narrowed his gaze at his officer.

Deveraux cleared his throat. "Briefly, yes."

Emily felt her face grow warm, realizing that by now her early morning visit with Deveraux likely had been the talk of the camp.

"I do so apologize for interrupting such serious business but I thought we might start making plans for our return to Bradenton."

The general nodded. "Please, join us. I was just going over my ideas with Mr. Deveraux. We were discussing his new assignment—traveling with you and your uncle back to England. Mr. Deveraux was just accepting his orders."

Emily could feel the tension in the room rise a notch, but the surgeon remained silent.

Emily pulled her gaze away from him and back to the general.

"I never meant to be the cause of such division. In fact, I was coming to tell you that I believe you needn't worry about assigning more than a couple men to watch over us once we return home. I spoke with Uncle Aldus this morning and we're in agreement that we should hire outside help on a more permanent basis. But until that time, we welcome any added security you can provide."

"Thank you for understanding. I realize that this is quite an imposition into your life, Miss Durbin. However, protecting your uncle is of the utmost importance. So much so, that it's necessary to put personal inconvenience aside. My apologies to you, but I will be assigning several key officers to your protection, Mr. Deveraux included."

The general gave a pointed look to the surgeon. The younger man did not look away, as others might have, but instead held his head even slightly higher than before.

"Unless I'm otherwise detained," Deveraux said, the edge of a sneer in his voice. "Might I ask, am I to be standing guard duty the entire time? I wasn't trained for combat," he said, a sharpness in his tone.

"Of course not," the general answered tersely. "You would be useless with a rifle. I think it best for you to continue in your present role as physician. Less complicated that way."

The man bristled. "I'm not a physician, I'm merely a surgeon's apprentice. Unless Branleigh needs a carbuncle removed, I'm afraid I won't be much help to him."

"Not to worry, since you won't be performing any procedures while in your current assignment."

"My uncle is in perfect health," Emily supplied. A small tremor of anticipation went through her when Deveraux looked in her direction.

"I suppose there is nothing else to be said in the matter?"

The general barely hid the smile that teased at the corner of his mouth. "Not unless you'd like to spend the rest of the war in the stockade, there isn't."

With that the young man stood up and sent a scathing glance in Emily's direction before he left the room.

Henley said nothing as they watched the surgeon leave; the general was obviously enjoying his victory.

"Now, that's settled. If you'll excuse me, miss, I've much pressing business to attend to, the rest of the war, to be specific."

Emily nodded, and rose to leave as well, her attention no longer on the general, but rather on the wide set of retreating shoulders that was retreating to the army camp.

Tristan marched out of the tent, anger building inside him like a volcano about to erupt. Worse yet, while he couldn't read the general's mind as easily as some, it was easy to tell the man felt as though dealing with the wily surgeon was more a challenge than an obstacle. Damning the commander for all his arrogance, Tristan barely missed the young woman who pursued him now, doggedly gaining on his long strides.

"That's it, Tristan. Run away as fast as you can. So what if you catch a bullet in your back. It has to be better than living like this, don't you think?"

"Excuse me, Mr. Deveraux, I must speak with you."

Tristan was not in the mood for company. Thoughts of teaching her the truth about interaction between men and women roared in his mind for the briefest moment. Fortunately, the fevered rush of his emotions made certain that any thoughts of bedding the lady were put back at the moment, at least until her deep, luring voice touched his ears.

Whirling, he turned on her, fully intending to vent his

considerable anger in her direction, but the sight of the small, delicate frame, the full wash of moist, dark lavender eyes, and her small, completely kissable mouth took him by surprise. Instead of teaching her what interfering in his life might entail, the sight of her sent all of his emotions to a single focal point and much farther south in his own anatomy. Chagrined, he wondered what man would not look upon her and be aroused?

"You're a low, common beast, you know. Like father, like son, say's I."

If fighting his own natural male urges weren't enough, Tristan remembered his earlier mental encounter with the dangerous thinker who'd had terrible intentions for the beautiful young lady. Just the thought of what kind of deviant circumstances that sort of sick mind could conjure to harm a true innocent like Miss Durbin set Tristan's anger soaring.

The truth was, whether she realized it or not, her uncle wasn't the only one who needed protecting. She possessed a certain vulnerability. Not that she was of weak personality. From the beginning, Tristan had sensed an innate intelligence and sturdiness in her character. If she was threatened, he was certain she'd put up one hell of a fight.

But it was a man's world, and men, being stronger and the more depraved of the sexes, could easily overcome even the most well-intentioned female.

In short, Emily Durbin needed a hero.

Unfortunately, that was the one thing Tristan could never be. He had long known of his own shortcomings, in fact had spent his entire adult life atoning for them. But, neither could he turn away from someone in so much need. At least not until he was certain she and her uncle had found at least some measure of assistance.

"You can't save her. You can't even save yourself."

Tristan sighed. No, he couldn't really protect her. But neither could he abandon her. He simply wasn't adequate for the task, but for the moment, he was all she had.

"I'm beginning to think it would do no good to convince you that I am unable to really help you," he said at last.

She shook her head. "Before I entered the general's tent, I too believed that your involvement in my uncle's affairs would be most disastrous. I had every intention of saying so."

"For a defensive argument, you certainly had me fooled."

"The truth is, I have reconsidered. If the general is correct about your abilities . . ."

"Which he is not . . ."

"Then I would be remiss if I objected to a chance to protect my uncle."

Tristan withdrew a pace from her. How could he make her understand that she was placing entirely too much faith in his abilities without divulging the peril he would be in if the discovery of his gift became known?

"You might as well surrender now. Get it over with, get done with the trial and on to the execution."

Tristan shook his head to clear it.

"Let me assure you, the general is in error. I can no more read the thoughts of others than I can understand French. As a matter of fact, it is such a ludicrous idea that I find it hard to fathom that an upstanding, educated woman such as you would believe such a fantasy. Until now I never thought any well bred young lady would be the type who would be given to such fanciful thinking. Am I incorrect in believing that?"

His words caused her to step back as if she'd been slapped. It seemed, as he gently listened to the rapid spin of her thoughts, she took her own straightforward, logical mind to be quite her strongest suit. In fact, she took more offense at his suggestion of her frivolity than if he'd insulted her virtue.

"I assure you, sir, that I am neither fanciful nor frivo-lous in my manner. I love my uncle fiercely. I have no other close family. My parents died within months of each other when I was very young. He took me into his home and taught me to respect education and right thinking. I would do anything, even consider impossible circumstances if need be, to protect him."

It was at that moment that Tristan felt the true force of the woman's passion. Though she tried hard to dampen her rush of emotion, it was clear she was a mighty force to be reckoned with.

The only hope he had of deterring Miss Durbin's de-termination was to appeal to her rational, ordered approach to problem solving.

"Let's say, for the sake of argument that I do have this incredible ability. I can read minds. Fine."

"I believe you can." She nodded, crossing her arms in front of her.

"I suppose I'll have to prove the impossibility to you."

"I'm listening," she said.

"Do you suppose that there might be problems even if such a talent were possible?"

She considered his words. "Most things of value aren't met without difficulty. One would think that a man that can eavesdrop on someone else's secrets would be better able to prepare for every contingency. If one chooses to harm you or someone you care about, would you not be able to do something to prevent it?"

Tristan took a deep breath before answering her. At one time he might have agreed with her, but life and ex-perience had taught him differently. If he could have done such a thing, the lives he could have saved . . .

"We know all about that now, don't we!"

Tristan shook his head. No use in going down that line of thinking again. He knew too well it could lead to mad-ness. Without hesitation, he grasped her arm. Although touching her strengthened the mental bond between them, and Tristan could feel the rise and fall of her mind the same way he felt the blood rushing in the veins beneath his hand, he wasn't sure he could make her understand. She was a person who thought in a solid, pragmatic fashion.

So be it. Half walking—half pulling her—he took her to the perimeter of the camp. There, where the horses were corralled, was a large watering trough. Still holding her arm, he bent down and picked up a handful of pebbles.

"Let me demonstrate. When a person thinks, he often thinks in different directions, correct? For instance, one can be considering his next move on horseback, which direction the wind is blowing, and what is being served in the mess tent for dinner."

"I suppose."

"Even now, while you're considering my words, you're deciding whether or not to believe me, if your uncle is safe, and what the next London season will be like. Eh?"

Her face instantly registered the shock of his words. "How do you . . . ?"

"I don't know, but rather I suppose it's just what a woman in your position would be thinking."

"Mind reading?"

"Deduction."

"Go on."

Good, Tristan thought, they were perhaps on the right path. He plunged ahead. "Then, it would be much like this." Tristan tossed a single stone into the watering trough. It quickly sank to the bottom making a thunking noise. On the surface of the water small ripples spread out before them until they collided with the edges of the trough and then bounced back recklessly until the movement slowed to calmness once again.

"Chaos," he said.

"Is it?"

"One would suppose so if one were of a logical mind,"

Tristan said carefully. She flashed her concerned gaze up at him and then tilted her chin in agreement.

"Yes, I suppose one would."

"Good. This would be a benefit, you might think. I mean, knowing everything that was in another's mind. Now, imagine being the man who can divine another's thoughts. The scrambling of only one person's thinking could be very uncomfortable. Random ideas, emotions jumbling up, sounding and feeling very much like a hen house full of chickens who have just discovered a fox in their midst."

"It would be unsettling."

"Very. More than that, say our mind reader would be in the center of a crowd, several people, in fact. All of them independent minds, thinking about God knows what at lightning speed."

"It would become most worrisome."

"More than that. It would be very disturbing and excruciatingly painful if all those impressions from different directions were constantly bombarding one's senses. Add to that, most thoughts come also with unlimited emotions. Fear, anger, hatred, greed—every one overwhelming the person who receives them."

"Oh, dear."

Tristan went on. "Total disruption, twenty-four hours a day for an entire lifetime."

With that, Tristan threw the rest of his pebbles into the trough. On its surface, the water became a rush of movement, tiny waves battling against each other in all directions.

Tristan watched the water settle before them, but in his own mind he saw understanding settle over her. Closing his eyes he felt her concern arise and cover him like a soft quilt, wanting nothing more than to protect him from the harshness of such a plight.

A lump of ice took shape in Tristan's throat. Her concern rattled him completely. How easy it would have been to turn to it, to embrace it like a flower soaking up much needed warmth from the sun.

"I'm sorry. I never realized," she whispered beside him, the rise of true remorse filling her.

"It's all right. I, that is, this person, can also experience the good things as well, friendship, caring, sometimes love."

For a brief moment their eyes met and Tristan was overcome by the true sweetness of her. She was the embodiment of all that was good in a person. Soft, gentle curves but with strength of will that kept her from being too pliable, too unprotected.

Tristan gasped when she reached up to touch his face, a single perfect tear forming in the corner of her right eye.

At that instant, Tristan knew he had fallen in love with her.

As he stood staring dumbfounded into her beautiful violet gaze, he realized that Emily Durbin was a woman who had meticulously erected barriers around her heart, and who in the space of those few seconds, had opened them just the tiniest bit for him.

Unable to help himself, Tristan was nearly overcome by desire. With a rush of animal hunger, he wanted this woman—in his arms, in his life, and in his heart. He brushed his hand against her cheek. When she drew in a quick breath, a sharp pang of wanting stabbed through him.

"There's the boy. She's a right nice peach. Go ahead, have a little taste."

Leaning down, Tristan was about to act on his baser nature, to take her into his embrace, to touch and explore her with all his senses, not just with his physical self, but also with his mind and his heart.

Before he could barely take another breath, an intrusion of another's presence burst upon him. Glancing up he could see the general, standing at the door of his tent staring at them both. His expression was blank except for a knowing brace set about his eyes.

Tristan grimaced. Damn him. What the general had just witnessed had sealed his fate.

"He's got you now!"

Glancing down at Emily, he saw that her eyes had become impossibly wide. She was studying him now, perhaps deciding if she could indeed read his thoughts as well.

For the briefest of moments, he wondered what it would be like to confess everything to her. To tell her all about himself.

Before he could, however, old memories rose in him, like bitter bile climbing up his throat. The danger of such an impulsive idea thwarted his desire when he remembered another who had suffered from his once impetuous nature.

The reality of his existence punched him hard. Memories from his past rushed forward and he remembered that the life that most men craved was to be forever denied to him.

The best he could hope for was to convince her of the danger and get away from both her and the army at the first possible moment. He would add deserter to his list of other crimes. So be it.

Where he would go after that was another matter.

"You could always come home."

Letting loose of the lady, he stepped back a pace, then shaking his head only once, set off for the one place that would offer him refuge. The infirmary.

Henley watched the man flee from Branleigh's neice. Looking as though a hot poker had run him through, Deveraux glanced only once in the general's direction. It wasn't the same expression of anger that had burned between the two of them when they'd discussed his orders earlier in his tent. No, it was the expression of abject fear that marred the young man's expression.

A healthy thing, fear, Henley thought as he witnessed

Miss Durbin's observance of Deveraux's retreat. Best to let things work out on their own, he thought. Perhaps the chemistry between a man and a woman could achieve what he could not. Henley only shrugged, crossing his arms and putting his pipe in his mouth.

The general suspected that the surgeon's talent could be invaluable to the war effort, and combined with the lady's obvious sharp intellect and solid determination, they could be most instrumental in helping her uncle complete his mission whole and soundly. Yes, things were working much to his advantage.

"Mr. Watkins," he said to his second, "prepare Branleigh and his party to depart this afternoon, then, find my secretary. I've letters to send to General Wellington right away."

For now, there was a war to be managed and it was long past time he was about it. He meant to have his plans set in motion by the end of the season, and insuring Branleigh's healthy state was the only way he could see to achieve it.

Captain Jeffrey Hamilton was not an imposing figure of a man. He was not as striking as his older brother, Cyril, nor was he as dashing as his younger brother Courtney. But, he was honest and loyal, true to his word, and honorable, and in his own estimation that was good enough. It had to be. A second son of a viscount, and a poor one at that, Jeffrey had to be content with making his own way in the world. There would be no title, no inheritance, and likely little more than a mention in society at all, save for his mother being distantly related to the duke of Melbourne, though he suspected it was a dubious connection at best.

No, Jeffrey, being a realist, knew that the only way to ensure a good life would be through hard work and honor, the two things he seemed to excel at. So, having joined the army at the earliest possible age, he'd earned his place as an officer, something rarely done these days because all the officer positions were taken up by second sons of the higher titled and wealthier members of the *ton*. Nonetheless, he'd set out to make his mark.

Approaching General Henley's office, he had his suspicions, true enough. The general was famous for making exacting demands upon his officers, regardless of their social standing. He was a man who respected abilities and not what title one was connected to. A stern disciplinarian, Henley would not tolerate division amongst his ranks, and it was even said that he was most adept at handling the civilian population. Admired and revered, respected and honored, General Henley was the kind of man that Jeffrey aspired to become.

So, on the morning he was summoned for his next assignment, Jeffrey expected a challenge. He was not disappointed.

As he approached the general's tent, a young woman who nearly knocked him down in her haste passed him.

"Please, forgive me. I didn't mean to . . ." She paused, looking up at him. Her clear, amethyst eyes didn't waver as she took in his features.

A flush warmed her skin and the peach in her cheeks darkened. Jeffrey felt his own heat rise a notch in her presence. With dark brown hair, a complexion that rivaled a fine French painting, and the slender figure of a gazelle, she was the sort of woman men like Jeffrey dreamed about. Dreamed about, but never obtained.

"My pardon, madam." He bowed formerly. "I was not watching where I was going. Please forgive my clumsiness," he added, hopeful that she wouldn't instantly scorn him the way young ladies of society often did.

"Oh, no, the fault was mine. Uh, please excuse me. I'm in a dreadful rush."

"Indeed. Perhaps we will meet at another time and can be introduced properly."

"Perhaps." With that she nodded shyly, "well, good day, then."

Jeffrey nodded, and paused briefly to watch her retreat. It was a very lovely retreat, at that.

Entering Henley's tent, Jeffrey was met with a discerning eye.

"Ah, Hamilton. At ease. Sit, please."

After a quick salute, Jeffrey took the chair in front of the general's desk. The lady's soft scent still lingered.

"A lovely girl, Miss Durbin. Have you met her?"

"Uh, briefly on the walkway, sir. We've not been formerly introduced. She was set on some urgent task."

"Indeed. I've a new assignment for you, Hamilton. It's likely one of the most important tasks you'll undertake in the service of the crown. I trust you are up to it?"

Henley looked up from his paperwork, his hand still writing some mysterious missive.

"I am completely at your service, sir."

"You're a good man, Hamilton. I knew I could count on you."

"Absolutely, sir. What is it you wish me to do?"

Relatively new to command, Jeffrey's stomach clenched. He was good at handling the responsibilities that had been given him. "A true leader of men," was what the commander had proclaimed him after his leading a contingent of men through occupied territory and bringing back much-needed supplies. That had been nearly a month ago. Jeffrey was more than ready to set out on another mission.

"I want you to accompany Branleigh and his niece back to England. You will see to it that Mr. Deveraux goes with them as well. He will be on special assignment for an undisclosed length of time. You will make certain that he does not stray from his duties."

Jeffrey barely managed to bite back a course remark. "Deveraux, sir? One of Mr. Barton's men?"

"The same."

"I see."

Henley studied him for a moment. "You don't have a high opinion of the lad?"

"I find him abrasive, undisciplined, and generally disrespectful of authority." The army had been Jeffrey's passion for the past five years. Deveraux, while a relatively skilled cutter, was a far cry from a shining example of military presence.

"I see." Henley snorted. "Your expression looks as though you're not exactly enamored with the assignment."

"On the contrary. I am honored to be given the opportunity. I just don't understand why Branleigh would need a surgeon, sir. I mean, perhaps a physician from the Continent would be better suited if he's in poor health."

"Branleigh is not ill, nor is his niece, as I'm sure you've seen. No, Deveraux's responsibilities are of a different nature. What I require of you is to make sure he stays the course and remains with Lord Branleigh until such time as he is released from his duties."

"Of course, sir."

"Good. You are to take a small contingent of men and escort Mr. Deveraux, Branleigh, and his niece to the Continent. Once there, you are to stand guard. It is imperative that Deveraux stay close by the viscount at all times. Branleigh is a scientist who is working on several designs for our new weapons program. His safety is tantamount."

"I understand, sir. Have you specific men in mind, or do you wish me to choose amongst the troops."

"I'm certain you are aware of each man's strengths and weaknesses. My only suggestion would be to lean toward ones who would be respectful of Miss Durbin. We don't want them chasing after her skirts like hounds after a bitch, now do we?"

Jeffrey instantly understood. The lady was to remain out of the reach of the men. That was perfectly acceptable. Women of substance rarely turned their attentions toward the lowly enlisted men. Titled officers, perhaps.

The general held his gaze steady, and Jeffrey got the

impression that she was considered out of reach for certain officers as well. Himself, for instance.

"I understand, sir."

"I had no doubt you would. As to Mr. Deveraux, he is exempt from that rule. His situation with Branleigh and his niece dictates that he remains close in their confidences. It would not be unexpected that they might share common interests. You will instruct your men accordingly."

"Yes, sir." So, Hamilton thought ruefully, something was afoot, and he was sure it had to do with the surgeon and the lady. Was his commander trying his hand at matchmaking, then?

"By your thoughtful expression, I'm thinking you might believe that I'm trying to control the personal lives of the two of them. In fact, I am."

"Your intentions are none of my business, sir."

"Of course, not. However, I feel it important for you to understand. Deveraux is a gifted surgeon, more than that he has the makings of a damn fine officer. In my estimation, he has the potential to be groomed for higher office. As you have mentioned, he can be difficult."

"I hadn't given him much consideration. Mr. Deveraux is not under my command."

"No, but he is a thorn in the shoe of Major Cravens, as I'm sure you've heard on more than one occasion."

"Well, there have been rumors."

"Most of them based on some degree of fact, no doubt. As it happens, I believe Deveraux needs a steady hand, and Miss Durbin strikes me as the sort of woman who could manage such a feat. Heaven knows she's kept her uncle walking the chalk for quite some time."

"So your interest in Deveraux's well-being is strictly a military one."

"Exactly. I'll not mince facts with you, Captain. The army is in dire straights. Branleigh is in a position to be of inestimable value to the military if we're to gain the upper hand. Everything we do from here on is of vital importance. Protect Branleigh and his niece as you would your own family. The crown is depending on you."

Hamilton swallowed hard. "You have my word, sir."

Just then the general's tent flap opened and a young recruit poked his head inside.

"Begging your pardon, sir. I've a message for you from Mr. Deveraux."

"Really?" The general did not look amused. "Bring it in, man."

The youth hurried inside and placed the parchment gingerly on the general's desk. Taking out his quizzing glass, the military man studied its contents.

"I see," he muttered. Looking back at Hamilton he nodded once and handed him the message. "It appears your task has begun. Good luck and Godspeed, Captain."

Chapter Five

Emily paced the short length of her small tent for the hundredth time in an hour. How could General Henley even consider sending them off so soon? She'd hoped for at least another few days to come up with a better plan to protect her uncle.

After her last encounter with the surgeon, she'd decided once again that her uncle was in more peril than ever. Even if he could read minds, how adept was he at sorting them all out? She thought it very possible that her uncle's would-be assailant might slip past Deveraux's ability, and then disaster would surely befall them.

Peering outside the enclosure, she could see the army men loading up the last of her belongings.

Her mind made up, Emily reached for her bonnet and made a final decision. Her confrontation with Mr. Devereaux had placed things in a new light. He was not the right person to protect her uncle. She would go to the general and make him understand how important it was to not place their trust in a single man.

After a short walk she arrived at Henley's tent just as he'd returned from a tour of the camp.

"Miss Durbin. I trust my men are doing a sufficient job of getting things ready for your journey?"

Emily twisted her reticule in her hands. "That's what I've come to speak with you about; I think we should postpone our leaving."

"Indeed? Why is that?" He motioned her into his office.

The general seated himself at his desk, noticeably not inviting her to sit as well.

Taking the initiative, Emily quickly took her seat across the desk.

"By the way, I thank you for your assistance earlier," the general said. "I'm sure your inclusion in our discussion will help to convince Mr. Deveraux of the need for his cooperation."

"That's what I've come to discuss with you, General. I've now had the chance to speak with him and I think perhaps I was in error."

"I assure you, no matter what he claims, his talent is a real one. He can read minds."

Emily bit her lip. "I'm not doubting that, sir. In fact, I'm more convinced of it than ever. This gift, or talent, as you call it, is rather disturbing. It causes him a great deal of pain. There's something else. I'm not sure exactly what, but something is terribly wrong with him."

"Wrong? As in a defect in his character?"

"No." Emily paused. How could she possibly make the general understand what she'd felt? There was certainly no way to prove her suspicions, no empirical evidence that would demonstrate Mr. Deveraux's complete inability to be effective. Still, she had to try.

"He's so sad. I mean, it troubles him greatly. The poor man is barely able to protect himself from the result of his ability, how can he possibly be of service to us?"

What she didn't tell him was that Tristan Deveraux was a distraction and she could not afford to have her attention diverted from her uncle's welfare. Too long in the surgeon's presence, and heaven only knew what disaster would overtake their lives.

Already, she'd entertained thoughts of kissing him! No, he simply wouldn't do at all.

General Henley sat back in his chair a moment. "I do not doubt what you're saying. In fact, it would seem to me that such an incredible ability would not come without its drawbacks. I have spoken extensively with several of the men who've worked with Deveraux over the last few months. They all agree that he is a fine, upstanding man who works tirelessly and has great care for his fellows."

"I believe so, as well."

"If you worry about him fulfilling his duties, don't. I'm a superb judge of a man's character. He is under my command and if he were an excellent marksman, I would have him on the field saving lives. If he were an outstanding strategist, I would have him in my offices every day, analyzing the battle. As a surgeon, he is extremely efficient. At the moment he is needed elsewhere. I require him to use his ability to read minds, however off the scale of believability the gift may be, to keep your uncle safe until certain tasks are completed. There is no other choice in the matter."

"But he's so very tormented," Emily blurted out at last.

The general held up his hand. "Your concerns are duly noted. Now, if you'll excuse me, I have a great deal of work to catch up on. My advice to you would be twofold. First, I suggest you get packed and be ready to leave by midafternoon. Second, if Mr. Deveraux's soul is in need of succor, perhaps you are the one person to give it. Heaven knows nothing heals a man's soul like the gentle touch of a woman. Good day."

Dazed, Emily rose from her chair and glanced toward the door. Turning back she meant to beg one final time but the general's attentions were already turned elsewhere. Her spirits sinking, she turned away.

How could she tell him that it would be far too easy to offer "succor" to Mr. Deveraux. In fact, it would be quite easy to give him anything at all that he asked for. Emily clamped down on the thought. The memory of her dream that morning was proof enough of that.

"One final thing, miss," the general said as she approached the tent opening.

"Yes?"

"Your uncle has every confidence in the abilities of this army to keep him safe. Perhaps you should as well."

Emily said nothing else as she left Henley's tent. Confidence was not a problem, she decided. She was set on watching her uncle with her every waking moment. But watching Mr. Deveraux was another matter entirely.

Inside the surgical tent, Tristan could hear the shouting. Although he held his hand steady as he made the last stitch in the soldier's cut, he knew that any distraction could be his undoing in far less stressful circumstances. No matter, he told himself. Surely once he reported to the general of Mr. Kelly's botched surgery, the old man would change his mind about forcing Tristan to take this outrageous assignment.

He'd been absolutely insane to think he could help Miss Durbin and her uncle and even more so to allow himself to nurture feelings of a romantic nature for her.

"That's the way to think, my boy. You're certainly not good enough for the likes of that one."

Suddenly the tent flaps flew apart and one of the camp's most promising young officers, Captain Jeffrey Hamilton, stormed inside the medical tent, his face red with fury, his fists clenched.

"What in blazes do you think you're doing?"

Tristan ignored the urge to look upward and deliver a scathing remark to the superior officer. He knew he'd not be doing any cutting or sewing in the stockade. His one night spent in the cramped quarters was more than sufficient to remind him of the consequences of army discipline.

"I said, what in blazes do you think you're doing?" Hamilton was clearly at the edge of his patience.

"If you must know, I'm endeavoring to sew back two split pieces of intestine. Not that it shall do much good, mind you. The poor devil will probably end up with a putrid wound under these conditions."

"I believe you already have orders. Is there no one else to perform the task?"

Tristan glanced up. "Mr. Kelly, also one of Mr. Barton's protégés, is very astute at putting away several bottles of port, but is not so good at stitching pieces of man's gut back together. He's the one who caused this mess in the first place. As to my orders, I've already explained myself to the general. I'm sure that once he sees reason, he'll decide that my skills are needed much more fervently here than on some pleasure trip with the nobility."

"I just left the general's quarters. It was he who sent me here."

"He hasn't changed his mind then?"

"Not bloody likely. You are to report to me within half an hour. If you fail to do so, I am to place you in irons and drag you away in front of the entire division. I trust you will take the prudent course without further objections?"

Hamilton then turned and abruptly exited the infirmary tent. Too steeped in anger, Tristan wasn't about to give him an answer.

"Sounds like he's bloody well serious," Harry remarked beside him.

"He can be whatever he likes. I've work to do here."

"Laddie, you'd best be on your way. No sense ending up in the stew."

Tristan pulled back. Why couldn't they leave him alone?

"It isn't right. There's plenty enough for me to do here. One would think it's far more important than standing guard over that woman and her uncle."

Harry chuckled beside him. "Quite a pretty woman, if you want my opinion."

"Which I don't. You cannot imagine how much trouble she could become."

"Laddie, a troublesome lass is not always a bad thing. Now, off you go. I'll finish up here."

Tristan found yet another surprise waiting for him in his tent.

"Hello, Mr. Deveraux." Emily smiled up at him. She was seated on his cot, her arms laden with several of Tristan's uniforms.

"What in blazes do you think you are doing?"

"I've come to discourage you from accepting the general's assignment."

For a brief moment he had a vision of her in that bed, not sitting, but rather reclining. With him. Without her clothing. With her hair mussed up from lovemaking and her lips dark and swollen from being kissed.

Tristan groaned.

"Madam, I believe it is not appropriate for a lady to be resting on a man's cot."

"I beg your pardon?" Although her tone was indignant, Tristan didn't miss the slight pink that rose to color her cheeks as she spoke.

He couldn't hold back his grin. "I am relieved that at least you know the rules of propriety even if you choose not to follow them."

Tristan felt as well as saw the heated blush steal over her. There was no denying it. Emily Durbin was beautiful.

"It's not the first time I've been accused of being inappropriate."

Tristan felt her struggle with emotions that he'd suspected had long simmered beneath the surface. A vein of hurt ran through her mind, he was sure of it. Something had scarred her deeply. He took heart when he realized that they shared more than just a physical attraction. Whatever had cut her, it was comparable to the demons that Tristan himself had long battled.

Tristan sighed. "I'm not accusing you of anything. Forget it."

For a moment the two remained silent. Tristan felt her anxiety growing by the moment but knew by instinct that anything he said would only serve to heighten her discomfort. Best to let her work through her unease, he thought.

"Mr. Deveraux, I apologize for being responsible for your being forced to accompany us. I mean, I didn't request you personally, but I am so worried for my uncle that I was desperate. Had I known what the general would do, I would have tried harder to sway him."

Tristan smiled at her admission. He'd known instantly that she hadn't approved of him. Still, he didn't exactly hold her to task for it. Knowing himself as he did, it's quite likely he would have agreed with her.

"That's very kind of you to say so. Might I ask, just what is it about me that you object to?"

"I want you to refuse this assignment. It just isn't conceivable for you to accompany us. I can see no way around it."

"I admit that I do agree with you, however, General Henley has other ideas."

The woman jumped to her feet then. She looked as skittish as a colt. No, he thought. It was something else. He watched her for a few seconds more and imagined that the quick, shallow breaths she was taking were not out of nervousness or fear, but out of desire.

Tristan wiped his hand across his moist brow and found that his mouth had suddenly gone dry. All sorts of images were crowding into his mind right at the moment and he suddenly realized that not all of them were of his design.

The lady paused in her movement and turned to look

at him, her wide-eyed gaze sending a shock to his very marrow.

"Yes, Miss Durbin?"

Then she did it. She touched her bottom lip with her teeth. Her lovely, wine-colored, perfectly shaped mouth made a worried gesture and Tristan thought he might die from the inferno that roared in his blood.

"You, sir, are a distraction. I mean, I simply cannot keep my attention on my uncle if you are anywhere in the vicinity."

If Tristan had any sense at all he would have fled the tent at that very moment. He would have run to where the horses were kept, saddled and mounted the first one he came to, and then escaped the army camp as though his life depended on it.

His life did depend on it, he thought. Of course, the army wouldn't take well to one of its own so blatantly deserting them. He'd probably get caught. He'd probably be hanged. Or at best, shot for his trouble. Either way, it would have been a more prudent thing than what he did next.

He advanced on her. Like a lion circling its prey, he moved, slowly and intentionally. He felt his blood roil in his veins like a slow-moving storm. His skin tingled as if lightning had struck nearby and his heart beat with the pace of a hundred horses rushing to battle.

For all his wanting, he knew that Miss Durbin could have put him down with a single refusal, a raised hand, or even the thought that she didn't want him.

She did neither.

Instead, beautiful, desirable Miss Durbin didn't appear as a doe about to be consumed by a lion. Her eyes narrowed and color rose on her cheeks. Her beautiful mouth made a perfect, round circle. When he towered over her, she tipped her head back and closed her eyes.

With every bit of her, Emily Durbin wanted him to kiss her, and kiss her completely.

Without further hesitation, Tristan did just as she demanded.

Leaning down, he paused just a moment, his mouth poised to touch hers, their breath touching, mingling as their bodies very much desired.

The telling mixture of lavender soap and the unmistakable mist of female arousal scented the air around her. Her skin flushed and heat radiated from her. To his delight, he felt her pulse beat as wildly as his own.

When their lips touched it was like fire scorching across an open field—unwieldy and erratic, both unquenchable and unstoppable.

Tristan didn't just kiss her, he consumed her. In that moment, he knew he must have her. All of her. He knew that, one kiss or a thousand, it would never be enough to ease the sweet agony of his craving for her.

He would have taken her, too, if not for the whispered voice that stole into his thoughts like a thief robbing him of his passion.

"Go ahead. Take your fill of her. It doesn't matter. Sooner or later she'll learn the truth and cast you off like you deserve. Enjoy her attentions now, boy, because they won't last."

Bracing as icy water poured over him, the voice of his consciousness shattered his desire.

"I'm sorry, Miss Durbin. You'll have to leave now."

Hours later, Emily paced the length of her tent. How could she have been such a ninny? First attempting to sway the surgeon to her way of thinking, and then instead practically attacking the man in his own quarters. How had things gotten so out of hand?

What happened hadn't been his fault. She'd been the one to confront him in such an inappropriate manner. Who could blame him? She'd practically trapped him there and then thrown herself on him.

She'd meant to make him see reason. She'd meant for

him to take her side and argue with General Henley once more, thinking perhaps if they presented a stronger, united front to him, he'd acquiesce.

Emily clenched her fists. It had been a daft idea, but she'd been quickly running out of options. To have Mr. Deveraux so close all the way back to England was unthinkable. Unbearable.

Unbelievable.

Emily shook herself. She must maintain control. She mustn't let the lingering taste of his kiss or the feel of his wonderfully solid, warm body against hers deter her from what must be done. Absolutely not. More than that, she couldn't let the memory of his strong arms embracing her take her thoughts from her task, and the way he molded his entire body around hers, cocooning her in endless sensual delight, sway her from her intention of ignoring him altogether.

It was regrettable, she thought, but she couldn't waver in her resolve. She would have to just pretend that they'd never kissed. That they'd never shared a dream, or that she'd ever felt such wanton desire for him.

Not only for their journey home, but forever, she realized. She was Emily Durbin, a woman seeking to make an acceptable match to a man she didn't love. She simply couldn't afford the luxury of a match of passion. It would mean certain disaster.

If she ever loved someone as much as she knew she was capable of doing, Emily would lose her center. She would be swallowed up by the strength of her emotion. Emily had lost her parents, her childhood, and even her dignity a time or two, but she knew one thing for certain.

She could not lose control.

Deep inside her, however Emily had the growing suspicion that it wouldn't matter if continents separated her from the surgeon. She would still be consumed with the wanting. It would have been far better if they'd never met.

She sighed. There was nothing to be done about it. She would just have to do her best to keep her distance. To do otherwise was certain disaster.

"Miss Emily?"

If the afternoon had been troubling, the early evening was now deteriorating into a full disaster. Jessup Pemberton was standing outside her tent, and Emily wished he would sink into the ground and disappear.

"Mr. Pemberton. How pleasant to see you again."

In fact, pleasant was the farthest from the way she felt. Before her uncle had put him off, the man had tried every way possible to gain her attention. He'd sent her gifts, flowers, and unsigned notes, all in his perfect, wooden script.

Attempting to spare his feelings, Emily had tried on several occasions, to dissuade the scientist in his pursuit of her. Instead he'd answered with a calm resolve every one of her efforts to sever his attachment. She desperately hoped that nothing had occurred which had once again given him hope of kindling her interest.

"Ah, miss, you favor my sight with your beauty." He bowed low, sweeping his arm in a wide, formal motion. A small patch of hair that he'd used to cover a smooth, balding spot on his head fell forward like a dead raccoon.

"Please, Mr. Pemberton. There's no need for such formality. I'd invite you in but I'm busy packing for our journey."

"Of course."

Emily noticed him lean slightly to the left, his eyes straining to see around her. She quickly moved in the same direction. Instinctively she knew he was trying to get a glimpse of her undergarments. The thought of Jessup Pemberton ever laying his eyes on so much as a stocking left a spoiled feeling in her stomach.

"Did you want something, Mr. Pemberton?"

Emily instantly regretted her question. She saw his beady eyes dart up to her and the full-out expression of lust rose in their murky brown depths. Irritated, Emily cleared her throat.

"I was thinking that our trip to the coast will be most dangerous." He said, giving her an oily smile. "We could be set upon at any moment."

"General Henley has assigned us a quite capable escort. I'm sure we shall be well-protected."

"I know, but soldiers can be such ruffians." He glanced around furtively. "I was thinking that you and I should share a wagon."

Emily bit back her reply to refuse him outright, a part of her longing to give him the cut direct. But she knew that her uncle so depended on help from the weasel of a man. The last thing she wanted to do was stand in the way of her uncle's work.

She had to find a way to refuse his offer in the most inoffensive way possible.

"I think that's a wonderful idea, but unfortunately, I will be traveling with my uncle."

"He could become a target . . ."

She raised her hand. "General Henley has already provided for such a circumstance. He's arranged someone to ride with us. A Mr. Deveraux."

A surprised expression lit his face.

"One of the enlisted men?"

"Yes, well, he's a surgeon, actually. A quite good one, as I hear it."

"But, how can a field cutter possibly protect you?"

"Well, Mr. Deveraux has special talents. Um, I really can't explain. Very, very secret, you know."

Pemberton's eyes narrowed in disappointment. "Of course. If you'll excuse me."

With that he spun around and stalked away. Emily watched his retreating figure for a moment. The usual trepidation she felt whenever in his presence had doubled in size. The man upset her, though she'd no idea why.

He'd never so much as touched her, but something about his manner affected her deeply.

For a moment Emily thought she should tell someone. General Henley, perhaps? Her uncle? Mr. Deveraux?

"Foolish girl," she muttered. Certainly not Mr. Deveraux. He'd truly think her a lackwit. No, it was nothing but her own anxieties that made her so jumpy. She would do as always. If Mr. Pemberton should become a problem, she would deal with it on her own.

Jessup stormed into his tent. How dare she deal him such a blow! The silly chit had no idea what the future held for them both. If she did, she'd be more careful.

The sound of the distant battle reminded the scientist of his precarious situation. He hated living inside the confines of the army camp. Being in the midst of such violent men made Jessup very nervous.

Lately, his lordship had taken on another project, one that was top secret and involved his writing notes in a small, leather bound journal he carried. Jessup feared that whatever his employer was engaged in might thrust them into even more intrigue.

It was all Branleigh's doing. The viscount had seemed easy enough prey in the beginning. He was far too involved in his books and drawings to pay much attention to the crush of events going on around him. Now, with the interest of other men to compete with, Pemberton feared that he might lose his precious quarry.

After a few moments of pacing and considering several courses of action that included threatening Emily, he decided against it. No, he would have to do his best not to frighten the little bird.

"Deveraux?" Jessup paused, trying to remember where he'd last heard that name. Sorting through his memories, he finally recalled the man's identity. They had met briefly in the infirmary tents. Jessup had been on the rifle range with Lord Branleigh, testing some new gun barrel designs when a shot went wild, hit a nearby stack of firewood, and sent shards of wood in all directions. A piece of the flying debris had lodged in Jessup's left arm.

"Let me take a look at that," the tall, lean surgeon said, roughly tearing away his shirtsleeve.

"Careful, you dolt! That's imported linen."

The man had only laughed. "It's no good to you now, there's already a hole in it and it's stained with blood. Still, if you'd rather go back to your tent and care for the wound yourself, it's no concern of mine." The impertinent fellow dismissed him as though he'd been no one of importance at all.

"Here now, you can't leave me like this! I've been shot. I could die!"

The bastard waved him off. "It's barely a scratch, sir. I'm sure you'll be fine if you just clean it and wear a bandage for a day or two. If you want, come back tomorrow and I'll check it over."

"Worthless scut!"

Angered beyond belief, Pemberton stormed out of the tent, hearing the surgeon's laughter follow him out.

Jessup's arm no longer bothered him, but he still burned over his treatment by the surgeon's apprentice. He would have to find out more about Deveraux. One thing Jessup had known for certain was that every man had a weakness—something that cut him to the quick like a sharp ax to the base of a weak sapling. He would find out what that was. Then, when the time was right, he would take care of this Deveraux once and for all.

Quickly gathering his wrap, he dug through his luggage until he located his writing pack. Pulling out a piece of parchment he hastily scrawled the surgeon's name upon it. Then, stuffing it into his pocket he set out once again.

Walking through the busy encampment, the music of distant gunfire to guide his steps, he made his way to the makeshift stables. There, among the horses, he saw his operative.

Diego Chavez absently brushed a horse's mane, his eyes watching the distant hills with the same concentration that Jessup himself used to study his mathematical equations.

"You require something?" The man's voice was low and soft, barely audible.

Jessup reached into his pocket and pulled out the paper. "This. I need information about this man."

The man stopped his rhythmic movement. "Why is he so important?"

"He will be guarding the viscount, that's why. I need to know all about him. His family, their origins, even his food preferences. Anything that I can use against him."

"Why is he so important?"

"I'm not sure. There must be something or the general wouldn't have assigned him to watch Branleigh so closely. I must know what it is."

The spy nodded, taking the paper. He scanned the name and shoved it back to Jessup. "When will you need the information?"

"As soon as possible. We're leaving at first light."

Chavez nodded. Without further comment he turned back to the animal and resumed his work.

Jessup could only hope that things would go in his favor. If not, there was always poison. It had nearly worked once before.

Chapter Six

Two days after they had left the mountain pass encampment, Tristan had had about as much of this adventure as he could tolerate. The sergeant had explained they'd not had the resources to requisition him an animal and he'd had to make do with riding with the civilians in the supply wagon. He was certain it was another circumstance suggested by General Henley.

Tristan knew they feared him riding off in the night and deserting the lot of them. At least he was allowed his medical supplies and some journals to keep his attentions along the long miles.

Not that the distractions did any good. Beside his own misery and that of blocking out the thoughts of the twenty-man troop that was safeguarding their journey, he had to ward off any attempts at civilities made by the viscount. Several times he tried to engage him in conversation and Tristan had given him only short responses, trying to send his attentions back to his reading.

Of course, it did no good to even try. Emily Durbin was like a burr that had worked its way under his skin. No matter where she was in the camp, he could always feel her presence. Like her uncle, she had tried to make civil conversation.

Worst of all, Emily and her uncle did their level best to

make him comfortable at every opportunity. Offers of tea or a change in the seating arrangement and other such amenities they conceived only served to infuriate him all the more.

Though he likely knew of Tristan's determination to remain aloof, the viscount accosted him at first light on the third morning.

"Good morning, Deveraux. I trust you rested well?"

"Yes, milord, well enough, thank you." Tristan finished his shaving, trying to ignore the man, but the viscount was not to be put off. Tristan could sense the concern and unease spinning inside him.

In addition to his worry for his niece and the continuance of his work, Branleigh was curious about Tristan as well. As a scientist, he wanted to gain as much knowledge as possible. Tristan was more of a subject to study rather than a person to be accepted for who he was.

"My lord? Is there something else?"

The older gentleman smiled. "I was just thinking that you don't like me very much, do you? Don't try to deny it. I'm superb at discerning dishonesty in someone, you know. I can spot a liar every time."

"You are far too clever for me, sir. I will confess that even dismissing the situation you and your niece have thrust upon me, I am at cross purposes with your line of work."

"You are direct. I like that about you."

Tristan said nothing as he continued to towel dry his face and hands and then carefully replaced his shaving equipment.

Branleigh cleared his throat. "Of course, you object to my armaments program. That's understandable. However, if you knew my objectives you would realize that you are in error."

"Am I?"

"Indeed. Perhaps you will have a spot of tea with me and I shall explain."

"I don't think . . ." Tristan began.

"Nonsense, I'm not inviting you to marry my niece, you know. Just share some refreshment."

"Very well," Tristan said.

"Easy boy, he means to trick you. They're all alike, these nobles. You have to be on your guard."

For once, Tristan agreed with his consciousness. Nothing could be more dangerous than an aristocrat.

When they had settled by a campfire, cups and biscuits in hand, Lord Branleigh cleared his throat.

"I must confess to enjoying this outdoor living. I've never had the opportunity to partake in the natural surroundings myself, so it is a treat."

"I'm glad you're enjoying it. I'm less an admirer of the outdoor lifestyle."

"You believe this is a colossal waste of your time, no doubt."

"I do. Many men will suffer with the shortage of good medical help."

"It's my intention to produce much more efficient weaponry; that way battles will be won quicker, there will be less loss of life."

"So I've heard. Forgive me if I find that a bit hard to believe, milord. Any weapon is an abomination."

Branleigh stirred his tea thoughtfully.

"You are against the war effort in general."

"I see the necessity to defend one's country. It doesn't mean I have to like it."

"Young man, I doubt you will find many a soldier who will disagree with you. Not many who have experienced the tragedies of battle would embrace war, I think."

Tristan was surprised to feel the note of regret in the other man's mind. Lord Branleigh truly did intend for his work to save lives. That was when he saw it. Branleigh was not being entirely honest about his labors. It seems there was more involved than carving new rifling designs in the barrels of firearms.

"I hope you are right, sir."

The other man paused and stared at him openly.

"You do understand what I'm talking about?"

"I believe you mentioned saving lives."

Branleigh nodded slowly. "I trust you to keep whatever you discover about my work in the strictest confidence."

"I don't know what you're talking about, my lord."

Tristan set his cup back on the bench beside them and rose to his feet. To admit more would sink him even deeper into this intrigue.

Branleigh stood as well. "I'll trust you to keep my secrets, sir, and I shall return you the courtesy as well."

Tristan said nothing more and watched as the viscount made his way to where his niece was speaking with Captain Hamilton.

Damn. Tristan sighed. He had a great deal to think about. Already his head ached from the effort of blocking the awakening camp's rambling thoughts, and he still had a long, tiring day ahead of him.

"You're doomed. It won't be long until they've bested you."

Emily watched the interaction between her uncle and Mr. Deveraux. She wondered if he was doing it now, that mind reading trick of his. Seeing him leave the campfire and walk toward the forest, she gathered her skirts and began to follow him at a discreet distance.

When they were out of hearing distance, he stopped. Straightening his spine he took a deep breath.

"You might as well find something else to occupy your time," Tristan said.

"I beg your pardon. I didn't mean to be a bother . . ." Emily lied. She had a dozen questions to ask him, not the least of which was exactly what he and her uncle had discussed. It had given her an uneasy feeling, seeing the two of them together.

Tristan didn't want to sound so short, but he did mean

to give her a bit of a dressing down, one that might, in the future, direct her attentions elsewhere.

"But you are, Miss Durbin. In more ways than you can imagine." He turned to her then, attempting to give her his best scornful expression. "It would be to your best interest to find other company."

The lady didn't relent.

"I see that you are quite out of your element, sir."

"I beg your pardon?"

It was her turn to be abrasive, but she chose not to, Tristan realized. "What I mean is, that you're likely quite comfortable with all manner of blood and gore, but as for personal communications, you are rather lacking. Not much time in the social whirl, I'd bet."

"While I'm not as socially adept as you, Miss, I can assure you that there is nothing wrong with my ability to communicate. A lowly surgeon finds little enough reason to intermingle with the high birds such as yourself and your uncle, unless my services are needed in a medical way, as in a boil to be lanced or a leg to be amputated."

He was rewarded when she blanched slightly at his comment. Served her right, he thought. He'd well warned her of his prickly temperament.

Tristan started to turn away, dismissing her with a wave, but she reached out her delicate lace-gloved hand and gently grasped his sleeve.

Her feather-light touch burned him like fire. The sensations of their embrace just days before flashed through his memory.

When Tristan spun back to face her, she gave him an expression of feigned innocence. He knew she was aware of her womanly charms, and that his closeness to her shot an arrow of desire right into his center. What she didn't know was how cursedly powerful and dangerous her touch could be.

He leaned forward, meaning to give her a proper set down, but the all-too-familiar lavender soap smell and her own mysterious scent washed over his senses, rendering him virtually helpless in its wake.

"I think perhaps I might be of some help to you, Mr. Deveraux."

"Really?" he answered, nearly breathless, the heat of her nearness now enveloping him entirely.

"You need skills to help you interact with others, and I'm just the person to teach you."

Thankfully, Tristan found his voice.

"In exchange for my helping you and your uncle, I suppose." Tristan assumed she might be at least slightly stung by his sarcastic tone. She was not.

"We could begin with the simple rules of etiquette and then proceed to the finer points of proper interaction in social circles."

Tristan didn't bother to explain that after this mission, he'd have no intention of ever being forced into interacting with any social circumstances whatsoever.

Instead, he decided that the way to best the gull was to de-feather her in mid flight.

"Miss Durbin, do you think your education might include a different sort of teaching?"

Leaning closer, he could almost taste the luscious cherry red lips she now formed into an almost perfect *o*.

"I don't understand?"

"Teaching about interaction between two people?" he explained.

He leaned closer still.

"Well, most interaction is between individuals." She faltered, stepping back a pace.

"Male and female individuals?" Tristan hardly breathed. Unfortunately, in an attempt to catch her in his net of deceit, he had trapped himself as well.

For the briefest of moments they were held in an unbreakable force. As if being pulled by a cord, Tristan leaned down farther still and brushed his lips ever so lightly against hers. The power of her touch was explosive.

Heat.

Passion.

Desire.

Innocence.

Those feelings hit him with the impact of a full-force cannon shot.

"Damn it all!" Tristan jerked back as if he'd touched a lit torch.

"Oh!" Emily swooned.

In an instant, Tristan was beside her, grasping her shoulders, he eased her to the ground.

His heart nearly stopped beating. Lying motionless, barely a breath coming out of her, she wore the most peculiar smile.

Leaning down, Tristan put an ear over her mouth to see if indeed her breathing had ceased. He quickly slid his right hand along the base of her neck and found a slow, steady pulse.

Exhaling since he'd first touched her, a dizzying spin of relief shot through him.

"Mr. Deveraux, please, not here," she said in a husky whisper.

Looking back at her, he read the emotion clearly on her face before he even had the chance to discern her thoughts. She was embarrassed.

Without knowing what else to do, Tristan swiftly lifted her in his arms and carried her to the wagon. Passing her uncle and the captain, he nodded.

"I believe she's had too much sun. It's best I take her inside."

"Of course," the captain answered, quickly averting his eyes.

"But, it's not yet noon," Lord Branleigh said at their passing.

The captain quickly took his arm. "Young ladies are very susceptible to the sun, you know. It has been my experience that this happens quite frequently to them."

"Really?"

Tristan set his charge on the bench at the back of the wagon.

"I'm so sorry. I think I've hurt you again," she said quietly, as he pulled the door shut behind them.

"No, I'm afraid I have injured you."

"With a kiss? I don't understand how that could be."

He turned quickly to her. "Didn't you feel it? What happened when we . . ." Tristan searched her face.

"Oh that, well, it was my fault, entirely." She shivered. "I'm so sorry to have alarmed you. I become so embarrassed when that happens."

Tristan stared at her, shocked that it had not been his touch that had affected her so.

"You mean you swoon quite frequently?"

"A nervous disorder, Dr. Stephens calls it." She laughed. "Without rhyme or reason, out I go, cold as a fish."

"Oh." Tristan sat back. So, it hadn't been because of him after all. He knew that on some level he should be relieved. Who would think that after only one kiss, the promise of another would wreak such havoc?

That should have been the end of it. Tristan should have dismissed it for the meaningless occurrence that it was. But, he was surprised to find that he was rather put off by it. Angered, almost.

"Have I upset you?"

He turned to gaze at her. "Madame, you upset me quite often, I'm afraid."

"I'm sorry. It seems I seldom meet anyone that I don't upset. My sincerest apologies." She reached out to him again, but he deftly dodged her touch.

"I think it might be best if we didn't become quite so personal, Miss Durbin. I do have a reputation to consider."

"Oh, I didn't know gentlemen had . . . That is to say, I hadn't realized . . ."

Tristan smiled. "It was a joke, Miss Durbin. A small attempt at humor."

"You're making sport of me?"

"No," he answered seriously. "I would never do that. You are a most intriguing person and I'm sorry if I've been rude or unkind to you."

She clapped her hands together, her expression lightening immediately. "There! You see? We've already achieved our first lesson. You are a quick study."

Tristan was dumbfounded. Of course, just seeing her eyes sparkle so and hearing the lyrical quality of joy in her voice gave him no small amount of pleasure. Perhaps it wouldn't be so much to give in to her attempts at controlling every situation and perhaps just enjoy her company.

Suddenly, a stark flash of pain lashed out at him.

Torture. Agony. Death. Fear.

Overcome by the sudden onslaught of emotions and pain, Tristan was knocked back. His chest squeezed impossibly tight. For a few seconds no air entered or left his lungs.

"Mr. Deveraux? What is it? What's wrong?"

Tristan heard her voice, saw her panicked expression, and even felt her hands go out to him.

"Please . . . get . . . the captain," he managed to ground out, the words jamming in his throat.

"Dear heavens!"

Tristan was certain he was about to die.

Men on a hillside. Soldiers scrambling for their weapons. Too late! Too late. They were hit, twenty to start with, only six remaining. Cannon fire. Bullets. Two men stabbed repeatedly.

His vision was cut short by Hamilton and his men hovering over him.

"Here man, what is it?"

"Two hills over. A small contingent of soldiers, about twenty or so, I think. Under attack. The enemy is all around them. You must help them!"

Tristan grasped the captain's coat sleeves, but the man was too quick for him. He turned, pulling open the wagon door.

"Secure this man!" He turned to two other soldiers who were nearby, "McGillis, Dennaly, get the animals in line. Hitch up the wagons. We're evacuating."

"No! Tristan shouted, fighting the hands that held him down. "Don't you understand? They need us. They need guns and medical help. We can't abandon them!"

Lord Branleigh stepped in front of Hamilton. "Surely you don't mean to leave them, Captain?"

"We are on a very crucial mission. We cannot intervene. I will spare only two men to ride back to base camp and alert the general. But we cannot help them."

"You bastard! They'll die out there," Tristan shouted as two soldiers pulled him to his feet. Hamilton's expression remained unchanged.

"I know."

Tristan lunged at the commander. "I'll go. Just give me a horse and I'll ride out . . ."

"I order you to stay with the company. My only concern is getting the civilians to safety. I intend to meet our objective and get us on a ship to England and to Lord Branleigh's estate at the first opportunity."

Tristan stepped back. "To bloody hell with your orders!" He couldn't let those men die. He'd wait until the soldiers were otherwise occupied and—

"Mr. Murphy," the captain yelled out, "bring me that set of irons."

"What in blazes?" Lord Branleigh stepped between Tristan and the captain. "You don't mean to chain him like an animal? Surely if you give the order for him to go with us, he will."

The captain turned a cold eye upon them. "I intend to make certain of it." Calling two of his men forward, he nodded to Deveraux. "Mr. Collins. Place him in irons. Tristan Deveraux, you are hereby under arrest for insubordination." He turned to his second in command. "Lock him in the supply wagon."

Chapter Seven

Jeffrey watched his men restrain the surgeon. Silently cursing Deveraux's stubbornness, the officer wondered if either of them would survive the trip to England, let alone accomplish their objective.

Branleigh remained behind after Deveraux had been taken away.

"I don't understand any of this," the viscount commented once he and Jeffrey were alone.

"My orders were quite clear. I'm to see to it that you and your niece are delivered safely back to London."

"Aren't you even going to investigate Mr. Deveraux's claims?"

"I have my orders." He drew in a breath. Of course it enraged him to know of the soldiers suffering on the field. Under any other circumstances he would ride to their rescue and orders be damned.

"I understand that, Captain. Still, it's difficult to think of those men suffering."

"I like it no better than you, sir, but I'm afraid it's out of our hands. If we were to attempt a rescue and were outnumbered, there would be no way to get you and your niece out of harm's way. The best we can hope for is a successful completion of our mission and an end to this war as soon as possible."

Branleigh nodded once and turned away. "With Godspeed, Captain Hamilton, with Godspeed."

Jeffrey sighed. This assignment was far more involved than he had thought at first. He glanced at the wagon thoughtfully.

Deveraux had been outraged at his assignment to this operation and Miss Durbin had accepted his ill temper without comment. She seemed drawn to him like a fish to water.

It was quite odd that not only did Deveraux not return the lady's attentions, he seemed to scorn them.

A woman like Branleigh's niece was not one to toss aside. Even he, with his lowly status in society, could tell what a gem she was. It would be a rare man who would not become enamored with Miss Durbin.

"The camp is secure, Captain." Becker, the second in command approached him from the perimeter of the camp. "Several of the men have volunteered to see if what the surgeon says is true."

Jeffrey gave him a stern stare. "As much as I'd like to allow it, Mr. Becker, I'm afraid it's out of the question. We must ensure the safety of our charges first and foremost. Prepare to break camp at first light."

Though he'd no reason to believe it, Jeffrey was certain that the surgeon's statements were true, though he'd swallow live ammunition rather than admit his suspicions to his men.

Becker saluted him and paused a moment.

"Is there something else?"

"It's Mr. Deveraux, sir. He's got the 'sight.' All of the men know it. At least in this company."

"I'm not convinced of the surgeon's abilities, Mr. Becker."

"Nay, and I'm sure that might be why you're in command."

Jeffrey studied his man acutely. He'd thought that his steady approach to command had put him in line for the position, but perhaps there were other factors at work. "Explain."

The other man shuffled sideways, carefully trying to hide his discomfort.

"You're well respected, a 'by-the-book commander,' is what's said. I'm sure the general has his own reasons. I, that is, we—um, the men and I were merely speculating."

Jeffrey's attention wandered to the prisoner's wagon. "Perhaps it's best not to dwell on the general's supposed intentions and pay closer attention to your orders."

"Yes, sir."

Jeffrey decided that when they neared their objective he was going to have a long discussion with Deveraux about his so-called 'sight.'

After an hour, Tristan thought he might die. The feeling of tight suffocation now wrapped around him, and despite his rapid, shallow breaths, the air suddenly seemed too thick to breathe adequately.

The door creaked open and Miss Durbin stepped up into the wagon. "I've come to sit with you awhile, that is, if you don't mind the company."

Tristan quickly looked away from her. He very much did mind, not that it mattered.

"I've little say in anything, it seems."

"I can't help but feel this is all my fault."

He shot her a sharp glance. "I'll have to agree with you on that. I'm supposed to be protecting you and your uncle, and yet here I am. Locked away like a criminal."

She gave him a sideways glance. "About that. The captain asked me to inquire as to whether you've had any more impressions?"

Tristan bit down on a curse. Now Hamilton was convinced of his ability. Could things get any worse?

"I keep telling them I can't help them. Now, the soldiers beyond those hills, the ones that lie suffering as we speak, I could be of use to them."

He felt the whirl of her thoughts. She had a dozen questions, her curiosity as boundless as her innocence.

"How do you do it? How do you know these things?"

Tristan regarded her for a brief moment. It was very tempting to tell her all of it. To lighten his burden and let the truth about himself and his past be known and the truth be damned for all it was worth.

"Don't be a fool. She'll see you for what you truly are, a pathetic shell of a man. Or, rather, not really a man, eh? A beast is what you are. An oddity to be stared at or frightened of. Not worthy of any real love."

Tristan shut his eyes and lifted his hands to his temples, rubbing vigorously, as if he could erase the words from his mind.

"I'm tired," he said, at last. Pulling his arms close to his chest, he did his best to ignore the rattling of the irons and the ache that throbbed in his chest.

Scooting back, he leaned against the wagon's wall and closed his eyes. He felt his body weaken with every passing moment, but he tried to ignore the effect of his imprisonment, or the memories that threatened to tear his mind to shreds. The buzz of thoughts outside seemed to blur then and tired of fighting, Tristan gave himself to the troubled sleep that awaited him. Like an unwelcome guest, the memories returned—to haunt his dreams.

The fire would surely catch him.

Young Tristan had spent most of his life hiding in the London sewers. Every doorway, every alley, any place he could secret himself away would do. Tristan was grateful that he was smaller than most boys his age.

He was also helped by the fact that he could easily tell when danger lurked—a drunk meaning to rob him or a prostitute ready to rat him out to her master. Too quickly he'd learned that there were men who found pleasure in the company of vulnerable youths like himself, unnatural attentions that made his stomach sick whenever he gave it much thought.

For the most part, Tristan had been adept at keeping himself alive, stealing what he must to eat, or when the opportunity presented itself, taking advantage of small jobs to buy a night of shelter from the winter. Time went by in a blur, one year flowing into the next . . . then he'd happened upon the one man who had offered him something more than a fleeting, terrorized existence.

Sir Alfred Brumly, a surgeon who specialized in the local hospitals, had seen Tristan one night, helping a man who'd been robbed and beaten get to the authorities. When Tristan had used his power of discernment to discover where the man's leg had been shattered, Brumly realized that he had a true healer on his hands.

That very night he'd offered Tristan a chance to carve out a decent life for himself, something he'd long thought he was to be denied. The years flowed on, not untroubled, but he had been safe enough.

Now it looked as if those from his past would kill them both. They would die the worst of all deaths: by fire.

"Easy does it, son," Brumly whispered beside him. "You'd best get yourself out of harm's way. That other beam will fall any minute."

Tristan shook his head. "I can't leave you!"

"Aye, you can and you will. I didn't spend all my time teaching you to be a cutter and a bonesetter so you could throw it away trying to pull my hinters out of the boil, now did I?"

"No," Tristan sobbed. The heat behind him was building. In minutes the whole building would be in flames. He knew from the hurried thoughts of the bucket brigade that had formed outside that his time was running out.

"It's all my fault. They did this to get me out in the open."

"Indeed they have, lad. But you're smarter then they,

aye? You know how to get around obstruction better than anyone I've ever met. Get going. There's a contingent of soldiers just marching into Latham. I hear they're looking for recruits. Tell them you've apprenticed with me and give them this." He reached into his pocket and pulled out a worn piece of parchment. "I wrote it before the beam fell. It's a certificate of your apprenticeship. Lord Fenton will testify to my signature. You remember him, I lanced that boil on his aristocratic backside last month."

"Yes," Tristan could barely speak. The smoke was thickening around them and it would soon be impossible for anyone to continue breathing. With any luck, Brumly would die from asphyxiation long before the fire touched him.

"I don't know how to thank you."

The older man just shook his head. "Don't fret about it, my boy. Just go on and do good in the world. You've a special gift. It'd be a sin to let it go to waste. Now, go."

Alfred Brumly coughed once again, his breaths coming in wheezing bursts.

Tearfully, Tristan gave his mentor a fierce hug. It was at that moment he heard the old man's plea. He didn't want to face the end gagging on smoke and feeling the fire. *No pain*, his mind murmured.

Nodding, his own lungs near to bursting, Tristan pulled his handkerchief from his pocket and, wrapping it around his hand, cupped Brumly's face. Seconds passed as his only friend gagged against the cloth, and then stilled forever. Tristan felt his passing as much as he did the escalating heat around him.

A single thought had drifted off with Brumly. Gratitude.

Any thought of grieving left Tristan as the groaning of the building around him heralded its imminent collapse. Gently setting his friend on the ground, he removed the cloth from his hand and covered the old man's face. Then, working his way around the flames, he finally made it to the street.

Three men carrying pistols waited at the other end of the alleyway. One of them raised his hand.

"There's the little bastard!"

In an instant, Tristan was running down to the other end of the alley, grappling at the wooden fence that separated him from freedom. It had been a near thing, but, at the last second, he gained purchase on the top of it and flung himself into an uncertain future. It had been a bare escape, but he'd made it.

Hiding in a wagon filled with casks of wine, Tristan crouched low. Because the men had already checked it for a stowaway, they only glanced once in his direction.

Tristan leaned back against the cool wood frame of the wagon and sighed.

Would this nightmare ever end?

Before he could consider any more he heard the old man's curse.

Lord Cantor, who had been searching for Tristan for years, had arrived in a coach that parked not ten feet from where Tristan lay hidden.

In addition to his mother and father, Tristan's Great-Uncle Cantor knew of his talent and had long ago tried to force Tristan to do his will. Thankfully, Tristan had escaped.

Cantor was the worst sort of criminal. He sold information to those who could afford it, rooted out secrets from those who were wealthy enough to pay for their indiscretions. A thief and a blackmailer, a traitor and a spy, George Cantor didn't care whom he destroyed as long as he profited from it.

Tall, bent, and looking as if he were nothing more than a skeleton covered with skin, Cantor struggled to get out of his rig. The old man's mind was far more agile than his body. His thoughts came bounding over in huge waves, making Tristan sink farther down, a sick feeling rising in his stomach.

"You fools! You've lost him yet again!"

"Not to worry, my lord. I promise we'll be tight on his trail in no time."

"Don't bother to attempt to placate me with your pitiful promises. It comes down to this. You have one month to bring the boy to me or I'll foreclose on your loans. Do you understand?"

The men grumbled in agreement, but their anger and frustration barely hid beneath the surface of their acquiescence as they left him.

Alone, Cantor shot a glance around the thoroughfare, his eyes scanning the nearly empty alley. Tristan knew that he'd much prefer to find his quarry himself. Visions of him beating Tristan came through loud and clear.

"Wretched lout." Cursing further about Tristan's lineage, he walked toward the inn.

As he listened to the other man's retreat, Tristan discerned something new. It was but a passing thought. Plans that Cantor had set in motion. Plans to murder someone within government. Someone who'd opposed him in Parliament.

It was to be a grisly scene, and the pain of his uncle's hatred pierced Tristan's psyche like a spear.

As quickly as the thought struck him, it was gone. Although he wasn't sure what terrified him more, the death that permeated Cantor's intentions, or the part in which his twisted mind had cast the youth to play in it all.

Tristan leaned back as the evil of the other man's thoughts engulfed him. He swore at that moment that should he ever fall into the beast's control, he would take his own life before ever being used for such horrible purposes. For now, however, he was safe, and escape was his biggest priority. At that moment, he knew he must find a way to stay out of Cantor's reach as well as the others who were bloody well like him.

Three days later he was signing his name on a parchment and consigning his future to His Majesty's army.

***

Emily had spent the better part of an hour watching Mr. Deveraux. Large beads of sweat formed on his brow and his color was ashen. She'd twice already gone to the captain and asked that he might be released, and twice he'd refused her.

Now, all she could do was sit beside him in the small wagon and wipe his face with a damp cloth. It was the least she could do.

"Please," he muttered. He'd been in this fevered state for hours and his condition seemed to worsen by the minute. Whatever had stricken him was a mystery and there was no sign of it relenting any time soon.

"Mr. Deveraux, please, try to drink some water."

He muttered incoherently, and Emily leaned closer.

"Please, don't hurt her! Don't!"

"Mr. Deveraux, what is it? What's wrong?"

The man only turned away, his eyes flashing wildly about. His nightmare still held him hostage.

"No," he muttered once again, but to her surprise he turned into her embrace. Guiding him gently down, she cradled his head in her lap. Gently caressing the side of his face, she watched his expression relax. A slow, whispering sigh escaped him. He was so stern, so furious when awake, but now he bore the expression of a young boy.

As she sat quietly, Emily marveled at the sheer heat that radiated from him. Not just physical heat, but a passionate burning. It was deep in the core of him, and she suspected any woman daring enough to touch it would have to risk being burned. Whoever it was that unlocked the puzzle that was Tristan Deveraux would gain something far more valuable in return.

The thought of getting involved with him both thrilled and frightened her, Emily realized. She, a woman who had yet to have a successful relationship with a man that didn't end in death or disaster, craved that elusive passion that always seemed to dance around her and never bestow its fickle gifts upon her.

Still, as much as she wanted passionate love, it frightened her more than anything on earth.

Emily was frightened because of what true love might really mean. She'd seen other women who'd given themselves so completely. They seemed lost to her. Changed. No longer able to separate themselves from their husbands or lovers. They became like an adornment for their suits, a jeweled tie clasp or a silky cravat. Always visible but never independent of the wearer.

Before she could ponder more on her own fears, Deveraux stirred again. His face now turned to an expression of fear and dread. The small child had disappeared in an instant, and a wounded, threatened man took his place.

"What has happened to you?" she asked in a breathless whisper.

Before Emily had her answer, a loud crash sounded outside and very near the wagon.

Suddenly the world shook violently around them. Screams and shouts followed and a smattering of gunfire. The next thing she knew, the supply cart tipped precariously. Trying to stay upright was futile. Emily felt what must have been a cannonball exploding a few feet from the wagon, which sent the conveyance rolling wild with a jerking tumble.

As the wagon rolled precariously one way and then the other, Emily hit her head on one of the benches. She was able to clutch the still form of Mr. Deveraux before another sharp jerk sent them flying in the other direction. Before she could think to call out or even guess what was happening, another crash shook them. Like a sweet siren's call, unconsciousness beckoned her, and unable to do anything else, she sank into its oblivion.

Tristan didn't know how long he'd been asleep when he heard the quiet hiss of a breath beside him. Cramped in the small wagon, he found that his muscles were screaming for movement, but he was crushed between a thick, soft bundle of quilts and the side of the wagon. Except that the soft bundle wasn't a quilt after all, it was a body.

Jerking sideways, he instantly surmised that they must have been attacked. He'd remembered pain and the sharp movement of the coach backwards. He thought that someone had grabbed hold of him, but then something from inside the wagon must have gone flying and struck him on the side of his head. That was when all awareness left him.

"Mmmm." Miss Durbin moaned beside him.

"Damn," Tristan muttered. Squinting into the dimness, he felt a sharp pain across his brow. Raising his hands, he felt the warm, dampened area. He was bleeding.

"What happened?" Miss Durbin whispered beside him.

"I'm not sure. I believe we were attacked."

"Oh, no! Uncle Aldus! He was in the other wagon."

She struggled to sit up, but they were tangled impossibly and her movements jerked him alongside her.

"Wait. You're only making matters worse."

Tristan felt her fear, thick and squeezing against her chest. He saw in her mind her terror at losing the only person she truly loved. Lord Branleigh was more than her uncle, he was her world.

"I must go to him. He could be hurt, or . . ."

Emily began to tremble as her worst fears threatened to overtake her.

Tristan reached out his hands to steady her. "Easy, he's with Captain Hamilton. I'm sure he's safe."

"You don't understand," she said, "there have been three attempts on his life already." Scrambling to get from beneath him, her movements tilting the wagon precariously sideways.

"Wait . . ."

Tristan did his best to hold her still, certain that they were about to plummet farther down, likely having been halted in their descent by a random tree or large stone.

Before he could explain, however, he suddenly had the sense that enemies were close. Their minds were humming with blood lust and killing. One was searching for someone.

"They've got to be here. How difficult can it be to find a weak old man and a woman?"

"You're certain this was the company? We've been wrong once already. If we stay longer in the area, we risk everything."

The other man paused. Uncertainty clouded his thinking. *"Very well, tell the others to pull back. We'll continue to search the grounds. Find that mercenary devil and tell him he's failed once again."*

Tristan pulled his companion closer.

"What are you doing? Let me go this instant!"

"Quiet!" He paused a moment, listening. The voices of the soldiers' thoughts drifted farther away.

For a moment both of them sat frozen.

Not daring to breathe, Tristan strained to hear more, but the men were gone.

However, with the danger past, he suddenly became all too aware of his companion's growing fear.

"Miss Durbin, Emily, listen. I'd know if your uncle was in trouble."

She turned a curious expression on him. He felt her emotions settle.

"You would? Are you sure? You don't feel anything bad, do you?"

In answer, Tristan took a deep breath, sending his thoughts out, searching for any sign of the stalwart commander or the intense Lord Branleigh. They were either unconscious or dead. No, Tristan thought, not dead. He'd know if they were gone.

There were injured soldiers and a few men dead, but he was certain that most of the company was yet alive, though for how long, he didn't know.

"We've got to get out of here," Tristan muttered.

He rocked gently back and forth. Again the wagon tipped sideways but stopped when it came up against something hard. Satisfied that if he worked on the opposite end of the wagon, he could maybe push the door open without sending them rolling into heaven only knew what, he began to throw himself against the door several times.

The wagon shuddered, but didn't move farther. Encouraged, Tristan hit the door even harder. Ignoring the growing pain in his shoulder as he hit it again and again, he continued his labor until he felt her hand on his arm.

"Please, stop, you're going to hurt yourself."

"I'll be fine," he said, wincing as she touched his newly bruised shoulder.

"What are you going to do? Batter it until either it breaks or you do?"

"I'm going to get us out of here, I hope," he muttered through clenched teeth. It wasn't just his shoulder that bothered him. He felt the woman's presence near and it unsettled him.

Even through the haze of discomfort she was like a fire beside him. In such close quarters he felt her every breath, her every heartbeat, her every thought.

At that moment she was considering how much she liked his form. Not one for heavy, thick-muscled men, she preferred his shape and the way she could see the muscles move under his skin.

Suddenly he saw himself as she imagined him. As though her thoughts came out of his own mind, he knew all that she had experienced in a single instant.

After her curious dream and subsequent meeting with Mr. Deveraux, Emily found herself wondering if indeed he had the power to enter her thoughts at will. If that were the case, she reflected, it should have upset her even more.

In fact, it should have enraged her. The idea of a stranger knowing her every thought, her every fear, her every desire should have sent off all sorts of alarms through her psyche.

It should have, she realized, but it didn't. And that

surprised her all the more. Emily Durbin was not a woman who let wanton thoughts run rampant through her mind. She was not a lightskirt; in fact, by her former beaus, she had been considered almost prudish.

Then why did her skin tingle as though he'd thoroughly caressed every inch of her? Emily shivered at the memory of her dream.

Closing her eyes she imagined his hands upon her, only not in gentle caresses, but pushing her toward the wagon bench, gently cradling her as she lay back. Those same hands slid the length of her body, across the tops of her thighs to push her knees apart.

A moan escaped her. It was heaven. It was a throbbing ache that grew stronger with each passing second until she could stand it no more.

"Please," she begged, although not exactly certain what she was begging for.

He moved closer, pushing her legs up and out. Kneeling down, he caressed the tender skin of her sex. Leaning forward, he kissed her labia, gently teasing her with his tongue.

Never in all her life had Emily ever imagined such a thing. She was suddenly embarrassed and flustered and totally consumed by the feeling of his mouth upon her flesh. He began using his tongue the way a cat laps up the cream, massaging her innermost parts, nibbling her as though she were some sweet treat and he could not get his fill.

Treacherous thing that it was, her body reacted almost instantly—her muscles tightening and relaxing again and again, each contraction growing stronger than the last until she was sure she would shatter like glass at any moment. Tighter and tighter, faster and faster, her muscles clenched, her desire unrelenting and beyond anything she could ever imagine.

At last her body seized, a single muscle clenching hard at her center. Then, an overwhelming heat flared through her as though she were a match struck against a stone.

Emily was sure she was about to die.

When she felt release start to come, he moved. Like a lion he shot up her length, his body pressing hers even harder. Before she knew what was happening, he was inside of her!

"Let go for me!" he commanded, and for the first time she well and truly understood another's thoughts. His need was as great as hers and he could not have release until she gave it to him.

The incredible feeling of sweet torture of her power over him nearly broke her.

"Yes!"

In the space of a single breath they were plummeting over a waterfall, soaring through the clouds, one man and one woman experiencing the totality of what their joining truly meant. Release came as an unbelievably intense explosion of their senses and the quiet nothingness of a single heartbeat.

As quickly as it had begun, their lovemaking had ended. Suddenly she was alone, standing behind him in the wagon, reaching out wildly and trying to regain her balance.

"Oh, my God," she said. Her knees were suddenly weak and her chest felt tight. "What did you do to me?"

Tristan only gasped in answer and braced his arms against the wagon's frame. Though they hadn't touched, his body felt as if he'd just ravaged her. Her scent was all he knew and the feel of her enveloping him still tingled on his skin. He turned to look at her, not at all surprised by her wide-eyed stare.

He felt a dozen things run through her mind. Had what she'd just imagined really happened? A moment ago she'd been sure it had been real, but now her certainty wavered.

Not only that, but what should she say? How would she begin?

Tristan couldn't help but feel the burn of embarrassment rise within her. Had he really desired her so much?

Or had it been her own selfish flesh forcing him to do such an unspeakable act?

Tristan nearly laughed. Had she forced him, indeed!

Emily stepped back a pace and then another until her back was against the wall of the wagon.

For a few seconds she wanted to confront him, to demand he tell her what exactly had happened between them. In her mind, the brave, ordered Emily Durbin did not exist and a cowardly ninny had taken her place.

She reasoned that it must be so, since he hadn't come forth and assured her that she hadn't imagined his desire for her.

Indecision warred within her. Perhaps he needed more time. Taking a breath, she closed her eyes opened her mind, inviting him in.

Seconds passed and Tristan did nothing. It tore at his heart that he couldn't tell her the truth of it. It was all he could do to keep from falling to his knees before her. He alone knew what their joining could become, but to give in to it would mean disaster for them both.

He felt the very instant her hope died. Realizing that she'd been wrong, Emily quickly wiped at a tear gathering in her eye. He felt her heavy disappointment.

She was sure she'd been a fool.

Nothing had really happened after all.

Tristan bit down on a moan. Her pain was almost unbearable.

Without speaking, he spun around and began battering the door again, thinking that a bruised fist was the least he should suffer for hurting her so.

The physical pain of his efforts did little to ease his conscience. Worse yet, the longer they were closed together the more he wanted her. It was becoming more than uncomfortable now. It was pure torture.

Finally she took a breath, her voice trembling slightly when she spoke.

"Please. Come sit down. I'm sure that when the captain and his men are able to, they'll start looking for us."

"And if they cannot?"

Tristan hated himself the moment he said it. The distressed sound she made tore into his heart like the claws of a tiger.

"I'm sorry, I didn't mean . . ."

"You didn't mean to frighten me. It's all right. I know this isn't the time to panic."

"Yes. That's it." Tristan let out a low sigh.

He felt a slow change in her demeanor. A new desperation rose in her. She was considering that they might not survive after all.

"Have you been doing it? Just now? Reading my mind, I mean."

"No," he lied. "I've been only thinking of how we might alert the others."

"Oh."

Tristan leaned back against the door and closed his eyes. He hadn't meant to lead her along.

It was a dangerous ground they tread.

Tristan knew that if he gave himself to her, that would give her power over him. Power to force him to her will, controlling him like a puppeteer pulling the strings of a marionette. She would own him.

As he watched her, his fear became like a snake, coiling around his spine, squeezing his chest, and binding his gut. She could force him to do anything.

He'd been controlled before. He would not let it happen again. Ever. Whether the mind of a cruel old man or the lovely Miss Durbin, Tristan would not let it happen.

"What is it? What's wrong?"

Before he could answer, something hit against the side of the wagon. Before they knew what was happening, the door was being pulled open. Relief flooded over him when he sensed just who it was on the other side.

Finally the broken wood gave way. Relieved at their

rescue, Tristan let out a slow breath. He felt her momentary relief as well, but it was a small victory. He couldn't help but feel the chasm of doubt and hurt between him and Emily broaden even deeper.

For a brief moment, Tristan wanted to turn and comfort her. To assure her that he did indeed find her beautiful and desirable. But to do so would endanger himself and the small, secure life he'd built. Without looking back, he took the officer's hand and made his way out of the wagon.

Chapter Eight

It should have been a simple operation. Attack the soldiers, find their weakest defense, take the girl and the old man. Never once had Diego Chavez thought his men could fail. The English soldiers had fought with the hearts of lions.

Chavez huddled beneath the outcropping of brush he'd been lucky enough to find for protection. The final spattering of gunfire rang out, the sound proving how distant his enemies now were. Relaxing back against the rocky wall, he wiped a damp hand across his brow. He was nearly out of ammunition. It was doubtful the British troops had called back their scouts, so determined they'd been to kill every last one of them.

It had been in the lazy hours of the afternoon, directly after the noon meal. The troops, twenty of them in all, not counting the two civilians, had eaten and were preparing camp for the night. It had been the captain's decision, likely based on the rumbling of storm clouds overhead.

In fact, when the first explosions had begun, the soldiers had likely thought it was the weather and not cannon shells being fired. That had changed quickly enough.

"To your guns!" the commander shouted. "We're under attack!"

The first hits had landed squarely, striking the supply wagon immediately. The rear right wheel split to kindling, and tipping precariously, it rolled down the steep hillside, tumbling bottom over top until crashing into the ravine.

Motioning to his compadres to mount a full attack, Chavez had planned to finish the troops off quickly, and then take the civilians back to his own base camp and the traitorous Englishmen that awaited them. But the soldiers had fought harder than he'd expected and his mission had been a failure.

"What do we do now, sir?" Chavez's second asked, scooting around the hillside, one arm across a wounded shoulder. Chavez grunted. His men were impervious to English tactics, but not their bullets. It galled him all the more to be humiliated in such a way.

"We wait, lieutenant. When the time comes, we will mount another attack." Next time, he promised under his breath, the scoundrels would not be so lucky.

"Thank heavens you've come!" Emily shouted as the wagon door was nearly torn from its hinges.

"Miss Durbin? Are you hurt?"

Captain Hamilton's concern clearly colored his tone.

"We're both well, in case you're interested," Deveraux said.

Emily watched as the surgeon gained his footing. She noted he was unsteady at first, a twist of pain crossing his expression.

In a few minutes the two of them were thankfully outside of the conveyance. Relieved, she took in a healthy lungful of the fresh air.

"Emily!" Lord Branleigh was instantly upon them. "Thank heavens you're all right. When I saw that cannonball land I was certain you'd been killed."

"Yes, Uncle. I'm quite all right."

Tristan sat quietly on the wagon bed, silent as another

soldier examined him. She saw that he'd been injured. He had a large gash in his right calf. The bleeding seemed to have ceased, but the edges were jagged and Emily thought they looked quite painful.

"I was so worried for you both."

Emily turned to glance at her wagon mate, but his attention was elsewhere. She watched as Captain Hamilton approached them.

"You didn't know of the attack in advance?" he asked the surgeon.

Tristan shook his head. Lifting up his still-manacled wrists, he explained.

"I must have fallen asleep."

The captain motioned for his second. "Remove the irons."

When the other man had done so and gone on to his next task, Hamilton scrutinized Tristan. "What of those soldiers now? Should we turn back and mount a rescue?"

Tristan remained silent for a moment, closed his eyes, and sat very still. His expression changed. "It won't be necessary. They're all dead."

With that he stood and limped off to sit alone at the farthest end of the encampment.

Emily patted her uncle's arm and then moved to the commander. "Perhaps if I speak with him . . ." she started, though her comments sounded flat, even to her own ear.

"You may do as you wish, miss." With that Hamilton straightened his spine and, turning abruptly, left her alone.

Wanting more than anything to separate himself from the rest of the party, Tristan quickly made his way to a small clearing just at the edge of the glade where they'd set up camp. Distance was what he needed. Distance from the living and the dead.

Without looking at the spattering of corpses that lay about the now disrupted area, he knew that men of both armies had perished. Bayonets and bullets alike had taken their victims. The heavy cast of loss weighted down the air like dust during a drought.

Unlike the other survivors of the attack, Tristan hung his head low. The pain of his weaknesses never seemed to fade and it was times such as these that were debilitating to him. Knowing of the suffering of others and being helpless to do anything about it.

Now he looked about the battleground and realized just what it was they were up against. This was no incidental attack. It had been planned. They'd been set upon.

Hearing the movement of another amongst the dead, Tristan glanced up. The strange little man, Pemberton, lingered at the edge of the encampment.

"It looks as though we've taken a rough hit."

Tristan didn't want to speak to anyone, and certainly not one of the civilians he'd been assigned to protect.

Meaning to tell the man to leave him be, he couldn't help but feel the indifference the other man felt toward the dead soldiers.

Glancing up, Tristan quickly noted that Pemberton, whom he'd been told was some sort of assistant to Lord Branleigh, appeared less burdened than the others. He also noted that the little weasel's clothes had not so much as a speck of dirt on them. His hair remained neatly combed and even his spectacles were unmarked.

A sudden suspicion rose in him. Tristan decided to question him rather than dismiss him as had been his first inclination.

"Rough enough," Tristan said slowly, scrutinizing the man, hoping that he could discern his thoughts as easily as the others.

Except that Pemberton was not a man who opened himself so readily to others. *That alone should make him suspect,* Tristan thought.

Except that it wasn't proof against him, and this bothered Tristan more than he would admit.

"Lucky I found a good place to hide or I'd have been killed like the rest of these poor blokes, eh?"

"Yes, lucky."

"I'd warned Captain Hamilton about just this sort of thing, you know. These Spanish devils are the worst, as I hear it."

"Really? The Spanish nationals are our allies."

"Yes, the nationals, but not the mercenaries. The hills are rife with these beasts, you know. Cannot trust a one of them."

Before Tristan could begin questioning the man further, the flurry of dark brown skirts with yellow trim caught his eye.

Miss Durbin had found them.

Tristan scowled. Did the woman not know how damned disturbing she was to him?

"Miss Durbin." Pemberton virtually lit up when he saw her.

"Mr. Pemberton. Mr. Deveraux," she said, pointedly walking past Pemberton.

Tristan eyed her curiously for a brief moment. Turning his gaze to the other man he noticed that his boyish grin of a few moments before had paled somewhat. The brightness of his expression soured when Emily didn't return his enthusiasm from a few moments earlier.

Though the idea seemed unlikely, the longer Tristan watched the expression on the other man, so totally absorbed in the arrival of Branleigh's niece, the more it was clear. The little man was more than enamored with her. He was quite frankly smitten. It was ridiculous, true enough. Like himself, Pemberton was not of the aristocracy nor was he anything other than her uncle's lab assistant.

An uneasy feeling passed over Tristan. Something dark had crossed the other man's mind, something bordering on sinister.

Just as quickly as it had come, however, it was gone. Not because he had lost interest in Pemberton's curious thoughts, but because of Miss Durbin herself. In short, nothing was normal where the lady was concerned.

He nodded to the lady. Suddenly a realization hit him. Whenever she was around the cacophony of thoughts that usually swirled around him ceased. They weren't gone completely, but they were quite a bit subdued. It was like the difference between being shouted at and a quiet whisper.

No thoughts, no rush of emotion, save for hers and to a lesser degree, his own. In fact, after their time together in the supply wagon, Tristan wasn't sure of much of anything at all. They had been at the edge of something. Something dangerous.

For a few brief moments, Tristan had been ready to sell his soul for hers.

"Mr. Deveraux?"

When he glanced up into her innocent gaze, he saw an odd reflection of himself. He almost didn't recognize his own doubting nature, his clouded gaze. It was as though she could see past all of that, deep into his psyche, into his heart.

Blinking rapidly, trying to push down the mixture of emotions that were assaulting him, Tristan turned away, rubbing his eyes furiously.

"Are you well?"

The sound of her voice had a soothing effect on his too tangled nerves. "I'm fine."

Beside him, Pemberton took in a deep breath. Seeing that the lady had yet again caught his attention, Tristan turned to her. The expression on her face nearly shook him to his core.

In that moment, for the very first time in many years, another showed genuine concern for him. Not since his mother's death had Tristan ever seen such an expression.

Eyes wide, brow slightly lifted, and the slightest flush to her cheeks, Emily Durbin now gazed at him as though she really did care about his well-being.

The thought of it nearly split him in two. So much he

wanted to trust in that deep well of concern, to let himself loose in her presence. To tell her about himself, all of him. Just as he was about to break down the barrier, however, he heard the hint of another's thought.

"Not fair! Bloody not fair!"

Tristan looked toward the little man who now stood, nervously shuffling from one foot to the other. A fine bead of sweat had broken out on his face, and it was clear that he wasn't at all happy with Tristan's attention to Miss Durbin.

Worse yet, the lady saw it as well. A look of discomfort crossed her face. Whatever attentions Pemberton had thrust at her in the past, it was clear that she did not want any part of them. She shifted as well, turning a slightly embarrassed gaze to him.

Her obvious discomfort, however, had not been the least bit noticed by the other gentleman.

"If you'll excuse us," he nodded to Pemberton. "Miss Durbin and I must discuss matters of her uncle's safety."

Taking her by the arm, he half pulled and half propelled her forward.

"Of course," Pemberton called after them, though the tone of his voice was of one who didn't particularly like being dismissed so thoroughly.

"Yes, yes of course," she nodded, breathless, quickening her step to keep up with Tristan's long strides.

Within moments they had left the little man behind, gazing anxiously after them both. Even at a distance, however, Pemberton's anger was palpable. Tristan pushed it away. His main concern was Emily.

"Thank you ever so much," she said, huffing slightly as they managed to make the end of the glade.

"You're quite welcome, but you must know, Mr. Pemberton is very besotted with you."

She sighed quietly. "Yes, he is, though I've tried to discourage him, to take care with his feelings. I mean, he's such an odd little man, and I'm sure the ladies aren't exactly pining for him.

Tristan gave off a short laugh. "His attentions are only for one particular lady. He has no thoughts of another."

"You can read his thoughts as well?"

Tristan sighed. He hadn't meant to encourage her. "I didn't have to. His feelings are written on his face as clearly as ink on parchment."

"Mr. Deveraux," she began, her face coloring again, a pleasing shade that touched a chord in him.

"Tristan," he said in a low voice, thick with an emotion he couldn't contain. The truth of it was, now that they were alone, now that the two of them had efficiently pushed away all intruders, she filled him to the brim. Her scent covered him like a blanket of soft, heady flowers, her vision clear-eyed and far more beautiful than any painting. The rough living of the camp might have diminished her, as it surely would any lady of the *ton*; instead it had left her with a healthy pallor, glowing almost. But beyond that, it was the peace that lived inside of her.

Peace that Tristan himself had been long denied. She was like a deep well, and one that he could so easily fill himself up with.

"What?" she asked, quietly.

"My name is Tristan. Please don't call me by anything else. I can't stand it any longer."

"My given name is Emily. I would be pleased if you would address me as such, too. I mean, with us being forced to live so close to each other, and so much depending on our managing Uncle's security . . ."

Tristan couldn't help himself. Watching the way her lips moved, so lush and alluring, she seemed to pull him to her. He couldn't push away the thought of knowing just what those lips would taste like, or how the feel of her breath against his skin would delight him.

All he needed was one kiss, he thought. One kiss.

Without really knowing why, Tristan acted on impulse. Leaning forward, he kissed her, long and deep.

The instant their lips made contact, Tristan knew exactly

what was at stake. She was more than a well, she was a chasm, long and deep, but not one which a man would turn away from. She was full of soft, gentle curves, a womanly body. She was love and heat and would protect him like a tigress protecting her cubs.

Though small in form, Emily Durbin was a force to be reckoned with. A woman alone, despite her doting uncle and history of marital ineptness.

"Emily," he breathed when they, out of necessity, ended their kiss.

"Yes?"

Tristan wasn't sure if she was answering his question or posing one of her own.

He was about to tell her that he would do anything for her, tell her about his life, ask her to spend an eternity with him. However, as blissful as their shared passion might be, Tristan realized that it was far more dangerous.

Glancing about quickly, he saw Captain Hamilton watching them. That realization shook him to his marrow. He'd not sensed the other man's approach. He'd not known they were being observed at all. Even now, with the cold force of his discovery, he realized with startling clarity that in Emily's presence the one gift he'd longed to be rid of was gone.

He could read no one's thoughts with her in his arms.

The realization hit him like a stone anvil. How could this be? Searching her expression, he felt her presence almost invade him. Her serenity became his, her thoughts consumed him. All in the space of a few moments he realized that she was the salvation he'd long sought.

"Is something the matter?"

Indeed there was, he thought ruefully. She was the matter. He couldn't protect them with her so close. He couldn't even protect himself.

A sudden knife of fear cut through him. He would have to end their affair even before it had begun.

"Miss Durbin," he began, putting up his hand when she began to correct him.

"It's Emily, remember?"

"Miss Durbin," he said again, this time his tone stronger, his words sharper. "I apologize for my behavior. I've not been myself lately. The fact is that whatever we'd thought might be growing between us is ill-advised. I'd appreciate it in the future if you'd attempt to keep your distance from me. Again, I'm sorry."

He'd meant to turn away from her then, meant to cut her from his life the way a surgeon severed a troublesome limb.

Except Emily was not just troublesome. She was dangerous. And if he wasn't careful, his affection for her—should he call it an affliction?—might end up killing them both.

Tristan meant to turn away, like the black-hearted coward he was. But the large, looming figure of Jeffrey Hamilton stood not ten feet away.

The atmosphere changed to that of thick, guarded mistrust. Tristan knew he was in a deeper stew than he'd ever considered. By the expression on the other man's face, he too was smitten by Emily.

First Pemberton, then Hamilton, and finally himself. Was there no man in camp who did not chase after the lovely lady's attentions?

Glancing at the horizon, expecting to see men silently watching their behavior, Tristan realized that indeed, there were none. Cursing under his breath, he turned back to face Hamilton and the accusations that rode high on his brow.

Jeffrey hadn't meant to intrude, but as he walked over the rise, he came upon the couple, arm in arm, sinking into a deep, passionate kiss. The picture of it both startled and upset him. He'd had no qualms about Miss Durbin, she had been indeed rather polite as her station required. Polite, but not affectionate, he reminded himself. He shouldn't have let the sight of them together bother him. But it did. The man certainly didn't deserve her attentions.

Once again putting away his tide of emotions for the drudgery of his duty, he clamped down on the recriminations that rose to his tongue and approached the couple.

When Deveraux glanced up at him, he wore an expression that looked as if he was both shocked and embarrassed at being discovered.

"You will pardon my interruption," Jeffrey began. He shortened the distance between them, careful not to appear to notice the slight blush of the lady's pallor.

"Please, join us," Deveraux was careful not to meet his gaze as well.

"I've assessed the situation. We were fortunate, our casualties are few."

"Fortunate," Deveraux muttered.

"I realize how difficult this must be for you. For the time being I'm placing you on the honor system. You may go about unshackled until we reach the ship. If you violate my trust at any time, I'll have you locked up until we reach our destination."

Miss Durbin stepped forward. "Is this really necessary, Captain? I mean, we're all civilized here."

"I have my orders, miss."

"Certainly you don't believe Mr. Deveraux would act irresponsibly."

"It's not up to me to judge, miss. Now, if the two of you will accompany me, we'll be under way."

Deveraux nodded, but then quickly looked away. "As you wish, Captain."

Jeffrey motioned for them to walk ahead of him. The lady moved forward, but Deveraux held back a moment.

"It's up to you what you do, Captain, but you must protect the lady and her uncle."

"I've made a thorough exam of the perimeter. I see nothing threatening at the moment."

"It's what we don't see that's the most dangerous. I assure you, Miss Durbin and Lord Branleigh are out in the open here. There is something about."

"Something about? Having impressions again, are we?"

Jeffrey watched as the other man started say something then halted his words. "No, but we've been attacked once; it doesn't take a mind reader to know that it will happen again."

Jeffrey nodded. "I'm ever watchful, Mr. Deveraux. Carry on."

The walk back to the camp was quiet and thoughtful. Jeffrey kept his vigil for the rest of the night. The words the other man had said were enough to keep him awake. That and his memory of the couple's embrace. It just wasn't possible that Deveraux had charmed the lady so completely in so short a time.

Jeffrey was certain that there was more to this than simple attraction between the two. He was certain the devil was manipulating the young woman. As soon as he had evidence of it he'd have the man back in irons.

Chapter Nine

Every time Emily looked at the surgeon, a thrill ran through her. It was too easy to think about him, about how his hands would feel as they caressed her face, or the warmth of his breath as he leaned forward for a kiss.

Emily scoffed. Would she never learn? The man wanted nothing more to do with her. He'd made it clear enough the previous night. Emily's sense of wonder at her new feelings for Deveraux had deteriorated to dread. Each time she looked at him she felt a sense of disaster creeping up on them and she felt ever more powerless to stop it.

"What is it, Em? What's wrong?" Her uncle leaned forward, concern growing in his expression.

"Oh, nothing, Uncle. I suppose I'm a bit fatigued is all."

It was true. The trip back to England seemed to be taking an awfully long time. Not for the first time she felt a longing for it all to be over with, for she and her uncle to be safe at Beldon Hall once again.

"I shouldn't have made you come with me," he said beside her. "The battlefield is no place for a young lady."

"I haven't minded it all that much. I just feel so inadequate at times. I'm sure I will be much more use to you once we're back home."

"Nonsense, my dear. Your companionship allows me to

keep my mind fresh, to have something to look forward to at the end of the day. I'm just sorry that you've nothing to occupy you the rest of the time."

"I haven't minded. I'm glad to have had the chance to meet new people. I mean, Captain Hamilton has been most cordial, and the other soldiers have as well." Emily clamped down on the thought of the other person she'd met, the one who had plagued her thoughts almost from the very first moment she'd seen him.

"I'm glad you've found a few new friends," he said.

Emily really didn't mind the rigors of the road. In fact, she now welcomed something else to occupy her mind. Anything was better than being curious about Tristan Deveraux.

As if he could read her thoughts, Branleigh nodded to their companion as he rode past them.

"A troubled young man, that one."

"Yes, I've not quite been able to figure him out."

"Perhaps it would be best if you didn't try. I mean, your life has been cast about enough, hasn't it? First with your dreadful wedding fiascos and now being pulled hither and yon by me. I'd think you'd need a season off from us all. Either way, that young man is definitely trouble."

Emily glanced at her uncle surprised. "But, I thought you were fond of him?"

"I am, my dear. He seems lost, like a puppy that can't find its way, I suppose. I feel more and more the need to watch over him."

Emily laughed. "As you've done for me on more than one occasion."

"Well, a man must be generous and giving or he has no sense of worth."

"As if working without respite to improve the army's defenses wasn't enough."

He shrugged. "I like tinkering, you know that. But that young man troubles me, and I'm thinking that may not be so good a thing."

"Well, if it's any comfort, I'm troubled by him as well. It's like we're drawn together, and yet whenever I get close enough to learn what he's really about, he just pushes me away."

"Perhaps he's wiser than I'd thought. I'll make no excuses. I don't think the two of you would suit. I'm sure the physical attraction would carry you for a time, but after that fades, what then?"

"Uncle!" Emily could feel her cheeks warm. "I doubt that Mr. Deveraux has the same sort of interest in me. Even if he did, I'd think twice about it."

"Ah, dearest, you deny the attraction between the two of you, but your heart may be a different matter entirely."

Emily wanted to argue with him, to deny that her heart was at all in question, but that would have been a lie.

Glancing in his direction, she saw that Tristan had his back to her. He must have known her thoughts again because his spine had stiffened considerably and she was certain his ears had perked up, just like a cat that knew you were talking about it.

"Uncle, please forgive me," she muttered to him, "but I've been in quite a pique lately. I think perhaps I'd enjoy a bit of a walk right now."

"In this heat?"

Emily nodded. "Don't worry, I'll keep up. Perhaps Captain Hamilton would be so kind to accompany me."

She watched the surgeon and could tell by the way he leaned slightly to one side that the devil was eavesdropping. She knew a way to teach the scalawag a lesson.

As she'd requested, her uncle signaled the driver to slow the carriage to a stop. Without even looking, Emily knew that Tristan had slowed his advance as well. Forget that he looked quite handsome mounted on his horse, or that the thought of him joining her on her afternoon jaunt left her nearly breathless. Emily was satisfied enough with the knowledge that she'd at least gotten his attention.

Though she'd only been jesting about the captain joining

her, she was surprised when the tall length of his shadow fell upon her.

"Miss Durbin, is there something you require?"

"No, I merely wanted to stretch my legs a bit."

"Of course. Might I ask if I may join you? With the uneven terrain, the caravan won't be traveling much faster than a brisk stride, anyway."

Emily looked into the wide brown eyes of the commander. For a moment she considered how unfair it was. She knew he was the second son of an aristocrat and he certainly was nice enough to look at. He was attracted to her as well.

Emily should have courted his attention. She should have considered him a very good placement for a woman of her station. After all, with her three such failures, she knew she wouldn't happen upon a stray duke or viscount that would be so willing. Marriage to a second son who had a nice military commission was very highly prized for a widow of her station.

Unfortunately her uncle was correct, while her mind knew Hamilton was the best candidate for her future, her heart was drawn to the tall, brooding figure up ahead.

Emily very much meant to deny the commander, but when Tristan glanced back at her, a smug grin growing on his face, something unforeseen happened. Emily decided to bait the tiger. Smiling, she slipped her hand onto the arm that Hamilton offered her.

"Why yes, Captain. I'd be delighted if you'd join me."

When she let her gaze wander back to Tristan, he'd already turned away. One didn't need to read minds to see that he was not at all pleased with her decision.

Still two days away from the coast, Tristan was exhausted. Though he had fewer minds to contend with, the emotions between Emily, her uncle, and Hamilton never seemed to cease.

Try as he could, Tristan wasn't able to block out the woman's thoughts. Like a burr under his saddle, she always seemed to be there. The resonance of her laughter, the way she'd let her gaze wander over to him when she thought he wasn't looking, even her humming when she was preoccupied with her sewing constantly tweaked his attention.

So when they sat for dinner that evening, he had to strain to give all of his attention to an important conversation between the commander and his second.

"I tell you, sir, if we continue to follow the road north, it will lead us too close to occupied lands. I'm not liking the looks of it."

"We've already suffered enough loss of time as it is. It's imperative to reach the arranged rendezvous location before the end of the week. Otherwise we'll miss the ship that's been chartered for us. General Henley made that very clear. Intelligence has picked up reports of the enemy closing off the channel. We've no choice but to forge ahead."

"It'll make no difference if we're all killed before we can get there."

Settling down beside the wagon with his plate of food, Tristan considered their words. It was true enough. Until this trip, he'd have been able to help the captain and his men. As it was, the longer he was around Emily, the less able he was to sort out the stream of thoughts that assailed him.

"Is this spot taken?"

Tristan looked up into Emily's sunny smile. He should have scowled at her and sent her back to the captain's admiring attentions, but instead he merely sat for a moment, practically staring at her sun-kissed radiance. As always, her mere presence left him practically speechless.

Without waiting for further conversation, she gracefully floated to the ground, her skirt billowing out like the petals of an apple blossom drifting from a high branch.

"Mmmm, I find the night air especially brisk this evening, don't you?"

Tristan sighed. He'd wanted to hear more of Hamilton's plans. How could he possibly help them out of this predicament when the devilish woman consumed his every thought.

"I suppose," he answered, though he spent his energy straining to hear any more of the exchange between the captain and his second in command.

Emily pulled her wrap a bit tighter and folded her arms beneath it. The movement had the effect of elevating her breasts just a bit higher.

Tristan groaned inwardly. Were it not for their being surrounded by a score of soldiers, her uncle, and the other members of the scientific staff, he very likely would throw himself upon her and smother her with kisses until she relented and allowed him to take her right there on the spot.

His groin twitched appreciatively. Of course his body would react that way. His lustful appetites didn't give a damn that they were leading him to sure disaster.

"Mr. Deveraux, I realize how difficult this all must be for you," she began, her voice like a balm on an open wound. "Please tell me, if there is anything I can do to relieve the situation . . ."

Tristan nearly choked. Anything she could do? How about lifting her skirts and letting him have his sinful way? Unbidden thoughts of long hours of sexual pleasure assailed him.

"Please, Miss Durbin, I must ask you again to keep your distance. It is most difficult." Not knowing what else to do, Tristan abandoned the remains of his meal and left her.

He knew he was running away again. It grated on him to think that he'd become the sort of man who never dealt with his problems. Even the very desirable, pretty ones, like Emily Durbin.

For the briefest moment, he considered stopping, turning around, and taking her into his arms once and for all. He thought to damn the forces that had conspired against him.

Tristan quickened his pace to the edge of the clearing. All he really wanted was a bit of peace. As he made it to the outline of trees that surrounded the clearing's perimeter, his attempt at solace was short lived. Jessup Pemberton stepped in his path.

"Mr. Deveraux, out for a brisk walk?"

"Yes, I am. If you'll excuse me . . ."

Pemberton grabbed his arm. "Do you think it's wise to stray beyond camp? I mean, the enemy could be lurking around in the dark."

"If he is, he'll find I'm not fit company for him either." As he said this, Tristan saw that Emily had risen from her seat as well. Giving him a dark look, she turned and started in the opposite direction.

Tristan felt like a scoundrel. He'd as much as cast her off. It certainly hadn't been his intention to hurt her feelings. He tried to turn away from Pemberton, but the smaller man tightened his grip.

"If you'll excuse me, I need to speak with Miss Durbin about her straying too far from camp."

"Listen, Deveraux. I've seen the way you look at her. She is none of your concern. She's far too delicate to be included in whatever black-hearted plans you have for her."

Tristan glared at him. "Just what is your business with the lady?"

Pemberton's expression darkened. "I've a fondness for the girl, and I've no intention of standing idly by whilst you scandalize her."

"You're joking, surely?" Tristan paused. "I can see by your expression that you are not. No matter. It's none of your business. Now, if you'll excuse me."

Tristan turned away, still feeling the small man's ire burning his back.

"Stay away from her, Deveraux. I'm warning you."

Scoffing at the other man's baseless threats, Tristan stayed to his course. He couldn't miss the angry thoughts the scientist's assistant threw at him. Bordering on a threat of violence, one that Tristan gave no credence to at all, Pemberton fumed behind him.

Like being hit by lightning, the force of a raging murderous intent fell upon him. Paralyzed momentarily, Tristan could do nothing to slow the rush of boundless rage that assailed him.

Spinning around, Tristan fought to gain his bearings. Who among them could harbor such hatred for another? As he searched the minds of those gathered, suddenly he came upon an intruder, just beyond the clearing. But the evil thread hadn't come from that spool. It was another who wanted the man destroyed and with hatred so fierce it cut Tristan in his tracks.

As he stood agape, a thought slithered beneath the surface of the murderous intent. A snake of malicious intent threatened another among their number. It was a huge python that burned a path through Tristan's mind, its prey only one person. Lord Branleigh.

But he wasn't the only target of the depraved mind.

Tristan closed his eyes and saw the vision of Emily perched upon her dressing room chair, gazing into a mirror. She'd been putting up her hair with ivory combs, but her attention was focused somewhere beyond the glass, her dark lavender eyes moist from crying. Then, behind her the wretched beast rose, its thick, green gaze bearing down on her.

Tristan could feel the animal's hunger as though it were his own. Turning toward the predator, Emily watched horrified as the beast slithered ever closer. Before she could cry out, it attacked, and in one quick motion, swallowed her whole.

"No!" Tristan screamed, but he was too late. The animal gazed up at him contentedly, its mouth bent in a sated grin. Then, the eyes bearing down on him wore a familiar expression. The green slits winked only once before transforming into the shape of a man, its face hidden from Tristan's sight.

The sounds of gunfire shattered the silence. The texture of his vision broke like a soap bubble and he was once again standing in the glade. Before his eyes, men were fighting and dying, enemy soldiers came out of the surrounding forest, bayonets raised, rifles blaring.

"Tristan!" Emily was knocked down as one of the attackers crashed through the melee and rode toward him.

"Emily!" Tristan ran into the battle, ducking around raised swords, trying to get to where Emily lay motionless on the ground.

As he ran, Tristan felt the fists of other men's thoughts beat against him. Anger, shock, betrayal, fear, terror, and panic bruising his psyche with each blow.

Still he continued, his feet moving with painstakingly slow motion, as though mired in thick mud. He experienced each man's pain, their deaths and suffering weighing him down with each passing second.

Like the true soldier he was, Jeffrey Hamilton fought with the fierceness of a lion, firing his rifle, and then swinging it like a club, pulling back to use his sword to cut away the fray, no less than five men bearing down on him.

Around him men and horses screamed, but Tristan continued moving toward Emily's still form, seeing the trickle of blood that made a small trail down the side of her face. A few feet from her, another man loomed, his gun drawn, Tristan could hear the man's shouting.

Tristan was certain he was about to die. When the gun's blast sounded he could have sworn he saw a bullet coming his way, time slowing to a crawl as his fate barreled toward him. In the very last fraction of a second, another rose from the smoke and pushed him out of the way. Lieutenant Becker had stood in the line of fire. He fell back, landing squarely on Tristan. Pinned to the ground, the surgeon tried desparately to free himself and pull the soldier to safety.

"God," the soldier grunted, "that hurt." Tristan felt the man's life energy flow from him.

"No," he whispered, but had little time to think of anything else. The weight of a shadow fell upon him and Tristan looked up to see the man who'd killed Becker now standing over them both.

Without saying a word, the soldier pulled a second pistol from his belt and aimed it directly at Tristan.

Emily awoke with the taste of dirt in her mouth and the feel of damp, sticky blood on her face. She was lying face down on the ground, the heavy form of Captain Hamilton pushing her into the soil.

"Let me go!" she demanded, but her protector remained unmoving.

"Stay still, Miss Durbin," Hamilton said above her. "I need to make sure the area is secure."

Emily couldn't take a deep breath for several minutes. She heard the volley of shouts between the commander and his men, more crackling of rifle shots, and finally the eerie sound of silence.

Then, as suddenly as the weight had fallen upon her, it was gone.

"Miss Durbin, I trust you will forgive the forwardness of my manner. I meant only to protect you from those scoundrels."

"It's quite all right," Emiy said, as she touched her ribs gingerly. She didn't think that anything had broken, but she'd wanted to make sure.

"What happened?"

"We were set upon, and very nearly were defeated."

"Oh." Emily quickly scanned the landscape. "Where's Lord Branleigh? Is he all right?" She searched the immediate vicinity and though many men lay unmoving, she was relieved to see that her uncle was not among them.

Hamilton shook his head. "I had him evacuated to the supply wagon when I heard the first shots. With any luck, he'll be about ten miles down the road by now. I think we've managed the worst of it."

"Oh." She searched the ground again. "I saw Mr. Deveraux before I fell. What's happened to him?"

Hamilton looked away a moment. "We're not sure. He may have led them on a chase or he may have been captured."

"Led them on a chase? You think he ran away?"

The commander bit down on his lip a moment. "I don't know yet what to think. For the moment, let's get you reunited with your uncle and the both of you to safety."

He started to help Emily to her feet. "Captain, please, don't leave him behind. I know he's not a coward and if he's run, it's likely he meant to lead them away to protect us. You must rescue him."

Emily held her breath as the captain considered her words. After a few moments, he sighed.

"I suppose you would think it unkind of me to leave him behind. Very well, I'll send you with my men and as soon as I've found Mr. Deveraux, I'll join you at the coast."

Emily let out a breath she didn't know she'd been holding. "Thank you so much, Captain. I know you won't regret it."

Chapter Ten

"What have you to say, English?" The mercenary soldier held his pistol higher still, aimed at Tristan's head. He began to circle around him, his gun hand never wavering.

Tristan held his breath. The soldier who had dived in front of him moaned.

"I'm a surgeon. Let me help him."

The mercenary shook his head. "Why should I care for the life of an English dog like him. No, I want you to tell me why I shouldn't kill you right now."

Tristan looked around the battlefield. Several men had died, at least twenty bodies were strewn about the landscape. A few of them still breathed, and unless he missed his guess, those that had survived were this mercenary's men. He saw no English uniforms among the living.

"I could help your men as well."

"They failed in their mission. Let them die as well. Get up." He motioned with his gun. "Over to that tree. I think it would be a waste of precious ammunition to shoot you. A piece of rope, however, that can be used again."

Tristan took a deep breath. He knew his chances of escaping alive were slim; still, he couldn't help his curiosity about the other man. Gently he pried open the other man's mind. Chavez was a Spaniard, one who didn't care for king or country. He only wanted gold. He'd been promised quite a sum of it in fact.

Tristan rose slowly, trying at the same time to probe deeper into his captor's mind. It was a grizzled and dirty place. This man had made his living killing and had absolutely no remorse.

"Turn around and put your hands behind you."

Tristan did as he was ordered, still probing the other man's mind. He felt the hatred in him, burning like fire across his psyche. He saw the other man lift the butt of his pistol and then both saw and felt the blow as it came down on his head.

Pain shattered all of Tristan's awareness. Grunting, he fell to his knees. Dazed from the blow, he couldn't even fight Chavez as he quickly bound Tristan's wrists together behind him.

"Get up," the mercenary ordered.

Slowly, Tristan rose to his feet, though a wave of dizziness made him stumble as he complied.

"Move over to the tree."

"Why are you doing this?" Tristan asked through clenched teeth. Nausea assailed him with every step.

"I was ordered to kill you and take the old man and the girl. They are beyond my reach now, but you are not. I hope I can at least get some of my payment."

The pain blazing in his head, Tristan could no longer focus on Chavez's thoughts.

"Who wants to kill me?"

The other man only chuckled. "Who indeed, sir. It seems you have enemies you don't even know about."

The assailant looped the rope around Tristan's neck. Still holding the pistol high, he threw the other end of the rope over the tree limb directly above them. Laughing, he pulled it taut.

"Just tell me who it is. In a few minutes I'll be dead anyway and it won't matter," Tristan choked.

The mercenary walked around to stand in front of him.

"I'll give you a small clue instead. You should never get between a man and the woman he desires."

The mercenary started to laugh, a loud, bitter sound. He yanked the rope again, again choking Tristan.

"Please," Tristan said again, "tell me who it is."

For a brief moment, Tristan could barely see the figure of the killer in the mercenary's mind. It was still within the shadows, still lurking, but the sight of him was just beginning to sharpen.

Tristan strained to see even as the rope tightened around his neck. Pain shot through him and his lungs were already crying for air, but he didn't give up his search. He wouldn't until he either died or knew the truth.

Just as the vision of the man was about to clear, a gunshot sounded. Suddenly the killer let go of the rope, and free from his hangman, Tristan bounded forward, landing on his knees.

Coughing furiously and enraged at not learning the identity of the man responsible for trying to kill them, Tristan spat out curses.

"Easy does it man," Hamilton said, suddenly beside him.

"Damn you!" Tristan whispered coarsely. "I almost saw the assassin's face!"

"You're quite welcome for my saving your life. Ungrateful scut," Hamilton said as he knelt beside Tristan.

Tristan could say no more, his throat burned and his eyes watered.

"Here, man, take it easy."

"Emily?"

Hamilton paused. "She's safe. Two of my men survived the attack, three others managed to get her uncle out of harm's way."

"Five men out of twenty," Tristan ground out. "So much violence."

"They knew what was possible when they signed on. So did you."

Tristan bit down on his next words. He'd known right enough, but he never dreamed it might be like this.

"Tired," he said at last.

"I only have one horse. We'll have to share it. We've got to get to the coast as soon as possible. The others will be there waiting for us."

Tristan nodded and followed Hamilton to where his mount stood waiting. A few minutes later they were both on the horse and heading for the coast.

Despite his attempts to block the thoughts of the other man, Tristan couldn't help but hear his ruminations. Hamilton practically roared in his head. The facts were very simple. He had every intention of finishing his mission. He was relieved that Tristan had not been a traitor after all. And he was anticipating the gratitude from Emily at having rescued the surgeon.

The situation had become ever more complicated. He simply had to get free of them all, the army, Hamilton, and most assuredly, Emily.

It occurred to Tristan that there was not only one problem for him to resolve, but two.

First, Tristan knew he must find whoever it was that threatened both Emily and her uncle. During the attack he'd had the glimpse of Emily in trouble. Somehow she was tied to this intrigue, he was certain of it.

The second problem was with Emily herself. With every minute they were together Tristan felt them drawing closer. He was certain it wasn't intentional, as much his doing as hers, but he couldn't refuse the growing power of their attraction.

Tristan lifted his arm and wiped his brow. The commander's closeness was making it even more difficult for him to think clearly. The man was besotted with Emily and his thoughts about her were, while not improper in any way, very much those that Tristan himself shared.

"Emily is beautiful."

Tristan had to agree there. She wasn't just beautiful,

though, she was beauty. Her hair, her eyes, her lips, her very form demonstrated such intense exquisiteness, that most women would have paled in comparison.

"She's deserving of far better than this lout can offer."

Tristan almost laughed at that. It was true, of course. But then, neither of them were worthy of Emily's radiance.

Still, Tristan knew that between the two of them, the better man was definitely Hamilton. He was strong, relatively well connected, and would spend a lifetime caring for her.

Tristan, on the other hand had no such high aspirations. His past pursued him at every turn, he'd no title to offer her, no home or the promise of children, for any of his offspring would bear the risk of receiving his terrible gift. No, Tristan was not the man for Emily.

As much as it tore his heart, he knew that he must arrange matters so that Emily was forever out of his reach.

While the rightness of that idea had settled in his mind, it didn't sit well in his gut. Wrenching pain of knowing he could never have her cut through him like a knife. He mentally shook it off. Emily's welfare mattered. There simply was no hope for them.

Emily waited until the very last moment before turning toward the dock.

"Come, miss, we can't wait any longer. I have my orders. You and Lord Branleigh must board now."

"Are you sure?"

"Aye, ma'am. We must keep your presence on board a secret. If we delay, it will give the enemy cause for alarm. They'll know something is about. The last thing we need is to be fired upon on the water."

Emily nodded and gathered her skirts. All she could do was hope that the captain had rescued Mr. Deveraux and together they would find their way back to England.

Walking up the plank, assisted by the young ensign, she glanced back one last time.

That was when she heard the unmistakable sound of hoof beats against the road. In the dimness the figure of two men on horseback appeared. She let out a heavy sigh of relief.

"Thank heavens they've made it."

The damn ship never stopped rolling. The entire trip felt like an eternity and for Tristan it was no easy journey. Emily hovered nearby, although he had sent her packing almost immediately.

"You're hurt!" She'd come to his side, hands out, looking as if she might have carried him on her back if need be.

"I'm fine," he said, pushing away from her, though he nearly stumbled in doing so.

"Of course, you're not fine." She turned to the captain. "What happened?"

"The man who led the attack against us clouted him a good one, by the look of it. Not only that, but nearly had him strung up when I arrived. Another few minutes and we'd be short one surgeon."

Tristan scowled at them. Although the captain had been correct, he felt their pity and that was the last thing he wanted. He turned to the ship's mate. "Sir, if you would show me to a place where I might sit down for the voyage."

"None o' that, sir. Taking you directly to the bay."

Tristan searched his battered mind and remembered the bay was short for sickbay, or infirmary. "Wherever I can lay my head, then," he said.

Emily started to follow but Hamilton held her back. "'Tis no place for a lady, Miss Durbin. I'll see that he gets proper care."

Tristan spun around to face them both. "I neither want or need any attention from either of you. Miss Durbin, I find your incessant coddling increasingly uncomfortable." He took a long breath before continuing.

"Mr. Deveraux," she began but stopped when he held up his hand.

"Captain, I have every intention of fulfilling my duty in regards to Miss Durbin and her uncle, but I cannot do so if I'm constantly under the woman's barrage. If you would be so kind as to occupy her time until we locate who it is that threatens the viscount, I would be most grateful."

The flash of Emily's anger was bright and hot. Although it was the last thing he wanted for her, he knew it was for the best. Best to put her off now before things got any worse, before he completely lost control.

Hamilton drew in a deep breath, his fists clenching at his side. Tristan thought for sure the man would throttle him.

"It is not for me to question General Henley's wisdom in this matter, but a more unsuitable protector for the lady and her uncle there cannot be. Just do your job, Deveraux, and I'll see to it you are shipped back to Spain at the earliest opportunity."

That was the last he'd seen of them until the ship pulled into port. While their immediate presence was not a problem, Tristan continued to be aware of their thoughts, buzzing along in the distance, like an aggravating mosquito just out of range of one's sight.

Thankfully, Miss Durbin and her uncle were taken off the ship before him. Tristan expected they were most likely halfway to Beldon Hall by now.

Unfortunately this was not the case. A groan escaped him when he climbed aboard the tack ready to take him to the final stop on their journey.

"Hello, Mr. Deveraux," Emily said sweetly. "I trust you are feeling better?"

Emily hadn't had a moment's peace since they'd left Spain. Now, standing on the deck of the *Embrace,* her rocky emotions were as unsettled as the sea. Instantly angered by Deveraux's disturbing display, she hadn't bought a moment of it. Looking like the devil himself, the surgeon's temperament was, at the least, understandable.

More than that, however, it was easy to see that he'd no interest in her beyond the physical. It did smart that he'd cast her off so easily, but then again, weren't all men that way?

"Hello, Miss Durbin."

Emily stirred from her thoughts. The captain approached her from behind.

"It's a rough sea out there," she commented, careful not to mention any part of their mission.

"Indeed it is." He stopped then, leaning against the railing. His dark brown eyes studied the dimness beyond their ship.

Emily wanted to ask after the surgeon's health, but thought it best not to. In a few hours they would be in England and she could get her answers herself.

"I want to thank you, Captain, for all that you've done for my uncle and me, and for Mr. Deveraux, as well, though I doubt he's given any thought at all toward gratitude."

"As a matter of fact, he's not faring too well. Been most under the weather, to be exact."

"I take it sea travel doesn't agree with him."

"He's been intolerably rude to you, Miss Durbin, and when we are finished with our mission, I shall see to it he is suitably chastised for it."

Emily couldn't help but smile. "I see. Some terrible task to make amends?"

"If he doesn't get a full court-martial first."

Though his words were serious, his tone was not. Emily was glad that the two of them shared such an easy friendship. It was certainly a sharp contrast to her stormy relationship with Mr. Deveraux.

"I imagine you'll have him plucking chickens or grooming the horses."

"In Mr. Deveraux's case it will take some careful consideration."

"Yes, well, nothing too severe, but I'm sure you know that."

"Miss Durbìn, I know it is presumptuous of me to speak to you this way, but I feel strongly that any 'considerations' you may have regarding Mr. Deveraux must be immediately stopped."

Emily sighed. "It's not something I meant to have happened," she said at last. "I mean, he's such a curiosity, I suppose. One finds oneself drawn to such an intriguing person."

Hamilton's voice softened. "Miss Durbin, I know that he is a gallant-looking fellow, whose differences might draw the attention of one such as you, but it will be for naught. He may give you his affection for a time, but I believe that a short acquaintance is all he is capable of. There are far more men available for you to consider."

"You would think that's the case, wouldn't you," Emily said evenly. "To be honest, I've not been fortunate in the marriage mart, as you've no doubt heard."

"I have attributed your poor results at the altar to be merely bad luck. You certainly have been blameless in all that's happened."

"Not if you listened to the gossips about town."

Hamilton took a deep breath, "It's been my experience that gossips rarely know the truth, and if they did, cared even less to share it."

"You are too kind, Captain."

They stood for a moment, watching the moonlight reflect on the water, its perfect countenance split on the sea's constantly moving surface.

Hamilton cleared his throat. "Miss Durbin, I know this is likely not the proper time or place to broach this subject, but I'm afraid that with events turning as they do, I might not get another chance."

"Captain?" Emily felt the cool mist of reason stealing over her.

"Miss Durbin, would you consent to be my wife?"

* * *

"Sir, I'm most complimented. We barely know each other," she said.

Of course, that had been her very practical nature, Jeffrey thought. How like her to analyze things down to the last thread and then speak her mind on the matter. There had been no malice in her estimation. He knew exactly what sort of logic appealed to her, for it most certainly did in his estimation as well.

"I know this seems rash, Miss Durbin. I can hardly understand it myself. Except to say that here we are, the two of us, myself with little hope for more than a passing glance in society, and you on the end of a scandalous affair. Very simply, Miss Durbin, no two people in the history of the *ton* have ever been as well-suited as we."

She looked at him for a brief second, her expression one of hopeless understanding and unfathomable defeat. "I accept your offer."

With that she slipped her small, delicate arm into his.

"I will speak with your uncle," he said, patting her hand and giving her his best smile.

Jeffrey knew instantly that her acceptance came not out of love, infatuation, or even a common understanding. No, it had been defeat, plain and simple.

Since he had long-ago accepted his lowly placed rung on the ladder of high society, he had well understood her decision to settle for what life had offered her rather than chase some nebulous ideal. Taking her hand in his own, he began their time together, certain that at least he would manage to give her a safe and settled life.

Jeffrey even held back a small part of his heart, thinking that if things went as he planned, Miss Durbin might yet gain some affection toward him. Not a raging love affair, to be sure, but it was more than many of their peers. He would be glad enough for that.

* * *

Emily returned to her cabin in a trance. In the end, there had been no reason to refuse the captain's proposal of marriage. He was positioned well enough for them to make a good match. He was strong and smart and very, very serious. To make matters better, or worse depending on how one looked at it, he was quite smitten with her. More than that, he was an honorable man.

He was simply all the things that Tristan Deveraux was not. And it was he, not the mysterious surgeon, who had asked for her hand in marriage.

Emily felt as if another had inhabited her body and accepted his proposal. Though her heart ached for another, she'd long known that any chance at a life with Deveraux was a small one. Now, her fate had been sealed. She would make Hamilton a good, reasonable wife.

For the first time in her twenty-one years, Emily hated being reasonable.

Chapter Eleven

If spending three days closed in a cabin two decks below Emily had been a distraction, sitting across from her in the tight confines of a coach was absolute torture.

They were less than a day from Beldon Hall when the second carriage's axle had broken. Forced to share the remaining conveyance, matters had been made worse when Emily's uncle decided that he and his assistant needed to walk a stretch and leave the young people to themselves. Even the stalwart captain's presence was denied them as he'd chosen to ride instead with the remainder of his company.

That left Emily and Tristan alone. Terribly, wonderfully, alone.

Of course, since Tristan's poor behavior toward her on board the transport ship, Miss Durbin's passions toward him had somewhat diminished. He found that her thoughts were focused even harder on her uncle and their return home than on any romantic notions toward him.

Tristan should have been overjoyed at the thought that the young lady no longer cast her affections toward him. He should have been, but he wasn't.

In fact, it near to drove him crazy to understand exactly what had happened that had cooled her passions so much. Not that they were entirely gone. Seated across from her, trying to focus on the landscape outside the carriage window, Tristan very much felt the struggle that warred within her. Her better judgment was losing, too.

Emily's battle with her rising discomfort should have been the only torrent of passion Tristan had to deal with. Not so. Worse yet were the captain's rampant emotions. It was as if Hamilton had been granted a general's commission and the title of a duke. Tristan knew better, of course. For days the man's mind had been filled with thoughts of Emily. Tristan knew they were mostly unsubstantiated, because she was not in the least returning his interest. Still, it left Tristan wondering.

Now, seated across from her in an empty carriage—which to allow her to be without a chaperone and in his presence would normally be considered unthinkable—he was beginning to doubt his own sanity.

Not for the first time, Tristan twisted in his seat. In addition to the pain of smelling her beautiful, alluring scent; seeing the prim way she pointed her chin slightly upward; feeling the hot, moist puffs of air as she let out one long, slow breath after another, he also suffered a constant barrage of her agony as well. In short, her discomfort and arousal were as painful as his own.

Not that she wasn't trying to avoid thinking about him, she was. Emily had labored for the last hour and a half not to recall the lovemaking dream they'd shared in the supply wagon days before. She tried ever so hard not to remember the touch of his lips upon her most private parts.

Tristan sighed. Thank heavens they'd been alone on the coach because even those who couldn't know of their brushes with intimacy could easily tell of their predicament due to the continual rise of the color red in her cheeks. Not to mention the tightening in his trousers.

Tristan swallowed a moan. This was pure agony.

It was torture to be so close to her every minute, knowing her much more than he had a right to, knowing how she would taste, feel, and react to his touch.

Tristan didn't think it possible but his arousal grew harder. He shifted in his seat once more. Yes, it was torture plain and simple.

"Mr. Deveraux," she said for at least the twentieth time in an hour. The sound of her voice, deep, breathless, and oh so alluring in its throatiness, nearly broke his resolve not to touch her.

"Yes, Miss Durbin?"

The worst of all was that he sounded like some young buck chasing his first lightskirt. It made him all the more uncomfortable and no small amount embarrassed.

"I know this must be difficult. It is for me as well. I've never experienced anything like this. What I mean to say is that I've never known a man, well"—she tipped her head slightly sideways, causing a rush of curls to fall alluringly over her forehead—"like that," she finished, her breath coming out in a full rush. "You must think me a wanton to react in such a way."

Damned if his trousers didn't get another notch tighter. Tristan bit down a moan and moved to the left. It seemed there was no position that would bring him relief.

As she waited for his answer, Tristan decided that indeed the most enticing, albeit the most frustrating, thing about his carriage partner was the way she sat unmoving, motionless except for the slight hitching of her beautifully proportioned bust. He nearly came undone every time it pressed against the tight confines of her white lace and ribbon bodice.

"Mr. Deveraux?" she asked again.

He shot a glance up to her. Best to look at her face, he reminded himself. Not her bust, nor the gathering of skirt at her waist that promised all sorts of delight beneath the soft, cotton material. And definitely not down to the marvelously petite black leather half-boots, which didn't begin to hide her slender little ankles and gave the merest suggestions of the shapely flesh of her legs.

But as he sat, trying not to think about Emily Durbin's too womanly attributes, he realized exactly what the most disastrous part of her anatomy truly was.

Emily Durbin had one of the most alluring, amazingly delicious mouths he'd ever seen. Not only that, but the way she pouted her cherry red lips just so and breathed through them was most distracting. Emily continuously did the one thing that made Tristan nearly crumble at her pretty little half-boots. She breathed through her mouth.

All the time. Every minute she wasn't speaking, which since the beginning of the trip had been almost every minute.

Tristan bit down on a second moan. Never before could he have believed that the simple act of breathing could undo him in such a way. And yet, he knew at that moment he could spend the rest of his life simply watching Emily inhale and exhale. When she drew in a truly deep, deep inhalation, he almost ceased his own breathing.

"Mr. Deveraux?"

Tristan shook himself, realizing too late that he was indeed staring, and he felt the alarm raised in her thoughts. She suspected she was the reason why, and that knowledge served to make her even more uncomfortable.

So, Tristan did the only thing he could do. It was so simple, really. He must put this ridiculous line of thinking out of his mind. He must put to rest once and for all the uncontrollable urges that flowed in him like the stormy sea at high tide. He quickly leaned forward and returned the favor of the perpetual stiff member she'd given him.

"Oh!" she managed when their lips first touched.

He growled back into her mouth, the sound vibrating back inside his own throat.

At first she stiffened at his attack, her senses twisting in a whirl of anxiety, desire, and surprise. But then, as his mouth ground against hers, his tongue plunging inward, his teeth scraping against hers, his breath filling her as he'd wanted to do from the very first moment they'd met, she gave into her own desire and turned the advance around. Emily took control of their kiss. In the space of a heartbeat she became the marauder and he her too-willing victim.

No one was more surprised than he when he realized his rash course of action was both an answer to his prayers and the hand of condemnation. Now both of their bodies sang with desire, a tug of war with the string of need pulled so tight between them that at any second one end of it might snap and they'd be cast forever into carnal oblivion.

"I want you. All of you," he demanded. *"Now!"*

"Yes," she answered. *"Yes-yes-yes-yes-yes!"*

Knowing that there simply was no way that he could not make love to her now, Tristan pushed himself forward and at the same time sent his hands roaming furtively to her endless layers of skirts. Raggedly pushing them upward, never breaking their kiss, he finally felt the warm, moist flesh of her womanhood, hot and damp and ready for him.

Twisting her pelvis upward, she sent him an invitation at the very same moment her mind sent him a command.

"Now!"

Tristan was both shocked and delighted by her wantonness and her eagerness to let him inside. All of her girlish shyness had gone, disappearing in the face of the animal instinct that had overtaken them both.

Her hands did not sit idle while he worked. She too had found the ties to his trousers, and with a force he'd never thought she was capable of, she thrust them down over his near-to-exploding member, down his clenched buttocks and leg muscles. In the very same instant he'd found her sex, she had freed his.

Like a hot iron against bare flesh, they met at the groin. Beautiful agony gripped them both. For a split second he was on the verge of thrusting into her, and she was chanting a single word in her mind.

"*Now, now, now, now-now-now!*"

For a brief second Tristan had the wandering thought that this was certainly no way to deflower a woman such as Emily Durbin. He should first shower her with fine wine and feed her delicate strawberries glazed in syrup and sugar. He should take her first, not on the seat of a dusty carriage and out in the open for any sort of low common lout to see, but in a bed of intricate lace, silken sheets, and endless softness to match the beauty of her soul.

Tristan's body, as demanding as hers, refused to wait for such a perfect circumstance to occur.

"*Now!*" She urged him again, and he gave her a sharp nod with his mind.

Then, as he prepared for his advance, her legs twined around his waist, his hands placed firmly on her round, exquisite bottom, his mouth sucking in her deep, moist breaths, a single thought flashed through her mind. So sharp, like a dozen razors it cut into his psyche and went straight to his groin.

"*I'm engaged to be married!*"

Chapter Twelve

"Come in, Captain. I hear you've completed a check of the Hall's perimeter."

"It's as quiet as a Sunday morning, my lord," Jeffrey said as he entered Lord Branleigh's study. A room consumed by shelves of books and globes and other items of interest to a scientist, the scent of ink and old parchment hung about the place.

Lord Branleigh was seated at his desk, a large, cluttered affair that likely hadn't been organized in quite some time. In the midst of the chaos, however, the viscount had centered a book, and he continued to study the text, not even looking up when Jeffrey entered the room.

Without waiting for an invitation, the army officer took the seat across from the scientist. The other man didn't even lift his eyes from his work to acknowledge Jeffrey's presence.

"I'm relieved that there's no one skulking about. It would look bad to the neighbors, you know. What's on your mind, Captain?"

Jeffrey cleared his throat. "I wanted to speak with you before the others come down for tea. It's been a terribly long trip and I think it best to put things out in the open as soon as possible."

Branleigh glanced up from his work. His round, blue eyes studied Jeffrey a moment, giving him a look that suggested he'd discovered more about the military man than he'd even known about himself.

"Frankly, I'm concerned for Emily. She was quite insistent that we marry as soon as possible. I fear there will be too much for her to do before the ceremony."

"Yes, the wedding." He returned his attention to the books in front of him. "Not to worry, she's put together three weddings already. I imagine she's got things well in hand. I'm sure things will continue along their intended course."

Jeffrey sighed. A true course to men like Aldus Branleigh meant only one thing. That no amount of intention would ever sway events from playing out the way they were meant to.

"Fate," the old man had told Emily that morning when they'd arrived at Beldon Hall, "is nothing more than nature's way of showing you that no man is ever in control of his destiny."

"I am in control of my destiny," Emily had argued at the time. She'd looked at Jeffrey as if to say his presence was proof enough of that.

"Nonsense, girl," Branleigh had argued. "If you attempt to force matters to your own choosing, you will either end up supremely unhappy or dead."

Of course, Jeffrey had well known the "matters" to which he'd been referring were their plans of marriage. Though he'd never voiced his opinion, Aldus Branleigh clearly didn't approve.

Now, sitting across from him, Jeffrey felt that it was even truer than before.

"I hope you'll believe me when I tell you that I intend to do everything in my power to make your niece happy."

The old man glanced up to him once again. "I know you'll try."

Jeffrey sighed. He wanted to argue, to list reason after

reason just why his plans were foolproof. He knew it would do little good. Branleigh was not a man who easily bent to persuasion.

A light tapping on the door drew their attention. "Lord Branleigh, Miss Durbin and Mr. Deveraux are in the parlor awaiting your arrival for tea."

"Please, let's not dwell on unfortunate possibilities," Emily said, pouring a cup of tea for them both. "I believe Captain Hamilton is correct. Between us, we can keep my uncle safe."

"I've told you all, I'm not some child that must be watched at every moment. Besides haven't you plenty enough to keep you entertained what with arranging your marriage? Surely you've no time to fret over me," Branleigh grumbled.

Jeffrey noted that he said the word *marriage* as though he'd had a mouth full of lemons.

Emily patted her uncle's sleeve. "There's plenty of time to finish with the wedding plans. We've planned the announcement party the week after next. My friend, Anna Davenport, has already chosen the hall. It will be a most adequate affair, I'm sure."

Aldus glanced up from his reading. "Adequate. That's a sterling way to start a marriage. Don't you agree, Captain?"

"I believe there are worse beginnings."

"Please, let's not start this line of discussion again. Uncle, I assure you, Jeffrey, and I will be most happy."

Jeffrey concentrated on Emily for a moment. Was that a genuine flush in her pallor? Indeed, it looked as if her cheeks had been painted with crushed cherries, and her lips seemed slightly swollen. Odd, he thought.

He also noted that her hair, which she usually wore tightly affixed in a neat chignon, looked somewhat contrary. Furthermore, her clothing that she'd always taken great pains to keep neat and completely without wrinkles, now seemed, well, mussed. In fact, if he hadn't known her better, he'd say she'd just had a lively tumble.

Of course, he did know her better. Such a thing was out of the question. He did find it odd, however that neither she nor Mr. Deveraux so much as looked at each other. Very odd.

The change in Emily's appearance was not overly noticeable, unless one was truly discerning of such things, and yet, her countenance seemed softer. Also, Jeffrey noticed that she kept to her usually closely guarded prim expression when speaking to everyone except Mr. Deveraux, who, throughout the entire meeting, had remained as silent as a specter in church.

Finishing her tea, she carefully settled the cup on the tray and smiled up at him. "I hope you and Mr. Deveraux will find your rooms suitable. Had I realized that we'd be having guests, I would have had the drapes and carpets replaced."

"I'm sure your accommodations will be most adequate, Emily." Jeffrey said. "If you'll excuse me, it's been quite a long afternoon what with the events of this morning and the long drive here. Gentlemen."

The captain rose from his seat, sending a silent summons to Deveraux. The other man for the first time since he'd arrived glanced briefly at Emily then nodded slightly before leaving them.

Branleigh closed his book. "I think I'll rest before dinner, as well. I've got some designs in mind for a new rifling, and as soon as I get things straight, I need to go over them with Pemberton. It could be the breakthrough that I've been searching for."

With that, he too left the room. Emily and Jeffrey were finally left alone, save for the butler, who was gathering up the tea service.

"The remainder of your journey went well?"

Emily looked down at her hands. "Yes, Jeffrey. It was enjoyable, but very long and tiring, I'm afraid."

Jeffrey wanted to press her for more details, but to do

so would have been ungentlemanly, and he was determined not to do anything that would make Emily uncomfortable.

"Of course. Perhaps you should rest before dinner, too. I'll see to all the arrangements for your guests."

Emily sat for a brief moment longer, looking at him as if she'd something important to say. She drew in a quick breath.

Jeffrey waited to hear the words he'd dreaded since their arrival. He feared she had changed her mind and decided to deny his proposal.

When she glanced up at him, Jeffrey held his breath.

She must have understood his expression of anxiety because when their eyes met, she quickly looked away.

"Is there something else?" he asked.

"No," she said, her voice sounding small and childlike.

Jeffrey wanted to turn away, to forget the irrational feeling of despair that was rising in him.

He actually did turn toward the door, but his sense of honor held his feet fast. He asked her a question, though he was not brave enough to face her when he did.

"Is there anything I've done that would make you change your mind? About our wedding, I mean."

A long silence stretched out between them.

Emily had reached forward and pulled a single white rose from the flower vase on the setting. She was holding it by the stem, her fingers placed carefully to avoid the thorns.

She glanced up at him, her eyes guarded. "A strange thing, a rose is. So beautiful and fragrant, and yet so dangerous."

Jeffrey's stomach tightened a knot. "I suppose that's true, yes."

A wan smile crossed her face. "So dangerous to hold and yet we're drawn to it, knowing full well that at any moment one of its thorns could easily pierce the skin. In spite of the danger, the petals are so soft and the scent so sweet, we cannot envision a life without it."

"I suppose that's true." Jeffrey tried to swallow the ball of ice that was forming in his throat.

Emily glanced up at him, clearly attempting to cover whatever melancholy had gripped her.

"You've been nothing but a perfect gentleman. You must never think anything but that. I adore the way you're being so kind and patient with me. Thank you."

Jeffrey nodded, the air of tension in the room settling to its usual calm. "I want you to be happy, Emily."

Jeffrey could have sworn he'd heard her sigh, but pausing outside the room, there had been nothing but the sound of an occasional breeze ruffling the curtains.

Yes, that's what it was. There wasn't the sound of a stifled sob, or that of a cloth being used to cover Emily's crying.

Jeffrey shook himself. Women were prone to getting a case of the bluebellies, now and then, weren't they? A slight pique, perhaps? Or maybe it was nothing but a bit of anxiety about the upcoming nuptials.

Yes, that's what it was.

It certainly wasn't anything that happened in the last twenty-four hours, nor did it involve the mysterious Mr. Deveraux. Jeffrey was certain of that.

To think otherwise would have meant disaster.

Although Tristan wanted nothing more than to run as fast and as far as his legs could carry him, coward that he was, he couldn't abandon Emily to the evil that threatened her. He'd have to face this messy business, find whoever it was that threatened her and her uncle, and be done with it as soon as possible.

"Well," Hamilton said from the door. "Any 'readings'?"

Tristan sat gingerly on the edge of the bed. The room was far more ornate than any place he'd ever slept. The furniture was solid oak, polished to a shine so exquisite that he could likely see his own reflection if he was so inclined.

Heavy drapes, embroidered with intricate geometric designs, covered the windows, and thick carpets covered polished hardwood floors.

"Well?"

Tristan sighed. "I am impressed by the amount of money it must take to build a place like this, pay the staff, and the indulgences of the wealthy in general, but no, nothing about your suspected killer."

"You'd best be about it. It wouldn't do to wait too long."

Tristan shook his head. "You don't understand how this works. You think I can just open up their heads and extract the information, like removing a bullet? It doesn't work that way."

"I think that the general was mistaken about your abilities. I think that you are crass and undisciplined. However, what I think isn't important. My orders are to support you in any way you deem necessary and work with you to end this business once and for all. Now, what impressions did you get?"

Sighing, Tristan rubbed his eyes. "Not many, save for the fact that Emily is worried for her uncle and giving little care to her own happiness." Tristan let that barb sink in before continuing.

Hamilton hardened his expression. "Who are they suspecting?"

"Miss Durbin? Everyone. Lord Branleigh is convinced he's safe enough, so he gives it little thought at all."

"I must say I'm disappointed in your abilities."

"I'm so sorry to have let you down. Perhaps you will see to sending me home and allowing me to return to my work."

"That is out of the question. General Henley believes the perpetrator, whoever he is, has a clear agenda. We must wait for him to show his hand."

"Wonderful."

"You will, of course, immediately inform me of anything out of the ordinary. Anything at all."

"Of course."

Once Hamilton had left him, Tristan loosened his neck cloth and then pulled off his boots. Settling back on the bed, he closed his eyes. Since his near lovemaking with Emily, it had been like a dozen carpenters hammering the same piece of wood to a bloody pulp in his head.

What was it about the woman that unsettled him so?

He'd been ready to surrender himself to her, to risk discovery, his very life for a few moments of losing himself in her womanly bliss.

Except that it was more than just lovemaking. It was total surrender. He would have been hers from that moment on, if he'd had the opportunity.

"Damn the fates that brought me here."

"You're not fit to wipe her boots. She's much better off with Hamilton."

Tristan sighed. His consciousness was right. He was a fool to think that he could ever have the kind of life that most men lead. Like the expensive furniture, fine clothes, polished floors, and all the other accoutrements of the wealthy. There was no place in Emily Durbin's life for a man like him, and he'd do best to accept it now. Hamilton's guarded expressions had told him that much.

Rubbing his temples, Tristan tried to relax. If only he could accept Emily's decision, but somewhere, deep inside, he held back a small hope. Damn his soul if he didn't want to try to gain her favor. It seemed that every moment they were together he was like a schoolboy climbing a tall tree just to impress his ladylove.

As if conjured by his thoughts, Emily appeared, tapping on the bedroom door, pulling him out of his reverie.

He could feel her presence, even through the thick wood. Like the scent of a rose, she lingered, teasing his senses.

Damn.

The woman was going to drive him mad before this business was through.

"Mr. Deveraux? I need to speak with you."

Tristan waited while she struggled to compose her thoughts, to hide her true feelings beneath her rational thinking. It did little good where he was concerned. The woman could have sung a symphony, but he would always hear the music of her sweet thoughts behind each note.

Emily drew a long breath before continuing. Tristan wondered if she knew what power she held over him. Instantly he clamped down on the thought. Clearly she didn't or the situation in the carriage would have surely come to completion.

"Yes, Miss Durbin?"

"I know this may sound absurd, but I feel we must face the truth of our situation."

"Our situation?"

The sound of her voice was sweet torture. Could he turn away the temptation of her closeness one more time? He began to perspire. Like a drunkard too long from the bottle, Tristan knew he could never refuse her.

"There's no other way. We must discuss what is between us, or I'm afraid we both shall say or do something which would prove disastrous."

"Go on," he said, still fighting the urge to throw open the door and draw her into his arms. In those brief seconds he battled in his mind too vivid memories of her smooth, silky skin against his own, her hungry, musky scent, and the taste of her skin. It was almost more than he could bear.

"I'd rather not discuss it in the hall, Mr. Deveraux. Please, you must let me come inside. I promise not to do anything rash."

Tristan leaned his head against the doorframe. A trickle of sweat melted down the side of his face. The heat from her, even through the solid oak door, was almost unbearable.

Suddenly Tristan had a vision of himself perched high

on a mountain, feet mired in the muddy slope with the rain pouring over him. It wasn't a matter of his feet losing their purchase, but of the entire mountainside disintegrating beneath his feet.

Emily was the rain that pelted him, and the ground of sanity he stood on turned into a morass of emotions that he could not withstand.

"Miss Durbin, this isn't . . ." he started, but the sight of her in his mind stopped his breath in his chest. It was no use. Giving in to his need to touch her, he opened the door, and grabbing her arm, pulled her inside.

"Oh!" She stumbled forward, but still holding her, Tristan promptly righted her, while using his foot to close the door behind him.

For a brief second, he held her. They stood unmoving as he searched her expression.

"Mr. Deveraux," she began, but her breath left her.

Tristan dipped down and touched his lips to hers.

That was all it took. As if a match were struck, a flame flared between them. Suddenly his hands were traveling over her and she answered him with a low, throaty moan.

Desire, hot and urgent, coursed through them both.

"Mr. Devereux," she murmured, pulling back from him. "This is not . . ."

Tristan would not be denied. He pursued her, his mouth chasing hers until she surrendered to his kiss. Before she could protest, he continued caressing her, his mouth moving along the line of her jaw and down her throat to settle in a spot between her neck and collarbone.

She moaned again. Then, taking a deep breath, she hurried out her next sentence, at the same time pushing him away.

"This is not a good idea. We could be caught."

"I want you," he said, his voice thick and hoarse as he spoke. "I don't give a damn if you're engaged. I want you now."

Tristan advanced again but was stopped short by her hands on his chest.

"No."

In the flash of a second, her command paralyzed him. It seemed that she did indeed have control over him. Somehow, Tristan didn't find it as disturbing as he might. It made him want her all the more.

"As you like," he said, pulling back from her, surprised at how easily he could do as she commanded.

"Good."

Although she'd gotten her way, Tristan felt her disappointment as well. Like his, her body throbbed to finish what they had begun.

That thought gave him no end of delight. At least he wasn't the only one drowning in delightful misery.

Taking a breath, struggling to steady his body's response to her, Tristan motioned her to the desk chair in the other corner of the room. When she sat down, he leaned against the armoire. Taking two deep breaths to steady himself, he began.

"What is it that's so important, Miss Durbin?"

As delicate as the leaves fluttering in a breeze, a small laugh escaped her. "Please, I cannot stand this continued formality between us. After we nearly, ah, that is . . ." She dropped her gaze downward as the delightful pink blush rose in her cheeks. "Please call me Emily."

The endearment startled him. Though he was adept at reading minds, emotions were quite another thing. Too often he found himself drowning in the feelings of others. White-hot anger was the worst, despair after that. But this?

This was something entirely different. He'd known those who had been fond of him. Women who'd thought him handsome and mysterious, and very attractive. In a few instances, some had pursued him like a hound chasing a fox.

Those occurrences had made him supremely uncomfortable. Though he had no idea why. Perhaps it was primal instinct but each female who'd pursued him wanted only to possess him.

But Emily hadn't wanted this power she held over him.

While she did lust after him, she hadn't given a thought to plotting how she would keep him either as a husband or a lover.

She simply desired him with an unbearable need that neither of them understood. It was raw and wanting, and like his own need, it was almost more than either one of them could bear.

When she asked him to use her first name, her given name, it had nearly been his undoing. Tristan would have given her his soul if she'd asked for it.

Without pausing, he found himself answering her in kind. "Of course, but only if you'll call me Tristan."

The smile she gave him was like seeing the sun after a hundred days of darkness.

Tristan felt his self-control slip just a bit more.

"Good. I'm so glad to be rid of formalities. I'm a simple girl at heart, you know. I get so tired of propriety all for its own sake. Don't you?"

When she gazed up at him, Tristan nearly fell into her deep indigo gaze, her eyes nearly opaque, except for the tiny bits of sparkling light, like stars littering a midnight sky.

"In my line of work, propriety rarely is a concern."

Her blush deepened, and Tristan decided that her scarlet hue was now among his favorite colors.

"We have done you a terrible disservice and I'm so sorry for it."

"Are you?" Though he asked the question, Tristan well knew the answer. He merely wanted to hear it from her. If she were brave enough to speak her true feelings, it would raise her yet another measure in his eyes.

"It was never my intention."

Tristan read her carefully and as if sensing what he was doing, Emily opened herself to him unafraid. She didn't try to hide from him, not like others he had known. People usually cloaked their secrets.

Hell, he had guarded his own.

"Who do you think wants your uncle dead?"

The question was simple enough, but the answer in her was not. A twisted logic spun in her mind now. Thoughts coming one after another, each one more upsetting to her than the first.

"I'm not sure," she said at last. "It could be anybody. I mean, Uncle Aldus is not an easy man to be around."

"Yet, you're very fond of him."

She nodded. "He's difficult for everyone but me, it seems. He feels I am his compatriot, his only friend."

"Why is that?"

"Because I always tell him the truth." She paused, a shadow of regret crossing her expression. "Well, almost always, that is."

"Until lately?" he offered, crossing his arms and leaning slightly forward. He knew already what had caused the rift between them. To her credit, she didn't try to defend herself.

"Until I accepted Jeffrey's proposal. Well, that and my other three proposals."

Emily's embarrassment went a shade deeper.

"I see," Tristan said, keeping his voice even. For no reason he could understand, the thought of Emily in another man's arms unsettled him greatly.

Emily sighed. "Three times to the altar and never married for longer than a day."

Tristan smiled. "You're scandalous."

She sent him a sharp glance. "You're making sport of me now. You've heard the stories, I'm sure."

He laughed. "I'm afraid that on my side of the town we're not indulged with tales of society's escapades."

Realizing her blunder, Emily started. "I'm sorry. That is, I didn't mean to insult you."

He shrugged. "It's the truth. You've said there are those who don't particularly care for Lord Branleigh? Perhaps we should make a list."

"That's an excellent idea. There's Lord Baker and all of Uncle's associates at the gentlemen's club. They say he cheats at cards. There's Lady Henworthy and her nieces.

My uncle insulted them at the party announcing my second engagement. He said that they truly were 'hen worthy,' in that they all sported beaks and chicken feet like their feathered counterparts."

Tristan laughed. "Did he? A most grievous statement."

"Uncle Aldus is like that. Whatever comes into his mind immediately falls out of his mouth. It can be most disturbing at times."

"And most entertaining, I'm sure."

Emily smiled. She had the most perfect mouth, Tristan thought.

He shook himself. Best to try to put down his growing list of Emily's positive attributes or he'd get nothing at all accomplished.

"Perhaps we should stick to those for now. At least it's a beginning. Will we be meeting any of these people soon?"

Emily paused. "There's the Harrington's ball. It's tomorrow night, though I wasn't really planning on attending."

"No? Why not?"

"Lydia Harrington is a spiteful woman who makes it her life's work to belittle me in front of the entire *ton*. Joseph, my second betrothal, turned her over for me. She was insanely jealous."

"Blames you for his demise, no doubt. How did he die?"

"Fell under a runaway carriage right before our wedding. It was a terrible accident. We'd gotten in the coach together, but I noticed that my reticule was missing. Just as he was getting down to help me find it, something spooked the horses."

"How terrible," Tristan said, quietly, trying to ease her distress.

"His jacket had become caught in the wheel, and when he tried to get it loose the carriage took off. The next thing we knew he was under the cab and being dragged down the lane."

"Indeed a tragedy."

Emily dabbed at her eyes. "You know what the worst

part of it was? I never really cared for him all that much. I mean, he was very sweet, and most attentive, but Lydia was truly fond of him and I came between them."

"You shouldn't blame yourself entirely, after all, your Joseph was a man, responsible for his own actions." He thought for a moment. "With three weddings you seemed quite in demand for the marriage mart. I've never thought that men of substance such as your suitors were so quick to dive into the river of the marriage mart. Why do you think that is?"

She shrugged. "I'm not really sure. My family never has been very wealthy. Uncle Aldus is the one with all the assets. After the first attempt on his life, the next thing I knew I had a list of suitors a city block long. Most distressing, you know."

Tristan drew in a breath. "Emily, do you and your uncle have any other living relatives?"

She shook her head, making the small curls on her forehead bounce lightly. "Some distant cousins to the north, but they were on my father's side. There is just the two of us. Why?"

"Perhaps all the single gents realized what a good catch you'd be. After all, it only goes to follow that your uncle's holdings would likely go to your husband if you were married."

Emily shot to her feet. "I never realized. I mean, it never occurred to me because I don't consider any of his possessions mine. But that certainly makes sense, doesn't it."

"I'm afraid so. At least we can understand why all the gentlemen are pursuing you so determinedly. Now, about your uncle's attempted murders."

Emily paused a moment. Something else began to skirt the edge of her thoughts. She gave Tristan a curious glance.

He sighed. "You have nothing to worry about in Mr. Hamilton's case. He is quite smitten with you. He doesn't even know about your potential inheritance."

"Well, that's good. I mean, no, that's terrible."

"You're going to break his heart, aren't you?" Tristan asked softly.

A worried expression rose in her eyes. "I don't want to. I shouldn't have accepted his proposal in the first place, but after three times, a girl becomes . . ."

"Desperate?"

She gave him a scathing glance. "Worried. It was never my intention to be a bother to my uncle. Besides which, I am one and twenty."

"Well past the age of freshness, eh?"

She gave him a sharp cut with her eyes. "You know, Tristan, even if you can read a girl's mind, it wouldn't be so difficult to be a bit more careful in choosing your words."

"You have my sincerest apologies."

Her expression softened. "I know you didn't mean an insult. Never mind."

"Thank you for understanding," Tristan said. Too few people in his life had ever been quick to forgive him anything.

"Yes, well. Perhaps we'd best stop here."

The tide of discomfort rose between them. Emily's heartbeat quickened and he realized that if they stayed too long in each other's company it would likely end in disaster.

"I agree," he told her. Walking to the door he opened it and felt the cloak of sadness now wrapping around her.

"I'm sorry," she said in a hurried tone.

Tristan wasn't sure if she was regretting their earlier encounter, or the fact that she'd yet again turned away from him. Either way, her words struck him hard.

"As am I," he said after her, and meant it.

Chapter Thirteen

The dinner had been expertly prepared, the lighting was to perfection, and the soft music provided by a violinist set the background for what should have been a pleasant evening ahead. Emily looked down at her plate and saw that even the vegetables had been arranged to please the palate. So, why was she feeling as if something horrible had invaded their serenity?

Seated at the dining table's head was her uncle, whose entire attentions were focused on the small, leather-bound book before him. Next to him was his assistant, Jessup Pemberton. Beside him, and directly across from her sat Tristan who had thus far kept his own eyes cast down, not daring to even glance in her direction. It was a small dinner party, but one would have thought it a funeral based on the silence that hung among them.

"I hope you gentlemen find the food adequate. I know it's not as fanciful as town fare, but our cook, Mrs. Stanley, does labor hard."

"It's a lovely set table," Pemberton nodded to Branleigh as he used his spoon to slurp up the very last of his lobster bisque.

Emily only smiled in answer, careful not to encourage too much attention from the man.

"Especially the soup," Tristan said, sending Emily a playful expression.

Emily bit down on her grin as Pemberton dropped his spoon into his bowl. He narrowed his eyes and cast them downward. Emily was certain if there had been more cutlery at the table, Tristan might have been a target for an "accidental" stabbing. As it was, she quickly cleared her throat.

"Mr. Pemberton, you must try the roast venison. It is quite well done tonight. I believe Mr. Stanley had quite a time hunting the other day."

Branleigh coughed once and reached for his water glass. "Mr. Stanley would do better to tend to the landscaping more and his hunting party a bit less, don't you think? The garden is a shambles this year."

Emily forced her smile to stay. "I fear it's the fault of too much rain this season, Uncle. Not even poor Mr. Stanley can control that."

"Yes, well he always seems to find some excuse or another. It won't be fit for the wedding at this rate."

Emily nearly choked. Jeffrey sat silent beside her. She could see his spine stiffen slightly at her uncle's statement, but to his credit he said little.

"Tell me, Deveraux," Jeffrey began, quickly changing the subject, "were you studying for your medical degree at university?"

"I was apprenticed here in London. My mentor, Sir Alfred Brumly, perished in a house fire prior to my signing up with the army. I owe him a great deal."

"Really. Poor devil. House fire, eh? That's a terrible ending. Personally, I'd rather die in battle."

Tristan swallowed hard. "Excuse me, this isn't fit dinner conversation in front of the lady," Tristan said. "Tell me, Miss Durbin, how are the plans for the wedding coming?"

It was Emily's turn to hedge. "Quite well. It's to be a small affair, at St. George's at ten o'clock in the morning on the fourteenth. I have a nice wedding breakfast planned. I hope you will join us."

Tristan set down his fork. "Surely you would want only family present."

Emily glanced down at her plate as well. "Uncle Aldus is my only close relative. Jeffrey has two brothers and they will be attending with their wives, I believe, so an extra guest would not be a hardship."

"A damned waste of time, if you ask me." Aldus never looked up from his book.

"Uncle!"

"Well, look at the disaster of the other three near misses. I'm not one to figure on curses or some such frippery, but rather on percentages. At this rate you might have a chance around the twenty-third or twenty-fourth attempt."

Tristan cleared his throat. "I'm sure things will go off well, Miss Durbin. A fellow would be a fool to not face down even death to get you to the altar. Captain Hamilton is a most fortunate man."

Tristan watched as Emily blinked back her tears. The pain of the conversation was weighing on her heavily.

"Thank you, Mr. Deveraux. I appreciate your compliments. I'm sure things will go well this time."

Emily glanced up. For a moment their eyes were locked together as if frozen in a glass sculpture.

Tristan sensed everyone's attention on them, but he didn't care. The sight of her gaze warmed him from the inside out.

"Emily?" Jeffrey said beside her.

The sound of his voice broke the spell Tristan held upon her. He could feel her embarrassment rise as a heated flush overtook her.

"I'm sorry. I'm afraid I'm not feeling very well at the moment. I need a spot of fresh air."

"Emily," Jeffrey said as she rose to her feet. "Are you sure? It's a rather brisk evening."

"You're correct, as usual, Jeffrey. Perhaps I shall just retire to my room and open the window. Gentlemen."

Tristan drew in a breath. Emily knew she was running for

her life, but she couldn't help it. The air had suddenly pressed down upon her, and if she didn't make her excuses and exit in haste, she would shout to the heavens her true feelings. It wouldn't do to break Jeffrey's heart in such a public way. She knew she would have to break their engagement soon, or this time it would be her fleeing the altar.

Tristan watched her go with a deep regret. They'd been very close to exposing themselves to the others present.

Any interaction with Emily seemed a path to disaster he couldn't turn away from.

"I see you and Emily are becoming quite close," Branleigh remarked to Tristan when all of them had returned their attention to the food.

"She has been very kind to me."

"Yes, I was quite taken back by her request to ride in the coach with you, without a chaperone, in fact," the viscount mentioned.

Jeffrey's head shot up. "You left her alone? With him?"

"I assure you, nothing happened that would have compromised your bride to be." Tristan could swear they would see through his thin lie at any moment. He may not have done the damage, but he'd surely wanted to.

"You should have refused. Only a crass, lowly bred cur would accept such a circumstance."

Branleigh cut another slice of his venison. "Nonsense. I rode quite closely by the carriage. Nothing happened between them."

Tristan instantly sensed the other man's lie. He'd seen them!

The viscount gave him a pointed look. It was dark and dangerous and Tristan felt as if he'd swallowed a cup of acid.

"Was this your idea, my lord?" Hamilton asked, turning his attention to Branleigh. "Were you attempting to undermine our courtship?"

"No, actually it was Emily's idea. She insisted."

Pemberton grunted beside them. "Miss Durbin is

above suspicion," he said, nodding toward Branleigh who sat unmoving.

"I concur. And she's an excellent judge of character"— he stared directly at Hamilton as he spoke—"at least in most instances."

After the meal concluded, the gentlemen retired to the library for a glass of brandy. Branleigh quickly finished his after-dinner cordials and ordered Pemberton to the laboratory, mumbling something about a new study of dynamic igniting materials. Tristan watched the two men go with interest.

"This Pemberton fellow," Tristan began. "Do you know him well?"

"He's been with Branleigh for some time. The two are nearly inseparable. Why?"

"I don't know. He's a bit of a puzzle, don't you think?"

"I don't understand," Hamilton said, tipping up his glass and taking a drink.

"He was watching Miss Durbin throughout dinner. I found his interest a bit disconcerting, myself."

Tristan had had several impressions at dinner. First, there was the way Branleigh himself had paid close attention to those present without ever lifting his brow. Pemberton had almost been totally consumed with thoughts of Emily, as had the commander himself, both men clearly pining for her.

"That seems to be the case whenever Emily's present. She's like the first spring flower. So beautiful, she can't help but attract attention."

Tristan gave him a sharp look. "You're a most fortunate man."

"Lord Branleigh is not enamored with the idea of our impending nuptials."

"It doesn't seem like he's approved of any of Miss Durbin's suitors."

"He believes that she's wasting her time. I suppose he thinks there is no one worthy of her attention."

"Perhaps, but I think you're about as close to that standard as anyone. I wish you both a happy marriage."

Tristan lifted his glass and feigned taking a drink. He detested alcohol. Drink too much and he risked revealing himself to others.

"Thank you. I am hoping the same. Emily and her well-being are tantamount."

Though he'd spoken the words well enough, Tristan could sense the ire rising in the other man's mind. He knew that unless Hamilton gave it voice, there was little chance of it dissipating. "Just be plain with it, Captain. What do you really mean?"

"I saw what transpired between the two of you at dinner. Emily has a delicate nature. She's already been hurt too many times. The loss of her family, her disastrous attempts at matrimony, and the hideous scandal that followed them, all have had a terrible effect on her. She's vulnerable."

"As she might have been when you proposed marriage to her?"

Hamilton's jaw clenched. "Just make certain that you don't disturb her anymore than you already have. I'll not stand for it."

Tristan nodded. "You've no need to worry about me. I plan to stay as far away from your fiancée as possible."

"I plan to stay as near to Tristan Deveraux as possible," Emily told her uncle. Concerned, he'd stopped at her door on the way to his own room.

"Do you think that's wise?"

"I think he is the key to your safety, Uncle. He's an excellent judge of character."

"Is he? I'm not sure he can even take care of himself. General Henley didn't believe so, at any rate."

"But he's the one who sent him here."

"Only to use his most improbable talent of reading minds. The man's a puzzle, to be sure."

"I've seen proof of it, Uncle. He has an uncanny ability to know things about people. I'm not sure how he does it, he just does."

Emily had decided not to tell her uncle even the smallest hint of her experience with Tristan. Not only was it a scandalous thing for an engaged woman, but she sensed he already suspected too much.

"It seems he has you convinced of his abilities."

"Yes, he does."

"Are you quite sure? I've seen tricksters who used subterfuge to gain the confidence of their audience."

Emily shook her head. "He's not like that. He's here under duress. General Henley forced him to come and given half a chance he'd return to the battlefield without hesitation. I believe his talent is genuine."

Branleigh nodded. "Then I'll accept your estimation. I only wish you could be so encouraging where your involvement in potential suitors is concerned."

Emily sighed. "If it makes you feel any better, I am thinking about ending my engagement to Jeffrey. I know he cares very much, I'm just not certain that's enough to build a life on."

Branleigh nodded. "I know your good sense will set you in the right direction. Just stay the course, young lady. You'll make the right decision."

Emily wished she could be so sure. "Good night, Uncle."

After giving him a kiss on the cheek, she turned into her room. Exhausted, she thought for certain she would surely have an uneventful, dreamless sleep.

Unfortunately, that was not the case.

After his verbal sparring with Hamilton, Tristan's only thought was to go to bed and for a short while forget the turmoil that had invaded his life. Even the voice of his conscience had remained silent.

But Tristan's intentions were short-lived. When he arrived at his room, he opened the door to reveal he had a visitor.

"Lord Branleigh?"

"Mr. Deveraux. I hope I'm not disturbing you."

Tristan looked up into the sharp blue gaze that studied him. He thought that if there was anyone alive who could see into his soul, it would be Branleigh. His eyes didn't just study him, they penetrated into his soul, formed a judgment, and passed sentence—all within the space of a few seconds.

"Not particularly. I was merely thinking how nice it would be to get a few hours of sleep. Please, sit back down."

The gentleman resumed his seat in the desk chair while Tristan settled on the bed.

"What is it you wish to talk about?"

The old man looked straight at him, without blinking.

"What are your intentions toward my niece?"

Tristan felt the breath go out of him. Suddenly, the entire evening's events came into focus. The old man had been paying close attention to him after all. He'd wanted to meet like this, to catch Tristan off his guard, to see if he had the mettle to be the man for Emily.

Tristan's conscience finally aroused, gleefully cackling at the surgeon's discomfort.

"Easy does it, man. He's trying to catch you up. He doesn't care for Hamilton and he's set on using you to oust him from his niece's affection."

Tristan didn't know whether to shout in joy or fall to his knees. He certainly did have designs where Emily was concerned, though it was his baser nature that seemed to rule supreme whenever they were together.

"I have no intentions, sir. "

"Liar!" his conscience fairly roared at him. With effort, he put his mind's accusation aside.

It wasn't exactly a lie. He knew that between their difference of class and the small matter of her already being engaged, anything more than what had already transpired was without hope. He'd answered as honestly as he could, given the circumstances.

"Is that why the two of you barely acknowledged each other during dinner? That is until the end of the dinner. I saw the look you gave her."

Tristan felt a knot begin to twist in his stomach. "I don't know what you mean."

"Of course you do. Don't play me the fool. I won't abide by it. You gave a valiant effort to distance yourselves from each other. I want to know why."

"Your niece is engaged. I'm sure Captain Hamilton seated at the table is reason enough for a gentleman like myself to keep his distance."

"Nonsense. He may be an upright soldier, but he's not marriage material for my niece. I've known Emily since she was a child and by the gods her interest was in you. I want to know your intentions where she's concerned. Are you going to act on them? Or are you going to break her heart?"

Tristan's mouth went dry, and the air escaped from his lungs. The audacity of the man's words struck him directly at his center and he, a man who could read minds like the headlines in a periodical, had not seen this coming.

"Surely you know that anything between us is impossible," he said, though even to his own ears it was a weak argument.

"Impossible? I know many impossible things, young man, but a joining of the two of you is not among them. Unless you think you're better than she?"

Tristan jumped to his feet. "No, never that. If anyone is unworthy, it is I. I'm the bastard son of a gypsy witch and a disgraced nobleman."

There, he'd said it. Years had passed since he'd heard that particular phrase. That was what his Great-Uncle

Cantor used to say to him. Even now his uncle's declarations still rang loud in his thoughts.

"Pah! Indeed. You're not worthy of affection. You're a disgrace to anyone of any real breeding."

Tristan swallowed his shame. "Your niece is beyond perfect, sir."

The old man studied him. The scientist possessed a crisp, ordered mind which allowed nothing frivolous or chaotic inside. He looked at all of life's problems like they were intricate puzzles, ones which, if he worked hard enough, he could manage solutions to.

Lord Branleigh's gruff expression melted into a smile. "At least you're an honest sort. The only thing that matters here is Emily's happiness. Regardless of your 'breeding,' and of whatever else you've imagined to be your shortcomings, Emily is fond of you and you are of her. You've nothing else to concern you."

Tristan looked away a moment. "If only that were true. There are, other things . . ." he said, evenly.

"I thought as much." Branleigh's tone grew softer. "Whatever troubles you, my boy, don't let it stand in the way of your happiness. I did once and have regretted it every moment since."

Tristan remained silent as the older man left him. There was so much that he'd wanted to tell Lord Branleigh. Yet, it would have done little good in the end. He hadn't known about the cloud of doom that lay over Tristan. A past he could not reconcile with, a future that was as dangerous as crossing the moors on a moonless night. No, he must stay the path he was on. Finish this business once and for all and forget that he'd ever kissed and almost bedded Emily Durbin.

Chapter Fourteen

Pemberton watched Branleigh leave Deveraux's room. There had definitely been something between the two, and he was certain it had to do with Emily. Leaning against the door, he listened with interest to their exchange.

As the minutes passed, his anger grew by bounds. How dare the old fool pass her off to a man like Deveraux! Especially since Branleigh had attempted to crush his own hope of ever courting the lady.

It was unthinkable, to match those two. Better to have the girl marry a gutter rat, than the likes of Deveraux.

Jessup was still unclear on the reason for the man's even being at Beldon Hall. He was a medical man, yes, but to Jessup's knowledge, Branleigh was in perfect health. It made no sense.

Returning to his room, Jessup dressed quickly and then slipped out of the house and down the lane. The Broken Crown, a small pub that sat but a mile from the center of the wealthy neighborhood, was as likely a place as any to learn what he needed. He'd enough coin in his pocket to buy information and when he did he planned to use it to his best advantage.

The brisk walk to the pub was not a difficult one. In fact, it gave him a chance to think. To consider his options.

Entering the Crown, he ducked beneath the notice of the barman and went to the back of the smoke-filled room. At a single table in the farthest corner sat his longtime acquaintance, Horace Beardsley, a man who, though nearly twice Jessup's height, had shrunken himself down to avoid notice by any but the most discerning eye.

Across from him sat an older man, bent and wrinkled with age, a scowl and a battered felt hat drawn down to cover his eyes, hiding his identity as well.

Glancing up, Horace's guest gave Jessup a frown and then excused himself from the table. Pulling his collar higher, the old man stooped even lower and made his way out of the tavern.

Jessup thought nothing odd about the exchange, especially since Beardsley was a man who had valuable things to offer many people.

"My old friend. Buy you a drink, eh?"

Beardsley looked up at him and gave him a grimace. "Are you trying to poison me with this pig's swill? Of course, I'll have to oblige you now, you old goat."

That was usually how any conversation with Horace started. He bitterly complained about the spirits but readily drank his fill.

"What brings a whey-faced townie like yourself out on a night like this?" he grumbled after downing his port and belching twice.

"Some bit of information, is all. Not worth much, no more than a shilling or two, most likely."

"If it's brought you out of your high-an'-mighty flop, it must be worth more than that. Go on, ask, and as usual I'll set the price."

Jessup cleared his throat. "You've heard talk of an investigation at Beldon?"

"I've heard that there's been some 'accidents' that might be something more than that, aye. Go on."

"You know my employer, Lord Branleigh has been placed in protective custody."

Horace shrugged. "'Tis old news."

"Well, it involves a strange fellow who's acting as a personal doctor to his lordship, though he's not even a physician proper."

Horace leaned closer. "Really? Anybody we know?"

Jessup shook his head. "The name's Deveraux, he's a surgeon's apprentice the military assigned to stay with his lordship. Though why they'd want a cutter is beyond me. It's all a puzzle, you see."

At the mention of the surgeon, Horace's spine stiffened. He sat up to his full height and gave Jessup a wary eye.

"Has he said anything about his mission since his arrival at the Hall?"

Jessup shook his head. "Not that I'm aware of, though I can tell you, he has his eye on Miss Durbin. He's a quiet sort, barely even lifts his eyes to you when he's speaking."

"What does this fellow look like? What's his age and all?"

After telling Horace all he knew, Jessup downed the last of his drink and instantly regretted it. The foul liquid burned the back of his throat and all the way down to his stomach.

Beardsley set his own mug back on the scarred wooden table. "I'll do a bit of digging for you, free of charge, if you keep your trap shut about what we've discussed. There was just a fellow here who was looking for a gent that fits yon surgeon's description. If it turns out to be this lad, then I'll give you ten percent of my take."

Jessup rubbed his chin. He wasn't interested in any profit from his inquiries, and had in fact been prepared to pay. However, this could yet turn to his advantage.

"Keep your money, just tell me who it is that's looking for Deveraux."

Horace shook his head. "Not this time, Jess. He's a bad one, I tell you. I once saw him cut out a bloke's liver, cook it up, and feed it to him as he lay dying right there before us. Let me handle it. I'll get you your information if I can."

Jessup nodded. It was best to go along with Horace, at

least for the time being. Once he had more information, then he'd decide best how to handle this new complication.

"Deal," he said, and tossed another coin on the table. "Have another cup of that swill, on me, won't you."

After Pemberton had left the pub, Horace pulled out the paper the old man had left him. Scrawling down the name and address of Lord Branleigh, he called to the barkeep.

"Keep my seat warm, I'll be back in an hour. If all goes well, we'll be breaking open a cask—on me."

The long hours of the night dredged on and Emily turned several times, restless and angry. Her life had turned to pure turmoil and she wasn't one to take it well. She liked a simple, ordered life. One that involved running the household, caring for her uncle, attending to friends, and generally keeping to herself. Although she'd been sick with grief after what had happened to Clive, Michael, and Joseph, feeling somehow certain their deaths had been her fault.

So now she lay, eyes wide open, thinking about everything, the danger to her uncle, her engagement to Jeffrey, and finally, her growing affection for Tristan.

Even now, hours after they'd parted, she could still feel his nearness, still delighted in how he'd held his breath when she'd touched him. She remembered the way his hands had felt upon her, and even the stirring of desire when he kissed her. Yes, she could easily close her eyes and imagine him nearby.

In the back of her mind he was there, the hum of his need for her constantly in her thoughts. Although she didn't understand it, she knew that if she so much as called out to him, he would come to her.

"Tristan . . ."

A moment later, a light tapping sounded on her door. Though she knew she was courting danger, Emily couldn't help herself any longer. With a desire stronger than she'd ever known, she wanted him. Her body trembled with the excitement.

Rising from her bed, she slowly approached the door.

He was close.

Opening the door, she peered into the hall. She hadn't had to look. She'd known it was him. She'd summoned Tristan with her mind, and like a marionette, he'd jumped to her pull of his strings.

"Please," he said.

"I'm sorry?"

"I can't stand it any longer. You've been torturing me for hours. You must let me make love to you this instant, or go to sleep."

"Oh." Emily's heart beat a pace faster. She stood for a moment, speechless.

Tristan waited for her decision, the evidence of his arousal tightening in his trousers. All at once the memory of their imagined lovemaking and the close call in the carriage came bursting into her mind.

"Well? Which is it?" he asked.

He didn't move, in fact, waited for several seconds for her to invite him in.

"Come inside and we shall discuss it," she said, though her voice quivered with anticipation.

He shook his head and sent her a smoldering expression written on his moist brow and in the way his teeth chewed just slightly on his bottom lip. Panting, he appeared as though he'd just run across the yard.

"No more discussion, Emily. Not now, not ever."

Emily licked her lips. She knew that if she did as her body begged her, she could never turn back.

"Which is it, then?"

"Come in," she said at last, and the next thing she knew he was lifting her in his arms, his mouth finding hers, and he was kicking the door closed behind them.

Leaning with his back against the door, holding her to him like a desperate man holding onto a lifeline, he kissed her deeply. Emily barely had time to take a breath before she was returning his passion, matching it with her own, devouring him with her mouth.

In two long strides, they crossed the room and collapsed on her bed, both of them working in a fevered rush to remove clothing and touch each other in every possible way.

"Tristan," she moaned when he kissed down the length of her neck and chest until his mouth closed on her left breast. Instantly, Emily arched her back, strained her body against his, and pushed her breast into his mouth even farther. He suckled her a few moments and then slid his mouth to the other breast where he continued teasing her sensitive flesh with his teeth, sending all sorts of riotous sensations throughout her body.

Emily cried out, begging him for more, and he did as she asked, tasting every inch of her, nibbling as he went, sliding his hand between her legs and massaging her until she thought she'd explode.

Feeling her so near to release, he growled.

"Not yet."

"Please!" She heard her voice and was surprised at the begging sound of it.

"Trust me," he said.

To her surprise and delight, Emily realized that she did indeed trust him.

Dragging his mouth from her breast, he took in a ragged breath.

"See what I see," he told her.

Emily saw herself, legs open beneath him, flesh pink and hot, her hips writhing on the sheets, her mouth round and her expression pleading.

She was both surprised and appalled at herself for such shameless behavior.

Tristan laughed beside her. "This is not wantonness, Emily. This is what every man desires. You are the most beautiful woman I have ever known."

"Am I?" she asked, momentarily unsure.

He smiled. "See for yourself."

Suddenly she was feeling all that he felt, knowing all that he knew.

She saw Tristan as a small boy, mourning his mother's death and fearing his father's violence. She saw an old man leaning over him, threatening him, preventing him from escaping into the black night.

She saw the first time he'd cut open a patient, and the time he'd helped deliver a baby, though he'd known that most surgeons considered themselves above such menial tasks.

Finally Emily saw him, wanting her as he'd wanted no other. She saw him being consumed by his need of her that night in the stockade, and then later, on the carriage ride home. He'd had many secrets to protect and now was willing to risk them all.

"Oh, Tristan," she said, caressing his face as he leaned over her.

"I love you," he said. "I know I will never be able to give you everything you deserve, but I will give you all that I have."

Emily nodded. "You are the only thing I want. Take me, Tristan. Make love to me."

She pulled him down, kissing him deeply and opening herself to him completely.

Moaning as he leaned over on her, he nudged her open, settling himself so that he was just at her opening.

"Make sure this is what you want," he told her, his voice straining against his need. "I can't hold back much longer."

Emily searched his face and knew he was telling the truth.

"I want you inside me," she breathed.

He nodded once and then placed gentle kisses on both of her eyes. Suddenly the pressure of him pushing inside her was all that she knew. A sharp pain cut her desire when he advanced into her, filling her with himself. The very next instant he was rubbing her temples and easing her pain.

"Focus on me," he told her in her mind. She nodded and realized that the moment she did so, the pain lessened, and a new fire began to burn inside of her.

Slowly, he began again, rocking her with a rhythm that stoked the flames. He read her thoughts and settled his body where she felt the most comfortable, though she could tell his need was growing with every second.

Emily began to pant, her body miraculously conforming to his. Seconds passed and the two of them quickened their pace until Emily felt she was about to explode. Together they became one—one being, one heartbeat, one soul. Faster and faster they went until Emily was sure she was about to shatter.

Then, pausing only a breath, Tristan pushed again and she took him wholly into herself. For a brief second they gasped together. Tighter, tighter, until there came the sudden, blessed release and they plummeted over the edge into oblivion.

Emily screamed.

"What in the blazes do you think you're doing!"

Vaguely, as if coming out of a fog, Emily became aware of Jeffrey's voice. Before she knew what was happening, he had reached out and dragged Tristan from the bed.

Enraged, Tristan turned and slammed his fist into Jeffrey. Before she could react the two were brawling before her.

"No!" Emily shouted.

The two men froze though neither acknowledged her. Jeffrey had a cut on his lip and a trickle of blood flowed freely down his chin.

"You despicable cur," he growled at Tristan. "What in blazes do you think you're doing?"

Tristan said nothing, but instead looked back at Emily.

Words and emotions lodged in her throat, and though she wanted to tell him the truth about her feelings for Tristan, she couldn't bear to hurt Jeffrey in such a way. Disaster loomed in her heart like a great heavy beast, ready to consume her no matter what.

Tristan cleared his throat and straightened his spine. Turning back to Jeffrey he finally answered.

"My apologies. I seem to have made a mistake."

Emily suddenly realized she could take no more. Seeing the two of them like that cut into her heart. "Get out!" Emily cried. "Both of you!"

"What the blazes is going on here?" Branleigh shouted from the hall.

Emily wanted to die. Her uncle, Jessup Pemberton, two chambermaids and her uncle's valet all stood gaping at the door.

"All of you! Out of here this instant!" Emily picked up her dressing gown from the foot of the bed and struggled into it.

Jeffrey struggled to his feet. "Outside, Deveraux. We will finish this man to man."

"As you wish," Tristan said quietly.

"No! Don't do this!" she begged, but he shot her one look.

"I won't hurt him," he said, pulling his trousers up and fastening them at the waist.

Before Emily could say more, he grabbed his shirt and left the room.

Emily pulled her own gown closed and went to the door to follow him. Her uncle stopped her there.

"Emily, it's best to let them settle this!"

"You don't understand. Jeffrey will kill him!"

"Nonsense. They're both sensible men. Now, cover yourself, miss, and meet me in the library. There are things we must discuss."

Emily had finally located her robes and with the help of her servant, had made herself somewhat presentable. She entered the library, immediately going to the window. Peering out into the dim night, she could just make out the figure of the two men who stood arguing in the garden.

"This is truly a disaster."

"And you've no one to blame for it but yourself, Emily." Her uncle said, now entering the room behind her. Though he spoke a reproach, his voice held no anger. As usual, Branleigh only spoke his mind.

"This is all my fault. I should never have accepted Jeffrey's proposal."

"Not to mention, disgraced yourself with Deveraux. A sticky business, this is. Of course, the two of you will have to marry."

Emily meant to answer him. Of course, she wanted to wed Tristan. But what of him? Did he want to marry her?

Emily had no further time to ponder the question. Suddenly, a single crack of a pistol shot split the night.

"No!"

She turned back to the window. Only one of the two men remained standing, the other had fallen to the ground. Emily's worst nightmare had come true.

Tristan felt the world crashing down on him. The instant that Hamilton pulled him from Emily's bed, he'd known the charade was finished. He'd done the unthinkable and now it was time to pay for his sins.

In seconds he made it to the front lawn where Hamilton waited, holding a set of pistols out to him.

"You've ruined her and I shall make you pay!"

Tristan stopped short. "I love her."

He knew it was a poor defense, even to his own ears it sounded inadequate.

"You have no right to say such things," Hamilton ground out.

"I know."

Suddenly the fight had gone out of him. He knew that if Hamilton won the duel, it would end more than just his life, it would free Emily to return to the life she deserved.

Hamilton ground his teeth. Pushing one of the pistols toward Tristan, he waited for him to take it.

"It's time to face your sins, Deveraux. Be a man and take what you deserve."

Tristan looked at the gun in his hand. It was already primed and it would be a simple enough act to point it and fire at Hamilton, though he knew his lack of experience with firearms condemned him to little chance of coming out the victor.

"I won't fight you." he said, but the other man only shook his head.

Hamilton raised his pistol, and Tristan could read his thoughts. His anger at Tristan warred with his pain at Emily's betrayal.

Though he hadn't wanted to, Tristan understood his rival. A man of honor and good intentions, he'd always been happy to settle for his lot in life. That was until Emily.

The truth was Jeffrey Hamilton had been smitten with her from their very first meeting and Tristan didn't begrudge him that. He'd known only too well what it was like to be so taken by Emily.

Nodding, Tristan pulled in a deep breath and took the pistol. As he stood there in the early morning hours, he knew his destiny lay but a few seconds away. He gladly accepted it, whatever the outcome.

"At your leisure, Deveraux," Hamilton called out.

Tristan didn't hesitate. Lifting his gun, he pointed it carefully toward the captain, and then moved it ever so slightly to the left. Sweat broke on his brow as he carefully squeezed the trigger.

A shot rang out and he felt the sudden burst of pain as it hit him, penetrating the muscle of his shoulder, the force of it knocking him to the ground.

But it wasn't the bullet that hit him the hardest. With the force of a cannon shot, another's thoughts burst into his mind. A blaze of burning pain ripped through him and he fell.

Murder. He could feel it, cold like the hand of death, and too ready to squeeze the life out of his victim. The target of the man's hatred was now coming down the front stairs, Emily in tow.

Flashes of vision hit Tristan's brain like a thousand shards of glass, splintering and then magically melding back together. He saw pictures of dead things, strewn about a graveyard. Animals, small and large, dead and bloated. On one side was a man, his carcass putrid and rotting. On the other, a young woman, her skin smooth and the gray-blue color of the recently deceased.

A man approached from outside the cemetery gate. He held a shovel in one hand and a rifle in the other.

"It had been so easy to kill them," he laughed. "So very easy."

It hadn't been his uncle's voice tearing through his mind, Tristan realized, but another whisper, stretched thin and higher pitched like a bow pulled across a sqeaking violin. Screeching laughter filled Tristan's mind, echoes of screams and a small boy's voice begging for mercy. It was more than Tristan could bear.

Tristan rolled to his side, pain shooting through him like a dozen knives severing his shoulder all at once. Gasping for air, he saw Lord Branleigh coming ever closer. Tristan tried to search the area around him, but the man who threatened him remained hidden in the shadows.

"No!" he called out, though his voice was barely above a whisper.

"Tristan!" Emily screamed.

In the corner of his eye, he caught sight of Hamilton charging across the yard.

"Emily, what have you done?"

That was when he saw her. Emily, the love of his life stood over him, her thoughts a whirl of desperation, pain, anger, and fear spinning out of control.

Tristan struggled to sit up, but the instant he did, the blood seemed to have left his head and he fell backward.

"Please, Tristan, stay still." Emily said beside him.

Tristan shook his head. "I saw him. The enemy," he whispered to Hamilton. "He's here!"

After that, the darkness consumed him, the ravenous thoughts of the murderer rushed into him and for a brief instant, Tristan was certain that Hamilton had indeed gotten his wish. Surely he must be dead.

Chapter Fifteen

Emily pressed the cold cloth on Tristan's forehead and he stirred under her touch.

"Easy, easy," she murmured, but her words did not calm him. They had settled him temporarily in the library, his long limbs now dangling off the end of the settee, his head pillowed by a blanket roll. He looked more like a disheveled child than a man who'd just been in a duel.

"What the devil happened?" Suddenly his memory returned with the force of a summer squall. "He shot me! Hamilton shot me!"

Emily hesitated. She wasn't sure she could explain her actions, or even if she did, that he would believe she'd had his best interests in mind when she'd pulled the trigger.

"Emily," he muttered beside her.

"No, it wasn't Jeffrey. He hadn't yet fired."

He shook his head, "Then, who?"

He must have felt the pain in his shoulder because he let out a hissing breath.

"We're not certain. Someone was hidden in the bushes. He was able to escape before Jeffrey's men arrived. He has searched the grounds twice and has yet to find the fiend."

Emily broke into a sob. "For heavens sake, Tristan! I could have lost both of you."

Tristan attempted to sit up, but it was clear that it was a vain effort. "Emily, please. You're engaged to Hamilton. It's best that way. I see the sense of it now." Tristan said. "You were right to send me away."

Emily shook her head. "You've got it all wrong. I didn't want Jeffrey to suffer for my foolish mistakes. I never should have consented to marry him. I was angry with you. I thought you didn't care for me."

He sighed. "It doesn't matter. Hamilton is the better man. He's loyal and strong, and you've seen to what lengths he'll go to protect your honor."

"But I don't love him." She said, unable to stop the words from coming out of her mouth.

"Well, you should. It's no good, you and I together." He shook his head. "Although, I can't help wishing it were otherwise."

He gave her a small smile and Emily delighted in it.

"If it's any comfort, the bullet went right through. It should be a few days, but I'm sure you'll be on your feet soon enough."

Tristan let out a slow breath, closing his eyes. "I guess I've made a mess of it, haven't I?"

Emily shook her head. "We both did. Listen to me. I don't care. I wouldn't have traded our night together for anything. You've done so much for me . . ."

"I've ruined you, is what I've done."

Emily touched his face gently. "Please don't say that. I'm not sorry."

"But your engagement, your reputation . . ."

"None of that is important to me. It never was. I've yet to officially break off my engagement with Jeffrey, and I feel awful that I've hurt him so terribly. As for my reputation, it was in shambles long before I met you."

She smiled at him, knowing he didn't quite believe her. It didn't matter. Given time, she was sure she'd convince him.

He took in a sharp breath. "I nearly forgot. I saw him, the man that threatened your uncle!"

"You did? Who is he?"

Tristan shook his head. "He was in the shadows but I felt his hatred toward your uncle, and now toward me. He's planning something."

Emily trembled. An uneasy feeling settled in the pit of her stomach. Was it someone they knew? Someone they considered a friend?

More than that, Emily knew that once Tristan revealed the man's identity, he would have fulfilled his orders from General Henley and it would be reason enough for him to leave.

She knew also that Tristan loved her as much as she did him. His love was not in question. He was an honorable man and would do nothing to compromise her.

On one hand she prayed he'd find the man responsible for threatening her uncle, and on the other she almost prayed he didn't.

Emily sat quietly beside him, holding his hand and giving him what comfort she could. She truly was fond of Hamilton, but her affection was nothing compared to the full out love she felt for him. If nothing else, his discomfort was well worth the delight of knowing that she cared for him so deeply.

Tristan closed his eyes. Now more than ever he needed to find the man who threatened her and her uncle. Sending out his thoughts, he hoped to find the fiend, to learn his identity once and for all.

It was almost there, he thought, as the specter loomed just out of his line of vision. If he concentrated he could still feel the essence of it, the man who wanted Branleigh dead.

He was filled with darkness and hatred and rage. There was something the man wanted above all else. Tristan took in another deep breath and tried harder.

It was a fever pitch, the way the thoughts came to him now. Anger, lust, fear, and death. This man knew more about death than life. He'd practiced his art of killing, sometimes with poison, sometimes with a blade, even a pistol on occasion. He'd spent long hours practicing, trying to improve his skill.

The killer was clearly not sane.

Then the vision was gone. Whoever it was had left Tristan's mind and there was no retrieving him.

"No!"

"What is it? Emily asked beside him, the scent of her lavender soap soothing his frayed senses.

"The vision. It's gone. He's gone. Damn the fates that brought me here, I can't feel him any longer."

"What in the devil are you going on about?"

Tristan looked up to see Hamilton at the door. He sighed. This was going to be more than difficult to explain.

"Nothing."

Hamilton narrowed his eyes at Tristan and then turned his gaze on Emily.

"I would have a few moments to speak with you, Emily. I believe you at least owe me that."

His words were short and clipped, and Tristan didn't have to read his mind to know that he was barely able to hold in his anger and disappointment.

"Jeffrey, perhaps later . . ."

Tristan reached out to her. "I'll be fine. He deserves to know the truth," he said softly. "Go on."

Emily shot him a worried expression but did as she asked. When the two were gone, Tristan closed his eyes.

He must have dozed because suddenly he awoke to another's presence in the room. Sitting upright, he faced his accuser with all the courage he could muster. Unfortunately, it wasn't enough.

Emily sat in the parlor with her fiancé, or rather soon to be former fiancé. Jeffrey stood staring at the fireplace and not looking at her for several minutes. She could see by the set of his jaw and the jerking muscle in his neck that he was trying to calm the rush of emotions that were running through him.

"Please, sit down, Jeffrey."

He sent her a sharp glance. "I don't think that would be a good idea at the moment."

"I know you're upset with me."

He gave her a mirthless laugh. "That doesn't begin to cover what I'm feeling."

"I'm sorry."

That likely was the last thing he wanted to hear, she thought, but it was enough to deflate some of the anger that must have been building in him.

"Why, Emily? Why him?"

She shook her head. It had all been so simple the night before. How could she begin to make him understand all that she had experienced with Tristan?

"I love him," she said quietly. "I don't understand it; I certainly can't explain it. I just do."

"What in blazes do you even know about him?"

She bit her lip before speaking, hoping to somehow make him understand something she didn't quite comprehend herself.

"He's a good man, Jeffrey."

"A good man? How can you be so sure? He's so guarded, so strange. How could you possibly love him?"

She shook her head. "I'm not sure I can explain it. I just knew it from the very first moment we met."

He scoffed. "That's impossible."

"It's the truth. Listen to me. I've almost been to the altar three times with men I didn't love. I would have settled for any one of them, and you as well. They were all worthy of a woman who loved them. I didn't."

"Emily, you don't have to explain . . ."

She put up her hand, determined to continue. "Clive was attentive and sweet. He promised me the world. I was very fond of him. No one was sadder than I when he choked at our wedding breakfast. Joseph would have done anything I asked and I knew he would have made a good husband."

Emily could barely go on, but she had to. She had to make him understand.

"I cried for three days when he fell beneath the carriage wheel. And sweet Devon, I didn't love him either, but he promised Uncle Aldus he would take care of me. What could I do? His death was the worst of all. There is no dignity to a man robbed and killed on his way to his own wedding."

"Terrible events, yes, but not your fault."

She shook her head. "I know I didn't cause their deaths, but I did something far worse. I never loved any of them. That was the biggest mistake of all. And, God help me, Jeffrey, I don't love you."

Jeffrey swallowed hard. "You are fond of me. I know couples who have started with much less."

"As do I, but that doesn't make it right. If you get the chance at love, Jeffrey, true love, you must follow your heart."

"Do you think that I don't care for you?"

"I think that you are a wonderful, sweet man, and that you deserve someone who is completely devoted to you."

"But Deveraux? He has no family, no inheritance. He has nothing but the army. Is that the kind of life you want?"

Emily had to admit she'd not thought beyond the moment of their first joining. That had been complete bliss. Surely he wouldn't leave her to go back to that life. Or would he?

"I don't know what the future holds, Jeffrey. I just know that I choose him. I only hope you can forgive me."

Jeffrey straightened his jacket and looked away for a few seconds. "I will always care for you, Emily. And when he disappoints you and you find that he is not what you think, I will be here, waiting for you."

Without saying anything more, he turned away, taking long strides out of the room.

Alone, Emily sat for a moment, the room growing cold around her. Of course she had her doubts, she'd had them from the beginning. An uncomfortable feeling grew in the pit of her stomach and she could find no way to put Jeffrey's words out of her mind.

What would Tristan do? Would he marry her? Would he agree to stay at Beldon Hall? So many questions flooded her mind that she thought of running back upstairs to ask him that instant.

Just as she rose, her uncle came to the door. "Emily, we have a guest. I'll need you to help me entertain him at dinner."

"Really? Who is it?"

"A Lord Cantor. He says he is Mr. Deveraux's uncle."

Earlier that morning, Cantor had awakened to the sound of pounding on his front door. His butler had answered it, but curious, he rose from his bed and after dressing, went downstairs to see who had had the audacity to call so early in the morning.

"Good morning, milord," Stanton had greeted him with a cup of hot tea and a plate of cakes.

"I heard someone knocking. Who was it?"

"A young lad, sir. He brought a missive for you." Turning, the butler retrieved it from the tea service.

Opening it, Cantor quickly scanned the page. It was good news indeed. Beardsley had made good on his promise. In less than one night, he had located the person that Cantor had been searching for nearly seventeen years.

Leaving his breakfast behind, he went to the library and quickly wrote out a card. Calling for Stanton, he gave his butler the note.

"Get this out immediately. Then, take this one hundred pound note to The Broken Crown and give it to a Horace Beardsley. Be quick about it."

Stanton bowed and set out to do as he'd been instructed. Once the task was finished, Cantor pulled out one more sheet of parchment. This message was the most delicate task of all.

> *Griffin,*
>   *You must return forthwith. An old acquaintance of ours has come home. You know whom I speak of.*
>   *Your Obedient Servant,*
>   *G. L. C.*

When he'd finished, he'd dressed and gone to the corner and called over one of the lads who'd been playing in the street. A quick exchange of information, a few coins placed in the boy's hand, and he quickly departed. Cantor watched him until he'd rounded the corner. Now it was time to take care of other business.

Hamilton cleared his throat. "You said something before you blacked out. You said you'd seen the enemy."

The first rays of daylight touched the windowpanes. Tristan stirred from his spot on the chaise longue and looked at Hamilton.

The man looked somewhat haggard, the events of the long, sleepless night were clearly written on the darkened circles that surrounded his eyes and the drawn lines of his face. Tristan sensed that he had found an uneasy peace with the events of the previous night, though he was far from happy about it.

"He's a good man, Tristan. You're not fit to clean his boots."

Tristan certainly agreed with his consciousness on that fact. Hamilton was definitely of a noble breed. Something that Tristan could never hope to aspire to.

"I felt something."

"Is it true? Has this devil managed to kill already?"

"Many times. I felt his hatred for Lord Branleigh, for

one, and his obsession for Emily as well. I'm afraid I've been added to his list of potential victims."

Hamilton grunted, not too disturbed by that thought.

Tristan sat up, the pain in his shoulder doubling and tripling as he did so.

"Who is it then? Someone in the house staff? His rodent of an assistant, Pemberton?"

Tristan closed his eyes. For all of his trying, he simply couldn't put a name to the enemy just yet.

"I'm not sure. I only felt his hatred, his lust for killing. Nothing else."

Hamilton scoffed. "You'd better make haste in discovering who it is, or the next bullet you catch might not be so kindly placed."

Tristan knew that all too well. "I believe he murdered Emily's former suitors."

Hamilton sat forward. "Really? Even the poor fellow who died choking on his wedding breakfast?"

"Of course, there's no way I can prove it, but I think he was given a poison that caused his windpipe to close up. I've seen men who've been stung by a bee whose venom made their necks swell up so tight that they stopped breathing. Sometimes there are those who have such violent reactions to foods such as shellfish or strawberries that it kills them almost instantly."

Hampton nodded. "And the others?"

Tristan rubbed his eyes. "The second man is a bit more difficult to explain, but I believe that someone might have tampered with the carriage's wheelbase and then spooked the horses. It's easy enough to do."

"Perhaps I could convince the local constable to recreate the scene, see if what you're saying is possible."

"For the last one, the devil must have hired someone to kill him and make it look like a robbery."

"To what purpose? And why threaten Lord Branleigh?"

Tristan shrugged. "Who knows? I did not have access to his thoughts that long." He sighed. "It's not that easy, you know, reading minds. With some people, it's like pushing yourself into a closed room. You must first find the door. Sometimes the door closes and you get trapped inside."

Hamilton nodded. "Why would this blackguard want these men dead? I take it he is smitten with Miss Durbin?"

"Yes, but it's not at all like a normal man's desire for a woman. He doesn't just want to marry her. He wants to own her, control her completely, shape her into his own idea of womanly attributes."

To his shock, brief visions burst to his mind. The devil's hands on Emily. Hands that wanted to touch her as Tristan had, to caress at first, and then to hurt her, punish her for lifting her skirts for another man.

First there would be beatings. The blackguard imagined Emily, crouched on the floor, begging him for mercy. Then, he would lock her in a dark room, keeping her from the sunlight until she promised to obey him in every way.

Tristan's gut twisted. The thought of his Emily controlled by this fiend made his blood boil. "We've got to stop him," Tristan said.

The captain must have noticed his expression darken. "I'll call up a few more men to search outside the house. If anyone's been there, there might be some trace of it."

Tristan nodded. He was tired and sore. His shoulder had begun to throb mercilessly. Frustration and anger still roiled in his gut, but there was naught to be done about it now.

Hamilton's tone changed from that of a spurned suitor to that of a commanding officer. "Get some rest. I'll have the kitchen staff bring you something to eat."

Tristan shook his head. "A spot of tea is about all I can manage at the moment. Thank you."

Hamilton nodded and rose to leave. "You've done good work, Deveraux. Could get you a medal, you know."

Tristan looked up at him. "I don't want a medal. I want to go back to my infirmary."

"And break Emily's heart?"

When Tristan didn't answer, he felt the smug satisfaction seep from Hamilton's mind. He was more certain than ever that Tristan would abandon Emily.

Tristan only shook his head. He only wished he knew what else he could do.

Emily followed her uncle into the dining room where an elderly man sat at their table, already sipping tea and fastidiously wiping his mouth. He rose on spindly legs when he saw them, reminding Emily of a long-legged spider winding its way through the rose garden.

"Lord Branleigh, I presume? And this would be the lovely Miss Durbin?"

Branleigh gave him a short bob of his head and Emily curtsied.

"Lord Cantor, is it?" Branleigh asked, giving Emily a sideways glance.

"I'm so glad to finally make your acquaintance. It has been so long since we've heard anything of my grand-nephew, we'd all but given up hope of ever finding him."

Emily watched with curiosity as the old man dabbed at his eyes. She wasn't fooled. The old charlatan was up to something.

It hadn't been much of a task to remember the fleeting emotions that had colored Tristan's thoughts the night before. He'd been afraid of this man, who'd been old even when Tristan had been a boy.

No, if ever there was a devil sitting at the dining table, it was Lord Cantor.

Branleigh cleared his throat. "Deveraux never mentioned he'd had any surviving family."

Cantor shook his head. "I'm not surprised. When he was a child, Tristan's mother had a terrible accident. His father was away in the military and the poor boy was left with me. He was devastated by his mother's death. I did my best, but I'm afraid I couldn't ease his pain. After a time, the poor boy ran away. It was a terrible time. I've been searching for him ever since."

"He's been serving in the army, with the fighting in Spain."

"Really? My nephew's a soldier?"

"He's been apprenticed with a military surgeon. He should have been easy enough to find, I imagine."

"Yes, well an error on my part. I never thought to look for the lad under his mother's maiden name."

Emily exchanged a quick glance with her uncle. "What is his legal name?"

"His father is Lord Griffin Whitehall."

Branleigh raised an eyebrow. "You don't mean the Earl of Kendall? I thought that Kendall had no heirs."

"I suppose you're thinking of the older son, Lord Charles. He died shortly after his father. It turned out, the second son, Griffin, survived to inherit. Tristan's mother, Vivian, was a gypsy girl my nephew had met shortly after his first wife's death. His marrying her was quite unexpected, as you can imagine. An embarrassment that the family chose to hold in confidence."

Branleigh nodded. "I suppose, that if it had become public knowledge, it would have become a scandal, to be sure."

Cantor smiled. "Of course, that was all before Griffin inherited the earldom. Poor Charles died in a terrible hunting accident." He sighed. "I'm afraid our family is fraught with tragedy."

Emily sipped her tea. "So it would seem."

Cantor cleared his throat. "His mother was actually running away from Griffin when she died. They'd had a terrible argument. Tristan must have misunderstood."

As the three of them continued with their visit, Cantor entertained them with fondness and stories of Tristan's childhood that Emily found difficult to believe. She was certain that the man was fabricating the entire thing. She'd felt no adoring family in Tristan's mind, no warm thoughts from loved ones, save those brief catches of his memory of his mother.

Time and childhood did have a way to make memories fade, though. Emily's own life had been proof of that. She barely remembered her own parents, though she'd been much younger than Tristan when hers had died.

"I suppose you'll want us to have Tristan come down as soon as possible?" Branleigh noted. "I do apologize for his not being here. A bit under the weather, you know. A terrible malaise going around."

Emily wondered if Cantor could read minds as well.

Her first inclination was that the old man did not have the same gift as his grandnephew. In fact, he seemed so eager to please that it sent a shard of warning through her.

"I do have a most peculiar favor to ask of you. I know this sounds terribly odd, but I'd rather you didn't tell Tristan of my visit. At least, not yet. There are some things I need to get in order before we meet. Papers to prove his legitimacy for one and letters that I'd put away from his mother and others in our family."

"If you didn't want him to know of your arrival, why even come to us now?" Branleigh asked, his gaze pinning the other man.

"I had to know if it was true. Tristan stands to inherit a great deal. I was afraid that an enterprising young lad might try to pass himself off as my long lost relative. I've made no secret of my wanting to find him. I wanted to be sure it was him."

"You're certain that the lad is your grandnephew, then?" Branleigh asked.

Cantor nodded. "Of course, I'll need to see him first. But I have little doubt. I only hope that old memories won't cause him to refuse my visit. I implore you to keep my secret a bit longer. Give me a chance to make proper amends."

"Old memories?" Emily asked.

Cantor's smile faded. "I'm afraid he blames me for his

mother's death. She and Griffin had been estranged. I wrote my nephew and told him that I'd taken her in. My intention was for them to find a way to reconcile. Unfortunately, Tristan's mother ran and while Griffin was pursuing her, she had a terrible accident. She fell into a river and was drowned."

"How terrible," Emily said. She searched her mind for Tristan's memories. Somehow, in the fleeting time their minds were together, she had a glimpse of something. Hadn't his mother fallen into a stream or something? The more she tried to remember, the more her head ached. To her surprise, the thoughts that weren't hers were fading fast.

"You have no idea. Griffin was stricken with grief. He thought he'd killed them both. Fortunately, I found Tristan and brought him to my home where he and his father finally had the chance to be together. Unfortunately the two didn't get on well. Tristan blamed his father for his mother's death as well. When he was eight he ran away. I have searched for him ever since."

"Where is his father now?" Branleigh asked.

"Poor devil died serving in India before the war. Most regretful."

Emily battled with her doubts. Glancing at her uncle, she saw that he too had not been entirely convinced of Cantor's sincerity. Still, if he was the only chance of Tristan ever knowing a real family, how could she refuse him?

More than that, if what the old man said was true and Tristan did stand to inherit, then he needn't return to Spain after all. He could buy off his service and be free.

He could possible stay in England, marry her, and begin a new, better life.

Emily's breath caught in her throat. It was a few seconds before she could speak.

"Of course, Lord Cantor, we'll keep your secret," Branleigh said at last. "It's late. Would you like to stay the night? We could have a room made up for you straight away."

Cantor shook his head. "I wish that I could, but I've got

arrangements to make for Tristan's return." He turned to Emily. "It's a pity my late wife, Lavinia isn't able to be here for his return. She so adored the youth. It had been my fervent hope that we might have found him in time for her to see him one last time."

"Oh." Emily felt a sudden stab of sadness. If what the old man said was true, Tristan had never known his family truly had cared for him. This was his chance for a good life at last.

Chapter Sixteen

Only able to manage a few sips of tea, Tristan had enlisted help from Branleigh's servant, Walters, and Hamilton, to get him up the stairs and to his room. Now, lying in his bed, he was way too awake for his own liking. Awake and alone. Worse yet, his shoulder wound had now deteriorated to a constant, unrelenting ache that set his teeth on edge and made it extremely difficult for him to find any position of comfort.

"Damn the fates that brought me here." How could his life be any more miserable? Suddenly, he found himself on the very edge of an emotion he'd not often let himself indulge. Self pity.

More than anything he wanted company, specifically Emily's company. As the midnight hour approached he thought more and more of their short time together and how wonderful it had been to lose himself in her.

Unfortunately, Emily and her uncle had had a visitor that had occupied them all evening, and in his present state he'd not felt up to attending dinner. Now, it was late and everyone else had since gone to bed.

His hope of spending some time with Emily had been dashed when he'd received a short note from her a few minutes earlier. She'd written that she thought it best for them to not be seen together so late, as the servants were surely spreading the news about the previous night's events.

Tristan usually didn't care about scandals, or for what anyone thought, for that matter. But Emily's reputation was important, and it was best not to test the newness of their relationship just yet. Also, when a man had spoiled a woman as he had done Emily, society expected that he would promptly marry her.

It was more than impossible, Tristan well knew. Yet a part of his mind couldn't help but imagine what it would be like to be wed to Emily.

Closing his eyes, he thought of waking up beside her each morning, the two of them sharing soft sheets and secrets before the dawn. He would take her into his arms, caress her awake, kissing each of her eyelids in turn. She would taste like heaven.

"Stop it!"

Tristan opened his eyes and examined the dark room. Emily?

A small laugh escaped him. He didn't realize he'd projected his thoughts into her mind.

"I miss you," he told her in his mind.

"Tristan, we can't do this. You're hurt and we've already set the gossips talking."

Tristan liked the way her mind worked. He loved that bit of hesitation in her tone and in fact, found it incredibly alluring. He wanted to touch her all the more because of it.

"Nonsense," he said. *"We've already done the deed. Besides, everyone's asleep. Who will know?"*

She paused and even though she was in another room on another floor of the manse, Tristan could hear her pull in a breath.

"I will."

He meant to argue with her. Or better yet, to coax her

to him with soft promises and images in her mind of what he'd like to do with her.

He was about to attempt to ease her fears when he felt something different in her demeanor. Her hesitation had grown to uneasiness.

Emily was worried about their being together.

"What's wrong?"

Emily paused again. He could feel her discomfort growing by the minute.

"Nothing."

It was a lie.

Emily was afraid. Of what? Of him?

"Emily. You know I'd never hurt you."

"It's not that. It's just, well, we're so new. I do care for you, but there are times you make me . . . nervous."

Suddenly, the memories of his mother's shattered mind rose from his past. She'd been terrified of him at first, then her fear had drove her beyond sanity.

Emily had cause for alarm. She'd had time to think about him, about what he was. He was different. He was an oddity. Someone she could dally with, but never more than that.

"Tristan?"

"Perhaps you were right. Good night, Emily."

"Tristan!"

He closed his mind to her. Or tried to. The pain in his arm had now slipped up to his neck and down his back.

"Tristan, don't do this. I do love you. But, this is so new. I need time. I need to be apart from you."

"Why? Because I'm not of noble birth, like you?"

"Never that."

"Really?"

"Tristan, please. You have access to my thoughts any time you choose. I'm afraid that you'll see something that you don't like. Or, I will think something that will push you away. You frighten me."

There it was. The plain truth and it hurt Tristan more than anything in his memory.

"I'm sorry. You're right to be afraid of me. I'm a freak."

Tristan closed his eyes. His father's words coming back to haunt him. What had he said? Demon spawn? Monster?

"Tristan, please. I just need some time. Time to assimilate it all."

"You don't have to pretend. I understand."

"Stop this. I do love you. This is just too new, too much, at times. I know I'm not making sense but . . ."

"You are making sense, Emily. Perfect sense."

"Tristan, please, wait a moment and just listen. I want to be with you, I do. I want to make a life with you, if you want to, that is. But I am still a person of my own. I need to know that if I choose to, I can close that door between us."

"It's about privacy."

"It's about trust. You have to trust that I love you and allow me a small measure of freedom."

Tristan paused. He'd grown used to being constantly assaulted by the thoughts of others. The invasion of one mind, even Tristan's mind, had been too much for her. He hadn't realized that he could ever become overwhelming to someone.

"Very well, Emily. I'm sorry to have ever caused you distress. You can close your mind to me for however long you feel you need to."

"I can?"

Her thoughts sounded afraid, unsure. It nearly broke Tristan's heart to hear the unease in her tone. He tried to reassure her.

"Put a picture of a house in your thoughts. Then, one by one, close every window, every shutter, and door until it is completely secure. When the last one is latched, I will be gone from your mind. Gone, until you decide to open your house once again and invite me in."

"Really?"

"Good-bye, Emily."

Tristan opened his eyes, but in the back of his mind he felt her doing as he'd suggested. What he didn't tell her was that with each time she closed an entrance it raised another scar across his heart. It was all right, he told himself. She did love him. She would allow him back inside.

At least he dearly hoped she would.

* * *

It was beyond believable. Pemberton paced the space of his small room for the thousandth time that evening. Everything was falling apart. First, Emily, *his Emily*, had betrayed him in the worst way. Spoiled in a tryst with Branleigh's physician. Then, when the man actually looked at him for a brief second as he'd fallen, Pemberton felt certain that the cur had guessed all of his secrets.

It had been unthinkable that any of his so carefully fashioned plans could fail simply because someone had guessed at them. Yet, the man had muttered something about a murderer, and Jessup knew instantly that it had been he that the man had come close to identifying.

Failure hung over him like a heavy cloud. He couldn't shake the feeling that his time was fast running out. He knew he must act soon or he'd lose his chance.

It had all been so easy until now. A bit of poison here, a few adjustments made in the carriage rigging, a few coins to a wharf rat in a pub, and his orders had been carried out. None of the residents of Beldon Hall had known it, but he'd ruled them all. Every last one.

Now, his kingdom was faltering. Pemberton didn't like it. Not one bit.

A light tapping came at his door and Pemberton started.

"Yes? Who is it?"

"It's Walters, sir. A gentleman is out front, he asks if he can meet with you."

Walters was a funny duck. He was fiercely loyal to Branleigh, but he was not above making a coin here or there. Still, Pemberton had to be careful and not let the man suspect that all was not well between him and his master.

"Yes? Did the gentleman give a name?"

"No, but he said it was of extreme importance. A delicate matter."

Pemberton nodded thoughtfully. It could prove advantageous if he had an ally from outside. Best to keep his thoughts close to his vest, however. He turned to Walters and nodded.

"I'll go see to him immediately. I've put out the word about town trying to find who it is threatening his lordship, you understand. Perhaps I shall learn something useful."

Walters smiled. "Of course, Mr. Pemberton. We are all most concerned."

"Indeed. Oh, and I'd prefer you didn't tell Lord Branleigh about my efforts. He wouldn't approve my using my own funds to gain information. Besides which, until we have something solid to report to him, it's best to wait these things out."

"Sir, as always, your meaning is understood. You may hold me in the utmost confidence. We must all work to protect his lordship."

Pemberton pulled a coin from his breast pocket. "For your troubles, Walters. You deserve far more rewards than my meager income can afford, but I hope you'll take this as a small token of my esteem."

Walters bowed low. "Sir, you honor me with your praise. I will indeed take it. Thank you and if there's anything I can ever do to help aid in the cause of protecting Lord Branleigh, you have only to ask."

Pemberton watched him go and waited a spare moment longer before grabbing his overcoat and following his messenger out the door.

Quietly descending the stairs, Pemberton could only hope that his clandestine meeting with this mysterious individual would provide him what he needed to put down Branleigh once and for all. Rubbing his hands together in excitement, he let his mind wander yet again to the familiar imaginings of what would happen on his wedding night with the beautiful Emily.

The thought was enough to spur him onward, finally hopeful that his grand plan would come to fruition.

* * *

A light steady rain had begun to fall as Emily lay awake in her bed. The tattering sound of the drops atop the roof wasn't the only thing keeping her awake. Closing her eyes she carefully replayed her exchange with Tristan a half an hour before. Was it true? Had he left her mind completely?

She knew the instant of his withdrawal that something drastic had taken place. His soft murmuring presence was gone, much like if someone had removed the top layer of a quilt, exposing one to a chill in the air.

Emily trembled. She was finding that she didn't like this new singular existence. That and the fact that she'd lied to him.

Emily opened her eyes and blew out a single breath. She hadn't meant to, but playing him false had been the only thing she could think of. If she'd not shut him out, he'd learn of his uncle's visit, and the last thing Emily wanted was to ruin Tristan's chance to have his family back.

Emily shook her head. Rising from bed, she pulled on her robe. Perhaps if she went to him and explained . . . what?

No, that wouldn't do. She felt she had to speak with someone, but whom? Who would hear her strange tale and not think her insane?

Only one person came to her mind, and she knew that if nothing else, her uncle might be the voice of reason in it all. Making her decision, she walked to the door, took hold of the handle, and found the one person in the world she needed standing outside.

"Uncle? What are you doing?"

Furtively he glanced down the hall in each direction before motioning Emily back into her room. She nodded and quickly stepped back.

"I don't understand."

Branleigh looked at her for a moment, as though he were memorizing every nuance of her appearance, every plane of her face, the color of her eyes, even the shape of her nose, and the puzzled expression she now wore.

"Emily, thank heavens I've found you awake."

"Uncle? What's wrong?"

Emily quickly pointed him to a chair. He nodded, and pulling out his handkerchief, he mopped his moistened brow.

"I have gained some information, Emily. Very, very startling information. I'm afraid we've fallen into a bit of a tangle. What's worse, your young man, Mr. Deveraux, seems to be at the heart of it."

The hours of the night stretched out long before him and Tristan could find no release. With Emily's absence, he felt as if a part of himself had been excised away. The most vital part, it seemed. His heart.

Rising from his bed, he managed to make it to the door and out into the hall. Emily's room was on the other side of the manse, in the west wing, and if he could have, Tristan would have run the length of both halls to reach her.

Aside from the fact that, in his current condition, he'd likely not make it that far, the small amount of pride he had left rose up to prevent his advance. No, he told himself. He must let her decide for herself, allow her to see the truth of his feelings for her, no matter what the consequences.

"Have you thought about what you're going to do now?"

Tristan turned, and found Jeffrey Hamilton leaning on the opposite wall, his clothes rumpled and reeking with the scent of brandy.

"What in blazes are you doing up so late?"

Hamilton coughed, and hiccupped. "Strange. I was wondering the same thing about you. Why are you out and about at such an hour? Going back to finish the job of ruining Emily, are you?"

Tristan scoffed. "Hardly. You may exhale, Jeffrey. Emily

seems to have cast me off as well. You may yet have a chance."

The other man straightened himself. "What are you talking about?"

Tristan shook his head and held out his arm. "Help me get to the nearest room that contains the largest amount of liqueur and I shall tell you."

Hamilton only paused briefly before taking Tristan's offer. In minutes the two of them were settled on the ground floor of the manse, ensconced once again in the library.

"Go on," he said impatiently as he poured them both a glass of the amber liqueur.

Tristan laughed. "You are quite hopeful, aren't you?"

The other man's eyes narrowed. "Don't trifle with me, Deveraux. I'll not tolerate it."

Nodding, Tristan took a drink and waited a moment while the brandy burned a trail down his throat to land in a warm pool in his gut. Instantly the effects of the drink calmed some of his anxieties. His fear of losing Emily had not gone, but rather settled in the back of his mind for the moment. He knew it wasn't a cure for his strange affliction, but it seemed to be enough to have a respite.

"There. That's better." Tristan looked up into Hamilton's expectant gaze.

"You said you had news of Emily. Well? Out with it, man."

"It seems the two of us are temporarily," he paused, searching for the appropriate term, "separated."

Hamilton took his seat on the chaise longue across from Tristan. "She's sent you packing, has she?"

Tristan sat back. "Not in the way you're thinking, but yes, we've come to an agreement. It seems the speed of our 'amore' has caused her a bit of anxiety. She's decided that she needs some time to step back from our situation."

Hamilton let out a slow breath. "Finally, she's come to her senses."

"At least for the moment."

"It's about damn time."

"Don't be too upset by the news. Your grief knows no bounds." Tristan took another long drink.

The captain straightened his spine. "She'll be better off without the likes of you."

Tristan sighed. "As it happens, Jeffrey, I do agree with you."

"At last, the voice of sanity." Hamilton took a drink from his glass.

Tristan closed his eyes briefly, and when he opened them he settled his gaze once again on his commander.

"I happen to agree, but not because of anything you've said. I'm not convinced that you're the best man to be her husband, either."

"But, a far better choice than you, don't you think?"

"That may be true, but it doesn't mean I have to like it."

The two men sat quiet for a moment, each one looking into his glass and into himself. Tristan finally felt the edge of exhaustion creep up on him and was about to say goodnight when Hamilton cleared his throat.

"When are you planning to tell her? That you're leaving her."

Tristan felt the cold stone of dread settle in his gut. Of course, that was the question, wasn't it?

"He knows you too well, Tristan. Much too well."

"When I find who it is that threatens her and her uncle. Emily deserves that much from me."

Hamilton nodded. "That's as it should be." He seemed settled on the matter. "Not that you are a bad sort. I'm sure that your intentions are of the best . . ."

"If not my bloodlines, eh?" Tristan laughed mirthlessly. "Either way, it's fine, old man."

Hamilton settled his half-empty glass on the table beside him. "Do you need help to get back to your room?"

Tristan shook his head. "No, thank you. I want to sit a

bit longer." He rubbed his eyes. "I'll ring for help when I'm ready."

Hamilton stood and lingered a moment. "I do care for her."

Tristan didn't return his glance. "I know."

Chapter Seventeen

The small pub was dark and filled with smoke, but Pemberton didn't mind the privacy that The Broken Crown offered. It was as good a place as any, he surmised. Seated across the table from Lord Cantor, he wondered at the sort of man who would brave such foul weather to coax a possible conspirator out in the middle of the night to a place of such complete degradation.

"Thank you again for joining me." He turned to the barkeep and signaled for two glasses of ale. In minutes the lukewarm liquid was set down before them.

"I must admit I was more than a bit curious, my lord. Your message was couched in mystery. I rarely get summoned so late at night, and even less often by such a distinguished man as yourself."

Cantor smiled, a wide, toothy grin. He could have been a corpse already, Pemberton thought, what with his leathery skin stretched over his bones and deeply sunken eyes.

"A lesser member of the peerage, still I should be happy that I'm not one to have to toil in the field or sell fish before dawn on Market Street, eh?"

He tipped his glass and Pemberton did likewise.

"I feel most gratified by my own station. Working as Lord Branleigh's assistant is quite a prestigious position."

"Yes, but not one that's profitable, as I hear it."

Pemberton sat back a moment, carefully setting his mug on the table. "I don't have need for much so my income is sufficient."

"I'm sure it is. A most generous man you are, too. I mean, you likely do the lion's share of the work and Lord Branleigh obtains most of the credit."

Pemberton's ire grew by the moment. "Working with Lord Branleigh has its positive points. He is a genius."

"Indeed. But then, to be up to his standards, you too must be quite the clever one."

Jessup was on the edge of telling the old fool that indeed, he was the main force behind Branleigh's work. More and more his employer saw fit to bury his nose in his manuals and books and less and less on the work the government was paying them for.

"I gain my largest rewards from the work itself."

"What exactly do you and Lord Branleigh do for the crown?"

Jessup knew that he couldn't divulge the details of their work, that the information was sensitive. But he could speak in generalities.

"It involves weapon development. Currently, his lordship is experimenting with rifle design and the impact of different configurations on speed and accuracy of the shot."

"Very important work, indeed. Which makes me wonder, why is my nephew involved in such work? His vocation is hardly that of a gunsmith."

"I don't understand? Your nephew?"

Cantor smiled. "Tristan Deveraux. He's my grandnephew. I'd heard from a friend of mine that the lad has been pressed into service to his lordship. Since he is but a field surgeon, I can't imagine what use Lord Branleigh would have for him. In fact, I even visited upon the Branleighs this very eve and found them not at all forthcoming with that information."

The scientist glanced thoughtfully at the man's half-empty glass. He decided it was best not to divulge too much of the viscount's affairs until he knew for certain what sort of man he was dealing with.

"My understanding was that he'd come as a medical aid to Lord Branleigh. We, that is the house staff and I, assumed that he was a physician and he'd come to take care of his lordship's waning health."

"Has his lordship been feeling sick of late?"

Jessup paused. Had he indeed? "Not that I've noticed. But you know the very wealthy, sir. Any malady, imagined or otherwise, and they run calling for a doctor." He paused. "What exactly is your interest in Branleigh's affairs?"

Pemberton felt the man's scrutiny like a hundred-stone weight on top of him.

"I am merely looking out for the lad's well-being. In the future, Tristan may be receiving an earldom. It's my concern that some wily female not insinuate herself on my nephew before even he knows of his good fortune. Not that I would suspect anything, but Lord Branleigh's niece is living in the same house. One must be very careful, you know."

Pemberton sat back. He supposed it was possible, though he'd never seen Emily do a single underhanded thing since he'd known her. But, with three failed attempts at marriage and the list of eligible and willing bachelors diminishing by the day, it was possible.

Cantor must have noticed his consternation. "Has something happened to my grandnephew that I should know about?"

Pemberton was hesitant at first to answer. Of course, what difference did it make? The deed was already done, and if left to their own courses, he was certain Deveraux would indeed offer marriage to Emily. In fact, it was very possible that the lad had been duped. But, what Cantor didn't know, as no one else did, was that Jessup would not allow things to follow their natural course.

"It seems he has indeed fallen into the stir. Your grandnephew has unfortunately already compromised Miss Durbin."

Cantor sat back, a thoughtful expression on his face. "I suspected as much. The lady seemed quite concerned with his welfare earlier tonight when we spoke."

Pemberton cleared his throat. "Of course, I've known the family for some time and it seems almost inconceivable that Miss Durbin is responsible for any deceit."

"You think the two have a genuine affection for each other?"

"I assume that's what they believe."

"I only want what's best for Tristan. I wonder, if evidence arises to prove otherwise, would you be willing to keep me informed of it? I mean, a few meetings like this would be perfect, if it isn't too inconvenient for you. I'd be willing to pay any expenses you deem necessary, as well."

Pemberton considered his offer. Of course, he could use the money, and the chance to remove Deveraux from the house without violence was quite attractive. Still, he'd need to make sure the man was permanently out of the way.

"I see no reason why I cannot keep an ear to the door, so to speak. Since it is that we only have the young couple's best interest at heart."

Picking up his glass, Pemberton nodded and drained the last of its contents. He was quite pleased with himself. Quite pleased, indeed.

"There is one other matter," Cantor said as he lifted his mug and finished the dregs of his drink.

"Yes?" Pemberton asked, suspicion rising in his gut.

"My nephew has an uncanny ability. One I'm sure which you might find a bit, disconcerting."

"What is that?"

Cantor smiled, looking very much like a cat that was about to feast on its dinner. A very plump, tasty morsel.

Suddenly Pemberton's neckcloth felt as though it had tightened around his throat.

"My nephew can read minds."

***

"Uncle, I don't understand. What's this about? Surely you don't suspect Tristan of any wrongdoing?"

"It's about my work, and indeed I do. The boy, whether he intends it or not, has been thrust into the center of it."

"What in the devil are you talking about?"

Emily watched her uncle closely. He wanted badly to tell her something but hesitated.

"Anything you say to me will not travel beyond the bounds of this room, I assure you."

He gave her a quick glance. "It isn't that I don't trust you, Emily, but lately your judgment has been somewhat . . . questionable."

"What are you talking about?"

"Mr. Deveraux, for one. You seem on edge whenever he's around, and after last night, well, I do question your alliances a bit more."

"My alliances? Uncle, you must know I would never do anything to jeopardize your well-being."

"Do I? Frankly, Emily, after what I've seen of late, I'm not at all sure what I know."

His words stung her worse than anything she'd ever felt.

He sighed, and reaching into his jacket, he pulled out his small, leather-bound book. "It's in here, girl. All of it."

"What is?"

"Top secret information." He sighed. "The delicacy of my work requires that I keep my activities under the wrap. However, an hour ago I came across this passage. Unless I miss my guess, this changes things quite a bit."

Emily took the book from him and studied the contents.

The small, leather-bound text felt warm in her hands, as though it were a living, breathing creature. Worse yet, it seemed to cast an accusatory spell, as though the thin parchment that comprised its pages could leap out at her, expose all of the hidden secrets of the beholder.

Opening the book, she examined the long scrawls of ink that formed undecipherable words on each page.

"I don't understand. What does this mean? Uncle?"

Branleigh pursed his lips, his hands clenching and unclenching, clearly deciding on how much he could trust her with.

"Emily, I'm not sure how much I can divulge. I've been trying to keep myself under the veil, you know. Now more than ever, it's important to keep our secrets close. If Deveraux is suspect . . ."

"Of what? Uncle, I can assure you that Tristan is as at odds with what's happening here as much as you and I. Whatever has occurred in the past, he's blameless."

The older man narrowed his eyes. "I want to believe you, Emily."

She shook her head. "You don't understand. Tristan has promised to not read my mind until I allow him to do so. Whatever he learns of your work, he will not learn it from me."

Branleigh let out a slow breath. "It's written in code. My work with rifle design for the army has all been a cover. My true task is to aid in deciphering the movement of Napoleon's troops, supply routes, battle plans, the lot of it. Several of us have been hard at work, and the 'grand cipher' of the French is beyond genius. Each word has several different meanings, you see, all of them intricately interwoven."

"I see. Then all this time you've been lying to me."

"Emily, you must understand this is war. The French generals send reports of their activities and orders back and forth across enemy lines. I am only one of a team of decoders. However, with this text, I fear the network of spies goes beyond just the movement of the army. Traitors, smuggling operations, arranged assassinations. It's all here, Emily, awaiting my translation."

"This book? It's part of that?"

"These are a compilation of letters from a spy network that

has existed for the last fifty years. Names, dates, locations—it's all here."

"Uncle, what has this to do with Tristan?"

He looked away a moment, his eyes focusing on something beyond the window and her small bedroom.

Sighing, he turned his attention back to her. "I wasn't certain at first. When I notified Henley of it, we thought the boy might be in some danger. There are mentions of a man of similar talents in these pages. After Henley discovered Deveraux's talents, he thought that by bringing him here we could discover if he and this man were one and the same and if so, just how he'd been involved. At the very least we would remove him from the center of the fighting, protecting the most delicate network of army intelligence."

Emily shook her head. "But what of the general's opinion that he could be of help in locating those who were threatening you?"

"It was a good enough excuse to get him here so we could determine what, if any, connection he had to those whom we've been investigating."

"In other words, you lied."

Suddenly, Emily's safe, little world, where only her uncle's safety had been paramount, expanded to unbelievable proportions. She had at least a dozen questions, each of them threatening to explode the very foundation of her life.

"Don't be so quick to judge me, Emily. I know it's not very forthcoming of me to keep things hidden from you. In fact, we'd thought it had nothing at all to do with you until the two of you became enamored of each other."

"I can't help it, Uncle. I care very deeply for him."

"I know, dearest. But, where will it go from here? Has he asked you to marry him?"

Emily shook her head. "There hasn't been time and we need to sort through some things."

Branleigh nodded. "Whatever his involvement, the men in these pages have been searching for him for a long time. What they intend for him is something unknown as yet. But if he's in league with those who traded in secrets against the crown, it won't go well for him, I assure you."

Emily shook her head. It was all too much for her to fathom.

"He's an honorable man, Uncle. I know that much. He strives every day of his life to care for those less fortunate. That sort of man wouldn't be involved in such heinous activities."

"It may appear so on the surface, yes. For those of us unable to read the minds of others, it's just that it's too hard to really know what's in a man's heart."

Emily drew in her breath. Of course, she did know what was in Tristan's heart, she'd seen it herself. Unfortunately, no one would believe her.

Emily shivered as a chill stole over her. How could she possibly explain her joining with Tristan? Somehow she realized that in this one instance, the question of her virtue was not measured in the flirtations of the flesh, but of the mind as well.

"What are you going to do?" she asked at last.

"Finish the work and keep our eye upon everyone around us, from the parlor maid to Captain Hamilton."

Branleigh looked away from her for a moment, hesitating.

"Surely, you don't suspect him as well? It's not possible."

"Anything's possible, Emily. Those missives were first intercepted by Hamilton's company in Spain, years ago. Since then he's been working with Henley to provide as much information as possible."

"Then why do you suspect him?"

"Because he's been too closely involved. It's war, my dear, and no one is beyond suspicion."

"Perhaps he's just a good soldier."

"These letters are no longer being passed through military channels."

"They're not? Where are they coming from?"

"The peerage. One book in particular."

A deafening silence fell between them. Emily sat back on her bed. "It's not possible."

"Think about it. Who was it that profited the most from the war? It wasn't the common people, or many of our counterparts. Only those whose hand had been in providing war materials earned profits. Mind you, I'm not accusing anyone with a title. Right now we've narrowed it down to five gentlemen in particular, one of which sat at our very dinner table tonight."

Emily sat back on her heels. "Lord Cantor is one of the conspirators?"

"I can't say for sure. They each took a code name and it's very difficult to identify who is who. The only descriptor that's clearly written in those pages is that of Mr. Deveraux."

Emily shook her head. "I won't believe that he is involved in this intrigue."

"I know it's difficult for you, my dear. If only we could tell if what he says is the truth. That is why I must ask you to do a difficult thing."

"What is it?" Emily's heart began to beat a bit faster and thumped like a hammer in her chest.

"I need you to stay close to him and find out the truth. It may be the only chance we have to learn how involved in this he truly is."

"I don't know if I can. Uncle, Tristan and I have decided to step away from each other for a while. We want to make sure that we're not rushing into anything."

The older man shook his head. "Emily, while I am in agreement with your levelheadedness in this matter, I must say that the boy's only chance at a fair assessment may be from you."

Emily clutched at her gown. "I'll do what you ask, but there are limits to what I can do."

"Of course, my dear. I'm only asking you to talk to him, nothing more. See if he will open his heart to you. It may be the only chance he has."

* * *

Tired and angry with himself as well as the circumstances he'd found himself in, Tristan cursed. There wasn't much chance now of reconciling with Emily. She would surely come to her senses and make a nice life with Hamilton. They'd have a house full of children and live out the rest of their lives, while he continued working in the poor end of town, drowning in cutthroats and thieves and his own self-imposed exile.

"Monster. Devil. Demon spawn. You deserve no better."

The voice came to him again. Only this time it wasn't his uncle chastising him. His father had been right. All those years ago, he'd been correct when he'd recognized Tristan's worth.

It had been all he could do to rise above the poor circumstances of his life, the tales of his bizarre birth and childhood never far behind him. He may have escaped his great-uncle's and his father's murderous ways, but the violence that haunted him was never far behind.

Tristan found a small measure of comfort sitting in the high-back chair in the library. At least upright, his shoulder didn't bother him so much and if he laid his head back just so, he could close his eyes and just let the remainder of the pain ebb away.

As soon as his physical discomforts eased, he fell into a half doze. He couldn't help it as his exhaustion pushed him further down. It was a dangerous place to visit, the place between sleep and wakefulness, but he was too tired and sore to fight it.

Chapter Eighteen

Emily had found him in the library. Sitting upright, he looked like a schoolboy who'd fallen asleep in the midst of his studies. She shook her head at the sight.

Leaving the room for a moment, she returned with a light blanket. He startled awake as she gently laid it across him.

"What?" He sat upright, focusing in the dim light.

"It's all right, Tristan. It's Emily."

Seeing him wince, Emily put out a hand to steady him. "Easy does it."

"I was dreaming," he began.

"I know. You looked chilled. That's why I brought you a blanket. I'm sorry if I woke you."

He shook his head as if to clear it.

"I hadn't realized that I'd dozed off." He rubbed his eyes.

"How do you feel?"

He laughed at that. "Like any man who was shot less than a day ago, I suppose. Sore as hell and not the least bit happy about it."

Emily sighed. "I'm sorry for that."

"Not your fault. As it happens, I've only myself to blame." He gave her a weak smile.

She watched him a moment. "What are you doing down here?"

"I couldn't sleep," he lied. "I thought I'd come down for a bit to escape the confines of my room. Unfortunately, my journey down seemed to have used more effort than I had realized. I sat down to catch my breath."

Emily nodded. "I had difficulty sleeping as well."

She let the silence sit between them for a moment. There was so much she wanted to tell him, and also to ask him outright about his involvement in her uncle's work.

Emily had always found her best suit to be an open, honest manner. She did not feel right about lying, and even more so with Tristan. To her knowledge, he had not told her a single untruth. Now she was about to lie to him for the second time.

"I was thinking about our decision to separate."

He nodded, rubbing his forehead with his palm. "You were right to want to do so, Emily. Don't doubt yourself."

"I'm not so sure, now. It's rather lonely without you so close."

At least she'd meant that. For the moment, it was close enough to the truth.

"I feel the same."

She took in a sharp breath. As she watched, he brought his hand from his temple. He wanted her as much as she wanted him.

Suddenly the room seemed to crowd around them.

"What shall we do?" Her words echoed around them, a question that really wasn't a question.

So badly she wanted to open her mind to him again, to invite him in and feel his wonderful presence in her thoughts. She knew he'd respect her need for privacy.

But now, there was too much danger of him discovering the truth. She couldn't risk her uncle's life if it turned out that Tristan was somehow involved in the activities of those missives. Worse yet, she knew that until she'd figured a way to tell him what she'd agreed to, she'd likely lose him forever.

He sighed. "We must wait, Emily. Wait for the right time. If it turns out that you and I are not meant to be together, well, it's better this way."

She felt a sharp stab of regret. "You mean it will be one less complication left for us to unravel."

He didn't waver as he answered.

"Yes."

Emily discovered at that moment that even though they had severed their connection, she still sensed the resonance of his feelings in her mind. It was as though being in the same room with him was enough to open the door even slightly.

The emotion that she felt growing in him frightened her more than anything else.

Despair.

Tristan had already made up his mind about their being together. He had already given up on her.

Turning away, she battled the tears. She knew he'd wanted her, desired her more than anything, but just as his mother had sacrificed it all for him when he'd been a child, Tristan now felt he was doing the same for her.

Emily swallowed. She'd just have to convince him that they really had a chance together and that she refused to be set aside for her own good.

Although it was the hardest thing she'd ever done, she left him alone with an ache in his heart that surely equaled her own.

It was a cold wind that blew across the plains. Griffin sat on his mount and watched the sun begin to rise over the distant mountains. It had been some time since he'd thought about returning to England. He'd traveled the world over several times in his life, doing the work he'd been destined to do.

"So, now you're going home?" his companion asked.

The two men sat astride their mounts, watching their prey with disinterested expressions. It was a simple assassination. They both knew it would be done by dawn.

The occupant of the small cottage pulled back the curtain to the kitchen window and peered out into the night.

A month before, his uncle had sent word of his inheritance. It had been years since his older brother Charles had died. That had left him an heir to the family fortune and the title of an earl. After years of estrangement, he hadn't wanted anything from his family. He'd thought to ignore it.

In all the time since he'd left his home, Griffin had not once considered returning. The family affairs had been taken care of by his older brother admirably. With the boy gone, he knew the business with his uncle had come to an end. That had left Griffin free to live the life he'd chosen after he'd dispensed with his family requirements.

As a younger man, he'd tried to meet his late father's wishes. At twenty-one, he'd married in haste to the daughter of a viscount, connecting his family to one of the wealthiest in the kingdom. When his first wife perished during childbirth, he was no longer bound to a woman he didn't care for, or outstanding family obligations.

His second marriage had been for love. From the beginning his family had spurned Vivian Deveraux, and many still referred to her as his mistress. But he'd loved her and it wasn't until her betrayal that he'd even thought of staying away. She'd been dead these many years, as had the child she'd borne him.

He should have killed the fiend that night at his uncle's house. He should have killed them both. He remembered the night clearly.

"I'm telling you, Griffin, the boy has worth. He can be a tool for us. We can use his gift of mind reading to learn so many things. Knowledge is power, and what this boy possesses is beyond our wildest imaginings."

At least the little scut had stopped struggling. Griffin cast him a dark stare. Huddled in the corner, he sat pressed to the wall. Pale, with a fine sheen of sweat covering his face, the demon child knew what fate awaited him at Griffin's hand.

The thought of strangling the lad came full force to his mind, crushing the narrow windpipe, the feel of the boy's spine crackling in Griffin's iron grip.

The fiend moaned again.

Seeing what was happening between the two, Cantor had pressed himself between them. "I tell you, he won't be hard to control. I know exactly how we can force him to do our bidding without even laying a hand on the lad."

Griffin turned his attention to his uncle. "I'll make him cooperate, or I'll kill him in the process."

Cantor shook his head. "No, no, I tell you. There is another way to hurt him. Deeper and far more painful than any physical discomfort you might deal him. Trust me in this."

The assassin considered his words. "First, buy off my commission. If we have an arrangement, I want to be here to make certain you don't take your little treasure and cheat me out of my share."

"But the cost . . ."

"Is the price you'll pay for my not killing the brat by day's end."

He gave Cantor a stone hard expression and under his scrutiny, his uncle practically wilted. "Very well, Griffin. I suppose it would be beneficial to have you close by. Just let me handle the boy."

"Done."

Griffin's mind snapped back to the present. "I've family business to attend to," he told his associate.

"To take your place as the head of your clan?"

Griffin shrugged. "For a time."

"It would mean the end of our business arrangement, would it not?"

Griffin looked at his "partner." Ten years ago they had

broken out of prison and immediately begun their mercenary service. It had been a profitable turn, but Griffin had
not done it for the money. Not exactly. Merlin, the name
he'd given to his friend, whose true name he couldn't pro-
nounce, had been a deposed prince, a castoff from his
own society.

They'd met in India, in prison, of all places, and formed
an unholy alliance. Mercenaries for whoever had enough
coin to pay for their services. It had been a lucrative
arrangement and one that Griffin didn't want to end just
yet. In the end, it came down to one thing. Killing had
come easy to them both. It was a vocation that Griffin enjoyed most of all.

He'd been happy to live in obscurity all these years,
killing men he did not know. In fact, so good at his chosen
profession, he'd amassed quite a fortune for himself, not
that he'd wanted the money.

All had been well with his life until the moment the
damned letter had arrived.

So now he would go back to the home that had cast him
off and the remnants of the family he despised. No matter,
he told himself. He would only be there long enough to
kill his uncle and the devil's spawn.

When Tristan awoke again, he was alone. Day had
broken and it appeared to be about late morning. The
noise of the house coming to life around him made him
wish that he were back in Spain, ready to begin his day in
the surgery and not tucked away in a London townhouse
with people he hardly knew and trusted even less.

All except for Emily, he thought. Like an old war
wound, Emily's absence from his mind ached. In their
short time together, he'd grown used to having her there,
always at the back of his thoughts, and now with her gone
it left him feeling painfully empty.

"You had no choice," he muttered to himself, pulling the blanket tighter around him.

Inhaling deeply, he could still scent her fragrance, lilac and lavender. It both heightened his arousal and deepened his despair.

"Awake at last, I see?"

Tristan looked up to see the captain leaning over the desk, hastily writing on a piece of parchment.

"Making your report to General Henley?"

Hamilton glanced up briefly and then returned his attention to his writing. He finished with a flourish of his signature, quickly folded the paper, and stuffed it into his jacket pocket.

"The army runs on reports, you should know that. Have you made any progress at all? Any more 'readings' on our friends?"

Tristan shrugged. "Nothing that I haven't already told you. Whoever it was that threatened Lord Branleigh has made himself scarce."

"At least his lordship's safe for the moment."

"It does look that way." Tristan motioned to the other man. "Come sit down. It's making my shoulder ache just having to look up at you," Tristan complained.

"Of course." Hamilton took a seat across from Tristan, his attention going to the fluttering of the morning breeze through the window.

"I believe our time may be running short."

Hamilton nodded. "Go on."

"Whoever our killer is, I think he may suspect we're on to him.

"How is that possible?"

"I'm not sure. It's just that the essence of his thoughts seems to have faded quite a bit."

"What do you propose we do?"

"First, we can rule out you and I."

"I should think so."

"I know I'm not the murderer, though I must say

there's a time or two I've wanted to do someone bodily harm; though, to be honest, my tendencies toward violence are directed toward Henley and the way he forced me into this God-awful mess."

"I had surmised as much."

"As for you, I'm reasonably sure that you're innocent of any wrongdoing."

"Your confidence inspires me." Hamilton coughed. "Who else might we suspect?"

"His assistant perhaps?" Tristan considered the little man. "What do we know about him?"

"Only that he's got a fairly good posting here with Lord Branleigh. It wouldn't be rational that he'd so readily toss it away by killing his employer."

Tristan nodded thoughtfully. "Whoever said that murderers had to be rational?"

"I see your point. Very well, then, Pemberton is as likely a suspect as any."

"I see him as a strong contender, but we must first find a motive. Why would he want Branleigh dead?"

Hamilton sat forward. "Perhaps because he is smitten with Emily as well?"

"As is every other man on the premises."

Hamilton sighed. "I see your point. Still, I don't like the little bugger. It's unsettling the way he stares at her."

Tristan again considered the assistant. True, he'd not had the time to really get acquainted with the man. He'd kept a fair distance from the beginning, reminding Tristan of a rat peeking out from beneath the wainscoting. "Very well, Pemberton goes into the suspect column."

"Whom else does that leave? Any of the servants?"

Tristan had spent time with several of them, Walters the main butler, and Timothy, Lord Branleigh's footman. There were also the groomsman and the parlor maid as well.

"No, I've found them all to be quite straightforward people, more concerned with retaining their posting here and keeping up their duties. Most of them are

rather fond of Lord Branleigh and Emily, seeing them as
fair and kind people."

Hamilton sighed. "That leaves for a rather narrow list
of suspects, then. Someone from the outside, perhaps?"

Tristan considered it for a moment, though it seemed
as good a possibility as any. "It might be. There's no
telling until we meet with some of Lord Branleigh's acquaintances."

Hamilton nodded. "Good, then. Perhaps you and I
should make the rounds to the gentlemen's clubs with his
lordship this afternoon, that is if you're up to it."

Emily had finished up her meeting with the housekeeper and was working on the dinner menu when the
message arrived.

> *My Dearest Miss Durbin,*
>   *It is with great hope that I ask you and your uncle to join
> me for dinner this evening. I would also ask that you con-
> vince my nephew to come along as well, although I beg
> you don't tell him yet of my intentions toward him. I would
> like to greet him myself. It is my hope that I can end our
> family rift once and for all.*
>   *I eagerly await your reply.*
>   *Your most honorable servant,*
>   *G.L. Cantor*

Emily read the note three times. It was too soon. She
hadn't had time to make proper inquiries about him, and
more than anything she wanted to find out the truth so
that she could convince Tristan that her duplicity had
been only in his best interest.

Emily decided the best route was as always the direct
one. She quickly penned her response and another note
as well to a friend of hers who would definitely be in the
know in regards to Lord Cantor and his true intentions.

That finished, she summoned Walters, gave him quick instructions for delivery of her letters and then rang for her maid. She'd need a special ensemble for her afternoon jaunt through the city. She'd decided to meet with her most formidable acquaintance.

"Yes, miss?" Anna answered her call and in moments the two were ensconced in Emily's dressing room, choosing proper attire for her afternoon walk. Wisely, Emily decided on an older fashion that would easily please the stately woman she planned to visit. A white muslin gown with an elaborate lace trim and her favorite purple knit shawl to be topped by her favorite high bonnet trimmed with delicate pink carnations and dark purple feathers. It was all the rage and had been a gift from her intended hostess.

Emily dressed as though she were a medieval soldier donning his armor and heading out to the crusades. Well, she thought grimly, it was very nearly the same. After all, it wasn't merely her life she was fighting for, it was her love. Never had a soldier been so well prepared.

Chapter Nineteen

Tristan hadn't liked Damen's Den much at all. The small parlor turned gaming hall was stuffy, filled with cigar smoke, and way too crowded for his comfort. Worse yet, the constant bombardment of extraneous thoughts had blasted him from the moment he entered the room, and it was all he could do not to stumble as he navigated through the crowd to a table that Hamilton had secured for him on the opposite, albeit farthest from the door, corner of the room.

"I don't recall it ever being so much of a crush," Branleigh noted as he led the way to their table.

Hamilton grunted. "I imagine with your work it's been some time since you've taken an afternoon at one of the clubs."

Tristan grimaced. He didn't know what was worse, being pushed into these ghastly surroundings, or having to bear the company of not only Hamilton, but Branleigh as well.

The truth was, Tristan had gotten used to the solitude of his surgery, and later even at Beldon Hall. Having to tolerate only a few people at a time had been relative heaven compared with this.

Even his jaunt on the battlefield had not been so bad. At least then he'd had the task of the healing arts to occupy his mind and thereby push the thoughts of others aside. Here, he had no defense at all.

"You don't look so well, Deveraux. Is something the matter?" the captain asked as he motioned for the servant to bring them their drinks.

"Nothing," he ground out, though he could tell by their expressions as they took their seats that neither believed him.

"I'm sure it's still the effect of his injuries from the other night. Although he served in the army, it's quite different from being on the other end of the barrel, eh, Deveraux?" Branleigh laughed.

"It is a bit of an aggravation."

"That's the spirit, my boy, never let them see your pain. I never had the opportunity to serve myself, though now I wish I had. Fear not, young man, a scar or two always gains the ladies' sympathies, you know. Isn't that correct, Captain?"

"I've had my share, to be sure."

Branleigh sat back. "Your share of scars or female attentions?"

Before he could answer, a tall, well-dressed man approached the table.

"I don't believe it's true? Hamilton, old boy? Have you come out of the caves to grace us with your presence?"

Tristan watched mildly amused as the army officer visibly shrank from the attention.

"Nicholas, it has been awhile." Hamilton turned back to the table. "Gentlemen, let me introduce an old family friend, Lord Nicholas Sennett, viscount of Bruxbey." Hamilton pointed to each of the men now seated. "Lord Branleigh, and his physician, Mr. Deveraux."

Sennett, reeking of stale cheroots and brandy, leaned over the table and greeted each one of the men seated.

"Deveraux, eh? You look somewhat familiar."

"Did you serve in Spain? You might have seen me there."

The other man shook his head. "I'm afraid not, bad leg,

you see. No, I'm sure we've never met, but dashed if you don't remind me of someone. Well, never mind, I'll figure it out. Good day, gentlemen."

Tristan watched the other man stagger off. Thankfully his mind had already gone to thinking about a late afternoon tryst with his mistress and he'd not lingered on Tristan's identity.

However, Tristan had seen a brief picture of a man whom Sennett had known, though he'd quickly dismissed the connection. There'd been no mistaking the face in the other man's memory.

It had been his father.

"I say, Deveraux, I didn't think it possible, but you've the look of a ghost about you. Are you sure you're well?" Hamilton asked.

Tristan returned his attention to their table. Both men were staring at him, each one wearing a questioning expression.

Suddenly he'd become that frightened child again, huddling in the cold, damp cellar, waiting for death to burst through the door and find him at long last.

"I tried to protect you lad. I did my best to keep him away. It's your own fault what happened you know. Yours and yours alone."

Memories he'd long buried bubbled at the surface of his thoughts. Pain and fear mixed together, torture of the flesh that left no marks on his own, except for bleeding scars on his psyche. Those would never go away.

Taking a shaky breath, he did his best to put down the past and return to the present, reminding himself that he was a man grown now. If he ever did meet with his father again, it wouldn't be as a small, helpless child.

"I'm fine," he said at last, decreeing it as though the simple act of doing so would make it true.

Thankfully their brandy arrived and the warm liquid burned a path of heat in him that served to revive him somewhat.

"Courage in a glass, eh, Deveraux?" Branleigh said, lifting his own goblet once more.

By the end of the afternoon, several gentlemen had approached Branleigh's table and introduced themselves. Each one had been more than a little curious at Tristan's presence, but his companions had covered his tracks well. Still, he found no respite from his uneasiness until two hours later when they'd climbed into the carriage.

It had been more of a relief than he'd expected. Tristan became lightheaded when the constant stimulation of the crowded establishment ceased and he'd finally settled into the peaceful surroundings of the cab.

He and Hamilton had climbed in first with Branleigh lingering outside speaking with another one of his gaming acquaintances.

"Well? Anything?" Branleigh asked as he settled into the seat beside Tristan. The sudden change of atmosphere caused no end of nausea to boil in him, and for a moment he considered tossing his stomach contents onto the lot of them.

"Nothing," he said at last, closing his eyes. "I read everyone of them, and no one seems to have any animosity toward you, my lord. You seem to be nothing more than a curiosity to some, an annoyance to the rest."

"That's preposterous, my boy. I certainly must be a threat to someone for this ghastly thing to continue. Three attempts on my life and not one among them knows anything about it?"

Tristan opened his eyes and examined the old man. That was when he saw it. A furtive glance passed between both him and Hamilton. Suddenly, the air of discomfort rose in the carriage.

"What is it the two of you two aren't telling me?"

Silence grew until Tristan was sure he was going to have to beat it out of them. Then Hamilton cleared his throat.

"Army intelligence was very clear in the matter. Lord Branleigh's life has been threatened. He has been doing 'other things' for the military and there are those in the upper echelons who are not quite happy about it."

"What type of things?"

He watched as each man set his jaw.

"Dear God," he muttered. "You're a spy."

Emily had been received in Lady Trevor's parlor as though she'd been related to the Prince Regent himself. Wife to an earl, Lady Trevor had reigned upon the throne of society gossip for nearly two decades. A dear friend to the patroness of Almack's, she'd had an ear to the newsworthy so long that if anyone needed information, she was definitely the one to ask.

Taken into the older woman's warm embrace, Emily nearly suffocated in the seemingly endless sea of lavender, white lace, and spun cotton ruffles.

"My dearest! I swear, I haven't seen you in over a season. My goodness! Aren't you the vision of loveliness!"

Emily gave her an embarrassed curtsey. The truth was she'd always been more than a little intimidated by the grand lady, but it was her great fortune that the woman had long ago developed an admiration for Emily's uncle. In fact it had always been the amount of pressing the woman did to learn her information about her uncle's daily activities that put Emily constantly on the defensive. The truth was, the woman could easily have been employed by the army to interrogate spies.

"Thank you. I am most appreciative that you could spare me a few moments from your busy schedule this afternoon."

"Think nothing of it. I was just speaking about you with my friend Lady Grayson the other day. Alma, I said, I wonder how our dear Emily is managing to cope with the loss of so many handsome beaus. Not one tragedy but three! I detest the ill-wagging tongues of those that would cast you in aspersion, as though you'd any hand in it all. Such distasteful business, gossip is."

Of course, Emily knew that the woman likely had been among the strongest and loudest of those "ill-wagging tongues." It didn't bother her, though. It simply was the way of things.

"My heart is still heavy. After mourning them each, I have found it incredibly hard to think of risking the life of another poor gentleman at the altar."

"My dear, you mustn't listen to those despicable wretches, they simply do not understand. Misfortune follows you so tragically. Tell me, have you found another young man brave enough to risk it all?"

Emily let out a slow breath. "Well, I recently became engaged, but I have to say, I don't think we'll suit in the end. I am far too fond of Captain Hamilton to risk his life for my sake."

"Hamilton? Would that be Cyril's younger brother? Oh, dear, he is quite a catch for a girl of your station. Think very carefully before you cast him off."

Emily nodded and swallowed hard. The truth was, they did suit very well. Financially, socially, and in every important way except the most important one.

"My dear, you'll overcome it. Perhaps this is the gentleman you were fated to be with after all."

Emily put up her bravest smile. "Thank you, Lady Trevor, you do my heart no end of good."

The woman smiled brightly and took a sip of tea. "So, tell me, what brings you to an old woman's lair on such a bright afternoon?"

Emily knew that her hostess was indeed fishing for more tasty morsels of gossip. It was one of the things that made her the perfect informant.

"I came seeking information"—she leaned forward—"of a confidential nature."

Lady Trevor's face lit like a gas lamp on a moonless night. "Do tell? Whatever I know I shall gladly share, though I hasten to warn you, sometimes knowledge can be a dangerous thing."

"I shall depend on your wisdom to advise me," Emily said, putting on her most serious face. "It has been rumored that my uncle may be in some jeopardy."

Lady Trevor shook her head, making her cascade of gray curls bounce riotously.

"These are indeed dangerous times. I had heard as much." She sat back, smug in the knowledge that little of the scandalous nature ever escaped her scrutiny.

"Well, we've been invited to visit a recently widowed gentleman, a Lord Cantor. Have you heard of him?"

"I have indeed," she said stoically. "He's a good enough sort, I suppose, though it is said that some of his dealings are under the table, if you get my drift."

"Really? How so?"

"That he's got deeper pockets than he divulges, for one thing. That his family wealth has had limits in the past, but he's been dabbling in the trades." She made a face of disgust.

"Oh. That's not very comforting."

"Nothing for you to worry about, my dear. Your family is safe enough. Fortunately, it was said in some circles that he'd been quite an asset to the war effort."

"Thank heavens."

"You and your uncle should be safe enough visiting, I should think."

Emily sipped at her tea, deciding on how best to approach her next question. "Have you heard anything about his family?"

Lady Trevor nodded. "Yes, indeed. His oldest nephew, Charles, met with a terrible accident some time ago. He was riding a hunt on his property and suffered a fatal throw from his mount. Terrible business, that . . ."

"Really. Is Baron Cantor in line to inherit, then?"

"No, Charles had a younger brother, Griffin. The last I'd heard of the lad was that he was off serving somewhere. But with the war, some of our boys were put to other, more clandestine jobs. We've not heard where Griffin is these days, though I'm sure what with family responsibilities and all, he'll come home one day."

"Does this younger brother have any family then? A wife? Children?" Emily was careful not to expose her dire need for answers, but still, she had to know.

"Well, it was a sad thing about Griffin, as I hear it. He was widowed twice. His first wife, daughter of a well-respected family, had died in childbirth. Both the child and the mother were lost, poor things. Then, his second wife fell into a river and was drowned. They'd had a young son, I think around seven or eight years old. He'd been lost in the water as well. As I remember it, they could never find the child's body, poor dear."

"Such a tragedy," Emily said.

"Very. It had been quite the scandal at the time, with her being a common girl, one of the local gypsies, as I recall. But a lovely little thing. So very sad."

Emily sat for the next hour listening to the woman discuss the goings-on in town, but she found her mind wandering back to Tristan. Then it was true, his parents had been legally married and he wasn't illegitimate. He stood to inherit quite a bit. That certainly changed things.

As she sat, stirring her tea and being a dutiful guest, Emily couldn't help her feelings for him. She'd missed him terribly already, and vowed that when she saw him next, she would quickly tell him of all she'd learned and then open herself up to him once and for all. Never again would she put secrets between them.

Pemberton watched the two carriages pull to the front of the townhouse. The first had been Branleigh's ornate rigging, and the second, the one that Emily had taken for her afternoon visit.

Cantor's words came back to him from the night before.

"What in blazes are you talking about?" Pemberton had asked, his stomach twisting at the thought.

"I'm saying that from a very young age, Tristan, whose mother was a gypsy, has had the uncanny ability to read minds."

"Like some festival magician?"

"Far more astute than that. I just caution you because I feel if you have any secrets, or plans that you wish not to become public knowledge, you might want to guard yourself well."

"How? How can I do that?"

Cantor took a deep breath. "You must make sure that you stay out of his immediate vicinity, for one. Oh, and don't let your mind wander. Strong emotions, anger, fear, hatred"—he paused a moment to take a breath—"and lust, for instance, are very easy for him to discern. No, I think the best you can hope for is to stay out of his way. Is there some way you might accomplish this?"

"The house is quite large. I'm sure if I remain in my room or the laboratory I'll be safe enough. Lord Branleigh is very succinct on the matter. He allows few to venture down there. It's also a sturdy, reinforced area. Extra thick walls. He designed it that way to protect the rest of the house from his work."

"Good. Keep yourself well hidden." He stopped, glancing quickly about before continuing. "One other thing. I was wondering. Are you particularly fond of Lord Branleigh?"

Jessup stared back at the other man, unease rising in his gut. "He's been my employer for a long time."

"Yes, but I feel that he might be placing an undue influence on Tristan. I worry for the boy, you know. If he's like his father was, he might be easily swayed."

"What do you want me to do?"

Cantor laced his fingers on the table. "I would be willing to pay a large sum, in gold, if his lordship was removed from the equation. Enough, say, to tide you through until you found another situation." His voice darkened. "I don't care for him meddling into my affairs. I want the boy home."

Pemberton had felt no guilt at accepting Cantor's terms. His only interest in Branleigh had been his niece. Besides, what did he care if one member of the elite class chose to put down another? Gathering up a change of clothes, a small meal packed into a bag, and three bottles of ale, he intended to do just that. He pulled the call bell.

Walters arrived five minutes later. "If Lord Branleigh inquires as to my whereabouts, please inform him I'm in the lab, working on those new designs he finished last night. I'm afraid I won't be at dinner."

Walters nodded. "Sir, your dedication to his lordship, is boundless."

"I am only his humble servant," he muttered, glancing once again out of the window. He watched as Emily climbed down from the cab, helped by Mr. Hamilton. She nodded her thanks, but then her attentions were turned wholly on Deveraux.

Damn the man, Jessup cursed. The scoundrel had taken her arm in his and the two were walking arm in arm into the house. The assistant did notice the scowl that grew on Hamilton's expression at the couple's obvious affection.

Pemberton paused. There might be something useful there, he thought. He'd think about it later, when he had time to consider it. He quickly grabbed his pack and hastily made his way to the basement.

Every muscle in Tristan's body ached, but it didn't matter. Climbing down from the carriage, glad to be in the fresh air and away from the clamoring crowd, he found his refuge.

"Easy does it man," Hamilton said beside him. "You'd best get inside. You look a bit worse for the wear."

Tristan nodded, meaning to do just that. That was when he felt her. A smaller, less ornate carriage trundled around the corner. To his delight, minutes later, Emily waved from the window. Seeing her acted on him like a tonic.

It had the same effect on Hamilton as well. He'd practically bounded to the cab and instantly put his hand forth to help her down.

Emily had been the picture of a shy, demure young lady until she set eyes upon Tristan.

He must have looked like the devil, because an instant expression of alarm colored her cheeks. Tristan didn't care. She was the picture of beauty to him, and just seeing her lifted his spirits.

"Tristan?" she said, practically brushing Hamilton off as she stepped past him to move to Tristan's side.

"Hello, Emily," he barely breathed. Even in his aching and exhausted state, she roused a burning desire in him.

"You look like death, what in the devil have you been up to?"

Hamilton cleared his throat. "Nothing for you to worry about, he's just had too much of an afternoon out."

She turned a startled glance at the captain. "Afternoon out? Are you insane? Why he hasn't yet recuperated from his injury."

Tristan tried to put a brave face on it, though secretly he was delighted at her concern.

"It was barely a flesh wound," Hamilton muttered behind them, obviously annoyed.

"Of course, Emily," Tristan said, though he had to admit, if getting shot garnered this much of her attention, he'd consider it in the future if her interest ever waned.

"Come inside. We must get you to bed immediately."

Tristan sent a sheepish grin to Hamilton who only grumbled something about seeing to some letters he had to write.

In minutes, Emily had him bustled into his room, in bed, and propped up on pillows. As she leaned over, adjusting one particularly uncooperative cushion, Tristan grabbed her about the waist, pulled her down on top of him and into his arms.

"Tristan!" was all she could manage before he raised up

and took her mouth into his own. Kissing her hard and deep, he felt that he must instantly taste her or he would die.

Emily responded by softening against him, guiding his mouth with her own, and heightening the pleasure between them.

When finally they separated he gasped.

"Emily, I've missed you terribly."

"And I you," she answered as he gently kissed her along her jaw and down her neck.

"I thought I'd go insane with missing you."

"I know how you feel," she sighed against him. "I want you so badly."

"Mmmm," he said, burying his head in her neck. He knew it was wrong, inviting sheer disaster, in fact. But he couldn't help himself. She acted on him like a drug. A powerful substance that heightened his desire and melted away any remnants of his resolve to do otherwise.

Before either of them knew what was happening, he'd lifted her dress, petticoats and all, and had her beneath him.

"Emily, I want you. Now."

She barely had time to nod yes, pulling at his trousers until she'd set free his sex. Moving as one body, he pushed up her shift and plunged inside her, feeling the heaven of her tightening around him in almost instant orgasm.

The little death, as he'd heard it once called, took them both to the edge of pleasure, tossing them about as the relentless sea of their desire continued to rock them, back and forth, until they both were plummeting over the edge of sensual pleasure.

Later when the two were sated, they lay arm in arm, still clinging to each other as if their very lives depended on their continued touch.

"I love you, Emily," he said at last, but he already felt the shame of his actions. "I shouldn't have done this."

"Nonsense," she said, stroking his face as she wiggled closer to him. "I've missed you so."

He felt her pain at her admission. "It's hurt me as well, us being apart."

"I don't understand," she sighed. "Where you're concerned, I have no control at all."

He pulled her closer, feeling her breath upon his face as he did so. "I feel the same. It can't be anything but disaster, this thing between us."

Emily sighed. "Perhaps we shouldn't think of it too much. Just accept our love for what it is, and enjoy it while we can."

He looked down at her, marveling at how beautiful she looked, her dark curls bounding across the pillow, her clothing rumpled, and her round soft, form melting into his arms. It made him ache just to look at her.

To look at her and know that soon he'd have to leave her forever.

Emily felt the strong pulse that beat under her palm. They'd had a fast and furious lovemaking, and in spite of their joining she found she still ached for him. Almost immediately she wanted him back inside of her, wanton thing that she was.

"Will it never end, this wanting?" she asked.

"I'm afraid not," he answered her, his voice thick with exhaustion. He sighed. "I want to make love to you again, but I'm afraid I won't have the ability to keep breathing if I do."

Emily smiled beside him. "Don't worry. We'll have plenty of time later. I'll have the maid tell my uncle that I've gone to my room with a headache. That way we both can rest."

"All right. But just for a moment."

Emily sighed. She listened as his breathing slowed into a low, steady thrum. When she was certain he was asleep, she gently pulled out of his grasp and rolled to the side of the bed. Her heart broke at seeing him so pale. The trip to town had certainly taken it out of him.

Perhaps she wouldn't be able to keep her promise to go to his uncle's for dinner. But then, it was too important not to go. He needed to know the truth. That done, he could dispense with this ridiculous nonsense of going back to Spain. He had family now, and an obligation, a chance at a better life, and she meant for him to have it. No matter what.

After she'd straightened her hair and dress, she slipped out of his room and down the hall to her own. In short order she'd had Anna help her get undressed for an afternoon nap, first setting out her dinner dress for the evening. Then she scrawled a quick note to her uncle and gave instructions to the maid that she was not to be disturbed for the next two hours and likewise for Mr. Deveraux. Then after the girl left, she slipped out of her room and returned to Tristan.

Slipping in beside him, she watched as he settled her in his arms once again.

"Missed you," he said.

"I missed you, too." She kissed him gently and then relaxed. At last she was sure they had a chance for happiness.

Chapter Twenty

Two hours later, Tristan awoke with a gentle tapping at his door.

"Tristan? You need to wake up. We have to talk."

He opened his eyes to see Emily peering inside the room. His hand went to where she'd been lying what had seemed like moments before. She was dressed for evening in a pale blue evening dress that was cinched above her waist, the neckline of which was plunging downward but girded by a white lacing that kept her ample breasts covered.

"Emily? What time is it?"

"Time for us to get ready for dinner." She seemed pensive as she entered the room, carefully leaving the door open. "Are you feeling better?"

He didn't miss the hopeful tone of her voice. Although he only felt slightly better than before, he wouldn't have disappointed her for the world.

"Yes." He patted the bed beside him. "If you'd care to come here, I'll gladly show you how much better I'm feeling."

A rose blush crept up her neck. "I'm sure you will. Unfortunately, we're expected for dinner."

Tristan watched as she came to his bedside. She had her hair piled up on the back of her head, and delicate brown ringlets trailed down her neck. God, he thought, he could have tumbled her right that very minute and not felt the least bit bad about it.

She must have seen his hungry expression.

"Not now," she mouthed, motioning her head to the door. "Uncle Aldus will be coming for us shortly. We've been invited to a small dinner party this evening." She hesitated slightly. Tristan could instantly tell that she wasn't at all happy with the idea, but felt compelled to go.

"All right. Send someone to help me dress. I'll be down directly."

A smile came to her lips and Tristan was instantly glad that he'd made her happy. In fact, to see the calm that came over her, he would have thrown himself at her feet if it could produce that sort of reaction again.

Ah, Tristan Deveraux, he thought, *you are indeed a fool.* Somehow, he found he didn't mind it so very much.

Half an hour later, he was climbing into the carriage to sit beside Emily, with her uncle seated across from them. To all appearances, it was just the three of them going to dinner.

"What about your other guests, Lord Branleigh?" he asked, a small niggling of doubt growing in the back of his mind. He could tell instantly the older man was unsettled about something.

A slight nudging of the other man's thoughts proved that his suspicions were true. He wasn't happy with the growing affection between Emily and Tristan, and secondly he wasn't at all pleased about leaving his work for some social event.

"Mr. Hamilton is otherwise occupied. Besides, tonight's visit is of a delicate nature, and I thought it best to keep it to the three of us."

"You're not worried for your safety?"

The old man gave him a penetrating look. "Are you? Worried for my safety?"

Tristan chewed his bottom lip a moment. "I'm not a soldier, so I'm hoping that you've some sort of protection arranged."

Branleigh sighed. "I've been told by Hamilton that our host has been cleared. It should be safe enough."

Tristan nodded, but he didn't believe it for the moment. Glancing back at Emily, it dawned on him exactly what was going on. Leaning slightly sideways, he saw another cab following behind them. He sent a knowing glance back to Branleigh indicating his understanding. The man nodded slightly and breathed out a sigh. He hadn't wanted to worry Emily.

Strangely enough, Tristan approved of Branleigh's subterfuge. She'd been through enough. Best to keep things under wraps.

It had been nearly three-quarters of an hour when they arrived at their destination. For some strange reason, Tristan experienced a sense of foreboding. A niggling of doubt tweaked his mind.

"Who are we are going to visit?"

Emily gave him a weak smile. Clearly she wasn't that happy about having to make this visit, either, but he supposed that like most things, if her uncle asked her to join him, she couldn't refuse.

"He's an old friend of Uncle Aldus." She gave him a quick glance and the old man nodded.

"Yes, I've asked the two of you to come with me because George enjoys meeting with young people. I thought it a fine time for us to indulge in a bit of a break from all the intrigue."

Tristan watched him for a moment. He knew one thing for certain. The scientist was not a good liar. Just the same, Tristan thought it best to go along with things until he had all the facts.

A few minutes later they were pulling up to the front of the townhouse and the three of them stepped down from the carriage.

"My lord." The doorman motioned them into the house.

Entering the ornate parlor, they were settled in and promptly served hot tea and an assortment of sweet cakes.

The butler bowed deeply. "His lordship will be with you shortly."

Tristan was too restless to remain seated. Something about the room bothered him. He decided to walk around, looking at the paintings of some obscure ancestors of their host. Imposing, thick-framed men and women stared down at him with stern expressions.

Tristan's uneasiness grew by the minute. He glanced back at Emily and her uncle, who both, oddly enough, sat quietly and sent quick, nervous glances at each other.

"You've known this gentleman long?" Tristan asked.

For a brief moment neither one of them answered. It was Emily who rose from her seat to join him at the fireplace.

"Tristan, there's something I have to tell you. I've not been completely honest and I hope you understand that there's been good reason for it."

He searched her face. A sudden blade of fear sliced through him and he reached out and gently touched her arms.

"Emily? What have you done?"

She bit her lip. "I've brought you here under false pretenses."

Tristan's stomach clenched. "What are you talking about?"

"I did this, all this, for you. I wanted you to know that you're not alone. You have a family, Tristan, and they wanted to have a chance to meet you again. There was this terrible misunderstanding . . ."

Tristan looked up, Emily's voice trailing off. Scrutinizing the paintings, his unease grew to gut-wrenching fear.

Desperate, he grasped her shoulders, shaking her as he did so.

"Emily? What have you done?"

Branleigh jumped to his feet, his cane at the ready as if he would strike Tristan if he saw the need.

Tristan's throat tightened, his heart beat rapidly, and his mouth went dry. He fought an overwhelming impulse to run. Just like when he'd been a child. Escape.

Breathing heavily, he let loose of Emily and backed away from them both.

He was here. The devil was here. And he'd come to claim Tristan at last.

"Hello, nephew."

Tristan whirled around to see the horrid old man from his childhood standing in the doorway.

"No," he said, backing away. "It can't be."

Emily watched in horror as Tristan retreated. The expression on his face nearly broke her heart. He was terrified!

"It's all right, my love. He's your great-uncle. He's been searching for you a very long time."

Tristan shook his head. "Y-you don't understand," he said, his face turning a ghostly white. He stumbled back. Instantly Branleigh was at his side.

"Here, here, my boy. Take it easy. You're among friends."

Tristan looked at him, his eyes narrowing as he studied the older man. His voice was above a whisper when he spoke.

"Emily, how could you?"

Cantor stepped into the room. "Tristan, it has been so long. Surely you don't think that I'd ever really meant to harm you?"

Emily watched as something indefinable crossed Tristan's expression.

"You can't hurt me now," he said.

"Of course not." Cantor turned to Emily and her uncle. "Please. If you'd allow us to visit a short time. I've waited so long to see my grandnephew, there is much for us to discuss."

Emily nodded, glancing at Tristan. He seemed to have righted himself somehow.

"Very well."

Cantor motioned to the butler. "Please take my guests to the dining room." He turned to Tristan. "Perhaps you'd grant an old man a few moments alone so that we could get reacquainted?"

Emily looked back at Tristan. Like a man walking to the gallows, he lifted his head high.

"I'm not afraid of you," he said, his voice barely above a whisper.

"You have no reason to be. I'm but an old man, widowed now. I just want a moment to talk to you."

"Tristan?" Emily asked. His eyes flashed at her, and she saw anger, betrayal, hurt, all mixed in with a quiet acceptance.

Instantly she regretted ever severing their connection. She should have prepared him for this. Reassured him. Now, it was too late. All she could do was hope that he'd forgive her.

In spite of the time that had passed since he'd seen the old man, Tristan noted that not much of him had changed. Still tall and gangly, Cantor's shoulders slightly stooped, the sparse hair on the top of his head remained as white as snow.

"It is good to see you again, my boy."

"What do you want?"

The old man leaned across the table and began to pour a cup of tea. The sharp aroma of the Oriental blend filled the room.

Cantor smiled, his expression softening, but Tristan knew the truth. There was no benevolence in that old carcass. No soft heart beat in that chest, so brittle that the slightest force would likely shatter it into many sharp pieces.

"I want only to renew our acquaintance. It's been so

long since I've seen you. We are the only family we have left, you know."

"No, I didn't know."

Cantor shrugged, the sharp, bony prominences of his shoulders tenting the fabric of his jacket.

"Well, you were there when your mother died, of course."

Tristan drew in a breath. The sting of that old wound had never left him.

"Yes, I was," he said.

"Unfortunate thing. Your father was never the same after that. She'd hurt him deeply when she left him."

Tristan gave him a brittle laugh. "That's a lie. They hadn't lived together for years. He'd been serving in the army and she'd been struggling by herself. Then, later—you know what his family did to her. Disgraced her, threw her to the streets. Why should I care any for the family I left behind?"

Cantor's gaze cut sharply to him. "Your father is dead. He perished in prison."

Tristan gave him a sharp look. "What happened?"

Cantor shook his head. "He was found guilty of treason. He'd been caught spying, of all things. High treason. His title and estates returned to the crown. It seems he'd been intercepting couriers and was selling the information to the enemy. It wasn't a long trial and neither was his imprisonment. Another inmate stabbed him in his cell as he slept." He sighed. "Griffin was a bad sort."

"Was he? Or did you make him that way? You raised him, didn't you? Perhaps you're responsible for the man he became."

"Nonsense, Tristan. I loved your father as my own son. After all, didn't I shelter you and your mother those long years your father served in India? I took you in when both families had cast her out."

"I may have been a child, but I remember what you did."

"I tried to protect you, Tristan. I really didn't approve

of your father's anger. You must realize. What happened was an accident."

"He strangled her."

Cantor pulled back, a look of surprise coloring his expression. "He said otherwise."

"He lied."

The old man sat back, feigning shock. "I never knew. How could I suspect him of such a thing? He was my nephew. Did you see it? Did you see him kill her?"

"Yes, I did. He didn't know I was nearby." Tristan stopped, the emotions building in him, choking off his words.

"Dear heavens," the old man muttered, shaking his head. "What a burden for you to carry all these years."

Tristan narrowed his eyes and gave his uncle a wary expression. He was buying none of it.

"You're lying," he said. "The things you made me do . . ."

"I swear to you. I had only your interests in my heart. I cared for you, protected you."

"You used me," he said, the heat rising on the back of his neck.

"Only to make a better life for us both." He sighed. "I was wrong for thinking that I could control you. I have regretted my actions ever since."

"When I escaped, you came after me. You hired men . . ."

"Yes, I did and I feel terrible about it all. I have to tell you, Tristan. I'm an old man, very sick. I'm afraid I don't have much life left to me. Your Aunt Lavinia passed a few weeks ago. I know the error of my ways. I mean to make things right with you."

Tristan's resolve wavered. He knew full well what Cantor's intentions had always been. Now, years later, it should have been just as easy to delve into the black pit that housed the thoughts of his great-uncle, but the tumultuous fear of what he'd find beneath the murky depths kept him at the edge of Cantor's mind.

Here was the one person that Tristan could never

fathom, the one mind he would never read fully because he knew that once he descended into that devil's pit of depravity, he would never find his way out.

"What do you intend? Do you plan to use me now as you did then? To continue your murderous, thieving ways?"

Cantor scoffed. "I no longer live that life, Tristan. Time has made me see the error of my ways. I merely meant to make amends with you so that I could end my life in peace. Your aunt begged me to do so years ago."

Tristan studied the man even harder. Could it be that his great-uncle had grown a heart? *Not bloody likely*, he thought. There had to be more than simple generosity at work here.

"I don't believe you. You used me then and you want to do so now. I'm no longer a child that you can beat and throw into the cellar."

Cantor's expression froze. "That was never my intention."

"Wasn't it? You profited quite well from my gift." He may have been just a child at the time, but even then he knew that evil ran deep in Cantor, as deep as the sorrow in his own heart. "You forget. I know what I saw when I looked into your mind."

"What you saw was only an example of a man's base nature. We're all Satan's spawn, even you yourself. Don't deny it."

"What are you talking about?"

Cantor smiled, which made him look even more like a corpse just fresh from the grave.

"I've seen the way you trifle with that girl. Her affection for you is genuine. Are you going to tell me you gained her attentions without your 'gift'?"

The knot in Tristan's stomach twisted tighter.

"It wasn't like that," he said, though to his marrow, he knew it was a lie.

"Nonsense, boy. If you choose to do so, you could use your talent to force your will on others, make them do your bidding the way Wellington commands his army."

"You're wrong," Tristan said, though he knew it was the truth. He could push his will on to others, making them believe it was their own desire and not his. But he hadn't because he'd seen the foul beast that lived inside of men like Cantor. To his very last breath he'd rather die than become like them. Still, it had been a choice for him. For others, perhaps not.

Sighing, he rubbed the spot between his eyes. "You haven't answered my question. What do you want from me? Why have you pursued me all of these years?"

Cantor shrugged. "It's only as I've said. You're the only family I've left now. Lavinia gone, Griffin left us years ago. All the others are dead. I don't have long left myself. You are the rightful heir to Kendall and all its holdings."

Tristan looked up, stunned. "Are you insane? I'm Griffin's bastard, remember?" He waved his hand. "Even if it were possible, I wouldn't want it. Leave it to someone else."

Cantor raised his chin. "There is no one else. If you do not step forward and take it, then it will revert to the crown. Besides, there's something I haven't told you. You weren't a bastard."

"What are you talking about?"

"Your father and mother were legally married before your birth. They'd posted in the banns of both of their parishes and followed the law to the letter."

"You're wrong. I know what my father knew. He said I wasn't his child. That I'd been born a bastard."

"Your father was wrong."

"He seemed quite convinced of it." Tristan said, turning away from him, not wanting to see the old man, much less hear the words he was spouting.

"I'd thought so as well. I went to your mother and demanded the truth. At worst, I'd thought you were another man's child, someone she'd dallied with while your father was away. That was when she told me of your amazing gift. She knew that you were somehow enchanted and had this remarkable ability to read minds."

"That's why my father killed her and tried to kill me?"

"Your mother was afraid that Griffin would not understand, or worse yet, that he would be afraid and do something terrible to you. I tried to reason with her, but she would have none of it. She was clearly insane."

"Did you tell my father the truth?"

"I told him what I knew of your 'special' abilities." Cantor shook his head. "Your father then grew angry, certain that she was covering up her infidelity and that was the real reason she'd fled, afraid of what he'd do if he found out she'd taken a lover and that you weren't his child. He was consumed with jealousy."

"Later, after my mother died, when he came home . . ." Tristan felt his throat tighten. The memories of his years controlled by the two men rose up in his mind. He turned to Cantor. "You did such terrible things."

Cantor looked away, clearly uncomfortable at Tristan's accusations.

"Yes, we let our greed rule us, no doubt. You were badly used. But I had no part in the killing. You must know that. I never laid so much as a hand upon you. Your father was the true blackguard."

"You never stopped him," Tristan said.

Cantor shook his head. "No, I was as much a victim of Griffin's cruelties as you. Surely you know that?"

Tristan sighed. "All of this is past, none of it can be changed. I've made a good life. Not the best, perhaps, but I've found a way to use my talents that won't hurt others."

"And what of Miss Durbin? What are your intentions toward her? If you accept my offer, return with me and accept your inheritance, then you will have the chance to woo her in a proper fashion, not as a commoner, but as a man with something to offer."

Tristan looked at his hands and wondered what he would do without that life.

"It would be living a lie. I've no place among the titled."

"What an elegant revenge it would be to take the title

your father disdained and use it to find your own fortune.
Think on it, man."

"I don't want revenge. I'm as much to blame for my
mother's death as he is. She died saving me."

Cantor scoffed. "You were a child. She gave her life for
yours. It was what she wanted."

Tristan felt a tide of ache rise in him. "It doesn't matter.
I don't deserve it."

"Take it. It's a chance for a better life. You're smitten
with the young lady, aren't you? Accept my help and you'll
be able to marry the girl. You'll be able to give her the life
she deserves."

"Why would you help me?"

Cantor sat back. Tristan felt his hopes rise though he
tried to deny them. Tried not to be lulled into believing
the old devil after all this time.

"Because before he left, your father hurt me as well."
Cantor reached up and began unbuttoning his shirt.
Pulling back the fabric, he revealed the line of burn scars
that went down his chest to the top of his drawers. "I want
him to pay for what he's done. You're the only tool I have
left to do that."

"So, you're the one who wants revenge."

"And why shouldn't I?"

Tristan shook his head, suddenly tired once again. "I
won't do it."

"You mean you'd return to that cesspool of a life you
had? Wading through bloody battlefields and living with
the stench of decay?"

"At least I'm doing my part," he said, "trying to make
amends."

The old man scoffed. "To make up for your part in the
crimes? Do you think you can save enough soldiers' lives
to repay the damage your spreading of secrets caused?"

The stab of that pain had never left Tristan. It hadn't
been his choice, his great-uncle and father had forced
him. Yet, he was the knife they'd used to slice open his

country's intelligence network. The information he'd learned may very well have set his country on the course of war.

"You can't save enough lives to make up for the lives you've taken," his uncle reminded him in a voice that had beaten against his consciousness for far too many years.

"Then I'll burn in hell for my complicity, won't I. Beside you and my father."

"Och!" The old man stood up, clenching his fists. "You're stubborn just like your father. I thought that would be your attitude. Very well then, don't claim it. It's your choice."

Tristan felt the rub of suspicion against his spine. "Why do you care so much?"

Cantor sighed. "I only want to have family around me once again. Surely you can see that. Not only your companionship, but the promise of carrying on the family's title. I've seen the way you look at Miss Durbin. The two of you would produce such wonderful offspring."

The sudden vision of himself and Emily together set Tristan's thoughts spinning. As a simple surgeon, he'd not much to offer the beautiful lady, but as an heir to a modest fortune, well, there were possibilities.

"Suppose I do as you ask. What would you require as 'payment' for my companionship?"

Cantor's smile grew wider. "What would I require? My boy, I want only the knowledge that I've done the right thing. That I've corrected the wrong that my nephew set upon you and your mother, nay, even my part in your mother's demise and the damage we've caused. Isn't that payment enough?"

Emily twisted her skirt in her fists. What was between Tristan and the old man? She'd felt it, the high tension and anger that filled the small space when they'd been together.

"I wonder what's taking them so long?"

Branleigh shrugged. "It's been a while since they've spoken. I imagine that they have much to discuss."

"I'm so worried about him. He was so angry when that man showed his face. You don't think he'd hurt Tristan, do you? I mean, surely we weren't wrong about him."

"It's difficult to say. The boy seemed able to handle the situation well enough."

"And he did just that."

The two of them turned to look at Lord Cantor as he entered the room. "You will forgive my poor manners. I hadn't intended for us to be so late returning to you. Tristan has asked for a few moments to consider things. He should be along shortly."

Emily cleared her throat. "Forgive my forwardness, Lord Cantor, but Mr. Deveraux doesn't seem all that pleased to see you. In fact, he was most distressed."

Cantor narrowed his eyes at her. A momentary flash of anger lit his expression but was quickly replaced in seconds by a demonstrative concern.

"It is unfortunate that Tristan and I have been estranged for all these years. I fear it's my fault. He's been harboring these feelings of disdain toward me for many years and rightfully so. I made far too many mistakes where he was concerned."

"Deveraux seems a good sort. Not one to rush into foolish conjecture without reason," Branleigh challenged.

"He was but a boy when he ran away. I'm sure his beliefs seemed quite correct at the time. Unfortunately, it was one of those situations which required a more mature understanding."

"Indeed," Branleigh sent a glance to Emily. The two shared a silent communication of disbelief. However, neither one would be able to authenticate the demon's tale at the moment.

* * *

Griffin watched as the small party entered the front gates. The first coach pulled to the house, the second remained at the end of the property. Several men emerged, taking their places around the perimeter, still watching the townhouse.

"Strange doings, my lord?" Merlin said beside him. He and Griffin sat in a gathering of bushes just beyond the garden. Crouched low, they had a good view of the entrance to the grand house.

"Disturbing is what it is. I wonder what the old bird is up to now."

"Your uncle? You don't believe what he's written to you?"

Griffin sighed, carefully stowing away his looking glasses. "My uncle never minded misrepresenting the truth."

Merlin shook his head. "Imagine his surprise when he finds his own family is spying on him." He laughed. Taking in a full breath, the foreigner's eye covered the property. "Truly a wondrous sight, eh?"

"My uncle's townhouse? Not so much for men of his wealth. Though the country house is magnificent. That was the last place I saw the old goat."

"Then why are we here?"

"I need to see what he's about."

"You know that you cannot come forth to expose him without endangering yourself. Why bother?"

"Because he's the devil. I knew so years ago. I'll wager the old snake hasn't shed his skin just yet. Besides, he may have acquired something I want. I intend to see if it's true."

"That your son's still alive?"

"That the monster who walks and carries his name still breathes. If so, I mean to do as I should have years ago and destroy it once and for all."

Chapter Twenty-one

Tristan emerged ten minutes later and nodded to Branleigh, but did not send a glance toward Emily.

"Please forgive my poor manners, my lord."

Branleigh shrugged. "'Tis no matter. You only missed the soup."

"Yes"—Cantor smiled—"it was an excellent sampling of my cook's talents. Perhaps we can coax him to prepare it another time. Still, the roast mutton is choice, don't you think, Miss Durbin?"

Emily swallowed. The thought of Tristan's anger had put her off.

"Most enjoyable, Lord Cantor."

Tristan sighed. "If you'll all forgive me, I've found that I really don't have much appetite. I'm afraid I'm not good company at the moment. Perhaps I should go and wait in the coach for you to finish."

"Nonsense, Tristan. We've so much to discuss and so little time. I beg you to reconsider my offer."

Branleigh set down his fork. "What offer is that?"

Cantor cleared his throat. "I asked Tristan if he might stay with me for the time being. This townhouse is immense and I've been rattling around it for weeks. I would greatly welcome his company."

Emily started. "Is that what you wish to do?"

Tristan looked at her and Emily felt the hurt in his expression as surely as if it had been her own.

"I've told my uncle that I must satisfy my obligations to Lord Branleigh before I can agree to such a thing."

Cantor picked up his wine glass and took a sip. "I'm sure that his lordship would release you under the unique circumstances we have here."

"It's not up to Lord Branleigh. It's a military matter. I'm under order from my commanding officer to remain in his lordship's company until certain matters are resolved. There are others whose well-being depends upon it."

Branleigh sent a look to Emily. It was clear that he'd already made up his mind on the matter. She knew her uncle well. He was a man who always took control of the situation.

"I will consult with Captain Hamilton on the matter. I'm sure I can convince him otherwise."

Tristan nodded. "You may try, of course, but I believe he will be most resolute on the matter."

Emily watched as the two of them battled silently. "Perhaps there is a way to resolve all of this." She turned to Cantor. "You've said that you wish to spend time with Tristan. Would you consider coming to Beldon Hall and staying for a few days? That way, Tristan would still be meeting with his duties and the two of you could spend time together."

Tristan sent her an alarmed glance. *What in blazes are you doing?* his face said, though she was sure if she allowed him to, he would say far more in her mind.

She turned a hopeful eye to her uncle.

"A capital idea. Lord Cantor, surely you could make the sacrifice for the benefit of family."

Cantor nodded. "I've heard tales of the infamous Beldon Hall, sir, and you are a legend of the *ton*. I accept your invitation."

Tristan felt his gut turn to water. His uncle would be returning with them and he'd have to deal with his conniving uncle in addition to a murderer who stalked Branleigh. The situation could not have been worse.

Glancing at Emily, he sent her a guarded expression. He'd not yet forgiven her for her betrayal. He'd seen it all so clearly an hour ago in his uncle's parlor. Her manipulation of him had been unforgivable. Though a small part of his mind echoed that she'd had his best interests at heart.

Still, she'd broken his trust. Would he ever be able to confide in her again?

The meal continued on pleasantly enough. Lord Branleigh and Cantor discussed local politics, the war, and several other society favorites. Emily sent a discreet eye to Tristan on several occasions, but he never returned her attention.

At long last the meal ended and they rose from the table. "Lord Branleigh, I have so enjoyed your company. It would please me to no end to resume our conversation where we left off."

"I've had an enjoyable time as well. You will consider my offer to come and spend time at the Hall?"

"Indeed. I shall set my valet to pack this very instant." He turned to Emily. "You are a true delight, Miss Durbin. I look forward to spending time with you as well, although I'm sure, my grand-nephew has intentions on monopolizing your time."

Tristan watched Emily's blush rise at his uncle's comments. Part of it was from her discomfort at being so discovered, he was certain, but was it also partly from shame, he wondered?

"Tristan," Cantor began, "you have brought peace to an old man's heart. I look forward to spending time with you, as well."

"I'm sure you do." Tristan stiffened his spine and turned abruptly away from them, making for the door. Behind him he heard Emily whisper.

"Please forgive him, Lord Cantor. This has been all so terribly upsetting."

"Not to worry, miss. I understand these things take

time. Rest assured it is my life's ambition to right the wrongs between us."

Once outside, Tristan paused to inhale the fresh air. He drank of it like it had been fine champagne in a crystal goblet. Though he'd not realized it, Cantor's house had felt like a tomb. His mind flashed on the morning he had fled the old man's country home. Even then he'd seen it as a prison.

At least now he was a man grown, able to make his own way in the world. He would endure the next few days, solve the mystery of threats against Branleigh, and return to his regiment. Yes, he would surely put this all behind him and would be glad to do so.

Tristan was careful not to think further about the one person whose absence would pain him the most. It would be hard, but he would have to forget sweet Emily. Forget the taste of her kisses, the feel of her warm, soft flesh against him, the memory of what their lovemaking had been like . . .

He refused to allow her sweet essence to haunt him. Tristan had spent his life controlling his thoughts and blocking out the minds of others. He would lock her out of his psyche once and for all.

Of course, deep down he knew that blocking her from his thoughts was the very least of his worries. It would be his heart that would never let her go.

Griffin watched as the creature stood idle in the yard. It'd paused once outside the house, oblivious to Griffin's presence. Perhaps its magic was not as strong as Cantor had suggested?

The beast stirred restlessly.

It is a thing, Griffin reminded himself. Oh, it had taken the shape of a man, one that looked strangely close in appearance to himself, but a creature nonetheless.

"He is the one?" Merlin asked beside him.

Griffin nodded. "That's him. The beast that killed my son."

Merlin drew in a breath. "He doesn't look violent."

"No, it doesn't. But it's a killer, I assure you."

"Are you planning to kill him now? You've not primed your pistol? A knife attack, perhaps?"

"The soldiers would be on us immediately. I want it destroyed, but I'd like to keep my neck from being stretched in the process."

"A wise decision, my friend. What do we do?"

"We keep a close eye on it, wait for the right moment."

"Ah, you are an assassin's dream, my lord. It should be simple enough. Do you think the soldiers are guarding it?"

Griffin chewed his lip. "I doubt it. I mean to learn the truth from my uncle as soon as they've gone."

"Then you will kill the old man, yes?"

"If he's no further use to me. I have a feeling, though, judging from his letter, that he has something to offer me as well. I suppose it'll make little difference exactly when he dies."

As they sat in silence, the rest of the party emerged from the house and climbed into the carriage. There were three of them—the old man, the creature, and a woman.

Curious, Griffin watched the creature and how it tried not to look at the female. It was as though it'd been purposely avoiding her attention.

She meant something to the beast, it was clear enough.

"What are you thinking, my lord?" Merlin asked beside him.

"I'm thinking of what would be the best way to lure it into the open. I believe I've found what I seek."

"Ah, the girl?"

Griffin smiled. Fingering the hilt of the small dagger he kept in his belt he smiled. His cohort knew him well. Quite well.

The ride back to her uncle's house seemed to take hours. Tristan sat silently across from her, his gaze wandering past her, through her even, but not at her. She'd already made several attempts at conversation, to have him merely ignore her. It was the worst sort of torture.

"I think it's a grand idea to have company. We rarely get the chance to entertain," she began again. "Don't you think so, Uncle?"

The old man sighed. "As long as it doesn't detract from my work, I see no harm in it."

"I'm glad. You seem to get on well with Lord Cantor."

"He's not as annoying as others of his ilk."

Emily sighed. From her uncle, that was a ringing endorsement.

Silence enveloped the small cab once again. Sighing, she turned her attention to the window. The hour was late and there were few carriages about. That had thankfully made for a quicker ride home.

Ten minutes later they were back at Beldon Hall and Emily was glad of it. She wanted more than anything to talk to Tristan alone, try to explain her deplorable actions and beg his forgiveness. However, once they entered the house, he turned on his heel and addressed them both.

"Lord Branleigh, Miss Durbin. I want to thank you both for your intentions to reunite me with my family this evening. I understand how difficult it must have been, especially owing to your recent worries for your safety. I also appreciate your inviting my uncle here. You are most generous."

"Nonsense, my boy. We've completely uprooted you from your life. It was the least we could do. I do hope you forgive Emily's and my duplicity in the matter."

Emily watched as he drew in a quick breath. It was then that he turned directly toward Emily. "I understand your actions," he said, his tone tightening as he spoke, "as well as your reasons behind them."

His words stung Emily's heart as though he'd thrown a poison dart.

He gave her a meaningful nod and then turned back to her uncle. "I'm sure you'll understand if I don't share your good estimation of my uncle's intentions. I know that I have acted deplorably and I understand if you both were to hate me because of it."

"It was my understanding that you were fond of my niece. Is this not so? Are you now planning to back out of this and not offer to marry her? After you've compromised her in such a way?"

Emily's chest clenched at his next words.

"If there were anything I could do to take back my deeds, I would. However, I cannot. It is fortunate that Mr. Hamilton's offer of marriage remains open. I heard him tell her so myself."

"Tristan, no," she began, but somehow she couldn't find the words to continue.

"It's true, Emily. Hamilton does love you. He would be a better choice for you. As soon as this business is over, I'll not trouble either of you again. Good night."

Emily's heart shattered when he turned his back on them.

Behind Emily, her uncle coughed, drawing her to him. "We could force the matter, you know. I could insist on him marrying you. It would be the decent thing for him to do."

Emily shook her head. "No, it's no less than I deserve. I've lied to him. He'll never forgive me, now."

"Nonsense. You only meant to help him find his family. What man wouldn't want to know that he wasn't alone?"

She shook her head. "You don't understand. He's never let himself love anyone before. With his gift, it's complicated."

Branleigh patted her arm. "Then surely he knows the depths of your feelings for him."

She nodded. "He does, better than anyone else. It's just that he's never trusted anyone in his life. His father and uncle were terrible to him when he was young. They tried to make him do things . . ." she paused. "I'm not sure what happened exactly. He only let me see bits of it all. But whatever happened, he's never gotten over it. Now I've gone and betrayed him all over again."

Branleigh sighed. "It's late, my dear. Perhaps you both will see things clearer in the morning."

"I hope so, Uncle, I truly do." She turned and walked toward the stairs. It was going to be the beginning of a long, painful night, one of many to come, she was sure."

Pemberton had watched the exchange with curiosity. Had Deveraux truly cast her off? The idea of it warmed his heart. His chances at Branleigh were few, but now, if he could get his employer alone, perhaps there was yet a way he could carry out his plans.

"My lord," he said, emerging from the parlor. "I was going over some new calculations. I was wondering if you'd care to join me in the study?"

Branleigh's attentions had clearly been on his niece. "What? No, not right now, Jessup. I'm exhausted from our trip to town tonight. I think I'll just retire."

"But, my lord. It will only take a few minutes. I assure you, you won't be disappointed."

Branleigh's expression was that of resignation. "Very well, what in the devil have you got in mind?"

Jessup led his prey down the hall to the door that led to the basement. A few short steps and his plan would come into fruition.

Oh, it hadn't been what he'd thought before. No, the soldiers gathering at the gate had made that impossible. Instead, he'd decided a more direct approach was warranted. So, thinking his next move out carefully, he'd left word with the groomsman to ready a small carriage for a trip into town. He'd explained he would be taking a friend for a late supper.

When they entered the study, Jessup quickly lit a lamp. "It's simple enough, you see. A matter of changing the design on the barrel to a diagonal pattern."

Branleigh sighed. "It's already in that pattern. We determined months ago that so small a change would not matter. The prototypes we designed were proof enough of that . . ."

"I know that, but if you'll only look at my drawings, I think you'll see the changes I've made will prove otherwise."

Branleigh pulled his eyeglass from his pocket. Fitting it in place, he leaned over the drawings. Pemberton took advantage of the other man's vulnerability and reached for the heavy paperweight that sat on the desk beside them. Grasping it with both hands, he lifted it high and brought it crashing down on Branleigh's skull.

A dull thud was the only sound it made, and his employer quickly crumpled to the floor. A trickle of blood poured down the man's neck to pool on the carpet beside him.

Exhilarated, Jessup stepped back. Now, he only had to retrieve Emily and his dreams would finally come into reality.

Setting the paperweight back on the desktop, he wiped his hands on his jacket. Reaching down, he found the key to the lab in Branleigh's pocket. He fled the room then, and once outside, quickly locked the door. It was only a matter of gathering his few belongings and collecting Emily and he would at last have his dreams in hand.

Alone in her room at last, Emily had allowed her maid to help her undress and then sent her to bed as well. Unable to sleep, she sat at her window, gazing out into the garden below. Her heart so ached for Tristan that she could barely stand it.

She'd thought of at least a dozen ways to approach him, to beg him to see her point of view. But even in her mind, they had fallen woefully short. At least as many times she had called to him with her thoughts, each time opening the doors and windows of her mental sanctuary, just as he'd instructed her, but it had been to no avail.

Her thoughts remained painfully her own. Her mind was empty of the companionship she craved. Their love affair truly had ended.

A low tapping at her door drew her attention back to the physical world around her.

"Yes?"

"Miss Emily? It's Jessup Pemberton. I must speak with you."

Emily cringed at the low, coarse whisper. She'd had problems enough to deal with, the last thing she needed was her uncle's assistant hounding at her hems.

"Mr. Pemberton, I really don't feel well right now. Perhaps we could talk tomorrow," she began.

Before she could say more, he opened the door and burst inside.

"Mr. Pemberton!"

"Forgive me, Emily. I wouldn't be so bold, except circumstances have arisen that are most dire. Your uncle asked me to come immediately."

"My uncle? Is he all right?"

"Oh, yes, he's quite well. The captain has insisted upon moving him from the house right away and taking him to a place they've arranged in case of an emergency. I believe they have discovered who it is that threatens him. For your own safety, you must come with me now."

Emily stepped back warily. "I don't understand. Why didn't the captain send one of his men to fetch me? What about Mr. Deveraux?"

"Oh, they've already been moved. The soldiers are all leaving as we speak."

Emily paused a moment longer. It was a ruse, she was sure of it. "Mr. Pemberton, I've neither the time nor the inclination to participate in your games . . ." She moved toward the door, but he was faster. Grabbing her about the waist, he pulled her to him. Though he was small for a man, he still had enough height and strength to overcome a woman.

Emily meant to struggle, but his fervor seemed to have fueled his intentions, because he struck her, his hand landing on her right temple.

She tried to struggle out of his grasp, but with the blow her limbs became heavy and her thoughts turned muddy. As quickly as his attack had begun, it had ended, with her falling limply into his arms and the world going dark around them.

Emily had wanted to cry out, to sound the alarm, but her thinking had been stifled as well. She simply could do nothing but allow the blackness to consume her. Her thoughts of her uncle and of Tristan followed her into oblivion.

Tristan hadn't been able to rest. The events of the day had drained him. It was as if the walls were closing in around him, and the bed in which he'd spent not so long ago loving Emily now yawned cold and wide before him.

He couldn't spend another night here. Add to that his shoulder had begun to ache again. He would get no relief this night.

Finding his shirt and trousers, he quickly dressed and then slipped out of the room. The house was quiet around him and he so longed for Emily's company, it nearly undid him. Several times she'd called out to him, begging him to come to her once again, and each time he'd ignored her call.

Now, her thoughts had gone quiet, and he was sure she had at long last given up on him and had fallen asleep. It was a dreamless slumber, he knew, but at least she'd find some respite. He would not be so fortunate.

Quietly making his way downstairs, he passed the parlor, the library, and the hall that led to the dining room. All were thankfully empty. He did pass Hamilton's room on the way down and found that even he had managed to fall asleep, but only after drinking quite a few brandies.

Tristan made his way to the door that led to the garden. It was still within the perimeter of the property, and though he knew one of the guards would not be far off, at least he could have some privacy.

Briefly, Tristan toyed with the idea of escaping them all. Of course, that would leave Emily and the viscount without protection. Whatever the pair had done to him, their intentions had been good, no matter the outcome.

He sighed. His situation could not be any worse.

The night had fallen to a chill, even with spring still hanging the air. A few weeks and the members of the infamous *ton* would be migrating to London to celebrate the social season. It was too early for much of the summer growth, but the garden was fragrant enough with the early blooms.

Without Emily's presence the garden seemed as empty as a desert. Finding a bench along the far wall, he sat down and tried to settle his thoughts. Although he always kept the buzzing of others' minds at bay, he wished he'd had Emily at his side to fill the emptiness around him.

That was, of course, impossible. In spite of his uncle's attempts to convince him otherwise, Tristan still felt suspicious. Either way, he couldn't bring Emily into his troubles. As it happened, her betrayal was just the tool he needed to push her away. Away from him and the past that pursued him.

Just then a noise sounded from beyond the far wall. At first he thought it a rustling of leaves, a cat perhaps, or a rodent. He stood slowly, his mind set on investigating the source when a shard of pain cut through his head.

He screamed, grabbing his skull. Someone was in terrible pain.

Lord Branleigh had been hurt! An attack!

Tristan turned, intending to make his way back to the house and alert Hamilton and his men.

Just as he reached the door, a dark figure stepped out. "Hello, demon."

Dressed all in black, the one being Tristan feared the most stood leaning against the doorframe. He calmly held a pistol, its hammer cocked and the barrel pointed directly at Tristan's heart.

"Father," he said, but he had no time to say anything else. Behind him another had approached. Before Tristan could turn to see who else had joined them, a heavy blow landed on the back of his head. With it came the quick understanding that his fate had been sealed.

He only spoke a single word, a plea more than a statement. He knew all too well the danger that now hung over them all, but he was powerless to do anything about it.

"Emily!"

Branleigh was injured, maybe dead. Emily now at the mercy of some unknown fiend. He had utterly, completely failed everyone.

A picture of her being carried out of the house to a waiting carriage exploded into his thoughts as his consciousness faded into darkness.

Chapter Twenty-two

When morning arrived, the house was in utter turmoil. The housekeeper had been the first to notice that Lord Branleigh had gone missing.

"He hasn't even turned back the sheets on his bed," she'd shouted as she'd pounded on the captain's door. In minutes he had dressed and summoned his men who'd guarded the perimeter. They had begun a full-scale search of the house. Within half an hour two of his officers had come to make a report.

"Not only is his lordship not present, but we've yet to locate Miss Durbin, Mr. Deveraux, and Mr. Pemberton."

Another officer entered the room. "Sir, Mr. Pemberton has been making late night visits into town on a regular basis. Last night he told the man on watch that he planned to spend the evening with a cousin in town."

"Really? Did he leave by horse or by carriage?"

"Carriage, sir."

"Was there anyone with him?"

"None that was seen by the watchman."

"Sir," another soldier entered the room. "We've located Lord Branleigh. He's been injured."

They ran below stairs and found the peer sitting on the floor in the center of the room. A trail of blood had dried upon his left temple and down the side of his face and neck.

"My lord, what happened?"

He shook his head, his eyes focusing wildly about the room.

"What the devil is going on? Has the whole house gone mad?"

"Easy, Lord Branleigh." Hamilton reached for his handkerchief and pressed it on the viscount's wound.

"One moment I was here looking at his sketches, and the next thing I knew, something hit me from behind and I blacked out. Now, here you all are. My head hurts like the devil."

"Easy, milord. I've sent for a physician," Hamilton said, kneeling down.

"A physician? What of Deveraux?"

Hamilton shook his head. "He and Emily have gone missing, as well as your assistant. Mr. Pemberton has gone to town to spend time with his cousins. It is our best estimation that he left alone. We believe that Deveraux may have taken your niece. We fear the worst."

"Deveraux? That's not possible. He wouldn't harm Emily. They must have been forced."

Hamilton cleared his throat. "Sir, I believe that he may have been the one hired to kill you and then convinced Emily to run away with him. Gretna Green is . . ."

"Out of the question. Emily wouldn't do such a thing, and Deveraux, well, he's not what you think."

"He's a cad and a scoundrel. He's already done irreparable damage to her reputation."

"Whatever happened between them, Emily was a full and willing participant. Never mind that now. We must mount a search. Besides I don't think it was Deveraux who attacked me."

"Sir, whom else could it be? A member of the staff? Pemberton?"

Branleigh shook his head. "Why would he do such a

thing? Someone must have snuck in here while I was looking at the drawings. I'm not sure. Something that Pemberton said. Damn, I can't remember."

"Easy does it," Hamilton said. "I've got men out searching for them all as we speak. We shall find them."

"Sir?" Lieutenant Van Fleet said from the door. "We found traces of a struggle in the garden. Also this." He held out a piece of cloth, a torn remnant of a cravat that had fallen to the ground.

"I recognize that," Branleigh said. "Mr. Deveraux was wearing it."

"There's blood on it. Whatever happened, he didn't go easily," Hamilton said.

"If whoever it was would hurt the surgeon . . ." Hamilton began.

"He won't hesitate to hurt Emily. Captain, we cannot waste time. We've got to find them."

Emily struggled against the darkness. Someone had bound her hands behind her, covered her eyes with a rough canvas, and tied a thick, oily cloth about her mouth. Being held upright, she staggered forward on weak knees and worked laboriously at not falling on her face.

"Mmmm," she tried to speak but the material had been pushed in her throat preventing her speech.

"Take care, Emily, I'll have you there in a moment."

The voice belonged to Pemberton, Emily realized as her head began to clear. When the covering over her eyes slipped askew, Emily saw that several empty barrels were strewn about. Focusing her eyes in the darkness, she saw that they were indoors, in some sort of warehouse. Behind the filthy cloths that wrapped around her face, she could smell the ripe odor of dead fish mixed with a thick, earthen scent.

The mixture of the atmosphere and her aching head made her stomach roil. With shaking limbs she progressed slowly, but the more she came to awareness, the more alarm rose in her.

"Nmmm!" She pulled against Pemberton and he jerked her forward.

"You must not fight me, Emily. It would mean sure disaster if we were discovered. There are all sorts of bad ones out there—thieves and murderers and their ilk. One never knows whom one can trust. But don't worry. I've secured us transport, my love. In a few hours we'll be safely out of everyone's reach. Then you and I can be married proper and we'll begin our life together."

Emily made a distressed sound and shook her head. She didn't want to go where she'd never be found, nor did she care to be married to Pemberton. She'd die before she'd agree to such a thing.

"There, there, my love," he said as he set her upon a crate which leaned against a wall. Turning to light a lamp, they were suddenly thrown into a coarse, amber light. Emily saw instantly that Pemberton now was dressed in a black shirt and trousers, in one hand he held a key and in the other a large, sharp dagger.

It seemed that meek Mr. Pemberton was capable of forcing her to do his will. When he turned to gaze at her, Emily saw just how serious he was.

Something terrible burned in his eyes. A mixture of evil and lust, and something else—triumph. He'd been a man who'd desired the world and now it looked as though he'd gotten his wish.

Emily shrank back.

"Don't be afraid, sweet Emily. I promise to take good care of you." He walked closer to her then, and leaning over her gently, caressed her face with the back of his hand.

"Ugh!" She turned her face away, pulling back farther from him, until the wall behind her stopped her retreat.

Pemberton scowled. "You don't care for my attentions now, miss, but you will. Very soon, you will."

With that he turned and, thrusting the key into the

door's lock, he twisted it savagely. The door creaked as he pushed it open, its rusted hinges complaining as he did so.

"You wait here for me," he said as though instructing a child, "whilst I finish the last of my business and secure our journey. Not to worry, dear Emily. You've nothing back there to bother with. Your uncle has passed away, poor thing. Rest assured he died quickly. He didn't suffer."

He smiled, and humming to himself, pushed her into the enclosure. It was no bigger than a pantry with several shelves on one side, and no furniture to speak of. Emily landed on her backside, bruising her hands as she tried to break her fall.

Pemberton held the oil lamp up high. Peering inside, he nodded. "For you, Emily, I killed him quick for you. Consider my humane treatment of your uncle as my wedding gift to you, sweet Emily."

With that he pulled the door shut, the hinges complaining bitterly from the use. The slamming sound rattled the walls around her and Emily found herself enclosed in darkness.

Hysteria threatened to burst inside her. She didn't know how long she'd been gone, or if anyone had yet discovered her missing.

"Tristan?" she called out in her mind. Despair washed over her because she knew that her only hope lay in someone finding her before Pemberton had the chance to carry out his plans.

Had Pemberton truly killed her uncle? Surely that wasn't so. Yet, dread filled her soul, and she feared the worst. Added to that, she ached that she'd not gotten the chance to convince Tristan how much she truly loved him. Her situation could be no worse.

The rustle of something skittering in the darkness drew her attention back to her surroundings. Rats. A new level of fear struck her. If she didn't die here, accosted by the vile creatures, then she was to be Pemberton's consort. At the moment, she couldn't decide which was the worse fate.

"Please, Tristan. I beg of you, don't let him take me!" Again she called out with her mind, at the same time scooting so her back rested against a wall. Peering into the darkness, whatever fate awaited her, she knew she had little hope of rescue. She cringed as her unwanted company moved again.

Grief, anger, pain, and fear warred within Emily and she fought them all bravely. Tears slid down her cheeks and she did her best to quell the sobs that now escaped her. Emily knew only one thing.

She couldn't give up hope. That's one thing her uncle had taught her. Never give up. Never give in. If Pemberton or these bloody rats thought they'd get the better of her, they were wrong. She had to believe that Tristan would come after her.

She had to. To do otherwise was unacceptable.

"Come, my boy. Time to wake up."

Tristan opened his eyes, still blurred from the combination of his injuries and his exhaustion, and saw that he was not alone. Alongside the road in an alley he didn't recognize, he awaited his fate. Two men stood in the shadows, just visible enough for him to feel their menace.

Beside him a more familiar, less threatening figure stood.

"Come, come Tristan. 'Tis no time to sleep. We've much work to be done."

"We're wasting our time," Griffin said behind him.

The force of his father's thoughts slammed into Tristan's mind like a hammer. Hatred and anger burbling to the surface, like a poisonous stew threatening to spill out of its confines and stain them all.

"Easy, my lord. We must be careful," the second one said. He was smaller and more lithe, but Tristan suspected just as powerful. A man from India, if the long, colorful robes and headdress he wore were any indication. He peered curiously at Tristan as though he were some puzzle that required solving. Tristan was relieved that whatever he'd been thinking, he kept it to himself. In fact, while his father was a cauldron of burning emotions, and his uncle a cold and calculating menace, this one exuded a calm demeanor, almost childlike in its innocence.

Still, beneath his curiosity lived a darker, more sinister edge. While Tristan's great-uncle was greedy and self-serving, and his father deadly and filled with hatred, this one's desires were drawn from the deepest pits of hell.

"Careful of what?" Tristan asked, struggling against the fog that seemed to have settled in his brain.

"Nothing, my boy. Your father and his friend have just come for a short visit. They mean you no harm."

As soon as Cantor spoke the words, Tristan knew he was lying.

"They've come to kill me," he said calmly.

In a flurry of movement, he twisted himself and threw himself backwards, attempting to run from the men who flanked him.

In less than an instant, they were upon him, their hands grabbing his arms, trying to push him to his knees.

"It'll do no good to fight us, boy," Tristan's father growled.

"Go to hell!" Tristan charged, and slammed into his father with shoulder, the pain of the attack knocking his breath from his chest. Though jerked back, his father grabbed Tristan about the torso, crushing him in a strong-armed embrace. Before he could struggle out of their grasp, the second man was upon him, covering his face and mouth with a bitter smelling, oily rag.

Gagging, he shook his head violently but he wasn't able to shake their hold on him. Muttering in his strange tongue, his father's accomplice continued a strange litany over him. The words, and likely the substance that had soaked the cloth, seemed to have a numbing effect on him.

Though Tristan struggled with all of his might, the effects of his injuries and his prior exhaustion conspired against him. The force of the men now pushing him to the floor was more than he could fight.

"No!" he choked out once, before his limbs became as heavy as stone.

Griffin was on top of him now, his knee pressing Tristan to the floor. The man grabbed a handful of Tristan's hair and jerked his head back quickly placing the sharp edge of a blade across his throat.

"Easy, Griffin. You don't want to kill the lad yet." Cantor hovered just beyond Tristan's sight. Already the two men's thoughts were crowding one upon the other. Tristan felt his attacker's hatred boil as well as his uncle's fear that the man might yet complete his task.

"It's an abomination."

"My lord, you cannot kill him yet. The old man is right. You must be cautious or it will be our undoing."

The foreigner's words must have had their effect, because Griffin let Tristan's head go and pulled his blade away leaving only a small, stinging cut in its wake.

Expertly, they pushed him to the ground, binding him at the wrist and ankles, and stuffing a cloth into his mouth. As a final act, they pulled a dark hood over his head. Tristan could not even call for help. He saw his father lift his pistol and bring it crashing against the back of his skull. Myriad visions flooded his mind. Hatred, rage, greed, and murder all crowded into his mind before the last remnants of his consciousness slid into darkness.

Pemberton rushed through the busy streets, past the vendors and carriages, to reach his destination. The Broken Crown loomed out of the near darkness over him.

It was his final stopping place before he paid for the rest of his passage to America.

The thought of Emily and him alone in the wilderness of the former colony filled him with excitement. He wouldn't stay long in the city of Charleston. No, as soon as he purchased the goods they would need to finish their journey, he'd take his new wife and go to the glorious west. Through the mountains and over rivers until they reached a place where they could stay isolated from any who might interfere in his plans.

"I've read books," he'd told the innkeeper the night before as he'd downed his last glass of ale for the evening. "I know how to train a good wife."

The barkeep only laughed. "Train up a wife, that's the spirit, eh. Like she was a mare or a brindle bitch, eh?"

"She's neither a horse nor a dog. My girl is as sweet a girl that has ever lived. She's the epitome of womanhood. She's every dream I've ever had. Sure, it'll take a firm hand to teach her how to behave, how to please her husband, but it will be well worth the effort."

Of course, the other man had done nothing but laugh, as though he were an expert in training women.

"I have books," he told the barkeep again, "ones that explain exactly how to do it."

Though his host had made sport of him at the time—in fact had announced Pemberton's intentions to those drabs in attendance, which resulted in tumultuous laughter— the little man didn't care. He would do as he said. He would show them all.

Entering the pub, he quickly located the man he'd come to meet with at his customary table in the back. Waving his hand, Pemberton pushed his way through the crowd.

The old man took a moment to notice Pemberton's advance. Seated at the table with him were two men whom he'd not seen before. One was a large, foreboding Englishman, by his dress. Seeing Pemberton's approach, he gave him a dark look. The second man was smaller and of Arabian descent—India, if Pemberton's knowledge of the colorful robes and stark, white turban were any indication.

Pemberton waved again. As he neared the table, he overheard the men's conversation.

"You should have destroyed it," the Englishman said. "It's an abomination."

"My lord," the Indian said, "It is not an it, it's a he. He is your son."

The Englishman slammed his fist on the table. "Continue to say such things and I'll cut your tongue out."

The Indian only smiled. "I've already had my tongue cut out. It grew back."

"Stop it, the both of you," the old man commanded. "Whatever you think the man is, he's valuable to us. Can't you see? All that we've discovered over the years, he could have learned in minutes. Think of the power of the lad's mind. We need only to convince him that it's to his benefit and he'll surely do as he's told."

"If it doesn't throw in with us, what will you do then, eh? It's no longer a child you can push to do your bidding. I tell you, it will only end up betraying us all."

Cantor shook his head. "We'll just have to convince him otherwise. Make him a partner in our crimes and he'll risk his own skin as well as ours."

The Englishman labored not to raise his voice. "It won't care about the consequences. Bloody hell. Can't you see *it* for what *it* is?"

"I see your son, Griffin. Whether you choose to believe it or not. Can't you see it in his face?"

"I see only a monster who wears a mask to fool us all."

"Nonsense. The story about the changeling was just that, a story. Only a dolt would believe such a thing."

"My lord," the foreigner interrupted, "I felt his mind. He thinks like a man, he has fear and anger, and even lust."

Griffin shook his head. "You don't understand. They are tricksters, his kind."

Cantor shook his head. "It doesn't matter what he is, I

tell you. Listen. There is something far more important we must attend to at the moment. I heard from Lord Bertram this morning. He sent me a message. The book has been located. We must have it, or all is lost."

"Book? What book?" Pemberton asked.

The three men looked up at him simultaneously. The Englishman wore a scowl and his hand slid down to a dagger nestled in his belt. Pemberton stepped back.

"Jessup, how good of you to join us." Cantor smiled and put a hand out to his friends.

"I came as you asked. The deed is done," he said pulling out a chair. Leaning forward he continued. "Branleigh is dead. I killed him myself."

"Good work. Then he will trouble us no longer."

"Indeed. I am here for the payment you promised. I need that money. My fiancée and I are taking a long voyage. We'll need financing."

Cantor smiled. "Of course, Mr. Pemberton, of course. I do have a small favor to ask of you, however. Nothing important, really. Just a mere formality."

A small thread of suspicion snaked up Pemberton's spine. "I would be happy to oblige, however, my transport leaves first thing in the morning. I daren't miss it. It could be months before another suitable vessel could be located."

"I completely understand, but not to worry. My request only involves a few hours of your time, really. Lord Branleigh had an article that belonged to a friend of mine. A leather-bound book. He would have kept it close to his person. Have you seen such a thing?"

Pemberton swallowed. "Yes, there was a book like the one you describe. Why?"

"It has sentimental value. I would dearly love to have it."

"Well, I don't know. He always kept it with him. In his coat pocket, if I'm not mistaken."

"See! You know exactly the one I speak of. I beg of you, go back to the house and retrieve it for me."

Pemberton shook his head. "That's not possible. If I were to do so and they suspect me, it would be my end."

"Do they know you're the killer?"

Pemberton shook his head. "I don't think so, but Deveraux, you told me of his talents. Surely he would read my mind and . . ."

"My grandnephew no longer resides at Beldon Hall. He's living with me now. You've no reason to worry on that count."

The assistant drew an uneasy breath. "So, no one suspects?"

Cantor smiled. "You were his assistant and closest associate for many years. Who would suspect you?"

Jessup considered his request. On the surface the plan seemed secure enough. Also, he and Emily would have enough funds to get them overseas and buy basic supplies, but a little extra gold might help expedite their venture.

"I'll need more money," he said, "to fund my journey."

He watched a quick flicker of distaste cross the old man's features. Then he smiled.

"Of course. I'll pay you double what I promised for Branleigh's demise."

Pemberton gave him a quick nod. "It should be easy enough. My ship leaves tomorrow at noon. I'll be back tomorrow evening. Have my pay here and in gold. I'll have the book."

Chapter Twenty-three

Cold and damp, Tristan awoke in a pit of darkness. Moving his head sent a dozen arrows of pain through him and he moaned at the movement.

"Quiet down," Cantor called coarsely.

Tristan managed to open one eye. He was still tied and not in a pit, as he'd first thought, but instead in a corner of a dark room, lying prone with his head on a stone floor.

"Be still," a thick, accented voice called out to him. "You shouldn't try to move. That's an awful clouting he gave you."

Swallowing back a wash of bile that rose in his throat, Tristan tried to speak. "Who are you?"

"The large, angry man, Lord Griffin, calls me Merlin. He thinks I'm a magician."

"Are you?" Tristan whispered, the ache in his head growing to full force.

The man only smiled in answer. "You don't believe I am, though you're not quite sure what I can do. What your people call magic, mine call by another name."

"My head hurts too much for riddles. What's going on?"

Merlin sat back on his heels. "You are quite an interesting young man. My associate is afraid of you, I think."

Tristan nodded, the small movement raising the daggers of pain once again.

"The other man? I'm not quite sure yet." He glanced over at the old man.

Tristan groaned. "I already know what motivates him."

The stranger sighed. "Greed, for the most part, I think. I would learn more, but there is something in him that is dangerous, like a python, an evil that could wrap itself around its victim, strangle the life out of a man. His mind is one best left closed."

"What do you intend to do with me?"

"I intend nothing. No, 'tis not me. Like you, I merely am a servant. Plans and adventures are not for me. I simply follow."

"You have free will. You could leave anytime."

"You would think that, wouldn't you? But 'tis not so. Long ago, I started a journey. Would you like to hear about it? It makes a wonderful tale."

Before Tristan could answer, the door to the room opened and Griffin entered.

"Come on, you lazy lout." He called to Merlin. "We've little time to spend. Go purchase some dinner from the innkeeper and bring it here."

"I don't like this place," Griffin said, turning his back on Tristan.

"It'll serve well enough. I've been here in the past. Give him enough coin and the proprietor will keep his mouth shut."

"So you say. But what if someone else betrays us? What if one of his customers or even a maid sees the boy? There'll be questions."

"No one's seen or heard anything, Griffin. Ease your mind. The sort who visit this kind of establishment really don't want to become involved in the affairs of others."

"All they need do is hear him cry out once and they'll be asking questions. I don't like it. What shall we say then?"

Cantor whirled on him. "You've never had the stomach for this, you know. How you've survived all these years in your chosen profession is beyond me."

"I am a careful man, George, if I weren't, I'd been dead a dozen times by now. You didn't answer my question."

"If they ask, we'll just tell them that Tristan is given to fits and must be kept under tight rein."

"They'll believe that?"

"They have in the past. Now, open that bottle of wine and let's get to planning what we'll do next."

Tristan had gotten himself to a sitting position, his back to the corner. He watched both of his captors with an uneasy eye.

Neither man gave him any attention for the moment. It wasn't until Griffin had pulled the flask from his bag and poured out three measures that he turned his attention back to Tristan. Then, pulling a small pouch from his pocket, he poured its contents into one of the cups.

Walking over to Tristan, he remained silent, his long, solid steps making a resounding noise on the wood floor. Then, standing in front of Tristan, he knelt down so that they were eye to eye.

"Drink this."

At first Tristan pulled back. "I'm not thirsty."

Suddenly Griffin reached out and grabbed Tristan behind his head, jerking him forward and holding the metal cup to his lips.

"I said drink it."

Tristan looked deep into the other man's eyes. Something rose within their murky gray-green depths. Something that was vaguely familiar and very frightening.

"I know you," he whispered.

For a brief moment, Tristan's mind skimmed the surface of his father's thoughts. Chaotic, spinning out of control, there was a rising flood of terror that surrounded his mind. Emotions wrapped around his thoughts, anger, hatred, grief, pain, all of them intertwined and inseparable.

For no more than an instant, Tristan felt all of the demons that resided in his father's mind. Murderous intent girded him like the insane visions of his imagined enemies. In every corner he saw the dead rising up to take their measure from him, each one waiting and watching for him to let down his guard.

Tristan realized that his father was far more tortured than he'd ever been. It seemed he had found his personal hell and it lived in his own head.

Tristan mentally pulled away from the pit of his father's ruined psyche. He could not risk staying too long in the miasma of this man's thoughts. There had been no clarity, no rationality there; his father hovered on the edge of madness.

Griffin's eyes narrowed. Somehow he'd sensed Tristan's presence. With a sudden movement, he drew back and struck him with back of his hand. Not expecting the blow, Tristan was knocked back, his head striking against the grimy stone wall.

"Griffin! What do you think you're doing?"

"He was here, in my mind! He was trying to invade my thoughts."

"Nonsense. The boy was merely curious."

Cantor knelt down to Tristan and helped him sit up.

"What do you want from me?"

Taking care to brush the dust from his jacket, Cantor then reached into his pocket and pulled out his handkerchief. Dabbing it at Tristan's mouth, he wiped a trickle of blood from his face and then showed it to Griffin.

"See? He bleeds red, just like you and me. He's nothing more than a man. With a man's weaknesses, no doubt."

Griffin only grunted and turned away, wearing a disgusted expression.

"Why are you doing this? Why not just kill me?"

"It's nothing so bad as all that."

"Then why are you keeping me bound like this and trying to poison me?"

"We're just being cautious. Things are happening and we must be very careful not to tip our hand."

"And I'm a danger to you how?"

Cantor smiled. "It's obvious, my boy, your talent at divining the thoughts of others. I've warned you before. You must be careful where you let your mind wander. The minds of men are dangerous things. That's why you need me to guide you."

Tristan shook his head. "You made me do things." Tristan closed his eyes, desperate to push the memories away.

"You wouldn't be trying to read my mind now, would you boy?"

Tristan wanted to pull away but the other man held him tightly. "No."

His voice sounded hoarse, frightened, just like the eight-year-old boy he'd been many years before.

"I'd thought not. You see, Griffin, he's not all-knowing and all-powerful. There are places he can't go."

"I don't trust him or you."

Cantor leaned down once again over Tristan. His face glowing with the mixture of lamplight and something else. Something born out of greed and evil.

"Of course, we only did what we had to. You had a choice all along. You knew what was at stake. You could have stopped at any time."

"You killed them, not I."

He shrugged. "True enough. But you did nothing to stop us, now did you?"

Cantor's smile widened. He reached forth and straightened Tristan's shirt collar. "All these years, I've kept it going, our business venture. There are five men who are partners along with me. Together we've managed to make profits and continue the network of information. We only had one obstacle, a record that was kept by one of my 'partners,' which ended up in the hands of the military. Now, it is rumored that a code breaker has it in his possession. Have you any idea who that man might be?"

Tristan swallowed hard. "Lord Branleigh."

"You have indeed turned into a fine young man. Such deductive powers."

"You ordered him killed. That's what happened, wasn't it?"

"I'm afraid so my boy."

"No." Tristan's gut twisted with the news. "Emily."

"I see you're worried about his niece. 'Tis a pity, to be sure."

"What are you talking about? What have you done with her?"

"Why, nothing, nothing at all. Of course, Lord Branleigh's assistant has nurtured quite a *tendre* for her. I hear they are leaving on an extended holiday."

Tristan lurched forward. "Damn you!"

His uncle may have looked the part of a decrepit old gentleman, but he was hardly that, and it was evident the way he shoved Tristan back against the wall.

"Now you listen to me. I have plans for you. There are things I need to know. Military secrets, trade routes, even the minds of those who call themselves my friends. No one can be trusted."

"You want me to work for you?"

"Yes, in exchange for the girl's life. Pemberton will be bringing me the book in the morning. You agree to do as I order you, to keep my secrets and learn those of others and make them available to me, and I will see to it that he doesn't make that voyage he's been spouting off about."

"Where is Emily, now?"

Cantor shrugged. "In her home, safe in her bed, I imagine. Of course, if you want her to stay that way, then you'll do as I demand. To do otherwise might result in misfortune for dear Miss Durbin. Do you understand?"

Tristan chewed his bottom lip. There was nothing to be done about it. It was Emily's life or his, and he well knew the path he would choose. At least, for now. Later, when she was out of danger and they let their guard down, he would then take action.

"I understand."

Cantor laughed. "You see how easy that was, Griffin. Tristan can be most amenable with the right inducements."

"I still don't trust him. He could turn at any time."

"Very well, give me that concoction of yours. You're right about one thing. We need to subdue him better until we get to the country house. We can't take the risk of someone finding out about him too soon."

"Of course."

Griffin handed him the cup and Cantor held it up to Tristan's mouth.

"Now, be a good boy and drink this."

The vision of another who'd suffered at his uncle's attentions sprang into Tristan's mind. He couldn't let them touch Emily.

"I told you, I'll do as you ask. Just stay away from her."

Griffin stepped closer but Cantor held up his hand. "You have my word. Now be a good boy and drink some wine."

Tristan hesitated. God only knew what was mixed in the murky liquid.

His uncle's smile widened. "We're only doing this for your own good, Tristan. Surely you've felt it too? The danger of being discovered? Besides, if we'd wanted to do you any real harm, wouldn't we have done it already?"

Tristan remained silent. What he said was true enough. Yet he could feel the fine thread of menace slipping between them.

Without speaking further, Cantor gently laid the back of his hand on Tristan's cheek. That was when he felt it. The ice-cold touch brought myriad sensations to Tristan's skin. Suddenly, his mind exploded with the other man's thoughts.

Burning, hellfire flames, and a danger so palpable that it threatened to strangle the breath right out of him. A vision of a python with a lion's head appeared to him. The long body twined around him, squeezing tighter and tighter, and then turning its tremendous mien toward him, it opened predator jaws to several gleaming white teeth hovering over him. The beast's hot breath over-whelmed him.

Paralyzed, Tristan barely breathed when the cold rim of Griffin's cup touched his lips. Tristan could do nothing more than swallow the bitter wine as it flowed into his mouth and down his throat.

When the great maw of blessed oblivion opened up to him, Tristan gladly welcomed its embrace.

Hamilton entered the parlor later that evening. Bran-leigh was pacing the length of the room, his face drawn and haggard. The viscount looked up at him expectantly.

"Is there any news?"

Dusk was setting and they'd not found anything more than the few clues that had emerged that morning.

"I'm sorry, milord. Nothing. We've combed every inch of the estate. Nothing of Miss Durbin or Deveraux."

"Sir," one of the soldiers called into the room. "It's Mr. Pemberton. He's returned."

Jessup drove his carriage down the lane to the town-house. Nodding to the soldiers as he went, he regally pulled his cab to the front of the house.

"Mr. Pemberton," Hamilton said from the door. "It's good of you to return. Much has happened in your absence."

Pemberton smiled and quickly nodded his head. "Have I missed something?" He feigned ignorance and looked from one man to the other. "Has something happened? Lord Branleigh? Is he all right?"

"I'm well enough," Branleigh said from the door.

Jessup felt the life go out of him, and suddenly he was lying on the grass, looking up at the clouds. Concerned faces hovered over him and the next thing he knew they were carrying him into the house.

"Easy does it, man."

The very next thing he knew, Jessup was lying on the settee, a cool cloth covering his head before he was able to speak again.

"Dear heavens," he said, his voice trembling. "I had this terrible vision of his lordship lying dead somewhere. It was terrible. Thank goodness he's alive."

Of course, that wasn't exactly what Jessup was thinking. He tried to slow the beating of his heart and dampen his sudden need for more air.

Branleigh was alive.

"You've had a terrible shock, Mr. Pemberton," Hamilton said beside him. "It's very important. Did you see anyone about last night after you left his lordship in the study?"

The assistant closed his eyes. What was he to do? Suddenly, unbidden, another idea came to him. "I only saw Mr. Deveraux. He told me he was in search of something to eat. I believe he said his appetite had waned at dinner."

Calm settled into him as he watched the faces of those around him change expression. Hamilton nodded once to indicate it was as much as he had believed. He shook his head, likely feeling disappointment that the man who'd been chosen to care for the viscount had betrayed them. But the best expression was that on Branleigh.

The old man looked downward, disappointment clearly warred with disbelief. He'd actually believed in Deveraux. That thought galled Jessup, that the viscount would think the man even worthy of his support. Especially after all the years he'd worked beside him. He swallowed back the bile that rose in his throat.

"Where is Mr. Deveraux?" he asked, innocently enough.

Captain Hamilton cleared his throat. "He has been missing since last night."

"Surely he can't be behind this, can he?"

Pemberton was quite pleased when no one answered his question.

***

Night must have been approaching because Emily could have sworn that the temperature had dropped even further. As it was, the rats lost interest in her a short while ago. Owing to her good fortune, a wild eyed feline had found her companionship pleasant, and after catching its dinner and feasting on the rodent at Emily's feet, had now curled itself up beside her and slept.

Relieved to have the protection of the cat rather than the attentions of the rats, Emily relaxed slightly. Of course, she grew thirstier by the hour and her bladder ached for blessed relief, but other than that, she fared well. Lying to her side, she tried to find a position of comfort, curling herself around the tabby and resting her head on what must have been an old grain sack.

In spite of her relative comfort, she still worried about Pemberton's return and grieved her uncle's loss. Add to that she missed Tristan sorely. Closing her eyes, she pushed away her thoughts for a moment, remembering their time together. It had been the sweetest moments of her life, and she didn't care if it hadn't been acceptable behavior for a proper young lady, she would likely go to her grave with those memories to gird her. She had known love and passion. How many others could say the same?

So, thinking of her lost love, his warm touch upon her skin, the gentle way he kissed her and their final moments of bliss before their world unraveled, she finally drifted off to sleep.

Branleigh sat alone in the study. Hamilton entered the room, still dressed in the shirt and trousers he'd donned that morning.

"My lord, you need to rest. The soldiers are out looking as we speak. I'm sure we will hear news soon."

The viscount shook his head. "Deveraux didn't take her, I'm certain of it. Something else has happened to him. He was taken against his will."

"I hope you're right," Hamilton said, rubbing his eyes.

Branleigh shook his head. "The army has every foot of this property locked down. No one would have come on the grounds unseen unless they were very clever or they were someone who had belonged here."

"What are you saying? Surely you don't suspect me?"

Branleigh looked at him a moment, then sighed. "No, I know you're as worried about my niece as I am. No, it's someone we just can't think possible of such behavior."

"A good deduction, my lord."

Both men turned to look at the door. Pemberton stood there, his figure stark against the dim light. Holding a pistol he entered the room, closing the door behind him.

"Gentlemen, I'm so glad to find you both here."

"Jessup, what in blazes are you doing?" Branleigh demanded as both men stood to their feet.

"What I should have done last night. I won't fail a second time. Too bad, Captain, that you have to be a witness to this. It won't matter. By the time they find out what's happened, I'll be far away."

"That's only one pistol," Hamilton said slowly, inching forward.

"Yes, it is. Don't think that I won't use it on the first of you who threatens me, either."

"Stand back, sir," Branleigh ordered. "He's got another one in his belt."

Hamilton dropped his eyes and saw that the viscount had spoken truly. He cleared his throat.

"They'll catch you, you know. Someone will hear the shots."

Pemberton shrugged. "It won't matter. I've my carriage ready to leave, it's a short jaunt to the drive. Your men are at the far end of the property where a small fire has been set. If you inhale deeply, you can almost smell the smoke from here."

Branleigh cursed under his breath. The scent of burning wood was noticeable now that Jessup had mentioned it.

"There's only one thing I want from you now, other than your demise, old man. Give me the book."

Branleigh tightened his gaze. "What are you talking about?"

"Don't play me the fool. It's in your right coat pocket. Give it to me. Now."

Branleigh slowly reached his hand into the pocket and pulled the leather-bound text out.

"Why do you want this? You don't even know what it is."

"I know that it has great value to someone. It will be the payment I require. Now lay it down on the table and step back. Both of you, step back and raise your hands in the air."

Both men did as he ordered.

"Why do this, Jessup? Why try to kill me? What have I done to make you hate me so?"

"What have you done? You with your fancy title and your money constantly lording over me that I'm not good enough for your niece? Bah! Treating me as though I were nothing more than your house staff. I have a top rate education, one of the most deductive minds in science, and yet you treat me like nothing."

"Jessup, you must believe me, I never intended . . ."

"You never intended what? To remind me of my inferior status? Well, it doesn't matter now, does it? I've bettered you, haven't I? What's more I've got something that you love above all else. I have Emily."

"No!" Branleigh lurched forward, but Hamilton was quicker. He saw the assistant lift the pistol, pulling the trigger.

A loud explosion sounded, but the bullet never found its mark, in Branleigh, at least. Hamilton, had jumped in front of Branleigh, twisting sideways, himself taking the shot.

"Jessup, no!"

It was too late. Pemberton staggered back, the still smoking pistol falling limply from his hand.

Suddenly a noise sounded from the front of the house. Pemberton, as if being shaken from a dream, stumbled backward, his entire body trembling.

He looked about wildly, and then dropping the gun, fled the room.

Branleigh knelt down beside Hamilton, his hand on the growing spot of blood on his shirt.

"Good heavens, man, you've been shot!"

"What happened?" he asked, staring around the room, his hand going to the damp spot on his shirt. He pulled it open to reveal a furrow of burned flesh across his abdomen.

Branleigh shook his head. "It was Pemberton. He was the one who tried to kill me earlier. He would have done so again just now, except for your leaping in front of his shot."

"Don't worry, just a flesh wound. We'll catch the blighter this time. My men are probably chasing him down as we speak."

Branleigh shook his head. "He came back for the book. The code book." He pointed a bloody finger toward the table. "He didn't get it though. You don't think he'll harm Emily, do you?"

"He won't if he knows what's good for him. Either way, he won't get far. Once my men have him, we'll force him to tell us where she's at."

Pemberton had barely made it into his carriage and off the property. Slapping the reins down hard on his animal, he took off in a heated rush, practically running down two of Hamilton's soldiers in the process. He heard the shouts behind him, but a mad fury drove him. Damn if he hadn't lost his final chance to kill Branleigh and forgotten the very thing he had returned for.

It didn't matter. Cantor still owed him, at least for the first part of his task. He didn't know that Branleigh still lived, now did he? Of course not.

He'd just get his original sum from Cantor and leave as he'd intended. It would be enough revenge for Branleigh to know that he had Emily and the old man would never see her again.

Thankfully, for a Sunday evening, the roads remained somewhat clear of traffic and he made his way to the Crown with little effort.

Half an hour later he was jumping down from his cab and running into the pub. Pushing his way through the sparse crowd, he found Cantor, true to his word, as well as the two men who been with him the night before, seated at the same table.

Cantor stood. "Well, do you have it?"

Pemberton eyed them carefully. Reaching into his waist, he pulled back the pistol and aimed it directly at Cantor's middle. "Give me the money you owe me!" he shouted, his hand trembling even as he held the weapon upon them.

The two men with Cantor slowly rose to their feet, each one with hands falling limp to their sides.

"Don't be a fool, Mr. Pemberton," Cantor said, his voice low and even. You don't want to do this."

"I only want to leave now, with Emily. Give me the money you owe me and I won't hurt you."

Cantor shook his head. "You have disappointed me, Mr. Pemberton. I owe you nothing. Now, leave. I have another who will do as I ask. I don't need you."

Cantor and his companions sat down again, dismissing Pemberton as though he were no more than a mere annoyance.

He could hear them whispering, though.

"Have you your blade, Griffin?"

"You know I do, Uncle."

"Good. I believe you can now put it to good use."

Pemberton whimpered, his legs and arms quivering, he spun around to look at the gathering of the pub's customers who had backed away from him. With hands shaking and tears sliding unbidden down his face, he began backing away from them all, toward the door.

"You're going to regret this, Cantor! I swear it, you will."
Spinning on his heel, Pemberton ran for the exit.

Breaking out into the night, lights from lamps of men
riding toward the pub lit the dark like noontime. Covering his eyes, Pemberton stumbled and nearly lost his
footing. Raising his pistol, he threatened the men who
approached.

One of the men shouted. "He's got a gun! Fire!"

A thousand small explosions sounded, and suddenly
pain burst in Pemberton's chest, blood flowing freely
from at least a dozen wounds.

Before he knew what was happening, Pemberton was
lying on the ground, this time staring up into the faces
leaning over him. He managed only one word as his last
breath escaped him. An epitaph, really. His final spoken
declaration of his love.

"Emily."

Chapter Twenty-four

Much to his surprise, Tristan awoke in a bed. Not just any bed, though. One he'd known from long ago. In a room that very much looked like the one from which he'd fled in his childhood. He shook his head.

He'd been dreaming that he was eight years old again. He'd been hiding in that cellar, but it hadn't been his mother's death he'd felt.

It had been another's.

"Please don't let him hurt me again!" the child cried. No older than Tristan, she backed into the corner. Her face was damp from crying, her hair was matted to her skull, the dark, old blood sealing it there. On her face and arms were bruises and burns. As he watched, she trembled.

"You know what to do, boy. Go ahead, get us the information and your little friend goes free."

Tristan shuddered at the old memory. Meggie had been a servant in his uncle's house. Alone and too glad to be off of the streets, she'd accepted his uncle's offer of work. She'd been brought to the manse during the night by his father. He'd taken a particular joy in beating her.

Although no blow ever touched him, he'd felt every strike his father had thrown against the maid. He'd felt the hot poker scald her time after time, and reeled at the deep cuts as his father fashioned his blade over her again and again.

Tristan had begged and pleaded, but it had made little difference in the end. He'd had no choice. He'd done all that they'd asked of him for the years that followed. Gone into the minds of whomever they'd instructed him too.

It was the night that Griffin had tortured Meggie, one last time, and then killed her that Tristan decided to run away.

"No! Please!"

Griffin advanced on Meggie, his hand to her throat, his fingers grasping her, tightening, tightening until her rasping cries could not be heard.

"No!" Tristan cried out, but he was frozen. His fear held him captive and he knew he couldn't help her, the way he hadn't helped his mother so many years before.

Meggie's mind cried out to him. "Tristan, please! Help me!"

The pain of the memory crushed Tristan's chest as if it were a great iron vise. Worse than the memory had been for him, he knew what would happen to Emily if his father ever got her in his possession.

"I see you've awakened at long last."

Tristan opened his eyes to see his uncle seated next to him.

Licking his dry lips, Tristan felt as though he'd had nothing to drink for days.

"I'm thirsty," he said. Though he still had that heavy feeling in his arms and legs, he realized that he was no longer bound.

"Of course. You've been out for quite some time. A day and a night, in fact."

Tristan forced himself to sit up, dragging his arms as he did so. It was as though cotton had filled his brain and his stomach lurched with the movement.

"Where are we?"

"At the country house. Surely you remember it?"

Tristan took a long swallow from the glass of water Cantor offered him, then focused his eyes on his surroundings.

"I remember," he said. It was true. The room looked as though no one had disturbed it in years.

"Little has changed here," Cantor told him. "It was Lavinia's domain, really. I rarely came back even when she was still alive."

"Why are we here?"

"I thought it best to stay here for the time being. You never know when a retreat from events will be necessary."

Tristan closed his eyes a moment. No one seemed to be in the house but them. "Or if you want to hide out."

Cantor smiled. "I just thought it would be appropriate. We're only a half a day's journey from town and I was thinking it was about time we came back, anyway. There are things afoot, you know."

"What kind of things?"

"You remember Branleigh's assistant, let's see, Pemberton was his name?"

"Yes. What of him?"

"He's dead. It seems he made off with Branleigh's niece and then went back to finish him off. Unfortunately, he's as poor a shot as he is an assassin. He bloody well missed his mark and didn't get the information I'd hired him to retrieve."

"So you killed him?"

Cantor scoffed, indignant. "Not I. Neither did your father nor his companion, for that matter. No, we were merely enjoying some refreshment at a local pub, and the next thing we knew, he came running in brandishing a pistol and threatening everyone. Not to worry, the army caught up with him. They mistook his wild ramblings for a threat. The rest you can surmise."

A shard of fear ripped though Tristan. "What of Emily? Is she safe?"

Cantor paused a moment, obviously enjoying Tristan's distress. Sighing he shook his head in mock sadness.

"We're not sure what exactly has become of the young

lady. Most likely she's closed up somewhere, alone and afraid. She probably won't last long."

"No."

"Now, Tristan, it's none of our affair. With Lord Branleigh's influence and the army? Surely they'll find her, sooner or later."

Tristan closed his eyes. He couldn't let her die. Cantor wanted something. He wanted it badly and had already figured Tristan would be the one to get it for him.

Tristan remembered his first few hours of freedom so many years before. He'd sworn never to let anyone own him, control him. Yet here he was, ready to give his life for one person.

Emily.

Tristan opened his eyes. "Whatever you want, I'll do it. Just let me go. Let me try to find her."

Cantor leaned forward. "If I did, there's no guarantee you'd come back to me. I need you, Tristan. I need your talents. I'm not fool enough to think I'll live forever, but as long as I'm breathing, I mean to collect what's due to me."

Tristan nodded. "What about Griffin's inheritance? You said he'd had an earldom."

Cantor waved. "His lackwit brother gambled away most of the family money. Your father inherited an empty title. Why do you think he's never come back to claim it?"

"I see."

Cantor sat back again. "When he left the army, it was in disgrace. Caught dallying with one of his commander's daughters, of all things. He wandered for a while, and then got himself into a fight in a pub. The damn fool killed a man and was sent to prison. That's where he met Merlin. The two of them managed an escape and have been employed by me ever since. They've been busy intercepting confidential information, bringing it here."

"Where you've sold it to the highest bidder, no doubt."

"I've done my share."

"I bet you have. Let me guess, you helped the war effort?"

"When it profited me. When it didn't, well, let's just say that the war office never really suffered because of my little venture."

"What do you want from me?" Tristan asked, his voice low, the dread of what he must do causing pressure to build in his chest.

"There's an item I've been trying to retrieve from Lord Branleigh for some time. I only learned recently that Mr. Pemberton had been trying to kill him, or I would have done it myself ages ago. I thought to let the man finish what he'd started. It would have been best for both of us."

Tristan shook his head. "You want me to kill the viscount?"

"Not particularly. That is, unless you're forced to. Besides, he's not important. The book he has in his possession is; he keeps it with him almost constantly. In it is code that my counterparts and I developed to communicate between us. If it is broken, our entire operation will be exposed. I need that book back."

Tristan sat back. "I'll get it for you, on one condition. Let me find Emily. Afterward, I'll return here with the book and you may do with me as you will."

Cantor smiled. "I knew you'd see things my way." He paused. Drawing in a deep breath. "Don't think that you can cheat me, Tristan. Your father is on a short lead. Should I choose to let him, he would kill you in an instant. Not to mention your dear sweet Emily. You wouldn't want poor Meggie's fate to befall her, now would you?"

Tristan had no doubt of his uncle's intent. He told himself it didn't matter. He loved Emily, and he'd gladly sacrifice his life for hers if it meant getting her home safely. He only prayed he wasn't too late.

Emily knew her time was growing short. So long without food or water. One couldn't last more than a few days at best. At dusk it would be the end of her second day, and likely she'd not see the next.

Twisting sideways, she tried again to free herself. Already her wrists were raw and bleeding; this she knew because of the sore areas where the ropes touched her skin and the stickiness that had covered her hands and fingers.

At least she'd managed to get the gag off. It had taken hours, but she'd gained some hope that someone might hear her cries for help.

Long hours passed as she'd called out. Still, nobody came.

"Somebody, please! Help me!" she'd tried again, but it sounded more like a whisper. Her throat was dry and sore and she heard her own raspy breaths as evidence of her peril.

She would have cried, except she'd long ago used up the last of her tears. She lay alone now, for the cat had long since abandoned her to find his meals elsewhere. Not even the rats had returned to keep her company. She knew they'd come back, eventually.

She'd nearly lost all hope. Dozing now, from time to time, she'd been visited in her dreams by her uncle, Jeffrey, and even once her parents had come, dressed for their Sunday outing the way they had when she'd been a small child.

That had been hours ago. When she no longer was able to call out, she used her mind to try again, calling out only one name over and over.

"Tristan."

Not once did he answer her call.

Tristan sat in the carriage, his hands twisting in his lap, his eyes on the scenery passing by. In each alley, each yard, each corner, he searched for her. He'd been sending his thoughts out to her hour after hour but no answer had come. He refused to think that something had happened.

"No luck yet?" his uncle asked, calmly.

"None. But I will find her."

"I dearly hope so my boy, such a beautiful thing she is. Would clearly be a tragedy if something has happened to her."

Tristan gave him a scathing look. "I will find her," he repeated, as if saying the words would make them come true.

Tristan leaned toward the window once again, letting the brace of morning air revive him. They'd been traveling the night with no luck.

"What in blazes?" Branleigh and Hamilton were standing in the yard as Cantor's rig pulled into the drive just after sunup.

"I don't believe it! It's Deveraux. Perhaps he knows something."

The viscount didn't wait for his military escort, but instead ran into the yard.

"Tristan? Have you found Emily? Do you know what's happened to her?"

The carriage stopped and Tristan stepped out into the yard.

"I'm sorry, Lord Branleigh, that I didn't protect you. I only caught a glimpse . . ."

Branleigh shook his head. "Never mind that now. What of Emily? Have you heard anything at all?"

"Not yet, but I am still looking. I promise I will find her."

"Deveraux! I should have you flogged." Hamilton ground out.

Cantor stepped out of the coach. "I'm afraid the fault is mine. My nephew, Tristan's father, he and his friend had a hand in abducting the lad. They simply wanted him to come home and when he so rightfully denied them because of his obligation to Lord Branleigh and his niece, they got into a brawl," Cantor said. Walking up the drive, he slipped his arm through Branleigh's and continued his explanation.

"The next thing you know, they'd wrestled him to the

ground and forced him to go with them. Imagine my surprise when they arrived at my house, Tristan trussed up like a Christmas goose."

Branleigh turned to Tristan. "Is this true?"

Tristan took a breath. "It is. Thankfully my father and his friend have left for the Continent. I've come to do whatever I can."

The viscount nodded, and shook himself from Cantor's reach.

"This is getting nowhere," Tristan muttered as Branleigh turned to go back inside the townhouse. Hamilton gave Tristan a scathing glance before he followed.

Alone with Tristan, Cantor yawned leisurely. "I must say, I'm not as enamored with travel as I once was." He glanced up, finally noticing Tristan's scrutiny.

"What?"

"What did Pemberton say to you? Tell me all of it."

"I've already told you a dozen times, he said that he'd plans for the girl. He was taking her on a long journey."

"How? Across country? To the continent? By carriage, by boat? What?"

"I believe he said something about a vessel. Yes, a ship."

Tristan sighed. "We've been to the docks three times. They've had no record or recollection of anyone fitting Pemberton's and Emily's description boarding any vessels in the last two days."

"I suppose he was lying."

Tristan sat back, rubbing his head. "No, it has to be around the docks. An illegal transport, perhaps. We have to go back."

The thought of Emily, alone, God only knew where, amongst men who'd use her for their foul purpose or sell her to those who might do the same sickened him. He turned and climbed back into the carriage.

After signaling the driver to turn around, Tristan and Cantor set out once again. Tristan had never been a man given to games of chance. Although with his unique talent, he'd imagined he'd be quite good at it. Though, truth be known, he would be cheating if he could read another player's mind.

"Read another player's mind . . ." he said quietly, though his mind was working tenfold.

"I've been such a fool!"

"What are you talking about?"

Tristan didn't answer, but leaned out the window once again, calling to the driver.

"Hurry! I know how to find her."

Emily wasn't sure just how she knew it, but she'd been dreaming for a very long time. It was rather strange, if she stopped to think about it. Her weakened state had finally dulled her aching thirst and hunger, and a sort of peace had settled over her. She no longer minded that the end was near, in fact, she'd the feeling that she'd finally meet with her parents once again.

And of course, her uncle would be there. Together they would share a heavenly reunion and she would be nearly as happy as she had been while still living.

Only one thing would mar her perfect existence in heaven. Tristan would not be there. Her heart ached for him, still, even though she was sure she'd get to meet him once again, when his life had passed.

It would be as joyous a reunion as the one she was about to have with her parents. Then they would all float to heaven on gossamer wings.

Emily sighed. It was a comforting thought. In fact, so pleasant that if she could have, she would have lifted her hands skyward and used them to guide her to the clouds. She had to be satisfied with lifting her chin only.

"Emily."

Emily roused from her half slumber. For a moment she'd thought she'd heard Tristan calling out to her.

Then she realized it was just likely her mind playing tricks on her. Yes, that's what it was.

"Emily."

The voice called out again.

"Tristan," she whispered. "You must stop this. Can't you see, I'm dying?"

"I don't want you to die, Emily. I want you to hang on. I'm coming for you."

Emily would have laughed, except that with her weakened state and dry mouth, she couldn't manage it. Still, she chuckled in her mind.

"Silly man. It's already too late. You needn't worry, it's a better place."

"Emily! Don't leave me!"

"I don't want to, Tristan, really, I don't. But it's been too long. Why even if you found me right this second, I doubt you'd keep me from dying. I've been too long without food and water, you know."

"Emily. I love you. I don't want to lose you."

"I love you, too, Tristan. I'm sorry that I disappointed you so. I never meant to hurt you."

Emily felt his chest tighten.

"I know that. That's why you must stay alive. So I can forgive you. But only if you'll forgive me."

"Forgive you? For what?"

"For being a stubborn, foolish man who didn't believe you had his best interests at heart."

"Well, there is that."

"Emily, I must be close by if you can hear my thoughts so clearly. I need your help to find you."

"I can't help you, Tristan, but it's awfully nice of you to try."

"No, Emily, wait. You can help me. Tell me about your surroundings. You can do that, can't you?"

Emily thought a moment. Of course, she could do that. At that moment she knew every inch of her small cell, though how it would help him, she had no idea.

"I'll try. Let me see. It's a small storage room. I didn't see the outside of the building, mind you, but there were several broken

crates, some empty barrels, oh and couple of empty grain bags lying around in the room beyond this one. I think the rats ate all of the grain.

"Rats? Emily? Have you been bitten?"

"Oh, no. I thought they were going to, but this lovely tabby cat came and feasted on a few of the devils and frightened the rest away."

Emily felt Tristan's sigh of relief. Well, she was rather relieved herself.

"Keep talking to me, Emily. Help me find you."

"I will try, Tristan, but I don't think we have very long."

"Nonsense. I'm coming for you. Tell me more. What do you smell?"

"Fish. Or more appropriately, dead fish. It's awful. Oh, and I hear water. Constantly dripping water. It's quite maddening, you know."

Minutes passed and Tristan hadn't answered. A well of pain sprang up in her. Somehow she'd lost her connection to him. Despair filled her and she gulped in deep breaths of air.

It wasn't fair! She didn't mind dying, and in fact had made her peace with it. But, she'd treasured those last few moments with him and hadn't wanted to lose him.

Tristan was frantic. Yelling at everyone he passed, he begged information from the dockworkers. All around him the shipyard had ceased its activity. Even the mighty Thames seemed to have calmed its roar to allow him passage.

Man after man denied him, shrugged off his inquiries, but still he did not stop. He was nearly at the end of the yard when he saw it—a single three-story brick building on the edge of the property.

"What's in that building? That one over there?" he asked another worker, who was backing away from him as though he were a rabid dog.

"It's not much used anymore. Used to store wine casks

in there, some grain, barley, and such. But the roof leaks something awful, so everything that needs to be stored until it ships out is in the main building over there."

Tristan thanked him and ran for the rundown structure. Just as he reached the door, he heard it. Emily had called to him one final time.

"Good-bye, Tristan! I shall never forget you!"

"God! Emily, no! Don't leave me!" Tristan clawed at the door, now heavy with rust and water warped wood. *"Don't die now, Emily! I'm coming for you! I swear it!"*

He had little luck with pulling the door open. He saw that someone had sealed it with a board wedged in the frame.

"Help me! Somebody help me! There's a woman trapped inside. She'll die if we don't get her out!"

Suddenly a dozen hands were beside him, some brandishing iron rods, hammers, and hooks. Together they pulled and fought, but time seemed to have slowed around them.

At long last a resounding crack sounded, and like parchment being ripped apart, the door splintered in their hands.

"Emily!" he called out, but no answer came. He turned to the confused men who cautiously entered behind him, wearing stunned and curious expressions on their faces.

"Spread out. We'll have a better chance of finding her that way."

The men nodded as one, and Tristan thanked the heavens above that not a one had questioned him.

"Over here, governor! This here's the old pantry."

"She said it was some sort of storage room. Quick, help me pry open the door."

Once again the men moved as one, each one tearing at the wood. Not as resistant as the outer one had been, the pantry door fairly shattered under their hands.

Light spilled into the room, and Tristan strained his eyes in the dimness. At first he didn't see anything. Just more broken boxes, crates and such, and a sack of grain covered with rags against the far wall.

He turned. Wait, he thought. The rags? Turning, he ran once again into the room, so frightened at what he might find, he nearly fell upon her.

"Emily!"

He lifted her slight frame in his arms and hugged her to him. He felt the wisps of her breath upon his chest. Feeling her neck, he sought her pulse, and for a few seconds feared that he'd been too late.

Then, like pure magic, she opened her eyes at the same moment he felt a single weak beat against his fingertips.

"Tristan?" she whispered. "I've missed you so."

Though small, and weak, and so frightfully close to dying, his Emily remained.

He wanted to crush her to him, but knew that he might just smother her in the process. So, very gently lifting her in his arms, he carried her out of the room and to the coach.

"Is she alive?" Cantor asked as Tristan walked past him.

"I'm going to take her home and care for her."

Cantor nodded in agreement. "Yes, do take her home." He leaned forward, grasping the coach door as Tristan reached out to close it behind him.

"Just take care not to forget our agreement."

Tristan nodded. "I won't forget, Uncle."

Chapter Twenty-five

Emily was certain she was dreaming. She didn't remember much except bits and pieces of the carriage ride and of Tristan carrying her up to her room where he laid her gently on her bed and bathed her with cool cloths. She was certain that she was burning alive, but Tristan had calmed her nerves and told her that she'd been severely dehydrated and that it was a fever.

Most of her time after her rescue, however, was much more pleasant. Tristan stayed at her bedside, regaling her with wild stories of faraway magical places. Old legends, he'd called them. But he hadn't just read the books to her. No, he actually formed pictures in her mind. Once she even saw herself as a fairy princess and her handsome prince, who looked suspiciously like Tristan, rescued her from a high tower.

Mostly, though, he simply stayed beside her, day and night, for how long, she wasn't sure. She did open her eyes once to find her uncle kneeling beside her bed, holding her hand and crying. She'd patted him lovingly, to comfort him, yes, but also to make sure she wasn't dreaming. A few times she'd thought that she had indeed died and gone to heaven, but awoke instead to find Tristan coaxing some broth into her and singing her silly songs he'd heard the soldiers sing when he'd been in Spain.

Once, Tristan's uncle had visited. She'd awakened briefly to hear the two of them speaking in low tones.

"You haven't forgotten our arrangement, have you?" Cantor asked.

Tristan shook his head. "As soon as I make sure she's going to live, then I'll do as you ask. I promise."

"I'll give you two more days. When you've obtained the item, I want you to meet me at The Broken Crown. When that's done, there is much that I need your help with."

Tristan nodded. Emily saw that while she had regained her health in slow, steady stages, his had slowly slipped away. His skin was sallow in color, and he'd large circles under his eyes, she knew it was from the long hours of worry and sleeplessness that he'd spent on her account.

"Tristan. You need to rest, too," she told him, after his uncle had left.

Seeing her awake at last, he bent to kiss her. "Don't worry. I've plenty of time to rest, later. For now, I want to make sure you get better. I have to. It's my duty."

"You're not going to perform surgery are you?" she teased.

He shook his head. "Not even I would dare touch perfection." He reached down and held her hand, placing a light kiss upon it.

"You silly man. You say such nonsensical things sometimes. It's a side of you I never knew."

He laughed. "Nor did I."

Emily took a deep breath, feeling like a large, lazy feline. "Come, lay down with me, Tristan. I've missed you so."

He smiled down at her, but Emily saw a shadow just behind his eyes.

"Not now, love. I have to go, soon. I've an errand to do for my uncle."

"Must you? I'm just starting to feel better."

"I know. I'm not sorry to say, I'm damned glad of it."

"Oh." She lay silent for a moment, just enjoying the touch of his hand in hers.

After a time, he moved forward and placed another kiss on her forehead. "I have to go," he said. Emily did not miss the tinge of sadness in his tone.

"Will you come back?"

He paused a moment, and then let out a slow breath. "Of course I will. I promise."

"Sleep now, my love."

Emily knew deep in her heart that he wasn't being truthful with her. But the suggestion of sleep made her lids heavy and she found she couldn't fight it for long. In the end all she could do was pray he would indeed find his way back to her.

Tristan walked through the dark house alone. The captain had pulled up his troops and gone once it had been determined that the threat to Branleigh had once and finally been put down. He'd made his good-byes, and apologies to Tristan and had left saying that he would see to it that Tristan would have transport back to his regiment as soon as Emily was well enough.

In the end, Tristan knew that Hamilton was a good man. He loved Emily, and when things had transpired, it was good that he would be there for her in the end.

He was about to finish the task that would forever tie him to his uncle's sins. He would be a criminal just like Cantor and Griffin. It didn't matter. Emily was alive and Tristan would do whatever it took to make sure she stayed that way.

He crept along the long hall to Lord Branleigh's room. The dear fellow had finally been convinced of Emily's successful recovery and was now in bed.

Tristan entered the room where the old man slept, carefully treading across the floor to his armoire. Behind him, Branleigh stirred, and Tristan hesitated, waiting to hear Emily's uncle settle back into sleep.

"Deveraux?" he whispered. "Is that you?"

Tristan turned slowly and faced the man he'd come to rob.

"I'm sorry, Lord Branleigh. So very sorry."

"What in blazes are you doing?"

Tristan shook his head. "I'm here to take the book."

Branleigh drew in a sharp breath. "No, not you, never you. This whole time it's been a lie? You're the villian?"

Tristan sighed. "No, but I'm working for the man that wants it. In exchange for Emily's life. He made me promise to bring him the book if he let me go to find her. I did that. Now, I must fulfill my part of the deal."

"My Emily's life for that bit of leather and parchment. Is it worth it? Betraying us all?"

"I'd give my own life for hers. But they don't want that. They only want the book."

Branleigh tilted his head back. "It's your uncle. He's the one who's been after it all this time?"

Tristan said nothing. There was no point in affirming what Branleigh already knew.

"Very well, take it and good riddance to you both. Just know that you'll be breaking Emily's heart if you do."

Tristan nodded. "I know it too well."

He then raised his eyes and looked at Branleigh, locking their gaze together, using the power of his mind that he hated most to employ.

"Sleep, Lord Branleigh. Sleep and forget."

Cantor had waited what seemed like an eternity for the package to arrive.

"I tell you, you should have let me accompany the creature. I would have made sure it would bring the book here."

"My God, Griffin. When are you going to admit the lad is your son?"

The knife that his nephew was using to cut his apple found its mark in the table only inches from where Cantor sat working on his accounts.

"It is not my get. Say it again and I shall cut your throat."

He rose and in one fluid motion, pulled the knife from the tabletop.

"What do I care what he is? The boy will be our gold mine, I tell you. Not long at all and we'll be trading secrets with kings. Already I've made two contacts that will pay heavily for information on the proposed silk tax that's being discussed. Not to mention they're willing to pay quite handsomely for the location of hidden diamond mines in the African continent, as I hear it. Most intriguing. I'm thinking of heading up a caravan myself, you know."

"You'll do nothing of the sort, you old fool. You'd have to cross a desert and then navigate thick jungles. You'd die from exposure before you ever set foot ten miles down the road from your country house."

"Mind your own business. What do you care what I do as long as your income stays steady. Speaking of which, where is that dog of a companion of yours?"

The door to the study opened and Merlin stepped inside. "The boy is back. He has the book."

Cantor shot Griffin a knowing look and rose from the table. The other man wordlessly continued slicing and eating his fruit, though his eyes never left the door.

Dusty from the long ride, Tristan had barely made it in the room and Cantor was upon him.

"Well, boy? Do you have it?" Tristan coughed once and then reaching into his coat pocket, pulled forth the text.

Like a child on Christmas morning, he pulled the text from Tristan's hands and returned to the table. So concentrated on the ink-covered parchments inside, he very nearly missed his nephew's and the Indian's advance on Tristan.

Glancing up, he saw the two of them grab his grand-nephew's arms.

"Here now! What are you about?"

"Take care, old man. I've got a score to settle with this one. It needs to learn its place in our business."

Cantor glanced from Griffin to Merlin. Neither one of them spoke.

So he sent his gaze to Tristan.

"Well, boy? You tell me. What are they going to do?"

Tristan closed his eyes, briefly. When he opened them, the expression of defeat drained all color from his face.

"They're not going to kill me," he said at last.

Tristan felt each kiss of the lash as it landed. Strike after strike, the unrelenting leather tore his flesh. He knew what they wanted. He had seen in their minds just what he'd have to do to make them stop.

Hanging limply and no longer able to fend off their advances, he didn't even cry out. No matter how many times they struck him, the pain would never be enough to cut through his defenses.

His betrayal of Emily and her uncle had already done that.

Twenty minutes later he passed out entirely, his last memory of the blood that now flowed freely to his feet and the frustrated, angry yell when his father realized the fruit of his efforts had come to naught.

It was Merlin who prevented Griffin from killing him. In the end, it had mattered little. Tristan knew the time would come that Griffin's rage would finish the job he'd started. It made no difference to Tristan how much time passed until he did.

"I swear I don't understand a bit of it," Jeffrey said as he sat in the parlor, sipping tea with Emily and her uncle. "My men have been scouring the countryside these last weeks and there's nary a sign of them."

Branleigh said little during their visit, and Emily herself

had only nodded pleasantly from time to time. It was a tedious visit at best and she wanted more than anything for it to be over.

"Emily, forgive me for talking so much. I know how hearing another word about the scoundrel Deveraux must surely grate on your nerves."

"Nonsense, Jeffrey. He saved my life. I bear him no ill will."

Branleigh coughed beside her. "Emily, dearest, I am not quite feeling well today. I think I'll leave you two young people to it, then."

Jeffrey cleared his throat. "My lord, surely you don't intend to leave her without a chaperone for the remainder of our visit?"

Branleigh looked from Emily to Jeffrey and sighed. "Well then, get on with it. Ask the girl to marry you."

"Uncle!" Heat rose up Emily's neck and she fanned herself furiously.

"Yes, yes, I know. I'm not a well man, and a woman in your condition has little choice in the matter. Let's be done with it all."

"Uncle, please. It's all right. You may go to your nap. I shall leave the door open, if it eases Jeffrey's concern."

Jeffrey sighed. "I hope you feel better soon, my lord."

Branleigh only waved them off as he left.

Emily watched him go and then waited a few moments longer until he could no longer be heard walking down the hall.

"I'm so worried for him, ever since the army discharged him of his duties, he seems to have been fading away from us, more and more each day."

"I'm going to speak plainly, Emily. He was a fool for not telling the truth. The authorities already know who has stolen that damned book, whether his lordship admits it or not."

"We don't know that."

"Emily, are you going to sit there and lie for him as well?

After he ruined you? After he left you with his bastard, and nearly got the both of you killed?

Emily couldn't stop the flow of tears that set upon her. "Jeffrey, you mustn't say such things." She stood and walked to the window. Her handkerchief clutched in her hand while her stomach cramped mercilessly.

Jeffrey rose as well, taking her arms and turning her so that he could embrace her.

"Dear, sweet, Emily. You're still waiting for his return. He's not coming back, my dear. Please. Let me save you from at least some of the harm he's put upon you. Marry me so your child will have a name."

"Jeffrey, I can't. I don't love you. I don't care what happens to me."

"I won't let you do this. Not now. Not when you have so much to live for. Think of the child, if you must. But don't make the mistake of wasting your life for Deveraux."

"My head tells me you're right, but my heart won't agree." Emily sniffed.

"You know I love you. You are fond of me. You even said so, once."

Emily nodded. What else was there for her to do?

It had been eight weeks when the army found them. Tristan had been closed in the room for days, denied sunlight, food, and he'd been given precious little water. The rope burns around his wrists had dug deep into his skin and now infection boiled in the wounds there as well as the ones on his back.

"Captain Hamilton, he's in here."

Tristan cracked open one eye to see the captain leaning over him."

"Ah, he stinks to high heaven, he does."

"Go fetch some water. We'll get him cleaned up and then interrogate him."

"Aye sir, you best be about it. Doesn't look as if he'll last long."

Hamilton knelt down beside Tristan. "We found the old man. He was headed south from here, trying to escape via the river. My men fished him out like a prized trout. He was spouting off about diamond mines of all things."

"Been talking about them for days." Tristan coughed.

The captain sobered then. "You know, Deveraux, I'm afraid it won't go well with you. Tell me where the book is and I'll see that things are expedited."

Tristan opened both his eyes and gazed at the man. "I don't know where it is. My father took it. Griffin."

"I'd thought as much. The slippery bastard has managed to escape my men on several occasions. Never mind. You rest. We'll get you decent medical care."

"So I can be healthy for my execution, Captain?" Tristan asked.

Hamilton laughed. "It does sound a bit off the center, doesn't it?"

"I'm afraid so. Do us both a good turn. Put a bullet in my skull and we'll call it fair. Tell them I threatened you, or some damned thing."

Hamilton looked at him for a moment.

Tristan gave him a dry laugh.

"Hell of a time to develop a sense of humor, Deveraux."

"Sorry, sir. It seems humor is about all I have left."

Emily paced the room for the hundredth time in an hour. She didn't want to get married. She'd said it often enough, why hadn't anyone believed her?

Looking down at her growing belly, she knew, of course, that it was the main reason no one was taking her seriously. Still, a woman ought to be able to turn down a man's suit if she chose to. Shouldn't she?

"Emily. For goodness sake, settle down. You'll be having that child in the churchyard, if you're not careful."

"I don't know why I even agreed to this. It's wrong. Perhaps we should wait until after the baby comes. That way I can fit into a real dress . . ."

"Emily, you know as well as I what kind of life the child will have if you are unwed at the time of its birth."

Emily's spirits sank. She knew only too well what Tristan had suffered. It was the only reason she'd agreed to this scheme. Of course, she was nowhere near ready to deliver, being only three months gone.

"I can't do this. I simply can't."

"I swear girl, you've been to the altar three times and you're still fighting it. Marry this one while he still breathes, for heaven's sake."

She looked at her uncle. It would soon be time to leave for St. James church. She felt like such a cheat marrying under these circumstances. She'd said so often enough.

"Emily, do you really think you're the first woman who approached that altar in this condition?"

Still, it was a bitter pill to swallow.

The front door knocker sounded loudly and Emily nearly jumped out of her skin.

"Fool groom. I told the man to come to the side entrance. Of all the mixed brain things to do with a pregnant woman in the house," Branleigh grumbled.

"Uncle! You mustn't say such things."

Grabbing her wrap she followed her uncle to the door.

"See here, young man, if I've told you a dozen times . . ."

Emily arrived at the front foyer just as her uncle paused.

"Uncle Aldus, what is it?"

"It's Jeffrey, my dear." He turned to her, his expression one of utter distress. "They've found him."

The carriage ride to the prison had been one fraught with peril, or so her uncle had said. He'd spent half the trip hanging out the window cursing at the driver.

Emily had sat stoically across from Jeffrey, her eyes already damp with tears.

"Funny," she said after a time, "that we should be riding together once again to meet with him. It doesn't seem that long ago that we were on our way to London to learn who threatened us."

"Emily, don't," Jeffrey began.

"It's all my fault. I couldn't protect my uncle, I was so afraid. Then we dragged him into all this and now he may die because of it."

Tears fell unbidden once again. Her uncle took her hands in his.

"Emily, this was as much my doing as yours. If I had been clever enough to see through Pemberton's subterfuge we could have prevented it all."

"Lord Branleigh, no one is to blame," Hamilton said. "Deveraux was a good soldier and is an even better man. We'll do everything that we can for him."

"He was forced to steal the book, I'm sure of it." Emily said, wiping her tears once again.

"At least we didn't find it with him. Still he won't defend himself. Says he's ready to take his punishment."

Emily was first to enter the infirmary, but Branleigh held back, tugging Jeffrey's sleeve.

"Tell me the truth. Does the boy have any chance at all?"

Jeffrey shook his head. "I'm afraid not, milord. If he lives long enough to go to trial, then he'll be at the mercy of the military court. And, trust me, with all the fear over what's been recorded in that text, mercy is in short supply."

Emily, meanwhile, had given her name at the main desk and was soon being taken through the various halls that led to the ward where Tristan was being held.

Though the sick and injured lay all around her, Emily saw only one person in the large room. On the narrow cot in the farthest corner, Tristan lay very still, a pale ghost amongst the stark, white sheets.

"Tristan?" she said, her throat clenching as she tried to speak.

"Emily?"

"Yes, I'm here."

She sat on the edge of his bed, taking his hands in hers.

"I've missed you."

"I've missed you, too."

"I've been dreaming about you a lot."

"I know. I've seen your dreams, too."

"I'm sorry. I didn't mean to interrupt your sleep. You need more rest now."

Emily laughed. "I know. Uncle Aldus keeps telling me the same thing."

"Good."

"Tristan, what's going to happen now?" she asked out loud.

He remained silent for a bit, then opened his eyes. When he spoke, his voice was strained and barely above a whisper.

"I'm guilty of treason, Emily. There will be a trial and then I'll hang."

"No." Emily leaned forward, laying her head on his chest and sobbing into the linen bandages there.

Weakly, he lifted his hand and tried to comfort her. Emily sensed his reverence as he stroked her hair.

For the longest time, they remained arm in arm, merely touching and not speaking at all. Emily knew she could spend the rest of her days in his arms and never be unhappy.

"Emily," her uncle said gently, rousing her from her sleep. She opened one bleary eye, and saw that Tristan had fallen asleep as well.

"I want to stay with him."

"I know, dearest, but the staff here won't allow it. We've

got to get you home. You don't want the baby to suffer for it, do you?"

Emily shook her head, and leaning forward, placed a soft kiss on Tristan's brow. She turned to leave but heard a sigh behind her and a few barely audible words.

"Good-bye, my Emily."

Chapter Twenty-six

Tristan found that his arrival at Newgate Prison had been fairly uneventful, as much as anything in recent weeks had been. He spent most of his time between sleep and wakefulness, and found that as his body mended, his mind was forced to as well.

The truth was, he hadn't wanted to get better. He'd wanted to die sure enough, but fate had another plan for him. So, forced to get better, he waited out the time left to him.

Emily came to visit him each day, regaling him with stories of her childhood and what her life was like growing up with a gifted scholar. She spoke also of society gatherings and the latest gossip as though he really had interest in those subjects.

In all of her chatter, however, Emily was careful not to say anything of the future. It was as if someone had paused time for their benefit.

Even twice, Hamilton came with her, quiet and more reserved than usual. When he'd left to get their cab, Tristan had motioned Emily to come closer.

"He's still smitten with you, you know."

Emily blushed, and Tristan was pleased that despite his infirmities he was still able to wield that power over her.

"Tristan, don't . . ."

He held up his hand. "When is the wedding?"

Emily looked away from him. "I've already canceled it twice. It's a wonder he doesn't throw his hands in the air and be done with me."

"He won't. He's quite a tenacious bastard."

"Tristan!"

He only winked at her in response.

Later that night, with the sounds of the ward settling all around him, Tristan endured his final change of bandages and the report that his back was healing nicely. He knew it wouldn't be long before his idyllic, if somewhat tortured, existence would come to an end.

Still, it hadn't been bad. He'd been able to watch the staff working all around him, and on occasion after sensing a patient's thoughts, he'd aided the doctors in their pursuit of healing.

In some ways, it made him miss his small surgery even more, but at least he could spend his remaining days around the hope of healing rather than the surety of death. He was smart enough to know that death visited both the prison and the infirmary, but sometimes in here, a few lucky souls did survive.

That night, after Emily's visit, Tristan saw them. Two soldiers posted at the entrance to the ward. It seemed the military was making doubly sure he was recovering as well.

Dozing fitfully, as he did more and more these days, Tristan was suddenly awakened when a hand came down across his mouth, nearly smothering him as it did so.

"Make a noise, demon, and you die."

Tristan instantly relaxed. The hand pulled back, and Tristan saw that Griffin and his minion, Merlin, now hovered over him.

"Here, put this on and be quick about it."

"What are you doing?" Tristan asked, doing as he was

told, or at least trying to. His injuries had weakened him considerably.

Before he could draw another breath he felt the blade against his throat.

"Don't make a sound. Do as you're told, or I'll cut you from ear to ear."

Tristan swallowed. He knew it would do no good to sound the alarm.

For a brief moment he saw into his father's mind. He had only one thing in mind for Tristan.

The two of them were standing on the embankment, only a few yards from where Tristan's mother had died. His father was a few feet from him then, a thick, long dagger in his hand.

"Why?" Tristan asked in his mind. "Why do you hate me so?"

"You're the reason they killed my son."

"I don't understand."

"My brother sired many bastards in his short life. He would have produced a few more, no doubt, except he fell from his horse the year you were born. His accident left him unable provide a proper heir. No bastard would be acceptable. That meant only one thing. My son should have inherited the family title."

"I'm your son." Tristan struggled to reason with him.

"You're not. She lied. She lied to me. She lied to you."

"Look at me. Don't I look like you?"

The other man's thoughts scorched him.

"Of course you do. You wouldn't know it, but your resemblance to me is incidental. You're the exact image of my brother. You always have been."

"No. It's not possible."

"It is more than possible. Charles had an affair with Vivian after I'd left for India. She'd just given birth to my son."

"I don't understand. My mother wouldn't have killed her own child . . ."

"She did. It was what drove her mad in the end."

"But how?"

"The how is not important. The babe was born early. She

merely had to abandon it and death came for it fast enough. Later, she tried to convince me that the child had been very ill his first few months of life. It made it easier to explain why you were so small. The truth was, my son had to die so that their lie would survive. I knew you were my brother's bastard from the first. They thought they'd fooled me, but I'd known the truth all along."

"Then the story about the changeling? It was false?"

"A convenient lie. One that she'd rather believe than know that she and her lover killed her first child."

"My brother died for me," Tristan muttered, the shock of those words striking him deeply.

So much sadness, so much death, he thought. All of it seemed senseless. His whole life lived without knowing the truth.

"He was murdered. And you? You should never have lived."

Tristan returned to the present, Griffin's hand crushing against his mouth.

"Let's go."

The two of them walked through the halls of the crowded infirmary to the front door. Keeping his head down, Tristan didn't look up to see the two soldiers who had been stationed there had been murdered, nor did he see the jailor turn a blind eye to them. He'd been paid well, it seemed. After all, what was one wretched prisoner to him?

Once outside, Merlin joined them. In a mad dash, the two men dragged Tristan along beside them as they ran down the yard and slipped through a break in the gate. A carriage was waiting at the end of the block. Half pushing, half lifting, they thrust Tristan inside.

A few seconds later, Tristan was alone in the cab with Griffin. Merlin had climbed atop the rig. They lurched to a start, and Tristan could feel the carriage weaving in and out of the late night traffic.

"So, this is it? You're going to kill me?"

"I'm going to finish what I started all those years ago. You should have died along with her. I was a fool to listen to Cantor. The sooner you are dead, the sooner we will all rest easier."

He said nothing else, but reached in his pocket and pulled out a small vial. Tristan knew instantly what it was.

"Laudanum. You've been injured?"

The other man only looked away. "It's none of your concern."

Tristan sat back and observed his captor. It was there, in the way he breathed. Something grew in his chest. It was thick and ugly.

"A tumor is invading your body. You're going to die," he said at last.

Tristan had seen cancer on occasion. None of the patients who'd had it had lived long. A man whose lungs gave out, another who'd had thick, black lesions on his skin. Then there'd been the woman who'd had it in her breast.

"I can ease your pain," Tristan said at last.

Griffin only looked at him, the pain evident in the way he clenched his jaw.

In the next instant he struck a glancing blow against Tristan's jaw.

"Stay the hell out of my head."

Tristan reeled for a moment, his vision blurring and a new ache consuming his already growing discomfort.

"I was only trying to help," he said as soon as he could make his jaw work again, though it did hurt something terrible when he opened his mouth too wide.

"Why? Why would you do this?"

Tristan looked up to see the conflicted expression Griffin wore. His eyes had darkened and his brow creased even more.

"Why, when all you want to do is torture and kill me?" Tristan gave him a dry laugh. "It's just what I do."

He settled back then, closing his eyes and taking refuge in the one person who would never hurt him. Emily.

* * *

The sun was just over the horizon when Emily's carriage pulled up to the prison. She'd not been sleeping well lately, and had on more than one occasion crept out of the house early, called for her carriage, and gone to visit Tristan.

The staff there knew her well and often allowed her to sit at Tristan's bedside. In return for their kindness she always brought with her small cakes for them. It was well worth the effort. She was extremely grateful for any time she could spend with him.

As she entered the ward she immediately saw that things were in utter chaos.

"I don't know the man who did this." The jailer shook his head. "It was as if he'd just appeared out of the shadows. Like I said, one minute he was there, the next he was gone. Then I found 'em, lying just as you found them."

He pointed to the two bodies on the floor.

The soldier shook his head. "Men do not come and go with the flickering of candlelight."

"I'm not saying he did, sir. It was just 'like' that."

Emily approached, a sense of alarm rising in her blood. "What is it? What's happened?"

The soldier glared down. Dark green eyes. A jaw the size and shape of a block of wood. He grimaced at her.

"Miss, I've no time to discuss it with you. Please move along."

"No, wait. It's Tristan, isn't it?" She looked frantically around the room, trying her best to see past the guard. "Please, it is Mr. Deveraux. What's happened? You must tell me."

"Miss Durbin, your friend has escaped. He was seen with two men fleeing the area in a carriage."

Emily shook her head. "It's not possible." Emily couldn't stop the flow of tears. "You've got to find them! They'll kill him for sure."

"Please, miss. Calm yourself."

The soldier's words were lost on Emily as she turned and ran from the infirmary. Hailing her carriage, she quickly gave instructions to her driver and set off. Although she had no idea where they were headed, she did her best to follow her instinct. His uncle had a country estate, she remembered. It wasn't much of a chance, but Emily knew that she couldn't give up just yet.

"Tristan! Where are you?"

No answer came.

Seeking out Tristan's thoughts, Emily called to him again and again. She knew he could hear her shouting for him. Hear but refused to answer.

"Hurry! Please hurry!" she shouted to the driver. The cab bounced her about recklessly. Emily prayed that her babe would not be harmed from her frantic flight. She had no choice. There'd not been time to send a message to her uncle. No one would know of her destination.

Hours passed as Emily rode out of the city and then down the country lanes leading to Lord Cantor's estate.

Three hours into her journey, a single, clear voice broke into her thoughts.

"Emily? What are you doing?"

"I'm coming to rescue you," she said, doing her best to sound confident in her thoughts.

"You can't save me now. Go back."

Emily shook her head. Did he think he could convince her otherwise when his life hung in the balance?

"I'm not going to lose you now. Not after all this time."

"Emily, I would only be hanged for treason in the end. This is better. No suffering."

"Don't you dare give up on me now! I love you and we're going to get you out of this somehow. I promise."

"Emily, please. He's gone completely mad. I won't have him hurt you. Go back."

Suddenly a pain so sharp, it nearly cut her in two, struck Emily's head. Her tenuous hold on Tristan's mind wavered.

She searched her thoughts, frantic to find any essence of him.

Only a single plea whispered into her mind before it faded altogether.

"Emily. Go back."

"Tristan? Tristan, come back!" A sob escaped her as she thought the inevitable might have happened. Was he merely unconscious? Or was he dead?

Grasping the doorframe, she leaned out the window once again.

"Hurry, Giles, hurry!"

Fifteen torturous minutes later, Emily could see the main house of the estate and beyond it, the narrow drive leading into the woods beyond. Instinctively she knew that Tristan was somewhere in that direction.

One minute Tristan had been talking with Emily, the next the blow came and had nearly knocked him senseless.

Now, opening a bleary eye, he realized that the carriage had stopped. Griffin was pulling him from the rig, dragging him to the very place where his mother had died.

Tristan glanced back once to see Merlin relaxing beside the carriage. There would be no help from him.

"You don't have to do this, Griffin. Don't stain your hands with more blood."

"I have no choice. It's the only way to put an end to this travesty."

"You're wrong." Tristan felt the blood from his head wound damp and warm against his face. "Even if you kill me now, it won't change the past. Your son will still be dead. My mother paid for her sin already with her life. You made sure of that."

"It will be my final revenge against them."

"It will be more death on your soul."

Griffin's rage struck at him full force. The throbbing in

Tristan's head increased to a furious pulse. His vision twisted and contorted everything he saw.

Unable to look away, Tristan watched the man he'd always feared change before his eyes. His head elongated and his mouth and jaw stretched to impossible length. He became at last the monster that Tristan had always dreamed about.

Tristan looked at him, and then into him.

Griffin only laughed. "You want to know the truth? Then look into my mind. See it all."

The memories came unbidden, and helpless, Tristan watched as the years peeled away, his father's life unfolding in his mind. The beatings and curses of Griffin's own father still rang in his ears, and the memory of the icy December night when the old earl cast him out of the house as a boy. Griffin had found only one refuge.

His uncle had taken him in only to beat him frequently. Griffin had gone many long days with little to eat, and spare enough to drink, until he had cried and begged for release.

"He did this to you," Tristan whispered.

A child's hell without end and Griffin had endured every bit of it, endured it until at last he broke and did the thing that Cantor demanded. First, to earn his uncle's favor, Griffin had killed his own father. Poisoned him when he'd come for dinner at Cantor's home. There had been a string of deaths after that. A local vicar who'd threatened the old man, a merchant who'd cheated him. Killing again and again until Griffin began to take pleasure in the act.

Then came the day when Griffin had seen Vivian. The willowy, dark-eyed minx had drawn him from the first. But she had been his brother's woman. Engaged to Charles instead of Griffin. Angered, he had threatened Vivian into accepting his suit, telling her he would systematically murder her family if she refused. Then the day came when they were married and it was one of the few in which Griffin had found joy.

Of course, his happiness hadn't lasted. When he'd returned from India, Cantor had told him the truth about his wife and brother and their ruse.

It's why he'd returned that night to murder her. Years later, when his brother had gone on a hunt, Griffin had found him, as well. Knocking his brother from his mount, Griffin had broken his sibling's neck with his bare hands.

He'd left the army then and killing had become his passion.

Tristan shuddered. The play of Griffin's life had been like an unending nightmare. One murder after another had stained his soul until it lay shriveled on the ground, a black and scarred thing.

Tristan swallowed. "Come see what I see," he said softly, opening his mind to Griffin.

The other man screamed, and letting go of Tristan, stumbled back, clutching his head. Half moaning, half screaming, he cried out, dropping to his knees and gulping in ragged mouthfuls of air.

"My lord," Merlin came running from the carriage, holding his blade out to Griffin. "Kill him and be done with it. Someone is coming."

Griffin jumped to his feet and advanced on Merlin. "Get away from me, you bloody bastard! Leave me alone!"

Pulling his dagger from his belt, and lifting it above his head, he sent it plunging into the other man's heart.

Merlin made a surprised grunt. Eyes rolling back, he slid backward off the blade and onto the ground.

For a moment Griffin only breathed. Standing there, staring at his dying companion, he said nothing. Then, looking at the knife in his hand, still wet with the other man's blood, he held it up as though it had done the deed and not he himself.

"It's over, Griffin. You need to stop. It's not your fault," Tristan said in a soft voice. "None of it is."

Griffin squared his shoulders and turned. "You did all

this. You cast an enchantment on me from the start. You made me this way."

Tristan saw that his eyes now blazed with an ephemeral glow. Whatever small thread of sanity that had held Griffin steady had now snapped. He became the demon that he'd accused Tristan of being.

Tristan remembered what his mother had once told him. That magic had not come from some pit of hell as Griffin had always insisted. No, instead it had been a gift from his mother. She had been a simple gypsy girl, descended from long-ago fairy royalty. In centuries past, he would have been born a prince.

Brittle laughter escaped Tristan as he considered it. Finally, he believed his mother's words. He'd not been born of evil, not the devil's spawn. No, that title had been more for men like Griffin and Cantor. They had been the true fiends in all of this.

Griffin seemed to have regained some of his stability, standing to his full height with arms spread, the menacing dagger in his right hand, his fist clenched around the hilt.

"It's time for you to die," he said, his voice solid and his tone resolute.

"It changes nothing," Tristan said again. "You cannot kill enough people to cover up your sins."

"You're wrong. One more death after yours will do the task. I shall fall on my own blade and see you in hell."

Griffin lurched forward, but as he did so another sound broke into the glade. A carriage roared through the woods, barely able to keep from tipping as the driver drew back the reins. The door flew open and Emily came bounding out.

A vision in a pale yellow gown, she pulled loose from the rigging. "Stop! Don't kill him!"

"Emily, no!" Tristan tried to gain his feet again, but his strength had not quite returned and he nearly toppled over from the effort.

"Please, I beg you," she cried. "Don't do this!"

Griffin spun around and froze when he saw Emily for the first time.

"Vivian?" he said, obviously confused.

Tristan felt panic crush the other man as he gaped at the sight of Emily in the clearing.

Tristan felt his terror. He thought that Vivian's ghost had come back to haunt him.

"No! Griffin, don't! It's not her. It's Emily."

His words were wasted because Griffin heard none of them.

"I've killed you once, witch! I will gladly do so again."

With a fury born from the pits of hell he set off after Emily, brandishing his sword and screaming at the top of his lungs.

Tristan's worst nightmare had become reality. Without thinking, he lunged forward, grabbing at the crazed man and he struggled to hold him.

But Griffin was too fast, and swinging wildly, he knocked Tristan to the ground. Without pausing in his stride, he then set off after Emily. Unable to do little else, she tried to run, but he was on her in seconds, grabbing her around the throat the way he had Vivian so many years before.

Tristan both saw and felt the crushing of fingers as he squeezed the life from her.

Emily fought valiantly, trying to break away as Vivian had done.

This time, however, Tristan's paralysis evaporated. He was no longer the frightened, weak child who had done nothing when the murderous beast had killed his mother. With a strength spurred by rage and fear, Tristan struggled to his feet, and grabbing the dagger that Griffin had dropped, dived forward.

Staggering, Tristan clutched the knife and knew for certain that he would only get one chance to use it. He intended to use it well.

Grasping the dagger with both hands, he approached Griffin from behind, and in a single motion, brought the knife across the side of the monster's neck.

With the precision born out of years of wielding a

scalpel, he pulled the knife down and back, effectively severing the artery in Griffin's neck.

A scream erupted from Griffin as he let loose of Emily and he staggered, his hands immediately going to his wound as he tried to stem the fountainlike spray of blood that had burst forth and quickly covered his shirt and Emily's bodice.

Twisting, Griffin lurched again toward Tristan, his hands abandoning the wound at his neck and reaching for him. But Tristan sidestepped out of the crazed man's path. The beast made only gurgling sounds, his mouth gurgling furiously, obviously attempting to scream curses as he flailed about. Blood spewed down his chin and shirtfront.

Griffin managed a few lurching steps before falling first to his knees and then on his face, with the very last of his life's blood pooling on the ground beneath him.

For a moment neither Tristan nor Emily moved, both shocked at the final grisly scene before them.

"Oh, God," Emily sobbed, her hands bloody and still at her throat. Tristan instantly went to her, reaching her as she started to fall. Pulling her into his embrace. This time, he would not let her go.

That was the way the soldiers found them, minutes later. On the ground, holding each other and rocking together.

"Oh, Tristan, thank heavens you're all right."

"And you. Why didn't you listen to me? What did you think you were going to do?"

Emily sighed beside him. *"I never considered it. I suppose I thought I'd convince him otherwise. Oh, and I had a pistol in my reticule."*

It was Tristan's turn to chuckle. *"Of course. And a hatpin as well? You could have shot him and then pinned a note to him to tell the army who he was, I suppose."*

Emily sighed. *"Silly man."*

Chapter Twenty-seven

"Well? What's happening? What the blazes are they doing in there?"

"Calm yourself, Lord Branleigh. The tribunal has heard the entire story, though I doubt they'll believe it." Jeffrey Hamilton stood outside the courtroom and paced beside the viscount.

"I don't believe it myself, and I was there for most of it."

"Yes, well, we've much to be grateful for. Emily's safe return, the book's final interpretation. You're sure you have all the names and dates correct?"

"To the last." Branleigh sighed. "Not much for a life's work, is it? All the damage old Cantor has done. Think of the lives that could have been spared."

"I know. Many a soldier's paid dearly for the trouble he caused. Too bad he won't be held accountable, though."

Branleigh chewed his bottom lip. "You think the old man is truly mad?"

"Crazy as a moth chasing a midnight lamp, he is. 'Tis a bloody shame he won't pay for his crimes."

"Perhaps he'll wind up in the same hell as Griffin Whitehall, eventually, that is."

"Or maybe he's already there." Branleigh sighed. "At least he had those moments of lucidity when he admitted it all. Threatening poor Emily, trying to pay off Pemberton. Such a miserable business it was."

Both men turned to see Tristan and Emily entering the hall.

"Well, what's the word? Am I to hang, or not?"

"Tristan!" Emily started.

"I'm sorry. There's a lot in my accounting that they might simply not believe."

"As I hear it, son," Branleigh began, "you've been getting quite a bit of attention."

Tristan took in a breath. "I don't understand."

Branleigh nodded. "The physicians at London Hospital have expressed an interest in you. Even the Newgate physician said that you gave him a wealth of useful information from your experience as a field surgeon and even offered comfort to others in the infirmary from your sickbed, of all things."

The doors to the courtroom opened and the clerk waved to them. "The tribunal has finished deliberating. They're about to announce the judgment."

Tristan's knees had turned to water. He stood in the center of the room now, the military tribunal staring down at him and each one wearing a disdainful frown. It certainly didn't look well. No, not promising at all.

He glanced back to where Emily sat, flanked by her uncle and Hamilton. Both held on to her, ready to support her if the worst occurred.

"Mr. Deveraux?" General Cabot's voice boomed over the courtroom.

"Yes, sir."

"The tribunal has reviewed the documents presented here, the charges leveled against you, and the report of your behavior over the last several weeks. It has been determined that though you were faced with peril to your own life, you acted solely in the interest of Lord Branleigh and his niece, Miss Durbin. After being pressed into service and accepting the duties therein, you performed to the best of your ability. Judging by the condition in which you were apprehended the first time"—he checked the facts in the paper before him and harrumphed. "And later, after having singlehandedly put down the threat against the lady and retrieving the stolen property to turn it over to the authorities in the second instance, it is the opinion of this tribunal that you did indeed act in a forthright and honorable manner. Therefore the charges brought against you have been dropped."

Letting out a breath he hadn't known he'd been holding, Tristan remembered to bow respectfully to the officers, and turned to make a hasty exit. He only had one destination in mind. Emily met him halfway to the door.

"It's finally over," she cried as he held her.

A mixture of relief, joy, and hope stirred in him as he embraced her. At last, he had the chance for a good life. One with Emily. One in which all of his ghosts had been laid to rest. No monsters would ever chase him again.

Epilogue

Emily gazed one final time into the full length cheval mirror. The wedding gown, no matter how she arranged it, did little to hide her growing middle. She sighed. It had been a near thing, but her child with Tristan would be born legitimate.

She laughed and touched the gentle mound of her abdomen. Finally, after the posting of the banns, the fact of her name having previously been in them notwithstanding, their day was at hand. At last she felt like the bride she'd wanted to be all along.

"Emily."

Her breath caught in her throat.

"Tristan."

"Who else were you expecting?"

"Silly man."

"I want you. Now."

"You must be joking! We've only half an hour until our wedding breakfast!"

"I can't stand it. It's been weeks. Surely you'll have pity on me."

"Yes, I do feel sorry for you. You've been a very brave man. Surely you can wait a few more hours?"

"I can't. I swear it. If I can't have you now, I shall die."

"Nonsense. No one ever expired from lack of . . . it."

"I might be the first. You don't know."

Emily paused. Thus far, her reserve had held strong. They'd struggled to maintain propriety until the last. There had been so much to do, so many people visiting and congratulating them. Emily thought she would perish from all the well wishing.

No. She must be strong. They must be strong. She was insisting for both of them, in fact.

Emily startled. Something touched her. A thought, really, a feather-light touch of desire that quickly blossomed, filling her with a warm, thrilling sensation. Like the very first time their thoughts had combined, it came over her again. Memories of what they'd shared, and promises of what their being together would bring.

"First, I shall kiss you. Like this."

Emily felt his lips on her mouth, then her cheek, her neck, and her breast. Suddenly his hands were on her, stroking, caressing, and worshipping every inch of her with his touch.

"Tristan . . ." she began.

"Then I shall touch you. Here, and here. And here."

Emily felt her skin tingle in several very intimate places. Of course her treacherous body begged to answer him.

"I want you. Please."

"I don't know . . ."

"Yes, you do."

She knew that she'd wanted him and only him from the very start. That he had been the one who had been made for her and her alone.

"All right, but if you make me miss this ceremony, I'm afraid it won't go well, for either of us."

"Don't you know by now I can deny you nothing?" He chuckled. *"At least, you would—if you could read my mind . . ."*

In the mirror, she saw the door open behind her. Tristan was there, his face flushed and his breaths coming faster and faster. His eyes met hers, and she felt his soul open up to her. She saw all the things they would do and be together, not just here and now, but for forever and for always.

Without another thought, Emily turned and went into his embrace. Theirs would be a love that would last the ages, steadfast and never changing. She didn't need to be a mind reader to believe it.

Celebrate Romance With One of Today's Hottest Authors

Amanda Scott

__Border Fire
0-8217-6586-8 $5.99US/$7.99CAN

__Border Storm
0-8217-6762-3 $5.99US/$7.99CAN

__Dangerous Lady
0-8217-6113-7 $5.99US/$7.50CAN

__Highland Fling
0-8217-5816-0 $5.99US/$7.50CAN

__Highland Spirits
0-8217-6343-1 $5.99US/$7.99CAN

__Highland Treasure
0-8217-5860-8 $5.99US/$7.50CAN

Available Wherever Books Are Sold!

Visit our website at **www.kensingtonbooks.com**.

Embrace the Romance of
Shannon Drake

More Historical Romance From
Jo Ann Ferguson